Aubry rubbed his eyes. Father was gone, vanished
like yesterday's newsfax. He was alone in the alley again.
He leaned his head against the wall, trying to remember.

"Hey!" someone yelled. Aubry looked up. At the far
end of the alley a unisuited Exotic glowed. He had completed what Promise had begun, all visible flesh covered
with plastiskin. His entire visual character changed as
Aubry watched, shifting subtly to resemble Aubry. A freelance Rapporter, seeking empath bits for the network. He
carried his feelie box with him, its antennae already wiggling toward Aubry. "Are you in pain? Could you use assistance?"

Aubry shook his head.

The man smiled. It was a big, warm smile. And suddenly
it wasn't quite a man's anymore. The processor shifted
the visual image into a woman's. Smiling. Warm. Dark-
skinned. Slightly overweight. Its best guess about Aubry's
mother?

"I can help you," he said. "Pain is profit—"

"Get the hell out of here!" Aubry screamed.

He stopped, taken aback. And grinned, glancing at his
empath meter. "That was good. Maybe twenty credits
right there. Would you do that again? A little louder?"

"If. You. Don't. Get. Out. Of. Here. I. Am. Going. To.
Kill. You. The Nets would *love* to buy that. I guarantee
you."

He seemed to be considering it, and then thought again,
and shrugged. "Your loss, boss."

Tor books by Steven Barnes

Achilles' Choice (with Larry Niven)
The Descent of Anansi (with Larry Niven)
Firedance
Gorgon Child
The Kundalini Equation
Streetlethal

STEVEN BARNES

FIREDANCE

A TOM DOHERTY ASSOCIATES BOOK
NEW YORK

FIREDANCE

Cover art by Royo

A Tor Book
Published by Tom Doherty Associates, Inc.
175 Fifth Avenue
New York, N.Y. 10010

Tor Books on the World-Wide Web:
http://www.tor.com

Tor® is a registered trademark of Tom Doherty Associates, Inc.

ISBN 0-812-51024-0

First edition: January 1994
First mass market edition: November 1995

Printed in the United States of America

0 9 8 7 6 5 4 3 2 1

In all the world, in all of life, the single most important question is: *"Who Am I?"*

This book is dedicated to those who never settled for the easy answers.

We have not even to risk the adventure alone. For the heroes of all time have gone before us. The labyrinth is thoroughly known. We have only to follow the thread of the hero path.

And where we had thought to find an abomination, we shall find a god.

And where we had thought to slay another, we shall slay ourselves.

And where we had thought to travel outward, we shall come to the center of our existence. And where we had thought to be alone, we shall be with all the world.

—Joseph Campbell

JULY 17, 2033. LOS ANGELES.

Naked, cloaked only in invisibility, San sat cross-legged within a circle drawn with her own blood, awaiting the target. The distortion field surrounding her shunted colors toward the blue, dissolved the external world into a swirling pastel collage. A cybernet wired into her optical nerves enabled San to pierce the chaos, allowed her mind to correctly interpret the visual input. Where another woman would have been blinded by the distortion, San barely noticed it. Reality's edges appeared . . . *harder* to San than to ordinary humans. If the average human being's senses were considered the norm, San was a goddess.

But if she had been modified in a thousand ways since birth, in her heart San merely considered herself to be *alive. Correct.* She was as her ancestors had been, even before distortion fields, cybernets, plasma-pulse rifles and the other technological abominations of a corrupt and decadent age. She was, at her core, a living memory of the time when humans pitted spear against fang and claw upon the veldt.

Below her, thousands of men and women clustered in the middle of a place called Pershing Square, a square block of statuary and shrubbery in the midst of Mazetown. They hovered around a podium where, in a few minutes, the target would appear.

San experienced a rush of visceral warmth at that thought, a sensation the average woman might have interpreted as love, or need, or lust. The target meant completion. The target meant victory. The target meant life for San, as San meant death for the target. Death which, in fact, had already been dealt. The order had come from the Master, and the Divine Blossom *keiretsu.* The Master was simply to be obeyed. No thought contrary to this lived in San's mind, or had ever lived there, since her birth fourteen years before.

Divine Blossom had trained San and her brothers. The emissaries of Divine Blossom treated the five of them with the same icy professionalism, the politely masked air of contempt, that Japanese always displayed toward those of African blood. All of the emissaries . . . except Tanaka Sensei. Tanaka Sensei saw beyond the black skin, beyond the disgraceful pseudobirth, to the warriors within.

Tanaka Sensei recognized their humanity. Tanaka Sensei subjected the Five to the same blessed, merciless discipline he imposed upon himself, with which he daily transformed himself into the greatest warrior in the world.

Tanaka was not one of the Five, could not be, but in his own way, he was the father they had never known.

Sensei's words lived in her mind: *If intention is pure, then what lives in the heart is made manifest in the world.*

Despite the changed circumstances, San's intention was pure. The target was already a dead man.

There came a ripple of sound and motion in the crowd below her, and suddenly her wait was ending. Something was approaching from the east, over the jagged horizon of Mazetown. Mazetown was the heart of what had once been downtown Los Angeles, a man-made forest, a jungle of glass spires and foamed steel struts. San could admire this—she had seen pictures of Mazetown after the great quake, and knew the extent of the damage. She also knew of the target's role in the rebirth.

Target: Aubry Knight. Age: 39. Weight: 230. Height: 6'4". Occupation: Leader of the organization most often referred to as the Scavengers, a nationwide network of laborers who had rebuilt a shattered metropolis.

Knight was a mystery to most. There were whispers about him. Some conjecture, some confirmed, and some mere fantasies. Stories that he had aborted an assassination attempt upon President Harris. Stories of his role in the destruction of Gorgon, the NewMan antiterrorist task force. Tales concerning his physical capacities, said to be unsurpassed.

All such rumors crumbled like straw before the shattering truth discovered by the Five. Such a truth changed everything.

It changed nothing.

I hope you have enjoyed the good life, my brother. I hope it has not made you slow, or soft.

I hope that the rumors are true.

I hope you are ready to die.

1ST SONG

EARTHDANCE

We do not own the Earth,
we merely hold it in trust
for our children.
Therefore, let no harm
come to either.

—Ibandi proverb

1

The Chevrolet passenger skimmer destabilized as it struck an air pocket. The pilot regained control in 1.47 seconds. Subadequate. Made a note: Manipulate Father into replacing her. Father made a short, sucking sound. Fear. Distaste. He said, "I hate these things."

Response mode: teasing. "Daddy, you are such a wimp." I thrust out my tongue, waved it side to side. Approximately eighty percent probability of a state change. I returned to the raveled cuff seam. Simple cross-stitch. Oddly soothing. Mira taught me.

"Leslie . . ." Father raised his right hand and swatted *fast.* Vision strobed. Visual faded to kino mode. Felt vector, danced to Father's blind spot. Evaded hand.

Question: Should I have evaded? Would causing me pain have reduced Father's stress level? Cost/benefit analysis: Judging by air pressure, effect would have been light pain, no damage. Father/subject Aubry Knight harbors subthreshold sadistic tendencies. Control tight. Likelihood of additional stress if Father/subject believes he has injured me.

I ducked in to kiss his cheek, making the sound they call giggling. Father's cheek is generally stubbled by thirteen hundred hours. His testosterone level is approximately 140 percent of average. Note: Is Father XYY? Scan files. Satisfy curiosity.

Scent strong, musk-based. His melanin content is thirty percent higher than mine. If my growth patterns follow projection, I will have his bone structure, modified for estrogen levels. Will have Mother's Polynesian cheeks and epicanthic folds. Ideal material for seductive subversion.

Father's massive chest rose and then fell as he sighed. Tone: irritated. "Promise, did you *have* to put him in a dress for this?"

Mother leaned back in her seat, looking over her shoulder at him. Her laugh is low, musical. Oddly pleasing. *"She* insisted, Aubry."

Father opened his mouth, then let it close. I hallucinate that he didn't wish to renew ancient combat concerning my genderic orientation. Wise. A fight he has never won.

My legal name is Leslie Knight. Official designation Medusa-16. I'm a bifertile hermaphrodite developed by Gorgon. Biological age: 10. Actual age: 8. Height: 4'11". Weight: 85. Have maintained same level of physiological maturity for six years, due to nutrient bath/accelerated input during formative phase. It may take thirty years to reach full adulthood.

Father leaned back into the seat, watching through the side window as Los Angeles passed beneath us. I never knew L.A. before the quake. It is now oddly pleasing. The colors and shapes fill the eye. Bright. Almost hypnotic. Confusion: visual input melding with preexisting emotional patterns re: parental role in rebuilding of city. Pride? Perhaps.

For now: play gender games. Father is pleased by martial performance. Easy. Personal coordination in 99.999 . . . percentile. Must keep him off balance to prevent certain questions from arising.

Easy. Play Father and Mother against each other. Mother is strange. Non-performance-oriented. Likes "girl" games. I play them. She approves. Play "boy" games. She approves. Throw tantrums. She gives affection. Disobey. She gives affection.

I do not understand. Further research required.

I have dreams. Death, blood, raving nightmares.

She wipes my brow. Places cool mouth against hot cheek. She dances her plastiskin for me, triggering color and light on the left side of her body. Soothing. I tell her I hate her. I will kill her. Twice, in delirium, I have broken her hand. Once, her arm.

She gives affection.

I do not understand.

I am afraid. For all of us.

2

From the front row of the Chevy's passenger section, Promise Cotonou-Knight surveyed the metropolis that she and her husband had helped rebuild. Her almond-shaped, gold-brown eyes were drawn first to one wonder and then another. In eight years, the leverage of property, money, and manpower, combined with generous grants and federal tax breaks, had created an empire. The Scavengers didn't really *own* many of the buildings they had built or enabled, but little moved or happened in the section called Mazetown without their blessing.

After the great quake, banks had abandoned the inner city. In response, the Scavengers created a thriving credit union. Industry fled, and there were no jobs. The Scavengers held to a simple philosophy: *Those willing to work will have food and shelter.*

Period.

A half-crazed visionary named Kevin Warrick had created the Scavengers. Aubry and Promise kept the dream alive, and expanded it.

"Beautiful, isn't it?" When the woman seated next to Promise spoke, her silver knitting needles ceased clacking and her head wobbled slightly, as if she were a doll crafted by unsteady hands. For most of Mira Warrick's fifty-two years she had stood strong and tall, but she had aged a decade in the last twenty-four months. Her shoulders slumped now, and her pale brown eyes seemed fixed on a horizon beyond Aubry's range of sight. Each brittle brownish gray hair seemed to repel its sisters by static, leaving her in perpetual disarray.

And yet the strong angles in her face reminded Promise of her brother Kevin, the man who had taught Aubry so many strange and wonderful things. Kevin had opened Aubry's heart and mind in ways he hadn't known since adolescence. If only for that reason Mira was family, an elder sister perhaps, the living link to a crucial moment of change in her husband's past.

Now her mood seemed restless. She had invested the last hour in knitting a red and blue cap of some kind. The design seemed almost random. Promise rested an elegant hand on Mira's shoulder and almost unconsciously stroked it with her fingertips. "What's the matter?"

The older woman was too frail, too pale, and had spent too many years underground. Even though the Scavenger network stretched from Seattle to Denver, with affiliated nodes in New York and Chicago, Mira still nurtured an unhealthy tendency to shun the light. Perhaps a part of her had died with her brother in the tunnels.

"This is a day for celebration," Promise said quietly. Leslie bit off the thread at her father's cuff. She climbed over into Mira's seat, looking up at her with dazzling earnestness.

Mira frowned, and Leslie batted her eyes. Her eyelashes were long and fine, her eyes a surprisingly soft black. Her lips pouted in a perfect Cupid's bow. Mira smiled, and hugged Leslie. "I can't believe you," she said. "How can you be so deadly and so darned sweet at the same time?"

Leslie giggled. "Just lucky, I guess."

Behind her, Aubry rolled his eyes. "Just lucky."

The pilot, a competent young woman named Cori, pointed out Pershing Square. "Mr. Knight—we're approaching the landing pad. Three circuits, as you requested."

"As Promise requested."

Promise clucked. "Nothing wrong with pomp, under the right circumstance."

"Medals. This is a load of shit."

"Daddy!"

"Crap. Sorry."

"You should be." Leslie's angelic countenance was alight with mischief. Her voice shifted, taking on the cultured, oleaginous tones of a virtvid announcer. "As the only person in the entire civilized world capable of spanking my adorable bottom, you have the solemn obligation to civilize me. To be, in other words, a sterling example of responsible male adulthood."

Mira's needles resumed their fitful clicking. "Isn't that an oxymoron, sweetheart?"

The Chevy floated in over the top of the Sears towers, spiraling down toward the platform where a thirty-piece brass band blared earnestly for a throng of thousands. Leslie watched, grinning broadly, and then—

Her face tautened, as if someone had run the cold flat steel of a knife blade across the back of her neck.

"Something wrong?" Aubry asked.

Leslie's lips were flat and unmoving, but her eyes were locked on one of the buildings, Tyson's All-Faiths. The half-finished web of steel and concrete was a multidenominational house of worship. Although unfinished, it was already in use, housing prayer services almost every day of the week.

Leslie was perfectly still, her body locked in the rigidity of a marksman preparing to squeeze the trigger. "I don't know, Father. There . . . when we passed a ninety-degree angle . . ."

"What?"

"I saw a distortion field."

Aubry chuckled. "A distortion field doesn't *leave* anything to see. That's the whole point, isn't it?"

"A popular misconception." Leslie's eyes never wavered. Her voice became unnaturally calm and precise. "While you cannot see the object concealed, the field itself has a visual presence much like heat distortion. We used them often during my period with Gorgon. . . ." His voice trailed off, as if that memory was still painful.

"Well," Aubry said doubtfully. "Distortion fields aren't

illegal. It might just be a virtvid crew. It's not like I'm the president or something."

Leslie's pretty face creased with concentration. The skimmer had made a lazy loop around the inner city. If there *was* something hidden on a rooftop, a momentary trick of light and angle *could* have revealed it.

Promise squeezed Leslie's shoulder. "Let it go."

"But Mother . . . Mommy . . ." The words were a childish plaint, but Leslie's eyes were huge and dark, as if he had dropped back into some other level of existence. Promise turned her child away from the window.

"There's nothing there, Leslie. If there is, then the security people will handle it."

"But—"

"Leslie."

"Sometimes . . ."

Her voice was as soft and strong as silk. "Sometimes you forget that you're just my Leslie. Forget about the things you were trained to be, and do, and see. Just be Leslie. That's enough. You don't have to see threats behind every corner, below every bush."

Leslie responded, sitting back in his seat, but her mind was still entangled by steel struts, enmeshed in shadow.

Aubry wagged his massive head. "Let it go. I've seen this before. There's a little bit of bird dog in Leslie. Give him a hint of a sniff of a whisper, and he's off. I think life's gotten a little dull for us."

As they laughed, Leslie's mouth softened into a childish, slightly abashed smile. But behind those youthful eyes the intensity was undiminished. Her eyes were a killer's eyes. Promise could never make herself forget it.

You cannot develop and nurture an ability, hone yourself to razor-edge preparedness, expand every capacity to its ultimate, and not have a raging desire to express those talents, be they creative or destructive.

There may have been few things natural or normal about Leslie Knight, but in this way, if no other, her offspring was typical. She could not remake Leslie. Could not give her a new childhood, could not make Leslie forget the terrible reality of her early years. All Promise could do was love her.

It was sad, in a sense. She had hoped that after all this time, Leslie would begin to forget. And yet . . .

Just because you're paranoid doesn't mean they're not out to get you.

3

The crowd was quiet as the Chevy spiraled down, momentarily eclipsing the sun and thereby haloed with its radiance. The platform doors dropped aside, revealing the landing bay beneath. Turbofan disturbance scattered papers and fluttered hats and cloaks at a hundred feet, and those very close to the stage experienced a brief but not unpleasant surge of heat. The skimmer sank down out of sight, into catacombs beneath the surface street. The platform slid shut above it.

Steam and compressed air hissed. With a hum, the turbofans glided to a halt. Skimmer and elevator platform came to rest.

They were underground now, in one of the subterranean catacombs the Scavengers had constructed over the last decade. Nearly a square mile of quake-ravaged downtown Los Angeles had been rebuilt by the Scavengers. Highly conservative estimates valued Scavenger holdings at six hundred and fifty million dollars. How much of that money belonged to Promise and Aubry was a closely guarded secret.

Not that it would be easy to translate it into liquid assets. Scavenger assets were immediately reinvested in human beings, one of the reasons for their overwhelming success.

An enormous sun-bronzed man strode to the landing platform. He was decked out in military dress, the interlinked vipers of the Gorgon insignia emblazoned on his jacket. He wrenched the door open and saluted smartly. "Aubry."

"Bloodeagle," Aubry responded. They clasped hands, expending enough pressure to crush Brazil nuts into meal.

Miles Bloodeagle was almost as tall as Aubry, and even heavier. His broad, weathered face was strengthened by the Asian-Semitic planes and shadows of his Cherokee blood. He was one of the hormonally altered beings known as the NewMen. Even among that elite fraternity, he was legendary, one of the leaders of the paramilitary subgroup known as Gorgon. Bloodeagle owed both life and honor to Aubry.

"How does the crowd look?" Aubry asked skeptically.

"Does the term 'feeding frenzy' strike a chord?" Bloodeagle helped Promise down from the vehicle. Although not physically attracted to her, he could and did appreciate a healthy animal. *If Aubry has to be hetero,* Miles thought, *at least he has good taste.*

"Looks like the whole Maze is here," Bloodeagle said proudly. "God, how it's changed."

Aubry grinned. "I guess it has, at that."

"Seems a lifetime ago that you brought the Scavengers in after us, saved a houseful of NewMen. Could have cost you everything, Aubry."

"Everything worked out fine."

"But you didn't know that at the time."

Aubry shrugged and mumbled something unintelligible, then turned to speak with the pilot.

For the thousandth time, Bloodeagle envisioned Aubry in Gorgon uniform. Aubry would never join, but Miles knew his friend had been born to wear the colors.

In Miles's circle, abnormal levels of strength and fitness were commonplace, an automatic aspect of being a NewMan.

Aubry was as great a freak as any of them. He had been tested, and his physical strength, stamina, flexibility, endurance, balance, and coordination were simply superior to ordinary human beings'. There was no evidence of chemical stimulation, or genetic tampering. And yet, the

indisputable fact remained—Aubry Knight was the fittest
human being the NewMan Nations had ever encountered.

If it wasn't genetic engineering, and it wasn't hormonal
tampering, then it might have been the morning exercises
that Miles had twice seen Aubry perform. It looked like an
odd combination of martial arts and yoga, and lasted over
an hour. Aubry said he had learned the movements at the
age of five, practicing them every day until his mid-teens.
Fifteen years passed, and then a man named Kevin Warrick reawakened the old habit patterns. Rigorous daily
practice had been resumed.

He refused to let Miles holo the routine. But twice,
Miles had watched Aubry's magnificent body flex and
twist and leap through the sequence, his breath hissing like
a steam engine at full boil. . . .

Bloodeagle felt a touch of vertigo when he looked at
Aubry, but had long since grown past any embarrassment
about it.

Leslie paused in the doorway, a coquettish smile on his
beautiful face, and dimpled prettily. "Uncle Miles!" he
yelled, and leaped from the doorway.

It was a hell of a leap. An entirely casual effort, it came
close to the city record for the standing broad jump. Miles
caught Leslie and spun him around, planting him on the
ground behind the screen. "Come on, now—no theatrics.
This is Daddy's big day."

Leslie grinned. "Isn't it like *muy headthunk*?"

"Uh . . ."

Leslie giggled and linked arms with Miles, and they
waited for Mira to emerge. She appeared in the doorway,
patting a stray hair into place and smiling wanly. She let
Leslie and Miles escort her down the stairs.

Aubry ran his fingers along the tunnel walls as they
walked past. The walls sighed, and whispered steam, seemingly in response to his touch. Miles watched him, without
covetousness.

*Are you happy, Aubry? You have all of the things that
men say they want. Family. Love. Wealth. Health.*

And now, public acclaim.

But why do you seem so coiled and brittle? Why the storm cloud hovering above your shoulders? Does the quiet life wear thin?

Do you miss the nearness of death?

They reached the elevator disk and stood in the middle, enveloped in a brilliant cone of light from overhead.

Leslie stood between his extraordinary parents, and linked hands with them, smiling so brightly he nearly glowed. At that moment, he seemed the proudest and happiest, most normal child that Miles could imagine. How different from the feral animal that the scientists of Gorgon had created from Promise and Aubry's seed. How different from the bloodthirsty creature that had been unleashed upon the president of the United States. . . .

The elevator disk began to rise. . . .

4

Promise Cotonou-Knight held her breath. The crowd's roar numbed the ear, rocked the ground, meshed with the swell of the brass band's Sousa marches, embraced them with its tidal thunder as they rose up into the staging area. Pershing Square was a rectangle of park in the very heart of Los Angeles. Ordinarily it held the Free Market, the last remnant of the bad old days, when Mazetown had been America's largest and most shameful ghetto.

Now, after years of backbreaking work, it was a showpiece. She had manipulated, finessed, and otherwise hypnotized industrial concerns ranging from Canada to PanAfrica into investing time and money and skill to make it so, and this was a gorgeous day to show it off.

The crowd surged against the police barricades like a joyous, volatile fluid. Many of them were still Mazies, the street people who earned their bread by selling physical services—anything from manual labor to quasilegal sex. But even today, the label "Mazie" seemed less an insult than a celebration of an individual choice. The world had changed. Skins tinted every color of the rainbow were cloaked in the raiment of a dozen lands. Painted and sculpted faces shone with love and appreciation.

Mazetown was an official suburb of the Greater Los Angeles Metropolitan Area, something that had always been a crazy quilt of neighborhoods: "a thousand suburbs in search of a city," as one wag had described it. But as the most culturally diverse area in the world, it had naturally split into uncounted overlapping zones.

Aubry stood quietly, flanked by Promise, Leslie, Mira, and Bloodeagle. He was conscious of Promise's steady, warm pressure on his hand, and he returned it. She seemed remote. Wherever she was, he wished that he could have been there with her, preferably the two of them alone. This, he decided, was a pain.

"This belongs to *you*," he whispered to her. She squeezed his hand and gave him a gift: her plastiskin, the light-conductive plastic on the left side of her body, crackled and arced in time with the music. After all this time, it still fascinated him. The artificial flesh was warm, soft, and resilient, porous enough to carry her sweat to the air, or to his tongue. But it was also pure visual magic, controlled by a processor implanted in her jaw.

A holofield above Aubry's head captured his attention as it transformed him into a giant. President Roland Harris's prerecorded voice echoed through the streets. "Born in the streets of this, one of the greatest cities of the world, with only his mind and his body to help him in his journey, orphaned at a tender age . . ."

A skimmer floated by above, carrying a banner of some kind. *Go Aubry.* A cheer? A request?

"—and so it is our very great honor to present to you, on this most solemn of days, this plaque, bestowing upon you officially what has already long existed in the hearts and minds of your people—"

5

San shut her mind away from cold, or fear, or excitement. There was, however, interest. She studied the target carefully. Knight seemed uncomfortable. And why not? He was playing a role, wearing a mask. And no human being can be happy wearing a mask. One must be who and what one most truly is.

And so, whither the charade? Shall it end today?

Certainly, for one of us.

The pulse rifle steadied itself, and San's finger caressed the trigger. Soon, now.

6

Leslie's head canted to the side, nostrils flaring, as if catching a whiff of skunk. His fingers closed on Aubry's hand tightly enough to crush ordinary fingers into paste. Leslie's small face was flushed, his gaze unsteady, as if struggling to keep raw emotion under control.

Suddenly Aubry regretted bringing Leslie with them. The child still hadn't accustomed himself to the notion of life above ground, out of the shadows.

Harris was a good man, as politicians went, but would this long-winded mouse-faced bastard get his fucking speech *over* with?

"—I give you now—Aubry Knight!"

Aubry stepped forward to the sound circle, and looked out. Promise, Bloodeagle, Mira, and Leslie. The closest thing to a family he had ever known. And beyond them, before him, a cheering throng of thousands.

His impatience melted. Some of that was merely butter-flies, after all. This should have been Promise's moment, and they would speak about that later. When it came to Scavenger business, she insisted upon thrusting him into the spotlight. And what Promise insisted upon, she usually got.

"I don't really know what to say, except thank you very much."

He accepted the plaque from the hand of one of the assistants, and—

Mira's head exploded.

7

In the last moment before the horror began, Aubry's peripheral vision flashed an image of Mira: standing to Leslie's right, hands clasped before her. Her face was sweetly serene, relaxed, somehow younger than the Mira sitting in the front seat of the Chevy. In the next instant she was a hideous scarecrow, her head a papier-mâché doll stuffed with tomatoes and cherry bombs, detonated as a schoolboy trick.

A sound wave slapped Aubry's ears as he dove to the ground, hurling Promise down with him, his left arm sheltering her, his right—

Where was Leslie?

Everything, including his thoughts, moved as if suspended in syrup. For the next few seconds his vision and hearing were painfully sharp. Smoke and the stench of charred flesh choked his nostrils. His eyes focused on something near him—too near him. Glistening. Shapeless. White, speckled red and brown, and black, with three strands of hair curling away from its base. As he watched, they curled and withered in the flames consuming Mira's emerald dress.

Christ. She was *burning.*

Pulse rifle. Plasma burst. One-hundred-percent kill rate, anywhere above the knees. Zero penetration: bystanders rarely more than singed. An assassin's weapon. A professional's weapon.

The killer hadn't missed.

Aubry realized he was screaming, and forced his mouth shut.

More sounds: running feet. A loudspeaker. His own breathing, rolling like lava.

Where was Leslie?

The air around the speaking platform churned in a varicolored whirl, seethed with the chaos of a Gorgon distortion field: automatic defense against a sniper attack. It screwed up the visual coordinates—an assassin would need the optical codes to pinpoint him in this mess.

The entire platform sank shuddering into the ground. On hands and knees, Promise scuttled over to the shattered, flaming remnants of Mira Warrick. She stared at her friend, stripped off her coat and flung it over the remains. Stinking smoke gushed from beneath the fabric. She stretched out her hands without daring to touch. Then she turned to Aubry, her eyes huge and luminous. The carefully conditioned autonomic locks that kept her plastiskin dormant slipped away. Sparks and whirls of color disrupted the warm brown skin on the left side of her face, transforming her into a creature of myth. She snatched her hand back.

"Where is my *child*?" Her voice was a terrible ragged whisper. Aubry crawled next to her and gripped her elbow.

Then the animal in the back of his brain, a thing ordinarily submerged, a thing that had once been the only Aubry Knight he knew, laughed sourly and stepped out of the shadows.

You knew you'd need me again.

Images flashed, lightning strikes against an arctic night. Again, he saw the platform in its fully raised position. Mira's head splashed into a cloud of flame and pink vapor as the fluids in her skull reached an explosive boiling point.

He visualized the platform continuing to sink into the

skimmer dock, without his child. Their child. Ten-year-old prodigy Leslie acted without hesitation.

"Damn," he whispered, lunging to his feet. "Did anyone see where that came from?"

"Nothing." Miles Bloodeagle had risen shakily to one knee. His ruddy face was almost ashen.

"Leslie saw something at the southeast corner of Tyson All-Faiths."

"Put your money down."

An alarm wailed distantly, melding with the more immediate confusion. Six-legged emergency 'bots clambered up on the platform, hoisting legs to squirt white foam over the smoking remnants of Mira Warrick. Part of Aubry watched in horrid fascination, an emotional shield sliding down over the rest of him, taking him into a dark and ugly place within his heart.

Miles jumped down from the platform and sprinted to his personal skimmer, a Lear airbike with triple hover fans. Twin Mitsubishi pulse rifles were mounted on the side. He opened the leather gear bag on the side and threw a pair of goggles at Aubry, who was already stripping off his coat and vest.

"This thing carry two?"

Miles looked at him appraisingly. "What do you weigh these days? Two thirty?"

"Two forty," he admitted.

"It'll have to do. Hop on."

Promise's cloak was burned and soaked with blood and firefoam. *The silk is ruined* . . . Aubry mentally slapped himself. "Aubry!" Promise screamed, the flesh of her beautiful face stretched taut over her cheekbones. "Bring back my child, do you hear me, Aubry?"

He nodded, unable to speak.

8

The air slapped against them, cold and hostile, as they rose up out of the dock. They were awash in a swirl of molten colors as the distortion field bent and twisted the light around them. Then they broke free of its protective bubble, and the world became sane again.

The crowd was still disappearing, screaming and streaming off in all directions. Aubry clung one-armed to Bloodeagle's waist, peering down at the police squads. Walking, driving, skimming—they strove to control the crowd, tried to keep them from trampling each other into the pavement.

Chrome security units whooped and shrieked in from all directions now. Searchlights dissected each building in turn. Nothing. Video would tell little, autopsy less: plasma-pulse trauma was too extreme to leave convenient, trajectory-revealing exit wounds.

The Lear airbike shuddered in the wind, dropping and struggling to reclaim altitude as gusts slammed them sideways. The wind deafened them as Bloodeagle fought his way toward the arching, emerald expanse of Tyson All-Faiths.

Aubry remembered Leslie's sudden, hawklike intensity, the bird-dog focus that he had disregarded. So strong. So quick.

So young.

Damn damn damn!

As All-Faiths' tangle of girders sprouted beneath them, Bloodeagle brought the Lear around toward the bare planking that constituted a temporary roof.

He had failed Leslie once. Not again. His child had focused on this building. Let the police search where they might—he would bet on his child's instincts—

As you should have trusted your own?

To hell with it. To hell with everything but Leslie.

And God help anything, or anyone, that stood in his way.

9

I was home. Father calls this his Dark Place. It is the only place in the world that . . . smells right. It is within me. Here, as nowhere else, I can feel.

I feel death.

In the Dark Place, sight, and sound, and sensation don't exist as most people experience them. Everything is immediate—as if I am a part of what is experienced. There is no spectator. There is no *me*. This is best.

I am very bad. I am evil. The Way is in killing. Death is life.

I remained within my breathing, floating on an air current. I am sounds too faint to hear. Am shadow-flickers too dim to detect. I am all of this.

And less.

Once, there were other Medusae. They understood. All dead now. Now, only Father. He has the Dark Place within him, but fights it. Sometimes wins. Mostly. I admire him.

I am terribly lonely.

A hundredth of a second before the woman Mira died I began to move OFF LINE. First order of action—move OFF LINE. Trust kinesthetic/visual flash. Cognitive correlation too slow.

Can't explain. Human sensory input processes a billion impressions a minute. Reticular activating system filters all but a whisper in a hurricane of data. Must trust older, more primitive cortical structures.

Once I got OFF LINE, cognitive backtracking and sorting began. According to Miles Bloodeagle this is a conditioned adaptation of the brain's holographic/fluid processing.

Tyson All-Faiths is a monstrosity. Mother called it neo-Byzantine. If this is a house of God, She has the aesthetics of a mud wasp.

Catholic, Muslim, Methodist, Hebrew, and Gaiac services are conducted in central shared area. Tyson was a wealthy agnostic, who left a building fund in his will. He had a nonsectarian religious vision a week before his death and took no chances.

I moved silently along a catwalk above a balcony, my senses open.

I heard a sound beneath me, and looked down on a police investigative team. At first I experienced anger—these idiots would muddy the water.

Or act as lure.

I stripped out of my dress. Strange. The softness and frills give me pleasure. This irritates Father. I need his approval, but it is pleasurable to irritate him. Strange.

Removed undergarments, and wedged all clothing into a corner. Ready for the night. I have five percent body fat. When people think I am too far away to hear, I have been called reptilian. I tell myself not to care what they think. I am Death. I am more silent than my own shadow. I was in automatic scan mode. The microreceiver in my occipital ran the electromagnetic spectrum, searching for relevant patterns. I can interpret them aurally, as visual, or as kino. At that moment, I needed audio, and selected police band. They were using encoded throatmikes. Using a primitive interpolation, I cracked the cipher before my next breath.

"—twenty-two-percent chance of vector origin mark Tyson. Perp still present."

"Has Knight and his family been secured?"

"All except for the kid."

"Jesus. That weird brat?"

"Keep your opinions to yourself. Keep your eyes open."

I do not care what they think.

I do not.

I caught something. Not light . . . but some variation on

the darkness. I wedged myself back into the shadows, and watched as three cops passed beneath me. They moved in standard inverted V, sweeping three hundred degrees a second, very alert, very "professional."

I watched them die.

One moment there was a shadow behind them, and in the next that shadow detached itself and merged with theirs for just under two seconds. There was a rustling sound, like pillows tumbling in slow motion. And then they were dead. I heard a single word spoken: *"Roku."* Japanese for the number six.

Efficient. Admirably competent. I climbed out along the catwalk, to get a better look. They were what Bloodeagle calls "body dead": broken, twisted as if fallen from a skimmer. I stopped breathing for a moment. Query: Who has such capacity for swift, silent violence? And the inclination to use hand-to-hand when sophisticated tools are available?

Gorgon personal-encounter protocols encourage such behavior. Were there Gorgons here? More renegades? Could some have survived the battle in Death Valley? Who else has the requisite skill and strength and power to bring silent death to three armed men . . .

Gorgon/not Gorgon. Irrelevant. This is Challenge. To whom? Father. Of course. Kill Mira, the old, useless woman. Spare the child, and the woman of childbearing years. Terminate, with contempt, the warriors you send after him. The message was clear. *I can kill anyone, anywhere, any time. Either meet me alone, or more will die. From a distance. These are my skills. Do not anger me.*

First frame: three human beings. Hale. Hearty. Second frame: pile of bleeding meat. My stomach flashed hot, and the urge to EVACUATE SECTOR began to override courage programming. All humans experience this sensation. Most call it fear. Some utilize it in the manner evolution intended: to stimulate combative or evasive potentials.

Some, ignorant, are ashamed of it.

I modified the submodalities of the kino impressions by

sending tendrils of thought out into my endocrines. I steadied my breathing and dropped respiration to two a minute.

I watched. Waited.

Nothing. Then, without warning, I felt the tingle. The strength seeped out of my fingers and arms. I barely managed to push back onto the catwalk.

I thought: *He* saw *me??!*

Next thought: *They?*

And then nothing.

10

Aubry's senses flamed the moment he entered All-Faiths. As he walked the hallways they shifted crazily from granite to steel to glass. Now a cave, now a glade, now a hall of mirrors infinitely reflecting a lone, armed man gliding through its corridors.

The environment processor wasn't fully activated. Crystal chandeliers. Now a row of Renaissance paintings: plump, haloed infants held by improbably pale Madonnas. Flickering candles shimmied in unseen winds. Now the faint echo of a ghostly choir, humming a Gregorian chant.

In the next moment, the tang of incense filled the air, and above him the ceiling assumed a mosque's concavity. Furniture and wall decorations morphed to fit the Middle Eastern motif.

Then the surroundings flowed again. Rugged mountain peaks soared overhead, sprouting out of the earth around him. Summer wind swirled from unseen vents, plucked at his hair, dried the sweat at the back of his neck.

It was a perfect site for Gaia worship. Promise's sister Jenna would have felt right at home. Aubry felt naked and exposed.

And vulnerable. And afraid. His body felt rusty. His

survival instincts simply weren't engaged. It was a terrifying feeling, akin to that of losing one's core identity.

Or for Aubry Knight, perhaps even worse than that.

A distant radio chuckled, then dissolved into echoes.

Aubry held his rifle at port arms, and slid from one doorway to another. He focused his hearing, striving to send his senses out in front of him . . . nothing but those echoes. He dropped to his knees and peered around the corner. Even the caution was something that he was unused to feeling. Before today, there had always been a quality of recklessness, a lack of respect for his own life, a willingness to throw himself completely into the fray. Today, it simply wasn't there.

He remembered Bloodeagle's fluid dismount from the bike, splitting off from Aubry, ghosting down the first of two rooftop stairwells. Where Aubry was torn, Bloodeagle was at peace. The man was still alert, and alive, in a world where lack of alertness cost lives—at the least.

With a single code word, Bloodeagle could have summoned a dozen Gorgons to the scene within ten minutes. But six hundred seconds was just too damned long.

Where was Leslie? And what could possibly be in this place that could endanger his child? Promise's last command still rang in his ears:

Find my child.

Aubry's mind chattered like a fevered monkey, lashing him with doubts. *What if this isn't the building?* Still, it was Leslie's likeliest destination. *What if he's dead . . . ?* He couldn't believe that. If Leslie were dead, Aubry's heart would be a stone in his chest. He would feel it, know it, though the corpse be a world away.

No, Leslie was alive. If Aubry could just find his child . . .

The vomitously sweet stench of human blood and body waste clawed at his nose. Even before he rounded the next corner, Aubry knew what he would find.

The three policemen lay sprawled in terminal angularity, splashed by the filtered, artificial glare of the stained-glass window. Aubry quickly scanned the surrounding room, then knelt to examine them. Their skulls had been shattered. Their eyes had been forced from their sockets by a hideous internal pressure. It reminded Aubry of something he himself might have done, in another life, if enraged to the point of madness.

He heard a shallow, childlike inhalation, and turned to see a tiny, slender figure slumped against a column, shrouded in shadow.

Leslie. Aubry was there in two steps, fingers checking the pulse. The sweet little face was unbruised, the chest rose and fell effortlessly.

Around his neck hung a silver medallion. Aubry examined it cautiously. His first concern was ungrounded: it wasn't an explosive device.

It was a receiver.

And even as he lifted it, it crackled in his hand.

"Greetings, my brother." A female voice. Deep, mellifluous, and strangely familiar. There was an odd singsong quality to it.

"As you see, we can kill you, or anything you love, whenever we wish."

"What the hell do you want from me?"

Another pause, during which Aubry heard nothing but the roar of his own breathing. *"We want you,"* the voice said. *"Not now, but when we say. Just you. Otherwise, you will never know."*

"Will never know what?"

"When we kill everything you love."

"There are more than one of you?"

"The woman died to show you we were serious. I want you, and you alone. The child is . . . interesting, but would be a distraction. Three nights from now. Come here, alone. Unarmed. And you will get the rest of your instructions."

"And then what?"

"And then? And then one of us will die."

The medallion became silent.

With a swift, fluid shuffle sound, Bloodeagle appeared at

his side. He hadn't seen Leslie yet. "Aubry? Did you find something?"

"Nothing," he lied, and slipped the medallion into his pocket. "I've found nothing at all."

11

Aubry and Promise took a security suite in Scavenger Towers, on the outskirts of Mazetown. Together, they watched over Leslie. The child had come out of his torpor, but still moved slowly, spoke with a thick tongue, had a frightening tendency to fall asleep. Doctors laid him on the white rectangle of the scan table, peeled him out of his clothing, inspected his prepubescent muscularity, and probed the moist, pinkish brown folds of his genitals. Eyebrows were arched in surprise and speculation, but their evaluations quieted alarm. They suggested that nature be allowed to take her course.

When the doctors and the well-wishers were gone, silence descended. Aubry stood at a video wall, gazing out over a night city where most of the citizens lived and loved and worked without thinking of imminent death.

Promise appeared behind him and wrapped her arms around his muscular waist. She pressed her mouth against his back. Through his shirt, her breath warmed his skin, but not his heart. "You're not telling me everything." Aubry said nothing. He crossed to their bed and slipped out of his clothes, and then under the covers. He stared at the ceiling. A thin, high snoring sound, almost a whistle, pulled his eyes down. Their child was curled on his side, asleep on a cot at the side of the bed. Promise wouldn't let Leslie out of her sight. The slightest variation in breathing patterns, the slightest shift in position, would rouse her from full sleep.

She knelt beside Aubry, the clinging film of her nightgown cloaked by her robe. It would require far denser camouflage to mute her physical presence: every movement, every inhalation or exhalation seemed to be carefully measured for impact.

Lashes half-lowered, she gazed at him, awaiting an answer. "What happened in All-Faiths, Aubry?"

"I don't know." *But you do know,* a voice inside him whispered. *You know too damned well.*

Aubry moistened his lips, buying time. "I found three dead police officers. Leslie was unconscious but unharmed. And there was a message. The assassin wants to meet with me."

A red and orange aurora crackled across Promise's face, shifted shadows on the wall. "Why?"

"Challenge. An affair of honor, perhaps. I don't know. But it's just between us." He didn't bother to tell her the rest.

Or we will kill everything that you love.

"You can't do it," Promise whispered. "You don't know who they are, or what they want."

"Yes, I do. They want me."

Promise spoke very calmly, very directly. "You can't do that, Aubry. You have obligations now."

"They killed Mira. They could have killed you, or Leslie. There must have been a reason. They could have killed me, if that was what they wanted."

If that bitch wanted to kill you like that, he added silently.

"What are you going to do?" Suddenly, quite abruptly, he was lost to her. There was an aspect of Aubry that remained beyond her reach. A part that she had striven against. With a sudden flash of guilt she realized that she had done her very best to conquer him with softness and love. With fame and money, security and family.

That was the aspect of Aubry which had responded to Leslie's warning. That part of him which Promise feared, because it seemed not only to detect trouble, but *attract* it as well. And now . . .

Mira was dead.

* * *

Leslie stirred slightly, still recovering from the effects of the nerve ray. He tossed onto his side and back again, lost in a world of phantoms.

Aubry sat at the edge of Leslie's bed, pulling the blanket up to the small chin with thick, dark, callused hands.

He studied the magnetic chess set in the corner of the room. Leslie and Promise's sister Jenna were teaching Aubry the game. Jenna was a master, and Leslie an intuitive genius at chess. Aubry was just beginning to understand some of the basic ploys and gambits.

But he could play well enough to lose gracefully. He studied his position. "Knight to queen's pawn six," he murmured.

Leslie stirred in his sleep. He didn't open his eyes, or take a look at the chessboard. "Queen's bishop to queen's knight four. Check."

Aubry studied his position. "Damn." He brushed one massive finger along Leslie's cheek. He took gentle pleasure in the ebb and flow, the steady river of life as its tides swept through the body of his child, the only creature in all the world he could call his blood. In repose, Leslie's angularity was softened. He seemed a chocolate angel, a picture of innocence and guiltless conscience.

How many people had Leslie killed? How many more would have died, if the Medusae hadn't been stopped?

Within Leslie burned a terrible engine of destruction. The fact that unknown assassins had managed to neutralize him was sobering.

He remembered Mira, lying in a pool of blood and brains and splintered skull, and made a mental transposition. Suddenly, Mira became Promise. And then Leslie.

And now, for the first time, he slid the emotional shields back so that he could actually feel the horror.

Dead. Shattered. His child. His woman.

Aubry's hand closed on the little bed's metal framework. It was a quarter inch thick along an edge, and bent beneath his hands like foil.

He would meet this assassin, this whore who wanted his life.

And kill her, whatever the cost.

12

JULY 20

The Maze was a fifty-square-block area in the heart of what had once been the most valuable real estate in the world, the heart of downtown Los Angeles. With the California Quake, it became an instant disaster area. As the exodus of business and residential tenants began, the social infrastructure crumbled.

Poverty and crime were rampant. The forces of law and order were completely overwhelmed by the task of preserving order in the midst of utter chaos. Bankrupt and water-poor, the State of California could do little.

The inner city burned.

After years, the group called the Scavengers began rebuilding. Today, when Aubry toured the city, with Promise at his side . . .

But that phrasing was a lie. The truth was that *Promise* toured the city, with Aubry at *her* side.

Whenever there was a function requiring their participation, wasn't it true that her presence was far more necessary than his?

Wasn't it?

But the sights and sounds and smells of Mazetown were still music to his senses. A hundred different ethnicities blended together to compose this melting pot. A dozen languages and a hundred dialects filled the streets. Office buildings sported signs in six languages. Dentists, acupuncturists, and certified public shamans shared office space. A thousand savory collations from around the world awaited the adventurous palate. Ten thousand street vendors peddled their wares to shopkeepers, street workers, and construction crews.

And everywhere they went, Promise and Aubry were offered condolences.

"Good day, Miz Cotonou," the men and women of Mazetown said over and over to her as she passed. Aubry hung back, watching as Promise made an inspection of Scavenger facilities.

"Why make the personal inspection?" he asked. "You can just facephone over, or scan the data vids."

"Doesn't give you a feel for what's going on," she replied. "We'll be back in Ephesus in a couple of days."

"I just want you out of here."

"We've already shipped Leslie back. If that assassin wanted me, he would have killed me. I can't neglect my duties."

Aubry sighed.

Every face had a sympathetic and concerned smile, and every hand that touched him touched in friendship.

Promise watched him. "You're not telling me everything," she said.

"What makes you say that?"

She gathered up a handful of mutant fruit. The mini-malls were serviced by mini-groves, mutant bonsai trees with different fruit on every branch. She hefted a banana-like fruit with an edible peel, then slipped a bunch into her basket.

"Because I know you."

"I have no intention of getting dead."

"Which isn't the same as not putting yourself in the position where it can happen. Don't play word games with me." She gripped his arm fiercely. "You say you love me. You promised to be there, for me, and for our child. Now some maniac hurls a challenge at you, and you're throwing it all away. For what?"

Aubry hesitated. "For Mira?"

That stopped her, but only for a moment. "Mira wouldn't want you to die for nothing. She loved you like a brother."

Promise watched his face, masking her own emotions. How do you tell a man, quite possibly the world's greatest expert in one very specialized area, that he can no longer practice his art? She had always known that, eventually, Aubry would find a challenge, a way to vent his fear and apartness, his frustration. And he would do it in the only way he really understood—through physical combat.

His eyes roamed the market, searching, and never finding the face he was looking for. The face of a woman he didn't know. Or a man? She had said *we*.

It *could* be a woman. He had known deadly women before. Jenna. His memory bubbled at him. What was that bitch's name . . .

Chan. He hadn't thought about her for years.

Hadn't thought about killing her.

Male or female, then. The assassin could be anyone. There—the butcher. The baker. The candlestick maker. Who in the world could know? How *could* they know?

After three hours, Aubry turned to Promise and said, "I have to go for a walk." She laid her fingertips lightly on his shoulders, and strove to memorize his face. Would he be dead and broken the next time she saw him? Or alive, with the smell of blood on his teeth? Could the civilized Aubry, so carefully nurtured, revert to the beast so quickly? Did it take only . . .

Only the exploding head of a woman they both loved, only the sight of that ghastly, splintered skull, and the smell of blood and viscera on the morning wind.

"Yes." She slid her fingertips up to his cheeks. If his lethal skills had been hers, she would have gone. If she were Jenna, she would go. And suddenly, for just a brief instant, she looked through his eyes and saw what he saw, a shadow world of reds and blacks with just a hint of subtlety beginning to creep into it. It was a dark and dangerous place. It was not a place that she wanted to spend more time in. It was Aubry's world.

And was, perhaps, a realer world than hers.

"Go for your walk," she whispered. "I'll be waiting for you." She kissed him, fiercely, crushing her lips against his, her mouth slightly open to receive the warmth and wetness of his fire. Then she spun, and was gone.

Aubry watched Promise disappear into the crowd, and sighed hotly. She understood. She might not have been able to tell him, but she understood. Someone had killed Mira, and harmed their child. Slaughtered three police officers. Threatened their lives, and the security they had so carefully established over hard years of labor.

Someone had challenged him on his home turf. Someone strong, ruthless, lethal.

Someone who was going to die.

13

Promise's eyes blurred as she moved through the marketplace, striving to immerse herself in the ten thousand small things that constituted her responsibilities in Mazetown. Where now? There were so many things to be done. She flagged a taxi drone and hopped in.

The Griffith Observatory had perched in its present position, overlooking the Los Angeles basin, for almost a century. Although it had performed no actual research for years, it was still a popular tourist attraction.

Now its coppered concrete dome was enclosed in scaffolding, and surrounded by cranes, bulldozers, hoists, and trucks. Air compressors hummed and hissed. Oxypropane torches seared metal and eye, and filled the air with acrid smoke.

The Scavengers were at work.

The observatory was being deconstructed, sold off by a fund-hungry municipal government. The University of

Osaka's science-fiction club had purchased it, and it would be shipped overseas in just under two months.

Promise exited the cab and slipped under the restraint lines. The screech of injured metal assaulted her ears, and her nose wrinkled at the stench of sizzling mica.

The crew chief, a squatly muscular man with a carrot-colored crew cut, waved and climbed down from the roof. He pumped her hand heartily. "Miz Cotonou! Didn't expect to see you here."

"How are things progressing, Kregger?"

Kregger flipped open a pocket projector. A hologram of the complete structure appeared in midair. He cross-referenced with the data, and an animated schematic disassembled the structure piece by piece. In the projection, the work proceeded with perfect fluidity. Reality, of course, was much more brutal.

"A lot of this concrete should be recast," he mused.

"Can't we negotiate that?"

"It'll bring the price down. These guys want the real observatory. Apparently, they shot a shitload of old sci-fi flatfilms around here. What does Osaka U. care if the structure is unsound? They've got the biggest movie souvenir in the world!"

"We need a connection to the board of construction and housing in Osaka? Put in a leak that an unsafe situation exists. If the order comes down from over their heads, then they'll have to change, and it shouldn't affect our price."

Kregger breathed a sigh of relief. "I like that idea. I don't want our name attached to a minor disaster." He looked back over his shoulder at the observatory. Its coppered dome shone brightly, "You know, I'm kind of used to this old girl. I'm not sure what I think about it going down."

"If the Brits can sell Windsor, I guess we can do without Griffith Observatory. Too many space-based telescopes," she said sympathetically. "Ground-based just aren't as important. Build a receiving station with display facilities and you get images from a dozen different 'scopes for the price of one." She shrugged. "Time marches on."

"So shall we all."

A crowd of spectators bowed the barricade lines. Beyond the cordon, wistful Angelenos watched as another link to the past was stripped down, packed, and trundled away. America had made its peace with the Japanese . . . the world was far too small for any other choice. By the end of the twentieth century, automated translation nodes linked Tokyo and Los Angeles. America wanted Japanese technology, but Japan wanted America's movies and television and music.

Japan had conquered America, and America had absorbed her. Perhaps the era of nations, and national enmities, had passed.

Time moves on.

She glimpsed a striking figure: female, quite tall, very dark-skinned, and beautiful in a severe way. When Promise caught her eye, there was a moment of blistering contact, heat so intense that she thought her legs would buckle. Then the woman turned—she moved beautifully, Promise noticed—and was gone.

She was left with the impression of broad shoulders and a narrow waist, a sinewy form that promised power as well as an almost overwhelming sexuality. For a brief instant, Promise felt something unusual—inadequacy.

She walked a step or two forward. Had this Amazonian been watching her? There was something about the woman that reminded her of . . . what?

Ephesus?

But by the time Promise had reached the edge of the crowd the woman was gone, leaving only a disturbing thrill along Promise's spine, and a whisper of trouble in her ear.

14

The corridors and video walls of Tyson All-Faiths were quiet. Seventy-two hours before, police cordons had sealed off the ground floor, but public curiosity had died down. Now it was yesterday's news. No one attempted to stop Aubry's entrance, or even question him.

He walked slowly through the hall, uncertain of what he was looking for. The mass of the shockrod along his side wasn't as comforting as he had hoped.

Was he wrong? Was this to be a straight assassination, one that the killers simply wished to complete in some ritualistic fashion?

There were no notes, no messages, but suddenly he heard a hop-o'-my-thumb whisper in his ear, in some sort of tight-beamed message: *"Come to the attic."*

This voice was guttural, and male.

He took the stairs carefully, senses open and alert. Somewhere, there was something that would kill him, or try to.

The wind sighed through the cracks in the building. Distant street noise filtered through, distorted by the space and building materials into a thin, discomforting chuckle.

Aubry tested the door at the top of the stairs. It was a two-inch-thick slab of plastic with a reinforced metal lock. He placed the flat of his hand against it, and pushed.

The assassin was a gigantic mass in the church's darkness, muscles knotted to an almost simian density. His dark bare skin was thickly crisscrossed with keloid scars. He crouched in shadow like some great nocturnal predator.

Lines of white ink were tattooed like webbing across his face. The lines spread across chest and back, and down to the naked groin. Aubry squinted, barely able to make out his enemy's features. There was something disturbingly *familiar* about them.

The slow, deep sound of the man's breathing filled the attic loft. "Shi," it grunted.

Shi? Half a word?

Aubry slipped the shockrod from under his arm, and aimed it. It hummed in his hands, ready to spit sparks. "Why?"

There was no answer, just that deep breathing. The creature shuffled toward him, spiderlike, apelike, something not wholly human.

Use the rod, he told himself.

And he couldn't, God help him. Here was a creature that seemed to have descended from one of his own nightmares, and he couldn't bring himself to simply burn a hole in it. *Why? Because that's not the way the game is supposed to be played.* Very simple, really.

All right, then.

Aubry disabled the rod, and placed it on the floor. He bent his knees, finding low balance.

The combat computer in his mind ran a dozen evaluations in a fraction of a second. Wrestler. Strongly grounded. Right-handed. More strength than intelligence, but incredibly strong. Tremendous endurance. Don't let the hands grasp.

They circled each other, shuffling on the balls of their feet, testing each other's awareness and reflex. Not touching, but connected by spider threads of intention. A war dance. For a full minute, the balletic mirror play continued, and then . . .

The assassin leapt.

Aubry snaked to the left, evading a tree trunk of an arm. His right fist hammered home, dead into the center of the solar plexus.

Tensed only at the moment of impact, Aubry's strike was less a sledge than a whiplash, but it landed with thunderous impact. It was like striking a skimmer's shock skirt.

Aubry spun away without trying to follow up, and just

as well. The assassin's hands were after him with invisible speed. Thick fingers raked, ripping Aubry's shirt, gouging his shoulders even as he evaded.

The man was *quick*—but not quite as fast as Aubry. Stronger, perhaps. As coordinated? He had no interest in finding out. This creature knew him, had studied him at its leisure. He could only assume that it knew his physical potential, and still chose to face him in hand-to-hand combat. It only made sense to grant the assassin superior physical strength.

But there were things that the assassin couldn't know. He couldn't know of Aubry's sessions with Leslie, where Leslie focused his analytical skills on Aubry's movements, ergonomically "cleaning" them, making them even more efficient.

He couldn't know of the time with Jenna.

Aubry had never been a classical martial artist—but Jenna was, with high ranking in aikido, pa qua, and a master's command of durga.

Aubry had always relied upon native speed and strength, and an uncanny capacity to replicate virtually any movement after seeing it once. Since marriage to Promise he had spent hundreds of hours with Jenna and Leslie—the three most unusual training partners who ever lived. They exchanged ideas, imitated and learned from each other . . . and improved.

Promise's coordination and fitness could have made her great, but she possessed no emotional inclination for combat. And it is a logical truth, denied only by the ignorant, that a great fighter, at least during his formative years, must love to fight, must enjoy seeing fear and pain blossom on his opponent's face. This Promise could not do. She could watch, however, and marvel.

Now Aubry would find out if that grueling effort had been in vain.

The assassin struck a pose, one shoulder higher than the other. He lurched forward and then retreated, rolling his shoulders like an ape. Back and forward, trembling on the edge of attack, and then haring off, almost as if performing some kind of ritual dance.

Was someone watching? A camera? Of course. We *will kill everything that you love.*

The moment of thought almost cost Aubry his life. The assassin was at him as if propelled from a blowgun.

In an instant, the assassin had one of Aubry's wrists. To pull back was to invite disaster; instead, Aubry pivoted, dropping his hips and backing into his attacker with perfect timing, in the durga version of the aikido throw known as *koshi nage.* The assassin tumbled over his head, and Aubry's steel-shod toe slammed into his solar plexus again. This time there was focus, that quality of mental and emotional control that brings a touch of magic into the physical realm.

The assassin was just a hair slow in pivoting. Before he could turn, Aubry was on him.

Aubry's arm clamped around his neck in a deadly naked strangle, crushing against the massive neck muscles, the edge of his forearm grating against cartilage.

The assassin threw himself backward, trying to crush Aubry against the ground. In midair, Aubry's legs twined around his enemy's midsection, and his heel crashed into the vulnerable solar plexus a third time. As they thundered to the ground Aubry eeled away, scrambling and making his breakfall at the same time. The assassin, disoriented by the solar plexus strike, fell poorly, grazing his head.

As the assassin rose again, his grogginess was obvious. Before the man could turn toward him, Aubry struck with his heel. His side kick, structure groomed by Leslie, timing perfected by Jenna, smashed into the muscle shielding the left kidney. It was a hammer blow, retracting faster than it was launched, and it lanced an explosive shock wave into the delicate nerves.

Ignore the muscles, Jenna had taught him. *Strike into the nerves. Strike into the blood vessels. Strike into the breathing cavities. Strike where no one can armor. Time and focus your blows to penetrate the sheath of muscle. For your size, you have the finest combination of speed and agility I have*

*ever even imagined. But you are crude, Aubry. We will train
your mind, and your spirit. Awaken your intellect. Fight with
both body and your heart, and think with the brain the Goddess gave you. Otherwise you are only an animal.*

The assassin roared with pain, and Aubry leapt on him
again. This time both palms slammed against the ears. The
assassin's tympanic membranes ruptured explosively.

The assassin wrenched his head down, and tore his face
away from Aubry's questing fingers. He shook himself like
a huge dog. Aubry's grip loosened, and he fought against
surprise, alarm, and momentary confusion. There was the
sensation of being caught in a whirlpool, and suddenly the
assassin was behind him, forearm crushing Aubry's larynx. Aubry curled into a ball, left hand scrabbling back
desperately. He found a handful of matted hair, dropped
his butt to the ground, and heaved the assassin over his
shoulder. At the peak of the arc he twisted savagely.

Neck twisted at an unnatural angle, the assassin's own
weight snapped his spine at the seventh cervical vertebra
the instant before he crashed to the ground.

Aubry stood. The world spun around him as he sobbed
for air. He took a halting step away from the dead thing
splayed on the floor.

Then it groaned. Aubry's head snapped around, fingers
spread.

The assassin wasn't dead. Not quite. He shuddered
there on the ground, eyes wide, as if transfixed by the sight
of his own impending death. His arms beat arrhythmically
like the wings of a half-squashed insect.

His fingers dug into the floor, and he began to crawl toward Aubry.

Aubry watched, fascinated, unable to move, or speak,
or think. The scarred and tattooed man humped across the
floor like a snake with a broken back.

The great muscles of lat and deltoid coiled and bulged as
he gripped at the ground, hauled, stopped. His bladder released, and a stinking puddle spread from his waist. As he
dragged himself, his knees spread the stain in twin tracks.

Aubry could barely breathe. Name of God, what did the man *want?* To attack? To beg for his life? What?

The assassin worked his fingers under his own chin, and somehow managed to lift his head enough to lay it upon Aubry's foot, like a large, untidy dog. He made a whining sound deep in his throat. It sounded like "She." Aubry's eye focused upon his enemy's face for the first time.

The world came apart, as if it existed only in a mirror suddenly twisted and fragmented into nightmare.

With enormous effort he pulled the pieces back together, and found his center.

It was him. His own face. The face was fatter . . . no, not fat. The face and neck were thick with muscles, grotesque with them. But it was *him.* Aubry saw his own death in those brown eyes, watched the life drain out of them, watched himself take a final, shuddering breath.

And then watched himself fall into eternal stillness.

Aubry fled from the room.

15

They were connected in virtspace, a realm of electronic reality, existing only in the screaming mesh of wires and fiber optics that encircled the globe. One at a time, they winked into existence. Though separated by thousands of miles, they were connected more intimately than most human beings could even imagine. Their images hovered against an electric blue background. One, two, three, they winked into being. A pause. And then one more. Three were male. African. Skin color identical to the dead man's. Physical characteristics very, very close. One was female, of the same stock.

"*My brothers. What do we see?*"

"*We see a man afraid of his own death.*"

"*He is not one of us, Roku. He is not a brother.*"

"*No, Ni. He is as we are. He is worthy. He killed Shi.*"

"Shi was but a beast, but I agree. I will kill him. He will have a good death."

"You cannot kill him as easily as you killed the woman, San. He will not die asleep, as did the policemen, Roku. He will kill you both, and then I will kill him."

"You have such pretensions. Go. You and your armor. After I kill him, we will match. I would see your blood."

"You are dreaming," Go said. "You will see. With your death, I will earn a name."

"What name?" Ni asked.

"I do not know. But to think of it, I rather like the name Aubry. He did not earn it. He will not miss it. He will be dead."

16

JULY 22. NORTHERN OREGON. 3:00 A.M.

The Chevy's headlight splashed across the green wall of forest surrounding Ephesus, weaving a shadowed tapestry of soaring pines and firs. The metallic oval bobbed on air currents, danced for Promise and then settled into its familiar path, snaking above the river. Her hands were light and sure at the controls: flying was one of the things that she loved, one of the few times when she could shed her cocoon of financial and political responsibility and be completely, exuberantly alive.

Ordinarily, Aubry enjoyed watching as her long, powerful fingers danced across the controls. Her joy was infectious.

But there was no exuberance now, not in this moment.

This early morning they carried both love and dread in human form, family and madness cloaked in human flesh. Behind them, in the Chevy's cargo hold, lay the remains of two human beings. The ashes of Mira Warrick, and something that could have been Aubry. It vibrated in the muffled roar of the turbos, limp and broken-necked, rolled in plastic and sealed in an aluminum coffin. It was still soiled with its own wastes.

He couldn't make himself turn around, to gaze back into the hold. More than quiet, decomposing flesh waited in those shadows. What lay in the hold was Aubry's destiny.

A broken neck. A final burst of light, a savage, certain *knowing*. And then the endless night.

His hand pressed against the tinted translucence of the skimmer's Plexiglas window. The plastic flexed slightly as his shoulder muscles bulged. The *other* had possessed shocking strength. Aubry wondered if his own adversaries experienced the same gut-wrenching shock when closing to grappling range with him.

Was that what terrified him, to look into the face of something more animal than human, and see himself?

He buried his hands in his coat pockets and stared straight ahead.

As they slipped through the trees, the wind whispered challenge and their muted fans growled greeting in return. The trees parted somberly for them. Promise drove the skimmer on and on, toward Ephesus. Toward home.

17

Promise touched them down tenderly, as if afraid to waken the golem in the Chevy's cargo bay. She spun out of her chair, then paused, looking down at Aubry. He sat unmoving, seeming not to breathe, or even realize that they had landed. "Come on," she said. There was no reply.

The skimmer door sighed open.

The first woman across the threshold had Promise's height and bone structure, but was more slender through the hips. Her breasts were flatter and harder. Her natural skin tones were lighter, but tanned deeply enough to affect the same general shade. Her eyes were tilted by the same

Asian caste. Whereas Promise had carefully, deliberately cultivated her sensuality as a weapon, refined it to the degree that it was no longer possible to turn it completely off, this woman seemed to have diverted the same sensual appetite, the same physical grace, into lethality. She was Promise's sister Jenna, combat mistress of Ephesus.

They embraced warmly. Jenna's gaze flickered to Aubry. "Is he all right?"

"He will be. I've seen this before."

There was motion and sound in the hold behind them, as workers struggled to move the coffin out. Six of them groaned beneath its weight, bending in respect to the flesh if not the spirit. Promise solemnly removed Mira's rectangular brass urn.

Jenna clambered in and sat quietly next to Aubry. He was still motionless in the copilot's seat. For a while neither spoke; then she laid her hand upon his.

"Aubry?"

He nodded. His fingers traced a circle against the window. He stared off to the east, across a deeply shadowed stand of trees. Soon, the sun would be rising. He ached to see it.

"It's good to have you back." She paused. "Leslie is fine."

This, finally, brought a smile to his lips. Aubry heaved himself up from the chair. "Leslie. I need to see Leslie."

He looked down at Jenna. Her nails and auburn hair were cut short. No makeup, no artifice, nothing in her face but concern and integrity. Nothing but love for him and for her half-sister, Promise. A ray of light brushed Aubry's heart for a second. Then the clouds closed, and darkness returned.

He tried to brush past her, to hurry from a suddenly confining cockpit, but she moved against him. As lightly as feathers her arms settled on his shoulders, and she pressed her cheek against his chest.

Through the windows of the skimmer he could see the buildings beyond the landing pad. Two steel-frame three-storied medical facilities, the cubical brick structure of the library, the wood and glass arch of the research and conference facility. All were set in a U-shaped clearing framed by hundreds of thousands of towering trees. All about him was was the scent of life and love, and Aubry should have felt at home.

But what was home? Was it the towers and spires, the metal and concrete forest that civilized man had rooted in the earth, and then raised to heaven? Or was home the calm center within him, found only in confrontations with death?

Or perhaps home was here, this place nestled in the Oregonian woods, where he was surrounded by people who loved him, who had nurtured him, and who accepted him fangs and all?

Or was home somewhere else . . . ?

Jenna leaned back from him, and looked up, smiling impishly. Her nose was pugged, slightly askew, as if it had been broken once too often. He found it endearing. She kissed the corner of his mouth. Her lips were soft, her breath scented cinnamon.

She pulled back, winked, and then linked her arm in his. She walked him back through the cargo hold, to the door. "Leslie tells me that you've been trying the Ludovico gambit."

"What?"

"King's pawn variations, favoring queen's knight."

"Oh." He was momentarily confused, torn. His moroseness struggled against Jenna's bright, questioning presence. And lost.

Tricky little twit. "I'm just trying to get through the damned middle game without that brat stripping away my pawn cover."

She laughed. "You're too aggressive. You don't leave enough defense. You have to refine your defensive structures, and stop trusting your damned invulnerability to protect you."

He rolled his shoulders. "I'm not feeling so damned invulnerable these days." He laughed lamely. "Father Time . . ."

"Is absurdly fond of you."

Promise handed Mira's urn to a burial crew, then joined Aubry and Jenna. She managed a wan smile. "All right. Where is she?"

"He," Aubry said automatically.

Jenna giggled. "That would be telling."

Aubry scanned the trees and the rocks as they left the skimmer. Within the next few minutes there would be an ambush. He was determined not to be caught off guard.

Without warning, the earth to his right rippled and cracked. Aubry barely had time to recognize the rectangle of tarp, comprehend the eruption of dirt, before Leslie's wiry body sprang from the ground. Five feet of half-naked, grinning child pounced onto Aubry's chest knees-first.

"Whoof!" Aubry staggered back, flailing at air. Leslie scrambled around him like a cat spiraling up a tree.

Leslie stood atop Aubry's shoulders, balancing there effortlessly, tiny fists clenched and raised to the clouds. The clouds, ever diplomatic, declined to comment.

"Taa-daah!" Leslie rode his thighs around Aubry's neck and hugged him, smearing dirt, giving his father a big, wet, dusty kiss.

The workers applauded and laughed.

"Gotcha!" Leslie chortled.

"Yeah . . ." Aubry pulled him around into a cradle position, gazing into Leslie's huge, beautiful eyes. How close had he come to losing this wonderful creature? Something inside him chilled at the thought.

"Daddy." Leslie laid his head contentedly against Aubry's massive chest.

Aubry crushed him in his arms and kept walking, not saying anything, afraid to say anything. For just that instant his heart went cold, certain that if he spoke the bubble would burst and he would awaken from a dream. And in awakening, he would find himself kneeling on a hydraulic stage in Los Angeles, shrouded with blood and brains and viscera, by the hearts and minds of the only family he had ever known.

18

"Any other words?" Promise asked.

Aubry shook his head. He had nothing to say to the bronze box of Mira's ashes. She was Warrick's sister. He had provided for her. In the end he had failed her.

Leslie set the box into its hole at the foot of a towering fir tree, and brushed dirt atop it. He stood, holding a pair of blue steel knitting needles to his chest. "Goodbye, Aunt Mira. I loved you."

He took his mother's hand. The four of them walked back toward the road, and the Jeep perched there.

"The government men will be here tomorrow," Jenna said. "You were right. They jumped up and scrambled around like little monkeys."

Promise's smile was a small, tired thing. She kissed her sister's cheek, and sighed. "Thank you for arranging that. Is there any business that I need to take care of?"

"Not just this moment."

"Then I'd like some time to myself."

She approached Aubry, her smile tentative. "Want some company?"

He nodded, and she swung into the Jeep next to him. Leslie bounced into the backseat, without bothering to ask. He threw his arms around Promise's neck and pressed his brown cheek against hers. Aubry started the Jeep and piloted it up the narrow fire trail into lumber country.

The road wound bumpily past the science center's ribbed dome. Four years ago, a terrible fire had destroyed it, and much of the surrounding area. It had taken Ephesus's characteristic stubbornness and dedication, combined with the emerging financial power of the Scavengers, to rebuild so quickly.

There was much to be proud of—the Scavenger/

Ephesus/NewMan empire stretched from New Mexico to Seattle to Denver.

His rough hands gripped the wheel, fighting the arrhythmic shocks as the tires slammed against the fire trail's packed dirt and uneven rock.

"Going to your special place?"

He nodded. The clouds enveloping him were still dark, but the first rays of light were silvering the edges.

The Jeep's headlights splashed against the trees. Oilskin-covered saws and winches and other rigs were stowed neatly at the sides of the road, awaiting the day's labor. Mazetown was beginning to slip away from him, fading to insubstantiality, shambling back to the ghost closet. Sweet green life was returning to Ephesus, a life that smelled and sounded and *tasted* more real than the life teeming in Mazetown. There, life milled, and churned, and endured.

Here, it grew.

It would be impossible to count the hours he had slaved in this country, the fires fought, brush hauled, stumps pulled, trees felled, children rescued.

Or, more darkly, men killed.

It was *living* that concerned him now. And at the moment, life seemed uncomfortably tentative.

An assassin who is me—but a slower, stronger, dumber version of me. An incomparable physique gilded in keloid scars and bizarre tattoos.

What in the hell is going on?

The fire trail wove up the side of a mountain, terminating first in ragged brush, and then in a dead end. If you knew the exact piece of brush to drag aside, a new and narrower road opened up. He felt mildly absurd, knowing that this bit of subterfuge was nine parts self-indulgence to one part security, but it brought him peace of mind.

While Aubry moved the branches, Promise slid over in the seat and drove the Jeep up the continuation road. She paused long enough for him to jump in, and then rumbled up a narrow dirt path, up and up the mountain ridge, as dawn's first powdery blush began to rouge the horizon.

Aubry swung out of the car, creaking the shock absorbers. Leslie bounced out, following him.

A white wooden gazebo sat at the very top of the mountain. Aubry took Leslie's small hand in his, and together they climbed up the path. Promise hung back, smiling almost dreamily. Somehow, the image of her man and her child, sharing this moment as they had shared so many others over the past three years, was absurdly comforting.

Aubry pulled a heavy, olive-drab weather tarp back from the gazebo floor, revealing polished hardwood. Promise saw his shoulders slump, tension fleeing his body, as if he had been clasped by an old friend. To one side lay a thick-walled wooden box, and from it Leslie removed a heavy woolen mat. Aubry and Leslie spread it out on the gazebo floor, then stood shoulder to hip, hands at their sides, facing the east.

As the sun rose, Aubry began the exercise learned in childhood, and reawakened under Kevin Warrick's severe tutelage. In time Aubry had not only reconstituted the exercise, but taught it to Leslie.

Promise watched them, her dancer's eye evaluating.

In some ways the movement pattern resembled a kata, the prearranged formal fighting exercises of Japan, Korea, and China. In other ways it seemed a dance. In still other aspects, it was similar to hatha-yoga's sun salutation, the *Suryanamaskara,* though infinitely more taxing. It combined the long slow limb extension of t'ai chi, the balance and flexibility of gymnastics, and the explosively dynamic tensions of karate. The limbs moved in arcs which, while not blows or kicks, were still frighteningly combative in their implication. In some way that she couldn't quite comprehend, each motion seemed the embryonic *form* of a punch or a kick, the essence rather than the reality.

She had tried the exercise for a month and a half. Oddly, its practice troubled her emotionally, as if the physical motions were shaping her perceptions of the world. She remembered completing her last and most intense session, walking about in a daze for the following hour. The first person she encountered was Kregger, who wouldn't quite seem to come into focus. There was something blurry about her visual field. When she concentrated, for a moment she had the ghastly thought that the crew chief wasn't a human being: he was an image painted on a sheet of glass, with groin and knees and kidneys marked in splashes of red ink.

She had never performed the exercises again.

Aubry called it the Rubber Band. Why? When pressed, he said only that Rubber Band was what he had always called it.

Aubry and Leslie worked it together, their limbs spiraling through complex changes, twisting and folding and lifting. Now they bore their full weight on the palm of a single extended arm; now the body projected to the side like a gymnast on the long horse. Now each arced through a spine-wrenching slow-motion backward somersault. Once the sequence began it never ended. Now fast, now slow, now soft, now hard, with a strange, sighing breath hissing in the backs of their throats, Aubry and Leslie seemed two animals engaged in a primal ritual of awakening, purging themselves of spiritual toxins, father and child together, welcoming the morning sun.

19

JULY 23

Silver and blue, a gilded eagle, a U.S. Department of Defense Boeing personnel skimmer was perched at the edge of the southern landing strip when the three of them returned. Two men waited, each holding an attaché case.

One of the two wasn't quite five feet tall, almost dwarfish but with a sharp face, light eyebrows, and piercing eyes. His nose was slightly hooked, and his thin mouth bore the barest trace of a smile, as if in memory of a half-forgotten joke. He wore a dark, impeccably tailored brown suit with a narrow gold tie.

The second man was younger, blond, thin, but almost as tall as Aubry. He wore a deep blue trenchcoat with a white scarf inside the collar. He was handsome in an arrogant way, brows creasing together to wrinkle his forehead. The trenchcoat was cinched with a tight knot, and the morning wind ruffled its edges.

Most of the tension had left Aubry. Once again, he moved with his customary effortless glide, and Leslie scurried to keep up with him. Aubry shook hands with the shorter of the two men, his grip as measured as that of a man holding the last egg of an endangered species. Leslie clung to Aubry's leg, looking up at the strangers with wide-eyed innocence.

"Mr. Knight?" The short man said. "I'm General Hayward Koskotas, Central Intelligence." He indicated the taller man to his left. "This is Kramer. We're sorry about your problem, and we're here to do whatever we can."

Aubry nodded. "Follow me, please."

Before they reached the medical building, they were met by Jenna, who measured the intruders with a practiced gaze. Koskotas she relegated to some emotional scrap heap in a moment, but Kramer she seemed to memorize. Their eyes locked, and for an instant, Aubry thought that there was going to be a challenge, verbal or physical. Then she stepped aside and let them enter the building.

Even at seven A.M. the med center bustled with white-smocked, efficient women. There was no mistaking the fact that this was a vital organ in the body Ephesus. Here were the biological labs, the places where small and delicate magics were practiced, human ova melded one to another, women breeding without the genetic contributions of males.

As the Intelligence officers were marched through busy halls, they were greeted with suspicion and distaste by the doctors and assistants. They were outsiders. They were *men*. They were not welcome, tolerated only because Promise and Jenna accompanied them.

Aubry was another matter. The women seemed amusedly fond of him, almost as if he were a mascot. Say, a pet leopard.

The six of them descended into the med center's basement. When the door opened again, they were in a glass-walled room. Two pale assistants—one of them, surprisingly, a balding man in his thirties—helped them trade their jackets for smocks. Their coats were treated like *contaminata,* and whisked away for irradiation.

In single file, they were ushered through a narrow door into a room bathed in wavering pink light.

In the middle of the room was a stainless-steel table. Upon that table was a sheet-draped lump of human dimensions.

Koskotas looked up at Promise, his narrow face creased with distaste. "Are you certain this is appropriate for the child?"

Aubry snorted amusement. Promise showed a moment's concern and then turned to Leslie. "Biological mode, Leslie."

Leslie's eyes grew sharp and then soft, and he nodded.

Koskotas whisked the sheet off. A younger Aubry Knight stared up at them. His features, relaxed in death, seemed deflated, void of all vitality, an empty vessel. The corpse had been rinsed, but otherwise remained untouched.

Koskotas opened his briefcase, revealing a screen and keyboard, voice and eye input apparatus, and three thin parallel lines of plastic touch-strip. He ran his fingers along the strips, triggering and adjusting the screen, spoke a few words, and allowed the case to read his retinal patterns. The screen lit with the words AUTOPSY ACCESS STYX HOT FILE. DIRECT INDUCTION ONLY. Koskotas touched the nape of his neck, and Promise caught a silvered glimpse of the implant linking him with the briefcase. The case itself was probably satellite-linked to some data pool in Washington.

Koskotas spoke as if to an audience of pathologists. "All right. I see a male of very pure Negroid stock, approximately seventy-six inches in length, perhaps three hundred pounds." He poked and prodded briskly. "The musculature is extremely dense. I've seen this only on professional athletes, powerlifters of international caliber, and members of that group known as NewMen. . . ." He turned to Kramer. "We're checking the geneprint for affiliation now." To Promise he said, "Would you have your main banks feed me the results of the blood and tissue samples, please."

"Frequency?" Jenna asked.

"Two-oh-nine. Alpha beta zeta."

"Coming right up." She tickled a transceiver pad built into her belt, and Koskotas straightened, eyes widening as the Ephesus computer system linked with the briefcase, and the case fed its information to the general.

Eyes wide and staring, he spoke again. Promise thought that it might have been her imagination, but it seemed there was a slight feminine lilt to Koskotas's voice now. "We have found no trace of any artificial ergonometrics. Present theory is that the muscular density is a direct adaptation to stress. The degree of adaptation suggests an override of pain thresholds, but no genetic or endocrinal modifications beyond basic acceleration technology. Physiological age—approximately twenty-five. Chronological age . . ." He paused. "No data."

Promise stared at the corpse, her eyes ranging from its cold, flat features to those of the man she loved. Again and again her gaze made its circuit. The likeness was shocking, beneath the scars and tattoos. These were almost twins—the same man, caught at slightly different stages of development. Her stomach soured and tightened.

"No evidence of plastic or thermal surgery, no alteration of the bone structure." Koskotas's thin, small mouth creased in a mirthless smile. "It's you, no doubt about it. Turn the body over, please."

Aubry and Jenna rolled it over, and the air in the room grew still.

Across the back of the corpse were two designs. One was a tattoo of a dragon, done in garish colors against the darkness of the skin. The other was a curlicue of keloid scars, running across the back and upper shoulders, down the back of the arms. The two images somehow blended into and reinforced one another.

Koskotas traced the scars with his finger, and then sighed. "Right here," he said. "Feel it." Promise reached out. Her fingers traced a roughly oval outline of keloid scars. Kramer's face was neutral.

She shook her head. "I don't understand."

"You will. Have the cameras been recording?"

"Yes. Everything," Jenna said. Her gaze was frozen to the table.

"Then let's go somewhere and talk."

20

The conference room could easily have held forty, and the six of them were dwarfed by its vaulted ceiling and convex walls. Kramer hadn't spoken during the entire business. Koskotas's lids were shut, his eyes moving rapidly behind them as if organizing file cards.

Finally, he opened his eyes. "Mr. Knight," he said. "What we have is what we were afraid we would find."

"Can you be a little more direct?" Aubry asked. His voice was flat with irritation.

"Certainly," Koskotas said.

Koskotas whispered in Kramer's ear, and they conferred quietly for almost two minutes.

So the sonofabitch can talk, Aubry thought. He had considered stepping on Kramer's toe, just to see if he squeaked. Aubry watched them, and listened, but couldn't pick up enough. Then he caught Leslie's eyes. The child was watching them in a defocused manner, concentrating on nothing, taking in everything. Aubry matched Leslie, matched his body position and his breathing. Oddly, something in his head relaxed, as if a door were opening.

Perception widened. Sounds and colors seemed a hair sharper.

Watching the two government men again, he noticed something for the first time: more than verbal conversation was being conducted. Kramer's fingers rested, almost intimately, upon Koskotas's hand. His fingers rolled and stroked in a ticktack rhythm. Two-level communication? Or more?

Finally Koskotas turned back to them. "Please prepare your processor to receive input. I believe they have already exchanged protocols?"

Jenna smiled thinly. "I will authorize a partitioned memory cell. You won't have access to our main banks."

"Young lady, I assure you . . ."

"Save it." Jenna's fingers stroked her belt. "Transmit."

"Very well. You are all involved in this incident, so it is pointless to request any kind of formal security arrangement. I assume that a verbal agreement will suffice." He paused, until all heads nodded shallowly. Leslie's was a precise imitation of Aubry's.

"Very well. I'd like you to take a look at something, something that we knew from the blood and tissue sample you sent us."

An image tweaked onto a holo stage, a three-dimensional red and blue animated helix. "This is the assassin's genetic structure. As you remember, we've detected no signs of tampering, or anything to lead us to believe he is a NewMan variant."

"That's a relief."

"In a moment, you may change your mind. Take a look at this." He flashed a second slide. It was identical to the first.

"I don't get it," Aubry said. The tone of his voice suggested that he "got it" all too well.

"This, Mr. Knight, is you."

The room was silent; then Jenna cleared her throat. "That thing was Aubry's clone?"

"An accelerated clone?" Promise looked at Leslie.

"Like your child, yes."

Aubry whispered, *"Shit."*

"Of course, we know that the child is one of the accelerated clones created by the renegade Gorgon division Medusa, led by Colonel Quint and Major Ibumi. Your child was designated Medusa-16. The Medusas were utilized for an assassination attempt on President Harris. All of the others died in that attempt."

"We've made certain of that," Koskotas said flatly. "And as long as Medusa-16 . . . ah, 'Leslie' . . . no offense, son—" His eyes were flat and hollow, like gun barrels.

"None taken," Leslie said in a remarkably adult voice. His eyes were defocused, and Promise declined to speculate about what had just flashed behind them.

"As long as, ah, Leslie, remains in your care, no action will be taken against him."

"Imagine my relief," Leslie said flatly. The singsong childish quality was completely gone from his voice.

"Ah . . . yes. At any rate, the accelerant technology is well understood. This clone was grown from a tissue sample, accelerated and trained to kill you."

Aubry was genuinely perplexed. "Why go to all of that trouble? Who would do something like that?"

"Much easier to determine once you take a look at the tattoos on the back."

A button was pressed, and the visual image became that of the slain assassin. Once again, the dragon and the lion warred upon his trapezius—the dragon in tattooed ink, the lion in ridges of keloid scar. "Yakuza," Jenna said.

"Yes. Specifically, the Yakuza *keiretsu* known as Divine Blossom. And do you recognize the scar patterns?"

Leslie cocked his head, but said nothing.

"Our computer says that the patterns are typical of the tribal scars of the Ibandi people. A mountain people of central Africa. The tribe which spawned Phillipe Swarna."

Silence.

"Swarna," Aubry said quietly. "I killed Swarna's son five years ago, in the battle at Death Valley."

"Yes. It makes sense now, doesn't it? One region of scar is in the precise shape of the Ibandi province, in what was once northern Zaire, and which has now been absorbed into PanAfrica. Are you familiar with PanAfrica?"

Promise nodded. "We have had business dealings. Opened contractual negotiations to build a dam. The PanAfrican Republic incorporates the territory formerly divided into Zaire, Tanzania, and Uganda. A military dictatorship, under a board of generals chaired by Phillipe Swarna."

Koskotas's thin mouth managed another smile. "Excellent. This is what I hypothesize. Phillipe Swarna wants vengeance against you. You foiled his plan to assassinate President Harris, and you killed his son. So he obtained a skin sample."

"How?"

Jenna rolled her eyes. "Give me a break. You've left tissue and body fluid all over the West Coast."

Promise looked stricken. When she spoke, her voice was small and somehow pale. "How sophisticated would this cloning technology be?"

"Extremely. Why?"

"Could they clone Aubry . . . and make a *female*?"

Aubry stared at her incredulously, and Jenna said, "Come on, now . . ."

Koskotas shifted uncomfortably. "I don't have that information at this time. . . ."

"Yes you do," Leslie said quietly. "But it's classified, and you're lying. Stupid classification. The technique was developed during the Gender Wars, back in '06 or so."

"Young man . . ." Koskotas said angrily.

Leslie ignored him. His eyes rolled back in their sockets slightly. Promise gripped his shoulder as Leslie began to recite.

"Human beings have a double set of twenty-three chromosomes, with twenty-two being identical, and one set being the sex doublet. Thus a girl is forty-six XX, with two X chromosomes, one of which doesn't work, and a guy is forty-six XY with one Y chromosome.

"There are at least three ways to accomplish the desired effect. The least difficult is a non-DNA-alteration approach." Leslie focused his eyes on them, and smiled slightly. "Artifically induce testicular feminization syndrome. Block the protein receptor for testosterone. The cells will automatically default to female development, even though their genotype is forty-six XY."

"This is classified . . ." Koskotas muttered.

"This is in any medical library in Canada," Leslie said snidely. "The TFS approach won't produce a uterus, so if you want a fertile female, you've got to lick the dispermy and recombination problems. They did it back in '05. Or you can take forty-six-XY blood-cell DNA and surgically or biochemically remove the Y and replace it with another X. Then implant it in an empty ovum and *bang!* Instant female. My guess is that someone whipped that problem, and did it for the government." Leslie's smile went nasty. "The ability to make women from men means that if something ever . . . *happened* to the women in North America, the U.S. could be up and breeding again in a generation."

The room was quiet; then Koskotas cleared his throat. "I'm certain that it's nothing so absurdly melodramatic."

"I saw one," Promise said. "I saw a feminized clone of Aubry."

"So there are at least two. And probably more," Koskotas said.

Aubry squeezed Promise's hand. "So Swarna accelerated the clones, then had them trained by a Divine Blossom assassination clan?"

"That's what we figure. Remember, Swarna wouldn't need the Japanese for their killing skills—he wanted them for their direct-induction educational techniques, developed in the late nineties. They created his brainwashing center." He flashed another image on the screen, a map of the African continent. "The Japanese own two and a half million acres in the center of PanAfrica. Literally millions of children have been trucked in from surrounding nations since its creation in the nineties."

Jenna seemed uncomfortable. "How did he get away with it?"

"He had the Five Songs. 'Five songs' is a rough translation of the word *ibandi*. It's some sort of crackpot Sufic
splinter religion, but he has every black military leader in
Africa under his thumb, using supposedly 'politically neutral' Ibandi bodyguards. That's what made the bloody
coup possible in the first place. Ibandi warriors had been in
security and assassination all over the world for four
decades. Known for intelligence, fearlessness, and skill.
Funny thing is—Swarna won't have any Ibandi around
him now. Seems to have had a falling-out with them. They
believe he broke some sort of covenant, one of the basic
rules of the Five Songs. His betrayal is referred to as 'the
Abomination.' We don't know exactly what this Abomination was. He rules with an iron hand—"

"Wow, Dad. Is that what they call an original phrase?"

"Hush."

"We tried to trim him back, but . . . well, you know the
result of that."

"Two failed assassinations," Leslie said, "and an abort-
ive coup."

Again, Koskotas looked startled. "Why, yes."

Promise listened to the information, and sat back and
closed her eyes, face placid. "What you are suggesting is
that this is a revenge killing, ordered by the enraged ruler
of the third most powerful nation on the planet. That he
grew the clone to do this in a manner than amused him, or
fulfilled some bizarre tribal ritual. And that, although this
attempt failed, there is no reason to think that he won't do
it again, and again, and again, until he succeeds."

Koskotas nodded. "Yes, I believe you grasp the essen-
tials."

"And what would you suggest?"

"We can provide security for you and your family. You
can stay underground—you have enough connections."

Beat. And then Aubry said, "Are you going to . . . take
another crack at Swarna?"

Koskotas coughed. "Not at this time." He switched
gears smoothly. "The clone was trained, and created, and

sent here for one and only one reason—to kill you. It fits with his psych profile."

"And just what is that profile?" Promise asked.

Kramer opened a briefcase and took out a disk, slipping it into the projector.

Koskotas continued. "We have limited information pertaining to the early life and actual physical presence of the man known as Phillipe Swarna. That may not even be his actual name.

"He first appeared on the scene in the middle nineties, as an Ibandi shaman. The history of the Ibandi is . . . colorful. They have never been conquered, partially because much of the terrain they inhabit is mountainous, and ideal for guerilla warfare. In the early eighteen-hundreds, the British tried to pacify them. A railroad was run into their territory, guarded by several hundred troops armed with cannon and mounted cavalry."

"What happened?" Aubry asked, quietly.

"They disappeared. To this day, the Ibandi's ceremonial knives are pounded from railroad spikes. Great embarrassment. The South Africans backed a commando operation against them in the fifties—again, a slaughter." The image changed again. Now there was what seemed to be newsreel footage—of a mound of human heads. Most of them were Caucasian. "This was found on the outskirts of Messina, in southern Africa near the border of Zimbabwe."

He cleared his throat. "Then when uranium deposits were found in the Ibandi province, in the late 1980s, the government of Zaire tried to confiscate the lands."

"And?" Aubry's voice rasped.

"Two million Ibandi just disappeared into the mountains. They waged such a war of attrition that the government of Zaire was forced to cut a deal with them, help them build factories. It was their fierceness that brought them to the attention of the world. Their young men became prized mercenaries. The first Ibandis competed in the Olympics in the nineties. Superlative distance runners and wrestlers."

"I know some of the rest of this," Jenna said. "Phillipe Swarna was the spiritual leader of their warrior class. The religion, this 'Five Songs' thing, began spreading into the regular armies of the dozen or so countries that hired Ibandian mercenaries."

"It's not exactly a religion," Koskotas corrected. "It's more of a philosophical approach to dealing with life as combat. Christianity, Islam, a dozen polytheistic sects— they were all absorbed. Fucking amazing, really. Apparently there was some feeling of alarm connected with the growth of his power and influence, and there was an attempt to kill, or disable, him. We don't have the details. It may have involved acid, or fire. We know that he went into seclusion, and disappeared into the northern desert for four years. During that time, his face was reconstructed to resemble a mythic hero of the Ibandi, a man named Erahs. These are the first reliable pictures that we have of him."

The image was clear, but not sharp-edged, as if the product of computer reconstruction.

What was displayed before them was a man in his fifties, with features more like those of a Negroid Pakistani than an African. Ridges of keloid tribal scars braided his face.

"He may not even be truly of Negroid stock. In recent years, Swarna has been too well isolated for us to get more current data.

"In 1999, the initial contracts were signed creating PanAfrica. This man united a dozen tribes and nations, played one off against the other, and seemed virtually unstoppable.

"The United States was experiencing its own period of collapse, and there were no resources for adventurism. After centuries of starvation, war, and disease, the world had wearied of Africa."

And here for the first time Koskotas winced a bit. "The decision was made to let Black Africa die. Swarna had a free hand. And he carved out an empire.

"You know the PanAfrican concept," Koskotas continued. "Nobody believed in it—but he made it work, by God. When he couldn't get cooperation from the Japanese government, he made arrangements with the largest criminal organization in Asia, the Divine Blossom Yakuza. Divine Blossom stole the technology he needed, and mass-produced it in prefabricated factories erected in Pan-Africa. Swarna became even more of a power. In the teens, we tried to prune him back, on the Zimbabwe plain, and PanAfrica crushed the United Nations forces. Through its deal with Swarna, Divine Blossom had the mineral resources to consolidate its power in Japan. It was the first 'Yakuza *keiretsu*'—a *keiretsu* being a sort of industrial and economic confederation. Divine Blossom possessed power under and above the law, within and outside of Japan. They are probably the largest multinational in the world, powerful enough to laugh at our embargoes. The technology continued to flow into Swarna's little social experiment.

"Then we . . . tried more direct actions."

Promise looked at Aubry, as if expecting a query. When none was forthcoming, she said, "You attempted an assassination?"

"Understand that the current administration had nothing to do with it. Yes. We tried to remove Phillipe Swarna. The attempt failed. We tried again. And failed again. Swarna expanded his political empire to Asia and Central America. Counting the labor, land, and material resources he commands or influences, Phillipe Swarna is almost certainly one of the ten most powerful men in the world, and he hates the West virulently."

"With reason," Jenna observed. "You raped his continent, abandoned them, and then when a leader finally rose with the vision to put things back together, you tried to stop him. When that failed, you tried to kill him. What are you angling for now?"

Her gaze was merciless. Koskotas met it for about eight seconds; then his eyes shifted. Some dynamo within Kramer seemed to activate at that moment—you could almost hear him hum. Without moving, he seemed to grow in size, to radiate heat. Jenna's attention was pulled away from Koskotas to the younger man. She didn't look at his eyes—she looked at a spot just beneath his chin. She nodded to herself, and to Aubry.

Aubry gave her a hard, flat smile, then spoke. "Thank you for the briefing."

Koskotas shifted, as if the room was too warm for him. "Frankly, I had no interest in this meeting. Certain . . . pressures were brought to bear."

There was silence in the room for a long moment. Some kind of energy whorl seemed to connect Aubry Knight and Koskotas, as if they were playing some kind of high-stakes poker game.

Aubry broke the impasse. "I used to be a professional killer," he said. "A 'soldier' for the Ortega crime organization. Part of my training was conducted by the American military, and part by former spooks." He paused, and smiled without humor. "Of course, they might have been current operatives on detached assignment—after all, you did use Ortega men in your first attempt on Swarna, didn't you?"

There was no audible answer, but Kramer nodded shallowly.

"I want to go after Swarna. I want you to help me."

"Jesus Christ—" Kramer hissed, speaking at last. He clamped down, silent again.

Koskotas raised his hand. "No. We understand your position, Mr. Knight, but cannot allow such a thing. In fact, United Nations policies directly forbid any such interference in the political or economic structure of another country. We cannot prove that Swarna was responsible for the attempt on President Harris—even though his son was involved.

"We cannot prove that Swarna was responsible for the attempt on you, Mr. Knight—although the killer bears tribal tattoos associated with Swarna's tribe of origin, and elite guard."

Promise was staring at Aubry, had stared since he first made the offer.

"We can provide you with protection," Koskotas continued. "We owe you this much for your efforts on behalf of President Harris. That is all we came to say." He pushed a silver envelope toward them. "In this envelope is our proposal for security, and a special number you can call, should you need more information, or support."

The two men smiled, shook hands, and left the room.

Aubry sat, staring at the envelope. Brooding.

21

Koskotas and Kramer rose up in the skimmer. They waited until they were hooked into the Pacific Coast guidance system before they began to talk.

"So," Koskotas said finally. "What do you think?"

"I've seen the reports," Kramer said. He spoke with machine precision, utterly bloodless. "His hand-eye stats were through the roof. Firearms almost as high. Explosives—good. Infiltration skills—adequate, with potential. But he was considered more or less a natural. Doesn't make a difference. We can't use him. He's an amateur."

"What about the kid?"

"Total freak. Makes my flesh crawl. But too unstable." He paused. "What about the chronological scan on the clone? What did the machine really say?"

"You know me too well. Thirteen years."

"Thirteen years!?"

"Yes. Interesting, isn't it?"

"So what do we do?"

"For now, stonewall it."

Koskotas opened a scrambled line and waited for the computers to handshake. The skimmer was already hopped from the Pacific to the Executive network, prioritized above the commuter and transport traffic, and routed to the preferred air corridors. In four hours they'd

be back on the East Coast. Current plans suggested a refueling in St. Louis.

"*General Koskotas?*"

The voice that came over the radio was soft but precise.
President Roland Harris.

"We've made our report, sir."

"*And?*"

"And he wants in on STYX."

Harris was quiet. "*Is that . . . possible?*"

"Absolutely not. Inappropriate in the extreme."

Harris paused. "*How many times have you . . . failed,
General?*"

"Never. The men before me . . ."

"*How many times have we failed?*"

"Sir, I understand your personal feelings—"

"*No,*" the president said quietly. "*I don't believe you do.
If Knight wants in, I want you to make a place for him. I
want to be kept briefed.*"

"But sir—"

"*Koskotas—I was against the operation. I don't like this
sort of thing. But if there is one man with a legitimate reason
to . . . participate in STYX, it is Aubry Knight. Military so-
lutions have failed. Covert intelligence operations have
failed. Perhaps a more personal approach is needed.*"

"But sir—"

"*I want you to modify your existing plans to include him.
And I want to stay current on those plans. Do you understand?*"

"Yes . . . sir." The connection died.

Koskotas slammed his hand against the panel. "God-
damn amateur fucking politicos!"

"Can we . . . stall him? Tell him that the pipeline will
close too soon?"

"No, damn it to hell. He received a full briefing last
month."

"Can Harris really shut us down?"

Koskotas glared at him. "It wouldn't be the first time."
He balled his hand into a fist, slammed it down again. "All

right. We use Knight if we have to. We keep Harris informed. But Kramer—"

"Yes, sir?"

"Training accidents have been known to happen. See that one does."

22

The moon was a swollen, pale blue portal into another, calmer time. It sat atop the pines, shining down, joining with the breeze that fluttered their curtains. The dew of their lovemaking was beginning to cool; the sighs, and the kisses, and the whispered affirmations of love and existence began to lose their urgency as heartbeats slowed to normal. All intensities eventually fade, and in the fading some of life's fears and sorrows hammer at the door, slip through the keyhole, slide through the windowpanes.

Love can banish shadows for a time, but in the end, night always prevails.

Promise ran her fingers through the tightly curled hair on Aubry's chest. Quietly, she said, "They can protect us. You heard them."

Aubry smiled wanly. "You don't know this business. They can protect us as long as we stay within their guidelines, as long as we don't go anywhere, don't do anything, and are never alone again."

"And what's so wrong with that?"

"Is that why we've worked so hard? For so long? So that we can run and hide for the rest of our lives?"

His voice was beginning to change, revealing a steely edge. She clung to him, afraid. "Aubry, listen. You don't have to do this. Dying won't solve anything."

But Aubry's ears were filled with a music Promise couldn't hear. "I killed myself," he said slowly. "I clamped my hand around my own neck. I twisted. I watched myself hit the ground, dead while living. I smelled my stench when I shit and pissed myself. How am I supposed to forget that?"

"It wasn't you, Aubry." She fought to keep her voice even, reasonable. "It was a piece of your meat."

"It was a clone. A three-year-old clone. That's even worse. I killed a baby. It was big, and muscular, and it had moves, but it was a baby." Out in the trees beyond their window, the wind shifted. The leaves and needles rustled, stirring from dreams. Distantly, a lonely animal howled, seeking its mate, hoping to share the moonlight. "That bastard Swarna did that to me. I don't feel . . . right." He searched for the right word. "I don't feel . . . *alive.*"

Promise turned her head away from him, pressed her face hard against a pillow. "I'm not sure that I believe you. I think that this is the first time in three years you've felt completely alive. You needed this to happen. This is your chance to get back into the game, and you can't let it go."

His gaze grew remote. "I can't expect you to understand it." He rose naked from the bed, and paused there for a moment. He was a man on the edge of a whirlpool, calmly considering its depths. He opened a corner cabinet and pulled out a pair of pants, a shirt, another shirt . . . he wouldn't need much, just a few items of clothing and some toiletries.

"No," Promise said. "Maybe I can't understand. But Jenna can. And Bloodeagle can. Will you at least talk to them? They are your friends. You can trust them, can't you?"

Aubry folded shirts and pants carefully. He tugged down a brown leather case and popped the lock. He tucked the clothes into a corner, and reached into the closet for another pair of pants.

"Can't you trust them?" Her voice was cracking now. "Can't you trust anyone?"

Aubry closed the lid, and then paused. Naked, motionless in the moonlight, he resembled a heroic statue, a guardian before some mausoleum. For almost a minute, he didn't move, didn't speak. Then finally, reluctantly, he said, "I'll talk to Jenna."

23

Archery was one of the four weapon disciplines of durga, the warrior art practiced by the women of Ephesus. Forty women were in Jenna's night class. They were positioned in staggered rows of ten. They drew their fiberglass bows, nocked their arrows with the tips raised to seventy degrees, and waited.

Aubry watched from his seat near the top of the amphitheater. The bowstrings remained taut for eighteen minutes. Even with leather finger guards, despite perfect posture, pain narrowed their eyes, arms trembled, sweat rolled in sour rivulets down strain-creased faces. Every few seconds a thin, shuddering gasp of exertion pierced the night air.

At a prearranged signal, the students released their arrows. A dark cloud flew toward the padded log target, buzzing like an angry bee swarm. They thumped *sh-shuck!* All but two furred the log. There was a sort of group exhalation; then they returned to the ready position.

To Aubry's way of thinking, they seemed more concerned with the ritual than the actual targeting. Somehow, they managed to produce accuracy without having it as a primary concern.

He had another impression, an image that remained in his mind regardless of his attempts to shake it loose: they were connected to the target in some manner. He couldn't *see* the connective threads, but he could *feel* them.

Jenna looked up at Aubry, a slight and secret smile shading her lips. Then she was guru again, her attention riveted to the class.

She drilled them with knives, with staffs, with a single twenty-inch stick, and with the empty hands and feet. She pushed them on and on, driving with her will and her knowledge and her hard-won fitness, until every one of them dripped with sweat and panted for breath.

She danced her women through their stretching exercises, then reclined them for deep breathing and a measured visualization.

And here she spoke to them, in measured tones. She spoke of hills, and valleys, and the animals of the Earth. Her voice lulled them into trance, and bade them dream of children and children unborn, of art and music and the gentle rhythms of existence.

"All that is of value is born of Woman," she said. "Of the female, and of the feminine side of men. All building, all creation. All dreams. But a child is safe only when protected, and dreams, unwalled, are torn by those who cannot sleep. . . ."

"Men, and the masculine force, cannot *be*. It must *do*. And it must analyze'—ripping the life from what it examines. When the knowledge is extracted from the body of a chimpanzee, all that remains is meat. The masculine has feasted. Science benefits. Civilization progresses. But the chimp is dead.

"If we would have life, in our way, we must be prepared to defend it. Beauty without strength is death. Strength without beauty is death. Only together is there life. . . ."

Aubry sat, listening to Jenna's singsong words, and felt as if a shell around him were cracking. As if the wind whipping in through the pine needles bore secrets, coded whispers for some part of him beneath and aside from the part he called *Aubry*.

And they make their knives of railroad spikes, to this day . .

Where had he . . . ?

How had he . . . ?

He *knew* those words. And some others, which flitted, unbidden, into his mind.

Come, they said. *Come to the Firedance. . . .*

Aubry shook himself out of the reverie, realizing that the class was over.

Many of the women waved or smiled to Aubry as he

trotted down the amphitheater stairs to the workout area.
A few averted their eyes, faces tight with resentment.

Jenna directed a trio of assistants in the packing of gear
as Aubry descended. Bows and arrows and staffs and
knives were slotted into hardwood cabinets behind the
stage.

Aubry descended and stood quietly, waiting as Jenna
cleaned the gleaming, curved length of her durga fighting
knives. She stroked them with an oiled white cloth with a
red border. Jenna's movements were very precise, very
controlled, as they were whenever she performed her ceremonial cleansing.

Finally, she hoisted her personal gear over her shoulder,
and came to him, sitting next to him. A sad, almost wistful
smile warmed her face.

"Well. Aubry. How was your talk with Sister Dearest?"

"What would you expect? Dreadful. She wants to believe that the government can protect us."

"And if they could?"

"What do you mean?"

"Well . . . I don't think that it would matter. You
brought Mira's ashes back with you. They killed your last
link to Warrick. They hurt Leslie. They disrupted your
ceremony."

His nod was barely perceptible.

"You've embraced civilization, as long as the civilized
mode works for you. When it doesn't work . . . well, let's
just say that you wouldn't bleed if you had to toss it
away."

"Is that so wrong?" He was surprised by the genuine in-
quiry in his voice. What was right, or wrong, in a situation
like this?

"It is true to who you are. But what's the truth here?"

"The truth." Aubry looked at Jenna, at the light cream
of her skin. Whereas Promise was a blend of African and
Polynesian and European bloodlines, Jenna was more
European and Asian. Much lighter-skinned, not quite as
pretty. Her body was made for movement, for combat, for
work. She was a finely tuned machine, in her own way as

finely tuned as Promise. But whereas Promise and Aubry created a balance, a certain yin-yang balance that was irresistible, Jenna touched him in ways that Promise had not. Could not. That, perhaps, no other woman could.

Jenna took lovers when she wished. Sometimes women, sometimes men. But she belonged to no one. She was the combat mistress, the security chief of Ephesus, and she had always walked alone.

But she was his friend. In a strange way, perhaps the best friend he had ever had. If Aubry Knight had to be reborn as a woman, he would want to be Jenna.

"I think," he said slowly, "that I've spent most of my life just reacting to what happened around me. That habit got me into deeper and deeper trouble. God—I only survived because of this body, Jenna. Because it is faster and stronger and has more energy than any body has the right to have."

"You talk about your body as if it isn't you."

"Sometimes I wonder," he laughed ruefully. "But now I'm in this position. Ephesus. The Scavengers. The New-Men. There are people who rely upon me, depend upon me. But the truth is that Promise is doing most of it."

"Which means?"

"That she's growing, and I'm not." He stretched his arms, and she heard his joints pop. Aubry's muscular density was astounding, as was his flexibility, his sense of balance, his muscular and cardiovascular endurance. It seemed that everything about him was in perfect proportion, but functioned at abnormal amplitude.

But sometimes his eyes were those of a child. Questioning. Wounded. Wondering. Looking out at the future, uncertain of what there was, or could ever be, for him.

"I feel cold." He wrapped his arms around his knees, and pulled his head tight against them. "I saw myself crawling across the floor like a dog, begging for death. And I know now, I *know,* that that's how I'll die. This thing inside me, this thing that pulls violence into my life, is the flip side of the skill. Unless I can find a way to heal it, one day my skills won't be enough. One day . . . it will happen."

She had to lean close now, to hear a voice that had dropped so low it was like the sound of leaves falling against grass. "I know what it is to have a family now. I'd die for them. Or for you."

Her hand rested against his shoulder. His skin seemed to burn.

"But that's not the death I'll get. I'll need to prove myself once too often. I'll draw some piece of unfinished business from my past. I'll stumble across a mugging in an alley. And I'll die, away from home, away from my family. A painful, meaningless death without honor or grace. Just death."

He looked up at her, and now more than ever his face was the face of a child. "I don't want to die like that. I want it to be for something. I just don't know how to get out of the loop."

"Does going after Swarna get you out of the loop?"

"My mind says no. But my guts . . . my heart . . ." He fumbled for her hand. "There's something going on here that none of us understand. And there is something inside me that says 'Come.' It laughs at me. 'Come to the Firedance,' it says. It promises nothing, but it says 'Come.' And it's not the same voice that has pulled me into violence. I don't think I've ever heard that voice before."

Jenna put her arms around Aubry and pressed her cheek against him. For a long time she remained with him like that, breathing when he breathed, her slender, strong fingers stroking the coarse, tightly curled hair at the base of his neck. Then she said, very softly, "If you have to go, Aubry, then go. But Aubry . . . you don't have to do this alone."

He pulled back, and she saw his eyes transformed from human eyes to beads made of glass. Somehow, she had said precisely the wrong thing.

"Yes," he said flatly. "I do."

24

Promise was still awake when Aubry returned to their bedroom. She said nothing, as if she already knew what had been decided.

"Where is Leslie?"

"She's in her own room in the south wing. We're alone."

He nodded and stripped out of his clothes. He sat on the edge of the water bed and looked down at her. She was probably the most beautiful woman he had ever known. Certainly and by far she was the most passionate.

He felt out of control around her—as if there was a part of him that surrendered completely, that would do anything, or try to be anyone, that she wanted or needed. But there was another, just as powerful, that remained hidden, carefully under control. A part that watched and waited.

He leaned forward, brushing his lips against her neck. Her body rolled slowly, richly, pressing against the gauzy nightgown, forcing the covers back and away. He ran his hands over her skin. Hard, callused hands, which could crush concrete. He wondered, not for the first time, if he ever inadvertently hurt her. He would rather die than hurt her . . . physically.

But he was willing to die, and hurt her, to accomplish something that might ultimately have no meaning at all.

Come. Come to the Firedance.

He felt caught, trapped by forces he didn't understand.

Now was the time, the moment, the instant when Promise might have said something, something that would change the course of action in his mind.

But she didn't speak, as if knowing that she might say the words, and save his life, but destroy some more vital aspect.

Instead, she drew him down onto her, raised her lips,

and found his, anchoring there, and for a time it seemed like they fed on each other, as if each contained some terrible, addictive nectar.

And when her fingers, questing, clasped him into heat and wetness, raised her hips to him in steady, urgent, kneading rhythm, he cried out and clung to her, clutching at her as if she contained within her the secrets of all the universe.

As if in the shadows that moved upon the wall there was all the truth that two human beings could find.

As if in the hot, salty sweet rhythm of sweat and lubrication and seminal fluid there were all the nourishment two human beings could desire.

As if they needed to stretch this moment, make it not just another evening's love but something terribly special. A final and ultimate time, something that each of them would remember always, even into the depths of that last long and dreamless night.

25

Leslie was asleep. The child slept with only a single sheet draped across his body, in a room carefully monitored for temperature.

Fine golden-black hair covered Leslie's body. It was the body of an animal, each and every muscle perfectly developed, perfectly placed, as if the child were half cat and half human being.

The light slanted in through the window, and the moon was high. In that cold, cool light, Leslie seemed even younger. The lines of his jaw, sometimes harsh, were softer, the feminine aspects of his face more apparent.

Aubry looked for himself in this child. So innocent now, so soft and vulnerable.

What was there in children that evoked that response?

And what kind of people would threaten a child to get to him?

So Aubry had made a mistake. Perhaps a terrible one—killing the wrong person. Swarna's son Ibumi. There had been no option. The combat had begun by mutual consent, and a ritualistic nightmare it had been. He had no regrets, and if he were to try to project feelings onto another man—something that he tried never to do—he would say that Ibumi had no regrets, either.

But that was entirely beside the point. Swarna had made a mistake—a fatal one. Aubry Knight was not alone anymore. He had resources, resources that extended all the way to the Oval Office, and by God he would use every last one of them to protect what was his.

When Aubry sat at the edge of the bed, Leslie rolled lazily into his arms. There were no words, but Leslie's thin body shook. Could it be the cold? Aubry felt no draft, no sign that the environmental seal had been ruptured.

Something to his surprise, Aubry realized that his terrible child was afraid. "Shhh," he whispered.

"Daddy." Leslie's voice was barely audible. "I don't want you to go."

Aubry stroked the very fine hair along the back of Leslie's neck. So beautiful.

"I have to."

There was a long pause, and then Leslie spoke again, without opening his eyes. "Let me come with you."

"WHAT?"

Leslie's eyes snapped open, flaming, and he was rattling words at a blistering pace.

"It could work, Father. I would be the perfect camouflage—no one would expect you to bring a kid along on a hit."

"Lone Wolf and Cub?"

"Well . . . maybe, except Daigoro was a wimp. I can learn any language in a week. I can break into any data net—"

Aubry shushed Leslie with a massive finger. "I know you could, sweetheart. I just . . ." What? What could he say to this hot-eyed creature, whose short life had seen so much mayhem?

"I want you to have a chance, Leslie."

"A chance to what?"

"I didn't have any choice. I had to fight. I had to kill. I want you to have choices that I didn't have. The doctors don't know quite what to make of you, but I do. You're my son. You're my daughter. You're the most beautiful, dangerous creature alive, and you're going to have a normal life."

Leslie's voice changed. It seemed that he was an automaton imitating human speech. "Father," Leslie said. "You are . . . all I have. You are . . . Without you, what chance would I have?" The machine's voice trembled, cracked. "If you die, do you know what would . . . happen? To me?" The tiny body was actually shaking, as if there were some windup apparatus under the warm flesh, something struggling to rev free.

Aubry drew Leslie to his chest, shushing him. "First of all, I'm harder to kill than you seem to think. I survived quite well before you were a twinkle in your mother's eye, thank you. Swarna won't be expecting me to come after him. I think I can pull this off. Secondly—what you'll have is a good life. You are respected and honored here. A good life, dammit, in Ephesus if nowhere else on this planet. You're going to have those things, Leslie."

Leslie's eyes shone in the dim room, and he held Aubry, as if seeking to meld bones with him through pressure. The child seemed all steel and catgut, something not at all human. His fingers sank deeply into Aubry's iron muscles.

Then some resolve, some well of strength expired, and Leslie held Aubry and wailed, the tears running down his father's chest. Aubry held Leslie in return, and felt himself pulled to the brink of some abyss beyond his understanding, as if there were within Leslie a Void, some great and utter vacuum against which all of his child's intelligence and energy warred.

All that sustained the child were his relationships. To Promise. To Aubry. To Jenna.

To Mira? Had Leslie cried for Mira?

And perhaps the tears now, a vast and endless flood of grief, were the tide of emotion held in check only by that monstrous will, the dike buckling under the thought of losing the only father he had ever known, or could ever hope to know.

They held each other, and Leslie sobbed until the first light of morning rose to meet them.

26

JULY 25

No security system in Ephesus can stop me. I see in the infrared and ultraviolet. I hear things that bats and cats hear. I can feel pressure traps, and sixty percent of standard movement sensors don't register me at all. I do not understand all modifications performed upon me for the Medusa Project. Some standard training. Some direct induction. Some implantation of preprogrammed fetal cortex. Some neural grooving of spinal tissue. And more: nanotech, genetic, hormonal, cybernetic. Everything Gorgon could do to produce a perfect killing and infiltration machine. Perhaps I was the best. I am certainly the last.

Father was gone. He kissed us goodbye and took one of the small Toyota transport skimmers. Travel plans said Los Angeles, and then Denver. From there to hell, by routes unknown.

If Father died not Mother, or Jenna, or anyone in the world would stop me from finding Swarna, and killing him.

And then myself.

The sheer wall outside Jenna's apartment was an engraved invitation. I disconnected the alarm, opened the window and sat on the sill, naked, four stories above the ground.

A guard passed beneath me. Quiet. Efficient. Unaware.

Jenna and a companion slept. The companion was female. Unidentified. I differentiated Jenna's breathing pattern. Jenna snores. It is one way I can be sure she is really asleep. Women rarely pretend to snore.

I began to imitate it.

I reached full rapport in just over thirty seconds. Began to change the rhythm, slowing it so that Jenna slid deeper. Listened and coaxed simultaneously. Jenna is intelligent, imaginative, sensitive. Thoroughly versed in trance arts. An ideal hypnotic subject.

Outside, the temperature was thirty-four degrees. I focused my attention tighter.

I hopped down from the window and crept to her side. Her breathing was deeper, and slower. Down to one-point-seven per minute. Perfect.

I whispered in her ear, timing each phrase to her natural exhalation cycles.

"Jenna. Your love for Aubry is almost as strong as your sister's—but you are even more capable of helping him. Only you can help him. Listen to me. You will go to Leslie, and ask her to help you to access the information concerning Swarna. You must know. And when you know, you will find Miles Bloodeagle. You will help Aubry. It is . . ." Jenna has an appreciation of the dramatic. I paused to build subconscious response potential. ". . . your destiny."

Jenna continued to snore. I allowed myself a brief flash of satisfaction and backed out of the room. I clambered back up onto the windowsill, and climbed down.

As soon as Leslie was gone, Jenna's right eye opened. She grinned in the darkness. Leslie. Little brat. Durga specialized in trance states. *Teach Gramma to suck eggs, sweetie.* Still, the muffin had a good idea. Aubry was waltzing into the meat grinder, and a little help might go a long way. There were resources available. The only real question was their appropriate utilization. . . .

27

Aubry hadn't been in this dead-end, red-bricked alley for a thousand years. It was still behind a refueling station near the corner of Century and Vermont, in South Central Los Angeles, beyond the invisible walls of Mazetown.

When Aubry was a boy, the station had sold unleaded, and diesel, and propane. Now it also dealt in liquid hydrogen, and recharge posts, and fast battery swaps.

That was the only landmark remaining. The neighborhood was still poor, but both ground and air traffic bustled. The pavement thrummed with the sound of the subway. It always seemed that it would be impossible for Los Angeles to grow more crowded. Or that the city would survive that overcrowding. So far, the first had always been proven possible, and the second remained to be seen.

In many ways he no longer recognized the alley. Peeling posters from forgotten political campaigns still cajoled, no longer shifting images and colors with the passage of the sun. Time seemed to have forgotten them. But to Aubry the pavement stank of blood, not garbage.

The air boiled with flies, drawn by the mountains of garbage, the boxes and cans and bags of offal. It was here, amid the filth, that Aubry's father had died.

Died trying to protect a woman who had been nothing but bait.

Aubry looked back into the years, ripped the veil painfully away. And he *saw,* as if the man were still there, as if the pain were still new, as if the crowd had just gathered to watch the death of the only family a boy named Aubry had ever known.

He knelt close to his father's body, close enough to hear

the hiss of breath from the ruptured chest cavity, where the blade had slid in, severing life.

"Aubry . . ." the man had said. And then something . . . Aubry didn't understand. Couldn't remember. Had never been able to remember. It sounded like gibberish,

or . . .

"Firedance. Iron Mountain . . ."

Aubry rubbed his eyes. Father was gone. Years vanished like yesterday's newsfax. He was alone in the alley again. He leaned his head against the wall, trying to remember.

"Hey!" someone yelled. Aubry looked up. At the far end of the alley a unisuited Exotic glowed. He had completed what Promise had begun, all visible flesh covered with plastiskin. His entire visual character changed as Aubry watched, shifting subtly to resemble Aubry. A freelance Rapporter, seeking empath bits for the network. He carried his feelie box with him, its antennae already wiggling toward Aubry. "Are you in pain? Could you use assistance?"

Aubry shook his head.

The man smiled. It was a big, warm smile. And suddenly it wasn't quite a man's anymore. The processor shifted the visual image into a woman's. Smiling. Warm. Darkskinned. Slightly overweight. Its best guess about Aubry's mother?

"I can help you," he said. "Pain is profit—"

"Get the hell out of here!" Aubry screamed.

He stopped, taken aback. And grinned, glancing at his empath meter. "That was good. Maybe twenty credits right there. Would you do that again? A little louder?"

"If. You. Don't. Get. The. Fuck. Out. Of. Here. I. Am. Going. To. Kill. You. The Nets would *love* to buy that. I guarantee you."

He seemed to be considering it, and then thought again, and shrugged. "Your loss, boss." And ran, carrying his precious bytes.

Aubry slammed his hand into the wall. He needed clarity, and balance. No one could sell that to him, or buy it for him.

The boy who had once wept over his father's corpse was gone. Aubry didn't know that boy anymore. He doubted that he existed. All there was now was a man torn between the worlds of emotion and logic, the physical and the ethereal. Robbed of his past, and denied a future.

A man, nonetheless. A man who would do what he must do for the sake of his family.

And his sanity.

2ND SONG

WINDDANCE

Watch the grass, the
clouds, the rain, if you
would know the wind.
Watch the difference
between a man's words
and his actions, if you
would know the man.

—Ibandi proverb

1

"There *are* no . . . *guarantees* on this sort of operation." President Harris laid the file down carefully on his desk, brushed the top sheet with the tip of his finger. Harris was a slender, bespectacled man in his mid-sixties, lean but withered by fatigue. His prim, thoughtful mouth was un-balanced by a nose just a fraction too large for the thin face that carried it. Behind the spectacles, his dark eyes were watchful, evaluative. A survivor's eyes. His carefully tailored brown suit hung on him like a cloak. His large, sensitive hands trembled.

He sighed heavily, and turned to peer out through the louvered window of the Oval Office. It wasn't really a win-dow: he was completely sealed in here, as every chief exec-utive had been since the assassination of President Quayle. But the vidscreen looked like a window, and piped in full-dimensional images of Pennsylvania Avenue just as if he were an ordinary human being, in an ordinary world.

The world outside seemed so placid, so quiet.

Roland Harris had survived two terms in office. He knew that he had done his duty, and served his country as best he could. There was no more that he could do. For the past few months, some weariness, some emotional cancer within him had grown steadily darker and heavier, as im-placable as a colony of rogue cells clusterfucking in his marrow. The time for change had come. The job needed a younger man. At least, it needed a man with younger eyes. One whose mind was a cleaner slate.

When Roland Harris closed his eyes, he saw blood, and rubble. He opened them again, focusing on a man who, despite his diminutive size, had absolutely nothing childlike about him. "I keep remembering that night, General Koskotas."

"That, sir, is almost inevitable."

He smelled concrete dust, and the burnt-orange stench of the explosive. "Sterling Delacourte almost killed me, on national television. He could have stolen the country, and God only knows what he would have done with it."

General Koskotas brushed imaginary dust from his knee. He was always impeccably tailored. His body was always in superb physical condition, posture absolutely erect, whites of his eyes so clear they crackled. Koskotas's face and body bore only one testament to his six decades of pressure-driven existence: facial lines which suggested that his expression, when unobserved, was one of contempt for everything and everyone in the world.

Harris had never trusted Koskotas, or any of his cohorts in the American intelligence splinter group referred to as STYX. He had learned of STYX almost accidentally, in conjunction with the final debriefing on the Swarna-backed assassination attempt. Too many dollars were flowing in the same direction. During a DEA briefing, he heard that a Nigerian grubfarm made payoffs channeled through Bank of Montreal. Bank of Montreal had been paymaster on a PanAfrican Gorgon raid, six years before. A blackmail sting against a pro-PanAfrica senator involved an ex-military attaché who had served with Koskotas in Ethiopia. STYX again. During that final briefing, Koskotas and Bank of Montreal had been linked to illegal arms sales to PanAfrican rebels.

Harris swore he would blow the operation to Congress unless he was given a full briefing.

STYX was the operation designed to destroy Phillipe Swarna, and to drive a wedge between the Republic and the Japanese. "Make the Japs need us again," he was told. "We need NipTech, and we're not getting it. America will fall behind the Common Market. In ten years it'll be too late to catch up."

Koskotas cleared his throat. "Knight performed great

service, Mr. President. To place him in this kind of risk is . . . completely unnecessary."

Harris listened to Koskotas, studied him. Who was this man, behind the medals and ribbons, the honors and degrees? As a hundred times before, he found that he couldn't penetrate. Try as he might, he got no further than Koskotas's blue glass-chip eyes.

Koskotas did not see Aubry Knight as a man who had saved a life, even so important a life as the president's. To Koskotas, Aubry Knight was just another civilian, a wild card, untrustworthy in an operation like STYX.

God. I want to sleep. I want to sleep forever. Harris composed himself. "They say that Harry Truman had a plaque on his desk that read 'The Buck Stops Here.' "

"I believe that that is true, sir."

"I never realized one implication of that. It is inevitable that we send good men and women into danger. Some of them die screaming, and probably damn us to Hell for the choices we've made."

"Probably, sir."

"How do you live with that, General?"

"With what, sir?"

The question was asked placidly, but for just a moment the facade had shifted, and Koskotas's face was clear to him. And what lay behind it was, simply, death for the enemies of America. At any price. Including Koskotas's immortal soul.

"With what, sir?"

There was emptiness within this man. Perhaps out of his own loneliness, Harris felt the compulsion to bridge the chasm between them. "Sometimes," he said, "I dream. I dream about the ceiling of the Democratic National Convention." Harris stared at the top of his desk as if his predecessor had carved cosmic answers there with the point of a knife. "And there is an explosion. And plaster and steel and wood burst out of the ceiling. And children, Koskotas. The bodies of mutant children. Pieces of bodies. They rain upon me." His voice was just a whisper now, and he looked grey and worn. *It isn't just that I can't make love with Juliet anymore. Or laugh, or dance . . .* Something flitted behind his eyes, something sad and dark, like the shadow of a wounded bird. . . . *or that I drink.*

He squared his shoulders and flipped open the dossier. "Aubry Knight. Former employee of the Ortega crime family. He broke away to compete athletically as a zero-gravity combat specialist called a Nullboxer. Ranked number eleven in the world." Harris paused, shook his head slightly, and then continued. "He was framed for murder, and sentenced to New Quentin and later Death Valley Maximum Security. He escaped during the riots of '24, and spent years in hiding. Somewhere during that time he took over the identity of one Kevin Warrick, head of the deconstruction group known as the Scavengers. And saved the life of the president of the United States by disrupting a plot by renegade Gorgon commandos."

"Sir," Koskotas reminded him. "You've done what you could for Knight. You pardoned him . . ."

"He was innocent."

". . . for escaping. And hardly without stain, sir."

"And in saving my life, he made an enemy of one of the most powerful men in the world." He paused, and looked up from the file. "He killed Swarna's son. I didn't know that."

"Yes. His son was using the name Ibumi, and was the lover and partner of Colonel Quint, head of Gorgon. Knight killed them both."

Harris's voice dropped to a whisper. "At what range? What kind of weapons?"

Koskotas cleared his throat. "Unarmed combat, sir. Simultaneously. Sir."

"Mother of God." The implications hit Harris in a delayed reaction. He sank back behind his desk, blinking. "How could . . ." He looked up. "I was always under the impression that the Gorgons were beyond human competition."

Koskotas colored slightly. "We had the same impression, Mr. President."

There was silence, except for the sound of the air-conditioning. Then: "I want you to give him his chance."

"Mr. President." For the very first time, something like passion crept into Koskotas's voice. "The . . . neutralization of a head of state who consistently expects assassination is not an easy thing. Short of an agent resolved to die in the attempt, it can be almost impossible. The American intelligence community discovered that in the nineteen-sixties when they tried to remove Fidel Castro.

"At least three different attempts were made to remove Swarna, including one armed intrusion under the auspices of an 'antiterrorist' action. We simply can't gamble the established networks on such a long shot. One good man, name of Kolla, has already disappeared."

"Swarna tried to kill Knight's family. I owe him my life, General. We owe him his chance." Harris brushed his right hand across his face, as if wiping away cobwebs. "Tell me honestly. How would you feel about him as raw material?"

Koskotas sighed. "We'll have a much better evaluation of that after training and testing. Of course, in hand-to-hand combat, his lethality is absolute. Possibly the best in the world. But that won't count for much against Swarna. Strategy and tactics, weapons skill . . . these are other things. Facility with vehicles . . . once again, we don't know."

"What *do* you know?"

"We have the records from his training under a man named Guerrero, back when he was with the Ortegas. He is credited with absolute hand-eye coordination. His facility with small arms falls well below what we would expect for an athlete of his caliber. Guerrero postulated that these were conceptual barriers, rather than lack of actual capacity. We do not as yet know what conditions he will face in PanAfrica. He may have to penetrate a fortress called the Citadel. Its security arrangements are somewhat unique. He must be prepared to utilize a wide range of weapons, including pulse rifles, timed explosives, and nanotech."

"And can you do it?"

"Theoretically, yes. Our task would be to implant the beliefs and mental syntax to use these weapons properly. We would also need to implant a language translator, and utilize a number of deep trance states." He flipped through the pages of his own report. "There is a possibility that he can handle a direct cortical input. That would be useful, if true."

Harris's eyes narrowed. "I thought that was only possible for cyborgs."

"It should be, yes. Some advanced yoga types can handle it. Reportedly the Medusas could. For most human beings there is simply too much input. Seventy-nine percent of our test subjects suffered cerebral hemorrhage."

"And you have no idea why he can do this . . . *if* he can do it."

"None."

Harris sat and folded his fingers together neatly, almost as if in prayer. "I want him to do this, General. I want him to have his chance. If I have any hint that he has less than your full cooperation, I swear I will shut STYX down. Do you understand me?"

Koskotas controlled his anger and changed tactics. "And if you are sending him to die, sir? Are you prepared to deal with that possibility?"

"If he dies . . ." Harris murmured. *My God . . . how have I done it all this time?*

"If he dies, he dies," Harris said quietly. "But this isn't a kamikaze operation. I want every effort made to get him out of there alive, do you understand?"

"Of course," Koskotas said.

But there was no light behind the glass-chip eyes, and Harris knew that the lie had been spoken, the death certificate signed and postdated.

Is this what you want, Aubry Knight? Is this how one repays a . . . friend? By sending him into death. Oh, God . . .

Quietly, Koskotas left the room.

2

THE CITADEL, PANAFRICAN REPUBLIC

Sinichi Tanaka stood just beyond the shadow of Caernarvon, waiting patiently for his primary to complete the kill. The dictator of PanAfrica stood at the edge of the castle's outer garden, the five hundred meters of man-made Jurassic forest stretching between the moat and the death strip. Beyond that strip lay a thousand-meter no-man's-land called the Menagerie.

Swarna's eyes were open, but his mind was out in Menagerie. At the moment he was joined mind and soul to one of the great carnivores, which hunted endlessly in its forest and swamp beyond the palace walls. His eyes stared, vacant, flickering as if in REM sleep, and his mouth made small trembling motions. His fingers crooked into claws.

Not long now.

Tanaka had no moral aversion to virtual addiction. His only concern involved security, regarding the potentially damaging aspects of neural link. To feel full satisfaction during a mating or a kill, ordinary virtual safety precautions had to be abandoned. Ecstasy on so primal a level was ... *sensation*, beyond any ordinary concepts thereof. Addicts had been known to go into shock. To suffer stroke. To exhibit stigmata during the playful, lustful clawing that preceeded penetration.

Deep within Caernarvon, that masterpiece of thirteenth-century Edwardian architecture, special safety breakers were constantly monitored. One day, the Americans might attempt to overload Swarna's nervous system. Sinichi Tanaka had never lost a primary. Nor had his father, or his grandfather, back through six hundred years of service. Tanaka's people had served Imperial Japan, and then Industrial Japan, and now PanAfrica by way of the Divine Blossom *keiretsu.*

Tanaka was huge and dusky for a Japanese, with close-cropped black hair and square shoulders, with thick fingers attached to thick palms, terminating in a thick wrist. At one spot, above the left ear, no hair grew, due to a sword slash that had glanced off his skull.

His dark skin was a tribute to his grandmother Grace Tanchala, a half-blooded Zulu who had married a Japanese tradesman. Their child, a mixed breed named Yoshi, had fought and struggled to attend college in Tokyo. A complete outcast, he had achieved academic success, and had, contrary to the wishes of her father, courted and married the daughter of a powerful Yakuza at the time when the Japanese crime lords moved into legitimate business, during the 1980s. Yoshi Tanaka proved so valuable in opening Africa to the Yakuza that he gained a reasonable amount of real power, although excluded from any of the family business.

His son, Sinichi, received an education fit for a samurai—but was never allowed to forget that he could never be such a man. He might know the intricacies of the tea ceremony. He might speak fluent Japanese. He might be a master of *iaido* and kendo, and hold certificates from the Kodokan and Kyukushinkan. But he was one-eighth black, and even worse, one-eighth white. And for that sin he would be trash, always trash, an animal fit only for service.

But on occasions of state Sinichi Tanaka still carried his great-grandfather's *katana* in its original scabbard. He was as muscular as a sumo wrestler on a liquid-protein diet, and held a doctorate in abnormal psychology from Tokyo University. It would have been a grave error to underestimate the man who lived behind those black, empty eyes.

Phillipe Swarna made a growling sound deep in his throat, and his eyes narrowed, and focused on Tanaka. They were reptilian eyes, hot and hungry. As he watched, they softened, they returned to sanity.

"Greetings, Swarna-san," Tanaka said.

Phillipe Swarna wiped the corner of his mouth, nodded, and turned. "Walk with me," he said finally. Each step was measured. His brow, once strong, was now grooved with age. His shoulders, once broad and powerful, were now stooped. Tanaka had seen many men of power, but few on whom the weight rested so heavily.

They paused at the innermost security strip, an invisible electronic curtain. The land without was just as lushly foliated, but Tanaka shuddered slightly. He thought of the creatures that stalked beyond it, and felt a touch of unease.

"You have words for me?" Phillipe Swarna said in perfect Japanese. Swarna's bodyguards walked four paces behind them.

In their light shock armor and faceplates, Swarna's bodyguards were dark twins. Both wore the PanAfrican security emblem, an abstraction of Caernarvon, Swarna's imported prize, symbol of his victory over the Europeans. The Japanese had outbid him for Windsor.

Swarna's personal guard belonged to no regular regiment. No one outside Caernarvon knew where he had found them. Some rumors said that they came from his home tribe. Others that they were his bastard sons. Sinichi Tanaka was one of the few men alive who knew that they had no names, only the designations Two and Five.

"You called for this meeting, sir," Tanaka said carefully.

Swarna nodded, but seemed to be lost in his own thoughts. He stopped and bent. A nearby bush rustled. Its triangular leaves looked nibbled along its lower extent. An avocado-sized head, perched on an impossibly long and slender mottled-yellow neck, poked out of the brush. Its body was the size of a medium Labrador. It had squat, powerful legs and a two-foot tail.

The miniature brontosaur peered soulfully up at Swarna and made a crooning sound. Swarna petted it, fished in his pocket, and fed it a nugget of Purina brontochow.

Tanaka marveled. The creature had the brain of a parakeet, but it still responded to Swarna with unmistakable affection. The little creature was collared. The collar was programmed to administer electric shocks. The farther it went from the control fence between the garden and outer Menagerie, the more discomfort it would experience.

Of course, the microsaur's discomfort was *nothing* compared to what the giant saurians endured. For them, the control fence was a literal death strip. Nearing it caused unendurable pain. Crossing it detonated explosive charges built into their collars. Of course, there was a physical moat separating the Caernarvon from both garden and Menagerie.

From time to time Tanaka could . . . hear things in the Menagerie. Rarely, very rarely, could he see anything— long before the big ones came into range of sight, their rudimentary brains were frying in pain. Most learned by the end of the first day. Only two had ever been decapitated. There was plenty of room in the outer Menagerie to roam, and mate . . . and hunt.

Primarily the precautions were for the benefit of the smaller, more docile herbivores, but still . . .

Tanaka pulled his thoughts back on track. Why the personal meeting? What business was there that might have motivated it? "We have received a proposition." Tanaka ventured. "LucasCorp Ltd. is looking for a white knight, a buyer to protect them from being acquired by EuroFilm. They would prefer one of our corporations."

Swarna's thick lips curled slightly. "And what would America think of me owning such a sacred possession? No. I will leave that."

Tanaka considered. What else was there that Swarna might take a personal interest in? Ah.

"The rex has been sedated, and is en route to the Iron Mountain, sir."

That deepened Swarna's smile. "Iron Mountain. They are mad, you know," he said, but there was an affectionate wonder in his voice. "Quite mad. But their madness has kept them strong."

"The *assagai* have passed security, and can be mounted in the throne room, if you wish."

"The present from the Zulus. Twin fighting spears, in stainless steel, yes. Very nice."

"Sir. You must have something else on your mind, or I assume that you wouldn't have suggested a personal meeting."

Swarna held a leaf between his fingers. The tiny dinosaur nibbled it gingerly, tasting. It ate with a delicacy that belied its awkward exterior. "The saboteur," he said.

"Kolla. At Swarnaville Spaceport."

"Yes."

"Working for the Americans—we think. Our mind probes revealed that Kolla was paid, and that he had a contact, but the timing was thrown off by the arrest. There was a street corner. A packet was to be exchanged, at exactly seven minutes past noon. It was impossible to break him in time to keep the appointment."

"We need . . . more effective methods," Swarna said. He stooped, grimacing as his back creaked. Nevertheless he sighed happily, as if the sight and sensation of the tiny creature eating from his hand gave him a corresponding pleasure. "They have such small minds. They must be . . . cared for. Protected. Even from their own impulses."

"Yes, sir."

Swarna gently scratched the microsaur's head. It nuzzled the last piece of leaf from his hand, and then scurried back into the bushes.

He stood and placed his hands at the small of his back, straightening his spine. "I want to know of the security arrangements."

"They are as full as I can make them, now, at this time. We must design equivalent security screens at each of two other possible locations. Disinformation. Unfortunate, but necessary."

The corners of Swarna's mouth moved down a quarter of an inch. The rest of his face didn't move. "Yes. Then we respond to this unfortunate incident in the standard fashion."

Tanaka was careful to keep his face neutral. "Kolla is only twelve years old, sir."

"Yes. No pain. Just kill him. And his father. And his brothers."

He smiled merrily, an ebon Father Christmas. "See to that. And stay for dinner, won't you?"

Tanaka's black eyes were expressionless. *Monster, you have purchased my services. I would die to protect you. My soul you cannot have.*

"Of course, sir," he said. And bowed.

3

JULY 27. MANITOU SPRINGS, COLORADO.

At 6:45 A.M. Aubry Knight awakened with a start, rousing himself from a dream of monstrous, angular buildings and predatory streets. In that dream he was an unborn child, floating within an eggshell. The egg rolled at the feet of two idiot, diapered infants who struggled for possession of an empty candy box, bawling out their mutual misery at hurricane decibel levels.

He wiped his forehead, disoriented, eyes focusing on the blur of brown and green around him. The skimmer settled into its approach pattern. To either side of him were cliffs, hills, low mountain ranges. Below him was a silver-blue slip of river. More formidable crags crested the horizon. His navigator screen gave him a tiny red arrow traversing a web of blue contour lines. Sugarloaf Mountain appeared onscreen. Ahead somewhere was Manitou Springs Federal Training Facility.

His skimmer dropped down into a primary approach path. Twice his guidance computer was challenged, warned that it was entering classified airspace. Codes had been requested and exchanged. Just ahead and below, Quonset huts glittered in the early-morning sun like a cluster of bubbles rising through mercury. As he swooped

near, three bronze VTOLs leapt from the ground and
flashed toward him.

They hemmed him in, thick metallic wedges rimmed
with pulsing strips of golden light. His control panel
bleated protest, and then submission as they overrode his
guidance system. Each security skimmer was twice the size
of his personal travel pod. Here in their midst there was no
turbulence and little sound.

They shepherded him along as if he were a puppet suspended by invisible strings, and landed him with surgical
precision. The skimmer's hydraulics sighed as he settled to
the landing pad. The metal superstructure sighed and
creaked as it began to cool.

The cockpit hissed open. Aubry smelled the air, scanned
the mountains, and was hit by an almost overwhelming
sense of déjà vu.

A tall, gaunt woman in a metallic grey flight suit strode
toward Aubry, hand outstretched. "Aubry Knight? Major
Gagnon." Her gaze was direct, open, and challenging. She
had shoulder-length hair that was as bright and fine as
spun gold. Her eyes were a bit too piercing, cheeks too severe and jawline too flat for her to be particularly photo-
genic, but she moved well, and spoke plainly. "I've heard
of you, and look forward to working with you. You were
trained by Guerrero, weren't you?"

A tickle of pleasure, tinged with regret, crept along
Aubry's back. He forgot about unpacking luggage, and
met the major's hard, flat hand with his own. Aubry liked
her instantly. She waved him away from the luggage, and
snapped her fingers for two junior noncoms to take the
load. "Yes," he said. *Guerrero.* "You knew him?"

"Know him," she said, her smile secretive.

"You . . . what?" Aubry stopped, and stared at her.

She laughed. "Not now. Later. STYX has a lot of secrets."

"STYX?"

"Code name. You don't need to know anything else
about them. *They* want what *you* want."

"Which is?"

"Phillipe Swarna, in a box. Now, we've got a tight schedule. Three weeks to teach you everything we can, and to refresh your memory."

"Why three weeks?"

"We may have more time, but we don't dare bet that way. There's a merchant route that's still sterile, but Swarna has a fuck-all intelligence network. He's using NipTech, natch." She sounded wistful. "We really shouldn't have blown that. Anyway, we have three different routes set up—but have to wait for additional confirmation before we make a commitment."

"All right, three weeks."

"Of course, we won't have to drill you on the unarmed. They say Colonel Kim is angry about that."

"Kim? Who is that?"

"Counterinsurgency expert. He coordinates a lot of the combat schooling for American intelligence. Created the Night Tigers unit. Almost as good as Gorgon. He insisted on having you go through his training, came out here personally to supervise it. We have to disappoint him."

"I guess we can work out, if you want."

Gagnon's golden hair bounced as she shook her head. The gesture softened but failed to offset the severity of her face. "You don't understand. He's heard your rep. Let's leave it alone. A broken arm or fractured kneecap for you right now would throw everything off schedule. We can't afford it."

Aubry thought about that for a minute. "You think he's that good?"

"He's magic. Leave it."

"All right."

"All right. Firearms, infiltration, we have to set up a communications link with you. Implant your linguistics. Instant polyglot. We can promise you the most intense twenty-one days of your entire life. Guerrero says you're the fastest study that he ever met. You'd better be. And something else, too."

"What?"

She led him toward a low building shaped like a reverse

L that had fallen onto its side. "Lucky," she said. "You had better be the luckiest man God ever let live. Phillipe Swarna is probably the hardest target on Earth. It'll take a touch of magic to get him."

4

Aubry's room was at the farthest end of a quiet corridor, at the end of a nested series of security gates. His thumbprint and voice opened the door. The room wasn't much larger than a cell. It held a shower cubicle, a commode, and a hard bunk. There was enough room on the floor for him to perform his morning exercises. A single window set opposite the bed was polarized blue. He ran his finger along the bottom, clearing it.

Snow-crested mountains clustered beyond Aubry's barracks window, jagged as splintered teeth. Beneath them sat the landing field, where wedge-shaped security craft dipped and lifted with metronomic regularity. He ran his finger along the vertical polarizing strip. Purple ghosts swarmed, devouring the light.

The cot creaked protest as he lay back, listening to the distant sounds. He struggled to distinguish voices and familiar noises. He needed to absorb the base's rhythms. He folded his hands together and slipped them behind his head. Little to do now, except be ready. Easy enough: *I was born ready. I'll die ready.* He grinned at the cliché.

And yet, there was a part of him that really, truly didn't care if he lived or died. It was a tiny spot, and he did not try to banish it. It was another tool. Within every human heart was an incredible range of emotions, from nurturing healer to psychopathic berserker. Each, in its proper circumstance, was appropriate.

Care too much about living, and you will die. This he had learned the hard way. So accept the inevitable—but do not seek it. Hope only that before that final hour comes, you can discharge all obligations. Beyond that, no man could do.

What had Jenna said?

"There are few things in life that matter, Aubry. There is knowledge. There is honor. There is family. Unless it benefits one of these three, what is the use of it?"

"What about pleasure?" he had asked.

"Don't seek pleasure. Seek knowledge, and honor. Protect and nurture your family. Pleasure will find you."

5

At 10:30, Major Gagnon escorted Aubry to the mess hall. Nine-tenths of the training complex was underground, or embedded in the mountain. No natural light shone into the room. In some ways it reminded him of Death Valley Maximum Security Prison, a genuinely scrotum-tautening association.

They filed through the mess line and found seating in a corner of the room. The major ate with a quiet fervor, her eyes sweeping the room like a lighthouse beacon brushing back the night.

Aubry ate in silence, absorbing himself in the task of slicing barbecued beef into strips. He inserted the fork tines between the grain, lifted it to his mouth and chewed slowly, extracting the juice before he swallowed. The room buzzed with unfocused conversation, general talk. Slowly, as if at a prearranged signal, the conversations died to a murmur.

A pale man with straight yellow hair and a crew cut rose from a table across from him and sauntered over. The man was built like an inverted pyramid, with narrow hips, and shoulders at least two inches wider than Aubry's. Stupefying pectoral development bulged an electric blue tank top. Deep networks of wrinkles radiated from the corners of his light grey eyes. It was difficult to determine the age—

face and neck suggested fifties. The man walked with eerie grace, his weight carried slightly forward, high in his chest.

A trancelike silence descended upon the room.

The combat computer in Aubry's head automatically judged and evaluated: tae kwon do, or one of the other kicking arts. Hwa rang do, maybe. Korean styles. *Kim is angry about that.* One of the colonel's boys? His hands were callused, so he wasn't a kickboxer. . . .

The man leaned over the table and cocked his head sideways. He reeked of animal challenge.

"Hey, Knight," Pecs said, not unpleasantly. "You were number eleven. Would have been the next to actually ride the torch, wouldn't you?"

"There were problems." Aubry chewed his food easily, steadily. One careful bite at a time. There was an eternity between mouthfuls. All the fucking time in the world.

"Yeah." Pecs was enjoying himself. "Well—all of the scandals hit right after that anyway. Whole Nullboxing thing is fake, isn't it? Like pro wrestling?"

Aubry flinched. Damn. "There might have been cheating. I don't know—I wasn't a part of it. They were still good, damned good."

"You think those techniques work against a real man?"

Aubry smiled thinly. "I think so. I've used them once or twice, with a little success."

"I was sorry to hear that you're not going to work out with us. Colonel Kim was disappointed." He laid one massive hand on Aubry's shoulder and squeezed. It wasn't hostile, more a subtle evaluation of the muscle density and striation. He peered into the depths of Aubry's eyes, into the cave, searching for the animal.

At first, Aubry just smiled coldly. Then he picked up a knife with his right hand. The table cutlery was heavy, institutional steel. He rolled the handle between his palms until it began to warm.

"There is something you want to know. This lesson is free." Aubry paused for emphasis. "The next one costs."

Aubry wound his fingers around the haft. Second,

fourth, and little fingers were on top, the third finger underneath.

The room was more than silent now. It seemed frozen, with every eye on the two men. One stood, the other sat. Aubry focused on the knife handle. A dark tunnel of concentration surrounded it, so that the rest of the world ceased to exist.

He contracted his fist. A roaring filled his ears. His shirt sleeve suddenly filled, as every muscle and cord in his forearm swelled. For two full seconds nothing happened. Aubry watched the knife as if it were held in someone else's hand and he were merely an intensely interested observer.

Then slowly, smoothly, the haft bent ninety degrees.

"Shit." Gagnon almost choked on her brisket of beef.

Aubry handed it to Pecs. "Here," he said. "A present."

The karate man looked at Aubry for a moment. He rubbed his stubbled chin thoughtfully, then broke out into a grin. "You are all fucking right." He held out a meaty hand. "Francois Belloc. Good to have you here."

Aubry shook it, felt the power and knew the man at once. In terms of raw contractile tissue, Belloc had greater physical potential than Aubry, but only a fraction of the mental focus. Still, Francois Belloc would be tremendously fast, and skilled, and tenacious, with an insane tolerance for pain.

And both of them knew that Aubry would kill him in under ten seconds. Despite that unspoken knowledge, Francois was damn near wagging an invisible tail.

Francois almost wiggled with delight. "Swear to God, man. Kim is gonna have a *kitten.*"

"Meow," Aubry said, and continued his meal.

6

The long, low-ceilinged room was darkened. Three cones of light projected down onto as many chairs, grouped at one end of a long, rectangular conference table. Aubry Knight, Major Gagnon, and General Koskotas sat. Behind Koskotas stood the silent Kramer. These four were the only human beings, but in the middle of the room hovered a relief map of Central Africa so vivid it seemed a living presence. No matter where in the room you sat, the map faced you. In the middle of the map, a landmass was marked out in dark red, like a bloated spider crouching in the middle of the continent.

"This is PanAfrica," Gagnon said. "It is ruled by two forces: the Yakuza Divine Blossom *keiretsu,* and the man known as Phillippe Swarna. Swarna is the greater power, but there is tension between them. That tension is the key to our plan.

"We don't merely want to kill Swarna—we want to make it appear that Divine Blossom is responsible. If and when we do this, it will destroy the partnership. All the king's horses and all the king's men will eat omelets for a month. The United States will be the only power the PanAfricans can turn to. The distraction will also allow you to . . ." Gagnon paused. "To be completely honest, I should say 'will increase your chances of' escape. Every step is crucial, because of Swarna's penetration of our security apparatus."

Aubry didn't like the sound of that one bit. "How severe is it?"

"In the past year, we've uncovered something frightening." Even in the dim light, Aubry could tell that Gagnon had flushed with discomfort. "We've had to come up with a new word for what he did to us. We call it Versa. Understand something—we can't manufacture all of the components necessary for our security systems. Millions of memory bubbles come from Europe, millions more from Japan. Literally billions of lines of code go into a single major defense network. Much of that is farmed out to contractors around the world.

"There is *no way* to keep total control of all of it. We try. Well, somewhere, with one of our suppliers, or one of our programmers, something went wrong. Someone slipped in a time bomb. One chip, one chip among millions, with a few lines of altered code. It got past us.

"The time bomb, which we call Versa, created a *virtual rom*. It read the original and created a new one—like a computer within the computer. It used partitioning techniques much more sophisticated than anything we have. It invisibly compressed and restored data, doubled our storage space. We never had a clue. At that point, everything we did went into the 'virtual machine', get it?"

Aubry nodded uneasily.

"Versa, the Niptech virtual rom, had duplicated all of the mainframe protocols. It sat in there for months, absorbing information, then sending it out of the building."

Aubry felt genuinely confused. "It did all that just in the software?"

"No. But the main computer has its own nanotech repair bots. Versa, ah . . ." Gagnon was searching for words. "*Subverted* them. Under the command of Versa, modifications were made to *the physical structure of the machine.*"

Aubry fought to remember something that Leslie had taught him. "Aren't your computers sealed from the outside? No lines in or out?"

"Yep. But every time we moved information out to another machine, it beat us. Say we moved data in physical storage, on a bubble chip. Versa created dual formatting on that chip, increased the storage, created an invisible island of instructions and information. When the chip reached a machine that *did* have communication with the exterior world, it executed its instructions, and conveyed its data to the outside world. Brilliant, simple, damn near unbeatable.

"It was in the telecommunications, it was was in data storage. It may have been there for as long as ten years."

"Still, how does that tell you that Swarna was involved?"

Gagnon looked at Koskotas. He raised his hand, quieting her, and spoke for the first time. "To tell you the truth, some of our sources are classified, and some is conjecture. We froze one of the virtual ROMs before it could self-destruct. We got into it, and took a look at the code. Brilliant. Linguistic idiosyncrasies will suggest the nationality of a writer or speaker. In the same manner, you can determine the cultural origin of a programmer. The interesting thing was that there were *two* major influences: Japanese and Ugandan. The only reasonable conclusion is Pan-Africa."

Aubry nodded. "All right. What's next?"

"The first thing," Koskotas said, "is to study the target."

The map disappeared, and in its place was the image of a man of perhaps fifty years. He was very worn, thin, the flesh stretched tight across his face. His face was covered partially by a burnoose, with all visible skin etched by tribal scars.

"This is Phillipe Swarna. Before he emerged into public light, he was incarcerated in a South African prison. This was before the Revolt, maybe as far back as '90. He had been starved and beaten. We believe that his parents died in the AIDS compounds that eventually bred Thai-Six. He blamed South Africa and the Central Intelligence Agency for the introduction of the retrovirus. Psy-op proposes this grudge to be the origin of his loathing for European culture.

"Some time around '95, he was involved in the Revolt, and was personally responsible for the death of at least seventeen Allied personnel."

Aubry leaned forward to examine the picture more carefully. "Seventeen? At what range?"

"At torture range," Gagnon said distastefully. "Information extraction by some obscene ritual of his people, the Ibandi."

"All right," Koskotas continued. "Much of what follows is conjecture, but some of it has been documented. In the late nineties, through means still not entirely understood, he united Uganda, Tanzania, and Zaire. By terror and political maneuvering, he constructed the nation now known as the PanAfrican union. Or New Nippon. But usually just called PanAfrica. What do you know about it?"

"Just the popular-press stuff. Swarna wanted Black Africa to be able to compete with Europe and Asia."

"Yes. Swarna believed that if Africa continued on her present path, it would never catch up with Europe. He blamed it on colonial manipulation of tribal lines."

Aubry felt a very slight stinging sensation. At first he considered it physical in origin, but then recognized it as annoyance. "And what do *you* think?"

"Well . . ." Koskotas said. He hawed for a moment, and then said, "I'm not a sociologist, or a cultural anthropologist, or a geneticist. We can just accept the truth that Africans were still in the Stone Age when Europeans were building cathedrals, and leave the answers to the academicians. If we can proceed?"

Aubry said nothing, but felt a burning sensation behind his eyes. A headache, perhaps.

Koskotas manipulated a console, and a holographic image of Swarna appeared. He was giving a speech before a throng of well over a hundred thousand cheering black Africans who were hanging on to his words like shipwrecked sailors clinging to life preservers. He pounded the flats of his palms on the podium for emphasis, and gestured sharply. He spoke in English. Loudspeakers simultaneously translated into French, Swahili, and Tradetongue. "Will we allow white men to destroy us, through conquest and rape?"

A resounding "No!" swelled from a hundred thousand

throats. "Or will we take control of our own fate? Meet
our future with pride, with our heads held high?!"

Koskotas froze on that last syllable. Swarna's face was
distorted, eyes glazed with ecstatic fervor, one thin, muscular finger pointed off to some far horizon.

"He's big on the 'head held high' routine," Koskotas
said dryly. "He took a lot of risks. It worked."

He dropped his voice. "In fact, frankly, it worked better
than anyone anticipated. The PanAfrican experiment
served two needs simultaneously. Swarna gave land-starved
Japan the growth space it needed, and in the process created a cultural implant which combined the best of Europe
and Asia. Japan's direct-induction educational technology
is the best in the world. We can't get our hands on it. He
brainwashed an entire generation of African children.
Thirty years ago the PanAfrican Union was a backward
laughingstock with nothing to offer the world market but
raw materials. Now it is the world's fourth-strongest financial power, with a GNP only sixteen billion dollars smaller
than that of the United States. The downside is that it is
the most repressive regime in the world. By Western standards, PanAfricans have no rights at all.

"Needless to say, in the process Swarna made many enemies. As a result, he is estimated to have the most complex
security screen of any ruler on Earth. He rarely sets foot
outside the Menagerie."

The map shifted. In the air now was a detailed representation of about six square kilometers of land. An outer
ring of forest ("the Menagerie"), an inner ring ("the Garden"), and, protected behind a moat and electronic fences,
Swarna's transplanted Welsh castle, Caernarvon.

"At any given time there are probably twenty different
plots against his life."

Aubry scanned the map, recalling the face of his enemy.
"It's hard to believe that one man could accomplish so
much in such a short period of time."

"Yes, it is."

"Hard not to admire him," he murmured.

"Don't like the bastard *too* much. During the upheaval

following the creation of PanAfrica, over seven million people died. Relocation camps the size of New England. Disease and famine sprouting like toadstools in April. *Millions* of children had their names, their language, their culture stripped away. You cannot *begin* to comprehend the misery this man created."

"But it worked."

There was an uncomfortable pause, a gelid void into which all sound plunged. Then: "True—it worked. But at what cost? The truth is that many other approaches might have worked. Democracy was coming to Uganda, and had existed in Tanzania for decades. If you factor in the human misery, Phillipe Swarna probably put Africa back a hundred years."

"Other approaches might have worked."

"Yes."

"But nobody tried them." Aubry listened into the silence that followed, finding only the sound of the ventilation system *shush*ing quietly through its hourly cycles. He stared at Swarna's image. Neither of them moved. Then, finally, he said: "All right. What *exactly* do you have planned?"

"Intelligence is sketchy. We expect a break within the next two months—perhaps as soon as three weeks. We have to stay fluid, and be open to changing conditions. If you're in the loop, here's our best bet: in five weeks, Pan-Africa celebrates its fortieth anniversary. Despite lack of official confirmation, sources suggest that Swarna will make a public appearance at one of three locations. We can place you near the prime possibility. As you will learn, there is one way in which you are uniquely qualified to penetrate the security screen, and actually come into physical contact with Swarna."

"You're kidding."

"Not at all. With the equipment and assistance we can offer—"

"Assistance?"

"Yes. When Swarna falls, needless to say there will be a power vacuum. We have . . . people in place who will be

ready to take advantage of this situation. Rest assured that
they will be ready and willing to help you."

"A rebel element?"

"We prefer to consider them the true voice of the people. Despite his messiah complex, Swarna is just another
power-hungry dictator who grabbed what he could when
he could, with no concern for anything other than his own
bank accounts."

"I see. And if this attempt fails?"

"It is absolutely crucial that it doesn't. Only the confusion following a successful strike will give you any chance
of escape."

Aubry tapped his finger on the table for a few beats,
watching them. "Let's put it another way. Are you suggesting that if I don't succeed, the rebel forces might not
want to help me escape?"

There was silence. Kramer muffled a cough with the
back of his hand. "The people helping us are human beings, Mr. Knight. They have hopes and dreams just as you
do. Just communicating with us is a horrible risk for them.
If you were to fail, well . . . wouldn't it be natural that they
be irritated?"

Aubry smiled. "I might even be considered an embarrassment, mightn't I?"

Silence, as dark and cold as the lining of a corpse's stomach.

"All right," Aubry said. "How long will it take to set me
in place?"

"Two weeks, give or take, depending on the insertion
route."

"Which gives me between three and seven weeks for
training."

"Yes, exactly. We need to be sure that you are familiar
with weapons, strategies, and tactics. We'll only get one
chance." The room grew bright again. Koskotas's expression was grim. "We may not even get that."

7

"**L**ie down," Gagnon said, "and wait."

The office was spare and narrow, with no windows. There was only a cot, and a small desk. Bare walls that *hummed.*

For almost three minutes nothing happened, and then the door opened, and then a small, pale, plump man shuffled in.

Only five and a half feet tall, of no discernible physical conditioning. Clothes neat, hair rumpled. Face unlined. No facial hair—not even eyebrows. A slight suggestion of glaze to his skin, a hint of reconstructive surgery.

"Good afternoon," Guerrero said.

Aubry's mouth hung open. "But . . ."

"You saw me die. Yes, so I heard." The figure crossed to the desk, with that gliding shuffle-step Aubry remembered so well. It had been . . . almost seventeen years? When he first joined the Ortegas . . .

"I died in '11," Guerrero said, conversationally. Aubry's shock was receding. He finally realized that the sound of Guerrero's voice wasn't quite coming from his lips. "You remember. It was the São Paulo raid."

Aubry's mind blurred for an instant, and his memory reached back to the year 2011.

Recent Supreme Court rulings had thrown the narcotics game wide open. Personal use of cocaine and heroin was no longer a felony offense, though trafficking still earned the death penalty. But power, as always, was accompanied by privilege. The Ortegas, with influence throughout the western hemisphere, were as firmly connected as it was possible to get.

They provided funds for covert ops. They provided

death squads for Central Intelligence. They kidnapped
foreign nationals untouchable by extradition treaty, and
delivered them to the Justice Department, gift-wrapped.
They provided safe houses for American agents in Latin
America. In return, they received a monopoly on the
American drug trade. Quid pro quo.

And the São Paulo raid was one of Uncle Sam's little
gestures of appreciation.

The Conquistadores were a tightly connected European
combine, moving in on Ortega territory. They were highly
protected by the Brazilian government. Intelligence was almost impossible to obtain. Where were they? Who were
they?

All that was known for certain was that they struck
from darkness, with brutal efficiency. Farms raided. Virtsex facilities invaded, lines overloaded. Needleheads
flipped into raving insanity by sudden surges of direct-
induction hyperpain and death imagery. Ugly.

The Conquistadores were paramilitary. Thus far, the
usual Ortega methods proved ineffectual. So . . .

The American government, grateful for past favors, decided to lend a hand. Manitou Springs Federal Training
Facility would be made available. One time. For a very
special black operation involving an Ortega hit team.

Twenty men and women: tested, brutal, efficient, nerve-
less. Twenty cold-eyed killers.

One of them was a seventeen-year-old kid named Aubry
Knight.

8

FEBRUARY 7, 2011. MANITOU SPRINGS.

The sun had almost set as the first of the helicopters
touched down to the landing pad.

Aubry Knight felt cold, although the air was warm. He

was a big, rawboned kid, a little thin for his height, with emotionless eyes and a remarkable fluidity to his movement, an understated lethality that marked him as *different,* even in this group of rough, hard men and women. There were twenty of them, the toughest and the best from the Ortega family.

Family. Aubry rolled that word around in his mouth, liking the sound of it. He was a part of something big, something important.

He bent, pulled his rucksack from the cargo chopper, threw it over his shoulder, and hauled it to the edge of the tarmac. The chopper's blades still rotated slowly, whipping up the wind, and Aubry narrowed his eyes against it. The ride in had been wild, fierce, a harsh wind whipping through the mountain passes. The choppers had come in from the north, avoiding civilian radar. This operation wasn't just covert—as soon as they were gone, the whole damned base would catch a quick case of amnesia. Who? Never heard of 'em. Where? Never been there. What? Wouldn't do that.

The American military might well agree to train a civilian hit squad for operation in foreign territory, against foreign nationals, but they sure as hell didn't want details of it in the Political section of the *Times.*

Aubry grinned. Shit. This was going to be *fun.*

There was a simple clarity to the boy's thoughts. When you hurt, you did something to stop the pain. If someone hurt you, you killed them. If someone had something you wanted, something that would stop the pain, you took it from them.

Simple.

He barely remembered the night in the alley, the night when an eight-year-old boy had watched his father die, for nothing. Trying to help someone.

A lesson had been burned into his mind. *If you stick your nose where it doesn't belong, it'll get sliced off.*

Not the lesson that Father would have wanted, but Father was dead. And all he had left Aubry was the exercises, the Rubber Band, which had strengthened his body, and had helped him to survive, and stay sane in the long years of deprivation following that night.

Aubry pulled his thoughts back to the moment, and sat on his rucksack, waiting. Some of the other guys were smoking cigarettes—Aubry never smoked. Never drank. Never used drugs. Didn't much care what other people did with their pain. As long as they left him alone.

The others were all big, eyes bright with animal intelligence. Some had done time. Others had been too sly, or had the right protection. For the last nine years of his life, Aubry had struggled to belong to something big enough to watch his back. It wasn't the life straight fucks went for, but then he laughed at citizens anyway. Their lives, their dreams, their hopes meant nothing. They were like birds trapped in a cage of cats.

The politicians, the multinationals, the union heads, the Ortegas—they were in charge of this world. Everybody cut the deck to get the best deal. The people who *made* the laws broke the laws. The people who *enforced* the laws broke the laws. There *was* no fucking law. There was only power.

Chan, the big Chink bitch with the flat, callused hands and the dead eyes, offered Aubry a cold smile. "You made the cut, Knight. Good. You're good action." Her hair was cut short, almost a shaved scalp. The hard, flat breasts beneath the saffron jumpsuit never needed a bra: pectoral development provided all the support she needed.

Maybe she was a 'Morphadite. Aubry didn't relish an opportunity to find out. All he cared about was that she ruled this roost with her cunning, and her terrible skills.

Most karate stuff that Aubry had seen was bullshit. Any good streetfighter could blow through it, and Aubry was the best he'd ever seen.

But Chan . . . she was something else. She kept control in the squad through rough justice and blind terror. Once he had seen her take out two men, so fast it was like popping balloons. Bam-*BAM*. Over. Aubry's mind was fast enough to reconstruct Chan's moves. His eyes could *almost* distinguish them. And someday he wanted to learn exactly what it was she did.

But for now he was content that Chan, the queenpin of the Ortega hit squad, ex-merc and flint-hearted killer, liked him.

Yeah. Life didn't get much better than this.

Aubry wanted to fit in in this group, more desperately than he could ever let anyone know. God knew, he had to fit in *somewhere*. He had to sound . . . straight on. "We'll get this handled." He nodded sagely.

Chan watched him as she took a pack of cigarettes out of her pocket, and shook a butt two inches out, wrapped her pale lips around it, and finished the extraction. She offered one to Aubry, and seemed amused when Aubry refused. "What're you saving it for, kid?" She laughed. "Like you'll live long enough for nicotine to make a difference."

Aubry felt his face grow hot, and tried to find a retort. His thoughts were interrupted by the buzz of a Jeep coming over the paved road leading from a group of dusky buildings. The man driving the Jeep was small, seemed plump, and his face was hard.

The Jeep halted in front of them. The driver vaulted from behind the steering wheel with surprising lightness . . . in fact, as if he weighed almost nothing at all. His right hand dug into his front trouser pocket, and emerged with a silver dollar. He flipped it and caught it, with a totally unconscious motion, as if he had done it twelve million times before.

He was Hispanic, a little bigger than he had seemed behind the wheel of the Jeep—but not much. He looked at them critically. A group of twenty men and women lounged on the tarmac, sitting on their duffel bags, eyes cool and disinterested. The little man's eyes were very bright. "I am Guerrero," he said. "I have six weeks with you." He looked them up and down with the expression of a man who has found a turd in his tuna salad. "*You* are the best that the Ortegas have to offer? No wonder they are in so much trouble, eh?"

Aubry watched, amused. Chan uncoiled from her seated position like a cat disturbed from its dinner. Guerrero stood flipping his dollar up and down, unaware of the shift in moods. Aubry was hypnotized. It caught the sliver of sun on the horizon, and threw it back. It glittered. It sparkled.

Chan towered over the smaller man, radiating challenge. Dwarfing him. Although both of them stood in plain sight, Guerrero in his crisp fatigues, and Chan in her rumpled jumpsuit, all eyes were riveted on Chan.

Except Aubry's. He watched Guerrero. And the coin. Up. And down.

Chan said, "What the hell are you supposed to teach us?"

The coin disappeared. Aubry was watching. It was almost as if Guerrero had tossed it into the air, and it failed to come down. Guerrero's right palm was there to catch it, and it didn't arrive.

Chan's eyes flickered there for an instant. The coin appeared in Guerrero's left hand.

"What kind of shit . . . ?"

"I'm going to teach you to think," Guerrero said. He tossed the coin up, and caught it. "Every one of you is here because you have proven yourselves in the kind of combat that the Ortegas call war. Well, it's bullshit. Bullshit, and if you go up against the Conquistadores with the training and the attitudes that you have now, you'll all be dead."

The coin flip-crawled across the back of Guerrero's hands as he talked.

Aubry watched, fascinated. It was perfect. The coordination was perfect, completely effortless. Like the jump out of the vehicle. The hair on the back of his neck prickled.

"What do you think you can teach us . . . *sir*?" The way she emphasized "sir" made it worse than if Chan had said "asshole."

Guerrero smiled. The coin flipped into the air.

Exactly to the height of Chan's eyes . . .

And seemed to hover there for a second.

And then Chan was on the ground, holding her left leg, up high near the groin, making a mewling sound. All of her wiry musculature was contracted, her mouth open in a silent O.

Guerrero caught the coin.

Aubry hadn't even seen the *move*. . . .

Suddenly, the group was very quiet.

They came to their feet, their eyes on the little man in the rumpled fatigues. He looked at them with a hint of amusement. He turned his back to Chan. "During the next six weeks, I am going to teach you to be soldiers. You will learn to use the most modern military equipment, using the most advanced teaching techniques in the world. And then you are going to execute your mission . . ."

As he spoke, Chan was getting up from the ground. She shook her head like a bull gorilla, clearing it. Her eyes were red with rage. For all of her size, she was almost silent, and she had dropped into kill mode. Guerrero's back was still to Chan, and he seemed to be unaware of what was going on around him. The coin went up and down, up and down . . .

"And you are going to execute your mission flawlessly, because if you don't it's not your ass on the line, it's mine."

"You'll be going in with us?" someone asked.

Guerrero nodded. "I am not a theoretician."

Chan drew her knife. It was a Loveless chain model, razor kill-strip whirring silently around the edge. She was only a fraction away from full commitment.

Aubry felt admiration for Guerrero. Liked the little man. And hoped that he had provided in his will for the doubtlessly plump wife and children who would shortly be widowed and orphaned.

Chan sprang.

Aubry's eyes couldn't catch what happened next, but Guerrero was behind Chan. Chan was on the ground, unmoving. The chain knife was three feet from her hand, whirring. And that damned coin was rolling on edge on the tarmac.

As Aubry watched, blood began to ooze from above Chan's eye.

The coin rolled, and slowed . . . and fell onto its side.

Had Guerrero turned, and thrown the coin into Chan's eye, deflected and disarmed and rendered unconscious all in one seamlessly meshed motion?

Whatever the hell Guerrero was, he was for real, and impressive as hell.

And just like that, the seventeen-year-old Aubry Knight transferred his allegiance from Chan to Guerrero, and promised himself that he was going to learn to do what Guerrero had done.

Or die trying.

9

FEBRUARY 15, 2011

Aubry Knight lay belly down against the cool plastic floor of a glide simulation unit, floating silently over the Atlantic Ocean, just a mile out from São Paulo now. He was under the military radar, above the civilian screens. His little stealth unit, towed up and cut free now, was guidance-linked directly in with his reflexes, his vision, his hearing. It was like swimming through air, close to flying. The little patches at the base of his skull and his temples fed information to some kind of computer thing. His goggles both recorded eye movement and provided additional visual input.

The villa was below him, a glowing series of concentric rectangles: guesthouse, pool, piazza, guardhouse. It sat on a bluff, overlooking the ocean. The cliff made penetration difficult. The electronics, more so. The entry had to be first-time perfect. Kill ratio perfect. Extraction perfect.

A team would ascend the bluff, coming up from the surf.

They would cover the escape route, take out the guards at the dock.

But Aubry had to get past the first defenses.

He heard a voice in his ear—just a buzz, really. "Course correction," it whispered.

And he felt himself respond. This was wild. He was in some kind of a machine, he knew, but it was easy to forget, forget that this was just a simulation, and—

A buzz, and a little electric jolt. The world went red.

Dammit, he had lost concentration. All right, mother-fuckers. Focus you want, focus you get.

He heard his own breathing rasp in his ears. Concentrate. Another loop, and—touch down. Barely a scratch. He was third down, behind the strike leader, Guerrero. He was supposed to circle around again, and land twelve seconds later. But, dammit, he could feel the approach, knew that he could get in *now*. He would beat Guerrero down— *that* would catch his attention.

Nothing *else* he had tried for the past week had done the job.

Guerrero's virtual image touched down. Aubry did everything that he could to imitate that smooth descent—

The world went white. Lights came up. He stripped the goggles from his eyes and wiped his forehead. He was breathing hard. (Just a simulation!? *Damn* that was fun!) And he turned, eager for praise.

The magnetic coils in the floor had calmed, and no longer levitated him into flight position. The room was white and circular. A series of concentric tiles ringed floor and ceiling. A door opened at the far end, and Guerrero entered.

The smile on Aubry's face died when he saw Guerrero's expression. "What the hell was *that*?" Guerrero's voice dripped acid. His face was livid. "You had your instructions. You were given your timing. Why the fuck didn't you stick to it?"

"I—"

"You *nothing*!" Guerrero's voice was scalding. "Six of you are coming in aerial. Anybody hotdogging it throws off the entire approach. You just killed your entire team, Knight, do you realize that? And for what?"

Aubry felt as if his face had been caught in a furnace blast. "I beat *you* down . . ." he began lamely.

The rest of the team came in behind Guerrero. Several of them smirked. Something was supposed to happen now. He felt it. He just didn't know what to do.

"Back off, man," he said.

"What?" Guerrero stepped a little closer.

"BACK OFF!" Aubry said. "I did the best I could. I was coming in low, and coming in good. I just took the window. You can't handle that, then fuck you."

Guerrero looked at him, and closed his eyes. Then, very quietly, he said, "You're out, Knight. Get your things. Report to the air pad at fourteen hundred hours." He turned, heel-toe, and left the room. Aubry stood, for a long moment disbelieving, shocked. And then ran after him, past the others.

He caught up with Guerrero in the hall, and said, "Hey!" Guerrero turned, just before Aubry would have . . . touched him? Or something. Their eyes locked.

The air between them shimmered. Aubry had never wanted to hit anyone so badly in his life. Not even the memory of Chan, bleeding and broken on the tarmac, could have stayed his hand.

Something else did.

Something made him swallow the hurt, and the pain.

What?

He had only been in Manitou Springs for a week, but he had seen . . . things. He saw men in uniforms, men who walked with purpose and pride. Men who spoke in calm, confident voices. Men whose laughter was not cruel. Men whose eyes seemed filled with something beside the constant, predatorial search for . . . what?

"Don't dump me, man. I want this. Want it bad."

"That's not enough."

Aubry paused.

Guerrero studied him. "You wanted to hit me. What stopped you. Chan?"

Aubry shook his head.

"I didn't think so. You're not afraid of me. Why?"

"Ain't afraid of nothing."

"Do you know the definition of a good lie?"

"What?"

"One that gets you through the night." Guerrero narrowed his eyes. "Why do you want another chance?"

"I don't want to fail," Aubry said. "Can't fail. Gave my word."

"To who?"

"To Luis."

"Luis Ortega?"

Aubry nodded. "He gave me this chance."

"To go and kill people you've never met, and probably die."

"I'm a soldier." When Aubry said that, his shoulders went back a little. If he struggled with it, he heard what might have been martial music in the background.

"No, you're not," Guerrero said. "But you could have been." He laughed sourly. "I'm probably going to regret this. Come to my office at thirteen hundred hours."

And then he strode briskly away, a plump little man who moved with a sense of self-possession that a boy named Aubry Knight had never known.

10

Seventeen-year-old Aubry sat in a straight-backed chair, in a room with plain grey walls. Guerrero sat behind the desk before him.

He had just asked Aubry Knight what he wanted.

"To do the job," he answered. He felt a little uncomfortable. What did he mean, "What do you want"?

Guerrero waited. "Why?"

"I want to fit in."

"Why?"

Aubry felt himself flare with heat. *What kind of game is this?* Still, he had to cooperate.

"I like it, man. Where I came from, ain't many things to like. Takin' out some motherfucker messed with you. Gettin' laid."

"And if you do this job, you get both?"

"Sure."

"And after you've done those things? After you have a steady supply of sex, and after you have killed your enemies, what then?"

"There's always more pussy. And more fools."

"In your vast experience."

"Yeah. In my experience." That heat-prickle was back, creeping down his neck, and spreading across his chest now. "What is this all about?"

"I'm supposed to go into São Paulo, supervise your mission." Guerrero shook a cigarette out of a pack, offered one to Aubry. Aubry shook his head. "I need to know what material I have to work with. Twenty men and women. You're the youngest. You have a street reputation. Tough man. No nerves. You like pain. Good skills." He pointed out through the window, to the obstacle course where the other Ortega men were drilling, turning themselves into a unit. "Physical skills are extreme. Fitness extraordinary. You are learning the weapon skills rapidly." He smiled thoughtfully. "Frankly, there is teaching equipment that I can't use with you—the clearance isn't high enough."

"You mean—we're not important enough."

"This operation is extremely illegal." Guerrero's grin was pure predator. Aubry liked that. "But you're important to *me*. *My* ass will be on the line."

Aubry waited. There was something more. Guerrero stood, looking out over the exercise yard. The distant crack of gunfire echoed from the mountains.

"So what do *you* really want, Guerrero?"

The little man stood, so that he was partially in the light, and partially in shadow. "I . . . wear several hats. I am involved in training. Covert operations. I occasionally act in the field. My commitment is to my nation." He paused. "But my interest is human beings."

"Well, you should be happy." Aubry slapped his chest flippantly. "All meat, no by-products, man."

Guerrero didn't smile, didn't change his expression or his voice. But suddenly, the atmosphere in the room was charged. Suddenly, the funny little man was gone again, as he had vanished during that first afternoon on the tarmac. The funny man was sometimes there during a lecture, but never present during tactical maneuvers. During anything physically stressful Guerrero seemed to split, and from the middle of the soft little man came . . . something else.

"Aubry," he said softly. "You have a potential for violence which is . . . exceptional. But there is more to you than that. With most human beings, there is a difference between our words, and our actions. A split between our heads and our hearts." He tapped his brow and his chest with a forefinger. "It is my job to take you, and make the different parts of you work together, in . . . congruence, for long enough for the mission to be accomplished."

"And for us to get out alive?"

Guerrero's eyes glittered. There was no spoken answer, and none was needed.

"Oh," Aubry said quietly.

"May I speak plainly?"

"Go right ahead."

"You're scum, Knight. A criminal. A hired killer. Ignorant. You have a small, petty mind. But there is something in you that goes beyond that. It will probably never have a chance to emerge. What I want to know . . . all I want to know is . . . would you like it to have a chance?"

Aubry felt that sensation of heat crawl down his chest, inflame his buttocks. It was a sensation similar to sexual excitation, but more generalized. "What do you mean?" He barely recognized his own voice.

"Are you tired of being an animal, working for animals?"

"What the hell are you doing?"

"I believe in our country," Guerrero said. "I believe in

the dream of America. And I am willing to do whatever it takes to protect her."

"What's the difference between what you do, and what I do?"

"You do what you do out of anger. Out of fear."

"What the fuck do you mean?"

"And I do what I do out of love."

The flush had grown into a roaring, and it was as if Aubry sat at the foot of a falls, and the roaring grew until it drowned out thought, and left only sensation.

"What do you love, Knight?"

Aubry didn't answer, still locked in his cocoon of roaring silk.

"Aubry Knight. If you survive São Paulo, would you like to come here, and work with me?"

The words reached him like echoes heard at the bottom of a rain barrel. His mind scanned back over his life . . . what he could remember of his life. It couldn't penetrate the blocks of dark, heavy, cold matter that stood between him and his past.

"I don't remember much," Aubry said thickly. He felt drugged. "All I can remember is trying to survive. There was one man, once. He was good. I watched him die."

"How did he die?" Guerrero asked, not unkindly.

"He was stabbed. And stabbed. I remember him holding up his hands. I remember his hands. They were bleeding. I remember that he tried to hold me. And couldn't."

He was in the room, and apart from it, sliding further and further down toward . . . what?

With a sudden effort of will, Aubry tore himself away from that path, and focused on the room again.

"I got a job, man," he said, putting as much flippancy into his voice as he could. And was not entirely surprised to find that he didn't completely believe it.

"We will talk, later."

"I got a job."

"Yes. But how would you like a *life*?"

11

Aubry Knight felt the movement of the air on his body as he fell through the clouds in the little one-man glider. The night was clear, and cool, and calm. The moon rippled on the water like a single cool eye, mocking his fears. Around him were five men and women. His Ortega family. But he already felt apart from them. Not one of them anymore. What he was was something joined to a man named Guerrero. And that was stronger than the bonds that he had experienced with the others.

And it gave him the possibility of a future.

He glided through the clouds, and ahead of him was the villa where, according to all intelligence data, the leader of the Conquistadores could be found. If the intelligence was wrong, the wrong people would be killed, and that was just too fucking bad.

"Not 'people.' Civilians. You don't kill civilians." Guerrero's voice.

Fuck 'em. If they got in his way, it was just their bad luck.

"You are a soldier, not a killer. . . ."

He wasn't sure that he liked the new voices in his head, or that he knew what to do with them, but he felt different. And he knew what he would do.

When this job was over, Aubry Knight would leave the Ortegas. And he would go with Guerrero, and become a part of what he was. There was something there that was more than Aubry Knight had known before, something that he hungered for.

The wings folded quietly, taking him into a descent arc. At the last instant he spread them again, gathering air to cushion his landing at the side of the swimming pool. The moon was low in the sky, and cast a pale silvery light. Ahead of him was a man-shaped silhouette. A guard. He whipped his machine pistol into position. The instant it sighted, it fired an almost silent burst. The guard tumbled back as if smacked in the head with an I beam.

Aubry dragged him out of sight, and continued on.

Guerrero had taken out his guard, and Chan had taken hers. They had both used knives—in the days following that first encounter, they had made peace, and Guerrero had shown Chan more about knife fighting than the Mongol had ever dreamed of.

As Guerrero disabled the patio alarms, Chan made silent hand signs to Aubry. *Cover the house.*

Aubry slipped between the sliding glass doors, entering a long, low stainless-steel kitchen. He was on the upper level. What he wanted was the bedroom.

The head of the Conquistadores was a Spaniard named Dominguez. Homosexual, bonded to a professional jock named Piccoli. Piccoli was said to be dangerous. The word was: Kill at a distance.

Why? The man was at least partially a bodyguard to Dominguez, but also a former champion of something called Nullboxing. As far as Aubry knew, that was some kind of karate stuff, and he wasn't impressed.

He would stick to the plans, though.

Stick to the plans, show Guerrero that he could be trusted, and then adios Ortegas, once and for all.

A short, quiet thump to his right. Someone had bumped into something. Knight and Guerrero looked at Chan. She made a "sorry" gesture, and they waited, listening in the gloom, waiting for the last echoes to die. The house guards were dead. The alarms were disabled. There were three bedrooms to clean out. Decapitate the Conquistadores. And get the hell out.

Aubry reached his target, the second bedroom on the left. His starlight lent the room an eerie amber glow. The bed was awry—had Dominguez and Piccoli had a last backdoor tussle? He hoped so. It would be a shame to blow a man to hell without giving him one last chance to—

And then something hit him savagely hard, on the shoulder. He tried to roll with it, and felt another, numbing blow on his chest as he spun.

Aubry's pistol flew from his hand as he took a step back, and dropped to the ground, gasping to himself as something whistled over his head with killing velocity.

Piccoli. The fucking Nullboxer. He was awake, but had only had time to roll out of bed, behind the door. Shit.

There was a *whumph*ing concussion from elsewhere in the house. As Piccoli leapt back in, the alarms blared to life.

The game was up. He could only hope that the mission had been accomplished. He had other fish to fry. He scrambled for the pistol, and Piccoli was there first, kicking it under the bed.

Damn that had been fast. One of the fastest movements he had ever seen. But there was no time to appreciate it. Aubry swept the lamp off the bedside table, hurling it at the man, for the first time forcing him to respond. Piccoli blocked with his forearm, eeling out of the way. Aubry was right behind the lamp, and *on* him.

All he knew, *knew*, was that he couldn't take this terrific man at kicking distance. He had to get close.

His momentary advantage turned to shit as Piccoli's arms wound around him, jerking him off balance, exerting enough leverage to drive the air from Aubry's lungs in an explosive gush.

He wrenched Aubry's left arm up, and hammered it down across a knee. If Piccoli had found the correct leverage, it would have shattered that arm like kindling. But Aubry's father had disciplined him severely in his youth, taking him through the paces of the Rubber Band exercise with merciless precision. Even if Aubry had slacked off in the last few years, he retained more strength and flexibility than most men dreamt of. He twisted, his shoulder screaming in its socket, and got just enough bend into the arm so that when it smashed into Piccoli's knee he felt pain, and shock, but the arm didn't break.

Aubry torqued savagely, and his right elbow crashed into Piccoli's jaw. The man's head snapped back, and Aubry wrapped both arms around the man's waist, burying his face in the juncture between ear and shoulder, knowing that if Piccoli could work himself free, the man would hammer him to death.

He sank his teeth into the hard rubbery flesh of Piccoli's neck. Crushing, tearing, savaging even as Piccoli screamed and convulsed, fists hammering for Aubry's kidneys, knees desperately seeking his groin. Aubry bore down, grinding flesh and whipping his head from side to side. Piccoli's blood filled his mouth. With a final, maniacal spasm, Piccoli tore Aubry loose and hurled him across the room.

Aubry had never felt anything like *this* before. This was a level of physical power beyond his dreams. And yet—

When Piccoli rose, hand to his neck, gore seeping between his fingers, there was something new in his eyes.

Some small, quiet animal within Aubry awakened him to the knowledge that Piccoli . . . this man, this champion . . . was *afraid.*

Piccoli leapt like a beast, his hands knives, his feet sledges. Blood slimed his neck and shoulders, and his scream was no longer a human sound.

He must have hit Aubry a dozen times in the next three seconds. The universe was filled with fire. Depth charges burst behind Aubry's eyes, and he heard his own ribs crunch, felt the sudden drain of his strength, knew sudden despair.

Something shifted in Aubry's mind. Suddenly, everything slowed down, and although his own movements were caught in the same torpor, he saw with great clarity, and greater calm. Piccoli surged in: Aubry dropped to one knee, and drove his fist into Piccoli's groin. The man's eyes rolled up in shock. His breath froze in his throat. He fell, scrabbling like a crab with a broken shell. Aubry slammed that fist into the vulnerable crotch again, and again, ignoring his own pain and exhaustion, oblivious of everything except the blind, irresistible urge to destroy this incredible human being.

And then a hand clasped his shoulder—he turned, and Guerrero was there, looking down at Aubry, and what he had wrought. Guerrero's face was lit by some tearing inner conflict.

Piccoli made a bubbling sound. The man was broken, mewling like a half-dead kitten, in diminishing echoes. Blood pumped out of his neck, then slowed to a trickle. And his eyes, yellow in the darkness, flickered as if searching for some elusive Truth. Then the light went out.

Aubry gasped. He stood unsteadily, the shock of the battle finally overwhelming him, swaying on his feet. His left arm throbbed, probably dislocated. His knees hurt. His face felt like it had been torn half away.

Smoke filled his nostrils. The house was burning.

Guerrero still stared at him, and what lived in the depths of those small, dark eyes was unknowable.

Aubry's world spun. He heard someone, a stranger, say something in his voice. "Did I . . . did I do right?"

It was, absurdly, a child's voice. Why he needed an answer, or approval, from this or any man was something that he couldn't answer.

Guerrero pulled him toward the door. "Come on— soldier," he said.

The unit was moving out. Distantly, he heard a whooping, as if the local authorities were finally responding to the alert.

Chan, eyes cold, watched as Guerrero and another man carried Aubry to the edge of the cliff. There was a nylon zip line set up there, and Aubry regained control enough to hook himself onto it. Waves crashed on the rocks below.

Consciousness wavered. The villa was burning. Guerrero smiled at him. "Step off, soldier," he said.

And behind Guerrero, Chan. The bitch's knife was out. Aubry couldn't speak, couldn't say anything, and Guerrero's hard smile turned into an O of shock as Chan closed with him.

"Bastard," Chan hissed.

And that was the last thing that Aubry Knight remembered, as he slid off the cliff and down to the foam and the toylike boats below.

12

JULY 27, 2033

Aubry shook his head, hard, as the sounds and colors of an earlier year suddenly fragmented, shredded, fluttered away like multicolored streamers in the wind, leaving him with a calmer, more familiar . . .

Somehow less disturbing reality.

He flexed his fingers. Examined his hand. His hands were thicker now, more muscular. Stiffer. Scarred, and possessed of weapon-nature. His body was heavier, with perhaps sixty pounds of muscle that he had not carried at the age of seventeen. Armor plate.

He missed that young man, with his simple vision of the world, his simple needs and drives.

"What," Guerrero said quietly, "did you see?"

"What happened to me?" Aubry said, rubbing his palms against his forehead. The world was still seen through a filter. He needed an aspirin.

"You are in an Optima-Two learning environment. Everything that you do, everything that you hear is intended to access you on the deepest levels possible. The couch you rest on is wired, with contact points every half-inch. The room is constantly bathed in subthreshold sound, with holographic subliminal flashes. When you saw me, it triggered a deep-regression memory surge, that's all. You are being observed, and your reactions recorded. All of it is going into a profile. We will use it to program you for your mission."

"But . . . Guerrero. I saw you die. I saw Chan . . ." His voice sputtered to a halt.

Guerrero smiled. The silver dollar appeared in his hand, and rose and fell, rose and fell, as hypnotically as if the intervening years had never existed at all.

"I'm not really here, Knight," he said, grinning. "I was a high-level trainer. The army had invested millions in me. Because I was also an active field operative, they recognized that I was likely to die on a mission one day. So, my memories were flushed, and stored. After I died, they created a simulacrum, for training."

"So . . . you know that you aren't real?"

"I'm dead, Knight. How can I be real?"

That stopped Aubry for a moment.

"By the way," Guerrero said. "Records showed that Chan died three months after the São Paulo raid. There are implications that you might have had something to do with that. Preliminary bonding had begun between us—I think that you were beginning to make initial Paternal Imaging transfers. You had already established a bond with Chan, which I interrupted. Tell me—did she kill me?"

Aubry was startled. "Didn't you know? I mean, yes, she stabbed you in the back, as you rescued me after the São Paulo raid."

Guerrero nodded, thoughtfully. "I thought so. My last memory dump was before the raid—I don't know anything that happened during it—my body was never recovered. The story is that I died heroically. Chan's lower lip actually trembled as she reported it." He paused. "Why did you kill her?" There was genuine curiosity in his voice.

Aubry's mind ranged back, over the intervening years. And with the perspective that only time can offer, he recognized new motivations in old and half-forgotten actions. "You changed my life," he said simply. "The Ortegas were a place for me to hide. You offered me a place to grow. After São Paulo, I was going to take you up on your offer—" He paused, eyes narrowing. "You do remember that, don't you?"

"Absolutely."

"Chan killed you because you shamed her, took her down in front of the others. She took away my passport."

Guerrero seemed to think for a moment, although Aubry had the distinct feeling that the pause was for his benefit. After all—Guerrero existed only as a computer image now. Where the human brain is limited by the speed of chemical reactions, Guerrero thought at the speed of light.

"I think it is more than that. We have a record that your father died, in front of you, in an alley in Los Angeles. Is this accurate?"

Aubry had to swallow past a hard lump in his throat before he could say yes. His voice seemed foreign.

"I think that you have spent your life looking for your father. For a family. And when Chan killed me, it awakened memories of your inability to protect him. Your own fear. So you bided your time, and you killed her. I think you've been killing as a way of easing your own sense of impotence. As a way of compensating for your inability to save your father. As a means of gaining the approval of a man who is dead."

"That is bullshit."

"Is it? Aubry—have you ever had . . . little talks with your dead father? Ever tried to justify your actions to him?"

"No . . ." he lied.

What about me? Warrick laughed. You've never gotten past me. And here you are again, talking with another dead father.

Aubry lowered his face into his hands. "What are you trying to do to me?"

"I am trying to give you a chance to survive." Guerrero paused. "You know . . . this is the first time I've dealt with someone I knew . . . before I died. It is interesting."

"How?"

"It is easy to find the opening in someone's armor. Any place where need exists, there is the potential for dependency. I think that all your life, you've been searching. Your father was a good man, but he died and abandoned you, and you became a criminal. Luis Ortega was an evil man, but you bonded to him. Then you bonded to me. I think that you wanted the possibility of military service—a healthier alternative, a healthier 'family' if you will. I died. You bounced back into the Ortegas."

"But I remembered you," Aubry said. "And . . . something else."

"What?"

"I remembered people's attitudes toward me, when they found out about the Nullboxer. That I took out Piccoli, unarmed. Streetfighting. I didn't have any real training. 'Streetlethal,' that was what they called me. And I started dreaming. I mean—what if I could be a Nullboxer? Make money. Do something legit."

"Please your first father."

Aubry found a little smile. "Yeah, maybe so."

"And that dream festered. Years later you left the Ortegas, and actually tried Nullboxing. And began to succeed. Luis reached out and destroyed your dream, set you up on a charge of rape and murder. You isolated yourself emotionally, and became numb. You lived only to kill Luis. You met your future wife, Miss Cotonou. She is both the mother of your child—and the mother you never had."

"Shit," Aubry muttered. "This is happening a little too fast."

"We don't have much time," Guerrero said. "Most of the programming will occur on a subconscious level—but I think it's fair for you to know what we have in store for you."

Aubry nodded. "All right. Go on."

"Conjecture here. You met this man Warrick. Can you describe him to me?"

"Weird." Aubry shook his head, laughing. "He was half-crazy, I think. His sense of time never worked right. But he taught me things . . . and reawakened things. I started remembering the joy of using my body. Not just the utility, the joy. I remembered the Rubber Band, an exercise my father taught me."

"Another father figure. All right. Aubry, according to

our reckoning, our testing of you, you are at a critical phase in your development. It makes you ideal for our purposes—which is tragic, in some ways."

"Why?"

Guerrero paused, his image actually freezing for an instant, before regaining full liquidity. "This is difficult. I have my imperatives, set by the program parameters. I exist to serve American interests—in this case an organization called STYX. On the other hand, I have my own personality. And must, in order to do my job. Aubry, you have been a child all your life, living in reaction to the world. The point—one point—at which we become adults is the point at which we take complete responsibility, and determine our future. In one case after another, you have allowed external circumstances to control you. For all your strength and skills, you are remarkably passive."

Aubry could only shake his head in weak denial. Then the truth of it sank in, and he muttered, "What the hell do I do?"

"Listen to yourself," Guerrero said. "You are asking a dead man for advice. You will trust anyone, or anything, but yourself. Tell me, Aubry. Look at me."

Aubry looked at Guerrero, and realized that his eyes were beginning to mist. What was this room doing to him? Where was he, what was . . .

"Aubry Knight, what do you want?"

He heard those words, and felt in some insane way that no one had ever said them before. And that had to be crazy, didn't it?

And the crazier thing was that he didn't have an answer.

And God, oh God, he wanted one.

13

Aubry Knight lay asleep. The apparatus scanning his body traveled slowly over its swollen territory, over the concavities and protuberances of his nudity.

On the other side of a glass wall, the apparatus that evaluated him had broken him down into a series of images—some of flesh and bone, some of heat and nerve. His organs lay in relief. The flush of each long, tortured breath ran through his body like a tide.

Gagnon looked at the numbers and studied them, put her attention on them as a means of keeping her attention off, or away from, Koskotas and his golem of a bodyguard.

"What do you think?"

"Preliminary mapping is complete. He responds to the Guerrero simulacrum, but that was predictable. What are the strategic reports?"

"Four plans still operative. We update every two hours. The Capetown scenario was compromised. The backup team's escape route was narrowed—one of the men might have been left behind. Worse yet, the man would have to have known beforehand that he was a sacrifice."

"I can see how that might be a problem," Gagnon said dryly.

Koskotas ignored her. "Swarna's security forces detained a suspected rebel yesterday. He was released after nine hours— possibly long enough to compromise him, and his brother *does* have knowledge of one of our routes. So the Mozambique scenario is declined. But it isn't all bad news. DEA uncovered a load of baby brains coming in from Ethiopia. Captain will make a deal." He clicked a button on his lapel, and a holographic world map appeared, swelled, and became a revolving sphere. The Atlantic Ocean expanded, continents contracted. A red line began to dance across the expanse of blue. "Captain's next assignment is a tanker heading to the port of Ma'habre in the Sudan. From there, Aubry can be smuggled to the south, through the Central African Republic, to Pan-Africa."

Gagnon's gaze remained level, on the figures and graphics sprouting before her. "I notice that you have never mentioned Knight's escape routes being compromised. I assume that is because they are exceptionally secure?"

Koskotas was silent. The machine hummed.

She waited for a long beat, and then realized that Koskotas's silence *was* all the answer she needed. She changed the subject. "Physiologically, all signs are perfect. Surgical invasion begins tomorrow." A red lozenge-shaped light shone on Aubry Knight's upper thigh. "Tracer implantation." A light near the base of his skull. "Translator. In connection with the posthyp work, the languages will be a snap. Is our top scenario still on?"

"If he completes training, yes. Otherwise, we have backup plans," Koskotas said.

"All right—we can compromise most PanAfrican files, but the standard X rays are unavoidable. We're implanting shadows. On the most recent tests, we've beaten better than ninety percent of the machines. Plastic surgery is commencing now—"

As she spoke, a robotic arm snaked down from the ceiling. With obscene grace, a needle extruded from the tip of the arm, and inserted itself into the flesh under Aubry's eyes. A small amount of silicon gel was injected. Then the arm traveled farther down, and inserted its tip here . . . and then there.

"Whether or not the spaceport scenario is effective, the physical transformation will be useful. Reduce the chance of accidental identification. After all—he did save the life of the president. His face was broadcast around the world."

"So we're destroying his face, and rewiring his mind. What do you expect to remain?"

Koskotas laughed. "His soul, of course." He laughed, and then frowned when Gagnon didn't join in with him. He straightened. "Is the subliminal channel open?"

"Of course."

"Good. Patch me in."

In Aubry's dream state, the image in his mirror shifted, and Guerrero was there once again. Aubry was startled: something was wrong with this. Was he still entranced?

"Aubry Knight," Guerrero said flatly. "Colonel Kim said that you could never stand in front of a classical karate man. He said that he would kill you in five seconds."

Aubry was shocked. "Why are you telling me this?"

"Don't you think a man should do something about that? He says you're a pussy."

Then Guerrero faded away. Blooms of pain, rage, fear blossomed in Aubry's head. He bent his face, clasped it in his hands, dug his fingers into it moaning until the headache subsided.

He looked up. He saw his own face, strained. And all he heard in his mind, over and over again, was a single syllable:

Kim.

"What the hell are you doing?"

Koskotas laughed, rubbing his palms together briskly. "We'll keep Kim and Knight apart for a while. Build up the potential. And then we'll put them together. We need to be sure that all this programming won't affect those wonderful reflexes."

Gagnon stared at him. "Jesus, you're a bas . . ." She dropped her eyes, stopping herself just in time.

"And you," Koskotas replied coldly, "are dangerously insubordinate."

Gagnon studied the sleeping man in front of her, her eyes cold with fury. She blinked twice rapidly, triggering

the computer, and spoke a few words. The couch beneath
Aubry shifted and hissed, and transformed into an upright
chair. Gagnon fitted a hood over Aubry's head, a black
construct of soft plastic that fit snugly at ears and jawline.
A clear visor lowered itself into place. The hood sighed
and wrapped itself closer to his head like a living thing.
The visor darkened, and Aubry was enshrouded by night.
Then dots of light began to dance in that darkness, focusing and defocusing, racing, blending, and spiraling in apparently random patterns.

If the major concentrated hard enough, she could pretend that Koskotas wasn't in the room with her.

"Now," Gagnon purred. "Place your hands in these
stirrups, and attempt to follow your eye movements with
your hands, go ahead and match them—"

The apparatus massaged and invaded him, rolled his
mind in its silver fingers, and let his consciousness surface
just enough to follow the directions. In his dream, her
words became Guerrero, coaching and leading him, as he
had almost two decades before.

At first, the entranced Aubry could follow the movements by bringing his attention to bear. It felt like trying to
read a book in a dream—if he wasn't careful, the words on
the page would fuzz away into meaningless squiggles. The
same was true with the light patterns, only here they simply accelerated into a glowing fog. He had an eerie sensation, as if one part of him were stepping back out of the
way, and something else, something different from the
waking Aubry, stepped in to take its place.

At that moment Gagnon, watching the readouts, inhaled sharply.

The images flew and split, bobbed and dashed. Aubry
slipped into a slightly defocused, dispassionate state, sur-
rendering to a mode of thought ordinarily available only
during combat. Despite the speed of the images, subjec-
tively they slowed down. Or did he speed up? He felt enmeshed in a cocoon, lost in a warm hypnotic reverie.

The testing, programming, and small insults to his flesh

went on and on. And as part of Aubry worked, and learned, and suffered, another part of him dreamed. Of Leslie, and Promise, and Ephesus. A dream within a dream, encased within a nightmare.

14

JULY 28, 2033

Sweat slicked Aubry's bare chest. For the past twenty minutes he had been strapped into a padded chair caged in gleaming chrome: a hydraulic strength training/testing system. It was similar to a piece of equipment in the Scavenger rehab center, except built for heavier duty. He had been performing various push-curl combinations on demand, warming his body up for the real work to come.

Gagnon passed a plastic card through a light beam, and the chair reclined. "We are going to build you to a maximal contraction," she said mildly. "And map your strength curve."

The chrome apparatus flexed, a giant spider attempting to mate with Aubry's chest. He grasped padded handles, and did a bench-press-type movement. "All right," she said. "Do a few more. The resistance is set at approximately fifty pounds."

With no apparent effort, Aubry pumped it a dozen times.

"All right. Let's take that up to a hundred." Aubry pumped it another dozen times, also without apparent effort.

"All right—"

They went through 150, and 200, which he also pressed a dozen times, although he hissed with effort and his concentration had become more intense.

Now the room lights dropped. Aubry was alone with his

efforts. Gagnon's voice drifted to him disguised as Guerrero's.

"All right. Maximal contraction please. Three repeti-
tions—" At 250 Aubry paused, adjusted his grip, hissed,
and pushed the weight three times. At 300 the veins in his
arms rippled like snakes, miming a relief map of Rivers of
the World. He was concentrating now, completely focused
in. At 350 he exhaled and got it halfway up, but then let it
drop again.

"Are you all right?" Guerrero's disembodied voice
asked.

"Why am I doing this?" Aubry panted.

"We're trying to understand you physically. Once we
do, it will be much easier to build our plans."

"What do I get if I push this?" His breathing was beginning to regularize.

"What?"

"What do I get?" Aubry searched for the right words.
"It's hard for me to motivate myself, unless I get something out of it."

"I told you—"

Aubry shrugged. "I'm not arguing with you, I'm telling
you that if I'm doing something for a reward, I perform
better. It's just the way I am."

Guerrero was silent, leaving Aubry alone in the darkness. There was a pause, and then a humming sound, and
the patter of feet crossing the floor.

Aubry heard Guerrero's whisper without being able to
make out the words. Then much more distinctly: "Just rest
there for a moment. I think we can arrange something for
you."

Aubry let his arms hang back, felt the sweat rolling
down his arms and off his fingertips, listened to the drop-
lets puddle on the floor. Dots of soft red light flitted in the
darkness. He relaxed more deeply, and his breathing
slowed. His eyes eased shut, but the red lights continued to
dance. Then images resolved in the gloom: images of brick
walls and trees and mountains, of death and prisons. And

of Promise, her beautiful face aglow with love and light and passion.

When his attention returned to the room, three technicians were adjusting cuff devices to the outlets from the ergometer. A connection was made to Aubry's leg, high on the thigh.

"All right," Guerrero said. "I can see the logic in what you say, and as long as you're willing to play the game, I'll work with you. Would you rather be motivated by pain or pleasure?"

Aubry chose his words carefully. "I'm not sure that 'rather' is the right word here. What we really want is to force me to perform at my best. If that's what we want, then forget pleasure. I've always done more to avoid pain than to get pleasure."

"You and the rest of the world," Guerrero said, and there was an undercurrent of regret in the admission. "All right. If you agree to cooperate with the experiment, we are going to give you a mild jolt of electricity into the iliopsoas muscle of the thigh. It will be decidedly unpleasant, and because of the proximity to the genitals, you are likely to feel quite a kick. Do you agree?"

Aubry's hands twisted in the grips. "Let's do it."

"All right, we stopped at three hundred and fifty pounds, one repetition—"

They started again. This time, Aubry's strength seemed to have decreased, as if a part of him resented the mode of motivation.

His struggles against the implacable bar took on a new dimension. He had ten seconds to break the connection, to lift it, and something had simply slipped within him. He watched the clock count down and—

"Damn!" He shrieked as the pain slammed into him. His thigh biceps contracted as if someone had whacked him with a bat.

The weight clattered down, and he heard voices in his head—along with something else. Lightning split his head, a flash of energy more *visceral* than *visual*—

He set his arms against the bar again, and pushed. . . .

15

It was three o'clock in the morning. Gagnon sat in her lab, surrounded by equipment. The air around her was alive with green, red, and blue dynamic hologram charts. They twisted like technicolor tapeworms. The door behind her opened. Gagnon didn't turn around, but knew that Koskotas was there.

"Strength curve estimates almost complete." Gagnon spoke so quietly that she could have been speaking to herself.

Koskotas closed the door behind him. The air-conditioning system pulsed in a hush against his back, drying the sweat. Koskotas waited without speaking.

Finally, Gagnon began to speak. "He's not strength-trained, not formally, in the sense of a power lifter."

"But?"

"Let me preface my comments. In addition to my work with the military, I was head performance kinesiologist for the AAU, and worked in the same capacity for the last two Olympiads. I've worked with world-class athletes for sixteen years, professional, amateur, and military. Some are 'natural,' some hormonally altered, and some are genetic or prosthetic modifications. I've seen class-three pain override, accelerated impulse, oxygen hyperload, tungsten bone implants, and hypnotic states so deep that the athlete literally couldn't remember the meaning of the word *failure*."

"And?" Koskotas said impatiently.

"And I've never seen anything like Aubry Knight. In the last contractions he was no longer able to extend his arm completely. We shortened the arc of movement so that he was exerting pressure through a shorter range. The apparatus was set for three inches."

"And?"

"We stopped the tests at five thousand, eight hundred pounds. That is almost eighteen *thousand* inch-pounds of pressure."

"*What?*"

Gagnon nodded. "Not a record. In . . . 1988, I think, a yogi named Sri Chinmoy set an AAU record at seven thousand sixty-three pounds. And Chinmoy weighed almost ninety pounds less than Knight. Whatever we're dealing with isn't 'sports performance.' "

"What the hell is it?"

"Hysterical strength? Maybe . . . oh, never mind."

"I don't want to hear any mystic crap. Just stick with physiology."

"All right. He eats pain. He has no brakes. He should destroy his own body when he exerts himself."

"What prevents him from doing just that?"

"As far as we can figure it, either a natural understanding of the arcs of movement and the rotation of joints, or . . ." She paused. "Somebody got to him early. Taught him something, I'm not sure what. Maybe a sense of rhythm which has evolved into perfect coordination. A sense of relaxation in movement which gives him . . . well, *total* speed. A reaction time of point-zero-three seconds. I mean, he seems to be reacting at the maximum physical speed the human body is capable of, given optimal nerve conduction, and absolute strength."

"What are you suggesting?"

Gagnon turned and stared at him. "I am suggesting that at some period in Aubry Knight's past, a period which he may not even be aware of, he was given a set of exercises. Technologies which have developed him physically beyond anything we can duplicate. He is, without a doubt, the finest physical specimen it has ever been my horror to examine."

"Horror?" There was genuine puzzlement in Koskotas's voice.

"Yes, dammit. Horror." Gagnon rubbed the bridge of her nose. She should have felt tired. Instead, she felt some variety of awful exhilaration. "For centuries, we have debated the relative contributions of nature and nurture in the creation of human potential. The horror of the 'nature' argument: What if Einstein had been born in a gutter in Calcutta? The horror of the 'nurture' argument: For lack of the proper environment and training, our jails and ghettos are filled with Mozarts, Jim Thorpes, Sun-tzus, Joans of Arc. We have squandered the greatest resource we have—the minds and bodies of our children."

"Why horror?"

"Because Aubry Knight's body and mind are, as far as I can determine, in absolute alignment. What I mean is that whatever the tolerance for error is, I cannot detect it. The average human being is probably in about twelve-percent alignment. A superb athlete might operate at forty-five percent. Aubry is something . . . else. Only his emotions are lost."

"Lost?"

"What would you say about someone who can only motivate himself through pain? If one considers the classic Greek triad of body, mind, and spirit, Aubry Knight is a spiritual cripple and an emotional child with a perfectly developed body."

Gagnon wiped a hand across her brow. "Coordination is a form of intelligence. Call it kinesthetic intellect. Sports performance is problem solving on a kinetic level, and only the Western schism between mind and body could possibly conclude otherwise. Plato would have given his left nut to teach Aubry rhetoric or logic or poetry. He might have been a great man—instead of that, he is one of the most damaged human beings I have ever seen."

"And one of the healthiest."

Gagnon's laughter mocked her own weariness. "Yes. Isn't that the bitch of it? And now we have him. For the next few weeks he is ours. Because of the situation, he has relaxed into trust. He needs to trust. The part of him who functioned without a father created his own father. His physicality, his deadly skills, are a paternal shell around a child. Striking at Aubry's family was the most suicidal thing anyone could do."

The lights in the room shifted, the environmental processor cycling intensities and directions to minimize the risk of eyestrain. "You know," Gagnon said, "I could help him."

The general, just beyond the cone of light, coughed. "We don't want you to help him."

"No," Gagnon said. "You don't."

"We just want you to prove he can't do it."

He waited. The smoke curled in the air between them.

"And if he can?"

"Then he goes in. But he won't."

Gagnon looked at the general, and one dark eyebrow arched in question. "If he goes in—he will, of course, have backups?"

"Of course. Our entire network is at his disposal."

"Odd," Gagnon said, her voice low and controlled. "I would have sworn that this was a suicide mission."

The general coughed and drew on his cigar. The smoke curled in the air, wreathed his face. Under his cap, his eyes glowed dully. "Confine your opinions, Doctor, to your area of expertise." General Koskotas coughed. He took the cigar out of his mouth and stared at the glowing tip. "I've got to quit these things. I really do."

"Some would say," Gagnon ventured, "that such self-destructive acts are indicative of deep self-loathing."

"Some," the general replied blandly, "should mind their own fucking business."

16

Aubry brought the fighter wing in low and upside down over the artificial lake, barely skimming the surface. He braked, and it hovered. He leaned back and looked "up" into the boiling water, grinning.

"All right," the voice in his ear said. "You have the manual down. System's had an opportunity to read your reflex patterns. We should be in the groove. Switch to Autonomic, and let's see how it goes."

Aubry switched it in, and held his breath. In simulator module-based practice, the switch to Autonomic had been a belly flop of an experience, a sudden expansion of his ego boundaries to include a great glider wing of metal and plastic, and all of the electronic guts thereof.

The wing shuddered, and Aubry *screamed*. . . .

He watched his body expanding, knew it to be illusion, but was still unable to reduce the shock and pain.

His skin peeled back, nerves and veins lifting free from his flesh, muscle *melting* into the tubes and wires cocooning him. He felt his fingers at the edge of the wings. His eyes and ears and nose joined with the sensors sandwiched into the skin of the fighter. What remained was some strange hybrid creature, man melded with machine, hovering above the lake.

If he concentrated, brought to bear every iota of his will, he could resolve a human image from the electromechanical phantasmagoria, a fading image that seemed now a dream.

He had always been a creature of steel and ceramic. His life as a human being had been an illusion, fading now, fading. . . .

Time trials. Disorientation stage four.

He didn't hear those words, or see those words. He just *knew* that it was time. It seemed natural for him to be tested, and to perform.

Aubry felt a stinging sensation on the underside of his left wing. A wave of frost passed over him, sweeping from left to right, leaving havoc in its wake.

The world was inside out and upside down, colors and sensations inverted. Panic. Then a hydraulic sigh, as he found a way to breathe that resolved the world into its rational form once again.

There was a moment of struggle, almost a tug-of-war, and something snapped. There was a metallic scream. . . .

And the flying wing was altered. It was Aubry Knight who flew, an Aubry with metal-ceramic skin, and fingers stretched wide. Aubry felt an electric tingle at the back of Aubry's neck, and knew, as he had often known, that there was danger. Something was approaching him.

His breathing thrummed, sonorously. The entire surface of his skin pulsed with each cycle of respiration. He reached into his own core, into his processors and turbos and metallic vitals, seeking some form of balance.

Knight— you have sixteen secondsssss. . . .

Behind him, the target drone released the first of its missiles. It stretched toward him like a finger of silver fire.

Missiles. Why not energy weapons? Oh, yes—to give sluggish human reflexes any chance at all.

He felt a flash of pain in his side. *Lock-on.* They had him.

They sought him.

Sought the boy.

(Slow motion now. The missiles were crawling toward him, and he was moving, moving away toward a tumble of snow-crested mountains. In the same moments another part of him, the part that embraced his humanity, that clung to his past, sank into fragmented memories.)

The boy was in the back room of a house, and caked in filth. Small, thin, black. Perhaps eleven years old. Eyes as wide as twin moons. Hiding. Hiding from what? Everything. Father dead. Blood. Everywhere. Danger, everywhere. Fear.

Everywhere.

Alert. You now have ten seconds before terminal impact—

The world switched and tilted through a crazy quilt of visual and kinesthetic options, each of them taking Aubry a click or two further away from reality, but also each and every one of them—

The boy lay, curled on his side, matted with filth. Crying. Little black boy, his little black hands stretched out into the dark, afraid, hearing doors open where there were no doors. Heard wind blowing, an evil wind, where there was no sound. Wrapped thin arms around his hungry stomach, and cried out for a father who could no longer answer . . .

There is no one there, little boy. Trust no one but yourself—

Aubry, in the grip of forces he could hardly understand, felt his emotions reach out to the controls—

Reach into yourself. If it isn't within you, it isn't yours.

And held on, as if his feelings, his intellect, his essence intertwined with the machinery, enmeshed with the machinery, combined with it—

And the boy screamed: I can't! There's nothing there. Won't Father, God, *someone* help me, find me, feed me teach me—

No.

It is time to grow up. You are not that boy anymore. It isn't your father. Or Luis Ortega. Or Chan, or Guerrero. Or Warrick. Or Promise.

It is time to be your own father, Aubry. Your own mother. Only then will that boy stop crying.

And the pod gently swayed, just enough so that the dummy rockets passed harmlessly this way and that beneath him, blossoming like flowers against the rocks, as the tears streamed down his forehead, and dripped into his hair.

17

Aubry lay asleep on the slab. Gagnon touched him gently, her thin, compassionate face relaxed.

The man Aubry was at peace. He seemed to have found something . . . comforting. From time to time the great fingers extended, and then relaxed. Almost as if he were holding an invisible hand. A small hand.

A child's hand.

"And what results this time?" Koskotas asked abruptly.

Gagnon monitored her face and tonal inflections carefully as she replied. "Well, of course his coordination is superb, but that just isn't enough with the neural net. We have to access a very early stage in development, what Piaget called the 'sensorimotor period,' from zero to twenty-four months. We're growing pilots younger and younger these days. He's done . . . all right. There are blocks that stand between the adult and a sufficiently youthful Aubry."

She paused, and then continued. "I was hoping to find that same adamantine quality all the way back to his youth. Apparently, that isn't going to work. I'm afraid to regress him any further. When we get back to around ten years old, he collapses. His father's death created massive trauma, and he built his physical walls around it."

"I see." Koskotas thumped his finger against Aubry Knight's chest, almost as if testing a side of beef. "So. What is next?"

"Languages. Implantation of linguistics. Then the map implantation. These have to be tied into his optical/kinesthetic track for instant recognition. There are a number of unpleasant days ahead for Mr. Knight—but he's getting what he wants."

The general concluded his impersonal inspection. He

pulled a handkerchief from his pocket and mopped his face. "Warm in here." He folded the cloth carefully and tucked it away, as if it contained something precious. "You know, I know that you disapprove of me. All I can promise you is that I didn't initiate the attack against Knight. I don't even want him. But—if he really can pull this off, I will damned well use him."

"And if he doesn't survive?"

"Then he doesn't. But do you know what?"

"What?"

"I know this man. I've known others like him. He was dying up there in Oregon, one day at a time. Chopping trees? Teaching bullshit karate moves to a bunch of dykes? Raising some freak kid? Do you really think that a man like this was built for that? Don't kid yourself. This man needs war like roses need rain.

"Hell. Blowing away the Warrick woman was the kindest thing Swarna could have done. Knight should kiss the guy."

The general turned and left the room. Gagnon moistened her lips. Then she whispered, "Bastard," sighed, and returned to her unconscious charge.

18

AUGUST 3, 2033. EPHESUS, NORTHERN OREGON.

Promise Cotonou-Knight sat in the central conference room. Its long, low ceiling somehow flattened the light. The paneling was genuine oak, the chairs upholstered in synthetic leather. An undeniable aura of power emanated from the room, a smooth and consistent sense that things *happened* here, that the person who sat in that chair had the reins firmly in hand.

But now there were no councils deciding the planting or harvesting of trees, or bemoaning market prices, or negotiating water rights between the lumber and farming concerns. For now, Promise was alone with her mental dragons, making a decision that she alone could make.

Finally she spoke a name and number aloud.

A window opened in the air before her. A man's head appeared, floating in the air above the table. The man had straight, shoulder-length brown hair, and intelligent eyes above a small sharp nose and a wide, sensuously Latin mouth. The entire effect was devastating.

"Hi there," the head said in a voice that dripped sex appeal. "I'm not available right now, but I can promise you that I want to be in touch. If you'll just leave your codes, and a message—"

Promise said, "Interrupt. Jeffry. This is Promise Cotonou. I need your help. Now."

The head froze, and rippled with static. The come-hither voice disappeared. "Yes, I remember you," the head said emotionlessly. "You would like to speak with Jeffry?"

"Yes, very much."

"Is this a priority message?"

"Yes, it is."

"Is this business, or personal?"

Promise paused for a moment. "Both," she said honestly.

"Thank you. I will try to reach him."

There was a pause, during which recorded music played. The computer-generated love-god's face smiled out at her with a dazed, meaningless smile.

The screen juddered, and Jeffry Barathy, aka Moonman, appeared. Jeffry Barathy was one of the heroes of the Virtual Underground: computer maven, phone phreak par excellence. He was also a disabled veteran of the first PanAfrican campaign. From the waist down he was stainless steel, hooked into one or another of his mechanized home transport systems. He had no facial fuzz at all, his skin was blistered pink as if with an eternal sunburn, and his hair was cut in a ragged mohawk.

"Promise. Lovechick. You look great. Listen—sorry about Mira. What a shit deal." He seemed to be dressed in some sort of snakeskin suit-shirt, and wore shades now. Video images danced along the lower edge of the shades, and she figured that he must be monitoring a small empire's worth of communication lines as they spoke.

"I've . . . been better. You're doing well."

"Well. Saving the president does wonders for your credit rating. And your rap sheet. Suddenly, I'm not underground anymore."

"Doing well by doing good?"

"The very thing. What's up?"

"Is this line secure?"

"Third-level merchant." Suddenly, his face was serious. "Do we need more than that?"

"Let's scramble." The air before Promise clouded and filled with sparks, the visual field temporarily destroyed. Jeffry's computer shook hands with Promise's, and made the requisite connection. Then it cleared again.

"All right," he said. "This will keep out everything but NipTech or maybe the NSA. Is that good enough?"

"It will have to do."

"I heard a rumor that Aubry was on the move."

How had he heard that? Promise was irritated and relieved at the same moment. "Yes. It's true."

"Does it have something to do with Mira's death?"

"Yes."

"What can I do for you?"

"We were told that the murder was Phillipe Swarna's way of saying hello."

"Shit." Jeffry threw some internal switch, becoming completely alert and aware. "Go on."

"Aubry is . . . trying to protect us. I don't want to say any more, even over *these* lines. Can I come to see you?"

"Day or night."

"I'm on my way. About eight o'clock tomorrow evening be all right?"

"Only if you can't get here sooner."

Promise felt as if a stone had been rolled off her heart. "Thank you."

The screen dimmed.

Promise turned the display off. She settled back into her chair, and rested her hand gently on her throat. Her pulse was erratic. She didn't know if she had done the *right* thing, but she had done the only thing she could.

19

"**H**ow did it go?" Jenna asked Promise.

"I'm not sure. He can help, I'm sure of that. Where's Leslie?" How Leslie was keeping herself under control, Promise wasn't sure.

"I'm not sure—I haven't seen her for a couple of hours. The last thing I saw, she was playing. With other children."

That was possible, although a picture that Promise found difficult to form. Skulking through ventilator shafts, yes. Teaching adults unarmed combat, yes. Hacking into the Japanese Consulate's direct-induction link and playfully scrambling programs, yes.

But playing with other children?

Jenna might have been reading her mind. "I think there are a few avoidance patterns running here. She doesn't want to think about what might be happening. So. What do we do now?"

"I go to Las Vegas," Promise said. Her face looked long. Her eyes cast dark, ringed shadows. She seemed to have aged five years.

Jenna watched her sister walk off to the communications building, shoulders slumped with care. Goddess. This was a mess.

There was a rustling in the brush beside Jenna. She didn't bother to turn around.

"Making an unusual amount of noise this evening, aren't we?"

"Well," Leslie said, "I wanted to announce myself.

Wouldn't want you to be all shocked and surprised and everything. Might be bad for your heart."

"What a considerate child you are."

"Lying a little to my mom, weren't you?"

"Just a leetle beet."

Leslie grabbed Aunt Jenna's hand and looked up at her. "Jenna, you made me promise to stay out of this. I promised you, and Mommy, and Daddy. A three-way promise is hard for me—everybody I love being pissed—"

Jenna looked at the child sharply.

"Sorry about that. *Miffed* at me. Is miffed all right?"

"Much improved."

"All right. Miffed." She drew her aunt down, and hugged her around the neck with thin arms. "But if one of you—just *one* of you—would let me off the promise. Share the guilt a little?"

Jenna pulled Leslie to her. Promise and Aubry would never forgive her if she let anything happen to Leslie. And yet, if something happened to Aubry, and there had been any way to prevent it, any way that Leslie could have gained knowledge or leverage . . .

She sighed. "All right. Information. Information only. And on a full-scramble circuit. And this is who I want you to contact . . ."

Leslie's eyes glittered.

20

AUGUST 4, 2033. LAS VEGAS, NEVADA. 7:45 P.M.

It was a boulevard of demons, of giants, of gilded titans who walked the night and beckoned, of goddesses of impossibly lurid proportions, a thousand feet tall, who licked their lips and shimmied, painted breasts barely restrained by brassieres the size of circus tents. Of galloping Lippizaners the size of the Dakotas, of Vesuvius in bloom, of starships alight and decending, of the Savior of the world, resplendent in his robes, beckoning to the faithful to come and render unto Caesars Palace.

It was a boulevard of dreams, of nightmares, an organic outgrowth of some not wholly explicable malaise, something that had taken hold in the 1930s in an obscure corner of the world called Las Vegas, Nevada. It had blossomed unendingly, until now it was a world unto itself, apart from and yet inexorably joined to the world, unique and yet as common as shattered dreams. The ultimate symbol of decadence and greed and yet in some small sad way, a cry for innocence lost.

For what eye but a child's could remember the feeling of being dwarfed in such a fashion? Adults know the girders and steel, the lights and plastic, the glass and electricity that go into the creation of such glitter. And so no matter how overwhelming, one can reduce it to its constituent flaws, and thus find refuge for sanity.

But a child . . .

A child still believes in giants, in steamboats that paddle-wheel their way through glittered streets at midnight, luring customers to the never-ending cacophony of spinning dials and wheels, its pasteboard fortunes. A child sees it all, and believes, believes in it more than he believes in the reality of the piece of green paper, or the plastic, or the trademark union scrip that represents hours of toil or promised toil. That child steps into the dream, agog, and awakens hours or days later, poorer but in some terrible sense, wiser.

Long ago, Promise had followed that dream. She had left honor and soul and skin here in this town. She had hoped never to return.

Promise turned away from the window, and back to her host.

"A bitch, isn't it?" Jeffry said. Moonman was happy today, and for that, she was grateful. He was doing better than the last time she had seen him, four years ago. He had a little more hair, and his chest had filled out. Only mechanics remained below the waist. Or, to quote Moonman more precisely, "There's nothing down there but eighty kilos of steel and seven inches of love."

Promise felt no inclination to investigate his claim.

He glided around his suite on the magnetic repulsor coils built into the floor. It played hell with watches and pacemakers, but he really didn't give a damn.

The suite was the top floor of a four-story communications studio. Virtual, multivision, data processing, satellite link, paced feedback, and a library of approximately eleven million films, television and radio shows, books, magazines, and newspapers.

"You seem to be doing very well."

"Notoriety does that to you," he said. "When the facts came out about our little to-do in Los Angeles, I became a bit of a poster boy. Some of the turbo-trunk lads and lasses decided to have me come and speak at their monthly gathering. Me being a hero and all."

"Of course."

"I went, and told them all about sliding down the line into the Fat Man's lair—" His little eyes suddenly turned shrewd. "Rumor says that McMartin is still alive, you know."

Promise felt a little sickened. "He is? Somehow I would have thought . . ."

"Yeah, well think again. Our wonderful government doesn't throw anything, or anybody, away. Anyway, I told them about the work I did in saving this great nation of ours, and several of the young ladies expressed . . . shall we say strong earthy desires?"

"Let's just leave it at that. It will save me having to eat dinner twice tonight."

"You wound me. At any rate, I talked to a number of the ladies, and it turned out that they made money running virtsex operations. Tied in statewide. It turns out that ladies who weigh three hundred pounds, and burn victims, and amputees are very popular for virtsex operations, because they can empathize with the needs of the clients. They understand a man who would rather stay home hooked into a sexsuit, phoning in his thrills, than go out and risk a relationship with a real woman."

Promise shook her head. With the blood-spectrograph equipment available openly, it was virtually impossible to contract a venereal disease without being suicidal or lethally stupid. Birth control was 99.99 percent absolute, with both abortions and fetal transplantation easily available. With the risks and downside of sex having been removed, the sexual revolution had actually begun in earnest. . . .

With the explosion of virtual technology, or the easy availability of all services and experiences pumped directly into the home, there were a growing number of people who simply chose not to interact with other human beings. Who stayed sealed into their homes, completely separate. And there they remained. They worked there, ate there, they pumped in their lovers over the fiber optics. And in that womb of apartness, of what others called terrible loneliness, they remained, encapsulated but safe.

"Interesting," Promise said. "In a straight psychological profile, they are as healthy as any average person. The shrinks are having a fit about it. They don't hurt anyone . . . they just don't interact."

Moonman looked at her. "And the question is—throughout human history, how many people would rather have had virtsex than the real thing? Less muss, no fuss, and nobody sleeps on the wet spot."

She smiled wanly. "There was a time I would have thought about it. Hard."

Moonman squinted at her. "Want to give it a try?"

Promise had a minor plug at the base of her hairline. She didn't have natural talent, and hadn't undergone the expensive, invasive neural educations and implantation procedures. But as an Exotic, she had had extensive cosmetic restructuring. It made little sense not to add a tiny input device. "Preset or live?"

"Oh, nothing but the best for you, babe. Preset. You control intensity." He brushed up her hair and felt around for the little socket, then clipped in a wire.

She dialed two on a scale of ten, and sat back into the chair behind her—

And fell through the leather, onto a bed. Hands were on her, spreading what felt and smelled like honeyed dust, smoothing it warm and soothing across, and over her body, evenly and penetratingly. Lips touched her, not sexually, but enough to make her body arch, and one pair of them nipped at her lips, and she—

Punched the button to jump out of that damned thing as fast as possible, and popped back into the office, with Jeffrey laughing at her.

"Well," she said primly.

"Well, indeed."

"I . . . uh . . . I think we had better get on to business. I need to know about a covert operation mounted against Phillipe Swarna. Involving Aubry."

"Time frame?"

"Maybe sometime in the next eight weeks?"

"Search strings?"

Promise counted off on her fingers. "Assassination. Close range. Aubry's past, and his physical capacities. Past efforts. Gorgon. President Harris."

"That's a good start."

"I'm going to try to go direct. Kanagawa, PanAfrican director of public works, once asked the Scavengers to put in a bid on a construction project. We were underbid, but I think I know someone who can get me another appointment. I'm going to Hong Kong. If you need to contact me . . ."

"We'll use a triple-X virtsex line. Government snoopers tend to be bluenoses. Blush easy."

Promise allowed herself a smile, the first real one she had had in days. "I like that." She leaned down and kissed him, holding his eyes with hers. "I like you. I owe you."

"Family doesn't owe," Jeffry said.

21

The stars were bright and clear above the NewMan Nations.

Miles Bloodeagle lay on his back against a blanket, smelling the breeze. He was a huge man, almost four inches above six feet tall, and weighed close to 260 pounds. At the moment, his flat, heavy features were at ease, and he was as contented as he ever allowed himself to feel.

Things looked much better. The NewMan Nations were now a genuine political entity, and that meant that the persecutions of the past were over.

But, while one whole species of problem had faded, there would always be new troubles. At the moment, his trouble had four legs.

In the past month, six of his sheep had been killed. After careful tracking he had picked up tracks, and was prepared to take the mountain lion in its own lair.

The lair was a crevasse in the blackness of the hills, tufted with grass and almost hidden with shadow. Bloodeagle lay hidden as well, watching the cave entrance, his Enfield rifle at his cheek.

He had no night scope, no thermal tracer or any of the other accessories that would have simplified the hunt. He had his eyes and his instincts. He would give himself one shot. If he missed, he would allow the cat to go free.

Another sheep—another bullet. He had to respect an animal that killed just enough to feed its young and keep itself alive.

There was something cleansing about this. It was so much better than the jobs he was occasionally asked to perform for Gorgon. The slaughter at Death Valley Maximum Security Prison a few years back, NewMan against NewMan, had covered him with blood enough for a lifetime.

But he still loved the hunt.

A hundred yards out, the grass fluttered. The moon was bright enough for him to make out the disturbance, even if he could see nothing beyond.

Bloodeagle raised the rifle to his shoulder and took long, slow aim.

The big cat's black-dappled muzzle poked through a moment later. It tested the wind, seeking danger, finding nothing. Bloodeagle had left no scent, no spoor. Just another couple of inches, and he would place one right in the cat's ear, and turn her out like a light.

Then . . . there was a buzzing in his pocket. The priority pager? *Damn.*

The cross hairs sat right on the cat's ear, and he exhaled harshly. *You live. Today, cat, you live at my whim. Go, go to your cubs. Feed them this last time. Tomorrow, you die.*

Bloodeagle rolled silently off the blanket protecting him from the stone and the barbs, reflecting wryly that there had been a time, not so long before, when he hadn't needed or wanted such comforts. In those days, he seemed one with the sand and the sky and the very insects crawling over his flesh. He had been another man then. Perhaps not a man, perhaps a boy. That had been long ago, in another life, before he had learned too many dangerous things about himself, and about his world.

Bloodeagle trotted down to his Jeep, carefully wrapped his blanket around his rifle, and pressed the top button on his heavy cotton shirt. He pulled it out and thumbed it into his ear.

"Bloodeagle," he said.

Who would this be? Department of Defense? Or . . . he hoped that it wasn't anything back at the Nations. He felt no panic, only a quiet anticipation.

It was a child's voice that came to him, distorted by some sort of scrambler, but still recognizable as a child's. For a moment Bloodeagle was taken aback.

"How, Big Chief. Tadpole here."

Bloodeagle's flat heavy lips curled up into a smile. "Well. It's the Sprout. Is this line secure?"

"They'd have more luck deciphering a bowl of Alpha-Bits."

"How are things in Greenland?"

A pause. Leslie's natural exuberance subsided. *"We need a favor. There may be a big problem."*

A second, feminine voice came on line. *"Has something to do with the little desert party you threw a couple of years ago."*

He recognized that voice. Jenna. Leslie was one of Bloodeagle's clan, a NewMan. Jenna was Leslie's aunt, Promise's sister.

Jenna. Mistress of a martial art called durga, originating in India. A good art, from what Bloodeagle had seen. But she had mostly practiced it against women or emasculated men. Making the requisite combative equations of mass and momentum work against a real man posed an entirely different problem, as she had learned in Death Valley. Still, she had taken out two Gorgons hand-to-hand, which made her very, very good indeed. And if she had been working with Aubry Knight . . .

"Does this concern the black Knight?"

"Yes."

"Do you need information or personal assistance?"

"Hopefully just the first."

Miles sat on the edge of the Jeep. He pulled his hat down over his head, shading his eyes against the rising sun, and closed his eyes. "Tell me what you need."

22

Only half-awake, Aubry Knight laced up his shoes. Within his mind, reality seemed to shift and slide, as if holes were opening and closing again, trapdoors to a consciousness that he had never explored before. He wasn't completely himself—he was possessed, controlled, by those who would use him.

They thought.

But he sat back in his cave, and watched as they gave him gifts.

Language: He had learned a thousand basic words in Swahili, Ibandi, and Japanese.

Flight craft: He could pilot planes, heliplanes, and skimmers. He could drive ninety-six percent of the ground vehicles known to operate in the PanAfrican Republic.

Tactics. He had eidetic recall of the street plans of six major PanAfrican cities. Recall was triggered by structured visualization. Implants improved the operation of neurotransmitters in his brain, creating an optimal environment for deep hypnosis to take root. All information was available at a moment's notice.

In two more days, he would be on his way. In some odd manner, he felt simultaneously half-awake and totally alive. A paradox, indeed.

He walked down the narrow stone steps leading to the combat-simulation corridor called the Pit. It reeked of gunpowder and high explosives.

Aubry had spent dozens of hours there, practicing until the flash of explosives and the roar of the exploding targets clouded his senses. Here in the Pit, he received refreshers in all of the old skills. Lock picking, explosives, the hundred deadly paths he had abandoned after discovering the potential of his naked hands and feet.

But here, they were reawakened.

He knew that he would be photographed here. He sensed that there was an air of finality to it, that there was something about what was about to happen that would spell an end to the previous period of training.

Still within a cocoon of dreams, he walked into the corridor. There was a flash of light, just a whisper of movement. Aubry spun and fired, his weapon braced against the inside of his elbow, its snout spitting flame. The target disintegrated. A wall of steel slid into place. He turned, firing without sight, and felt the grinding flash before he saw or heard it. In an ethereal slow motion, the plate ripped away, winging in pieces down the corridor.

The gun felt good in his hand, felt right. The child within Aubry liked the toy, liked its flash and glitter, laughed and clapped his hands as the targets disintegrated.

The chamber was empty. Young Aubry hesitated. A queasy fear-feeling rose in his belly.

Men will come. They will try to hurt me. Father . . .

The warning light flashed. Feet vibrated against the floor.

Father—

Aubry quietly laid the gun down and drew a knife from his belt.

He heard the child screaming within him, felt it scream. And laid the flat of the blade against his heart. Felt that inner child begin to calm.

"Shhh," he whispered. He felt the rage building within him. Rage that ate away fear. Doubt. Rage that·was a circle of flame surrounding his heart. "Shhh. Daddy's here. And no one is going to hurt you."

The knife gleamed in his hand.

23

The mood in the conference room was ugly. Almost as ugly as the images they had just witnessed in the holofield.

Major Gagnon looked pale. Although she had seen the images twice before, she still hadn't come to grips with their reality. She was still afraid that she was going to lose her institutional lunch.

Kramer stood just behind Koskotas, one steadying hand on the general's shoulder. Koskotas was still trembling with rage.

"This is where we went wrong, General," Gagnon said. "We sent in six men. We felt that the shock armor would protect them. That the mesh webbing would protect them. We were wrong. Look at this. . . ."

In slow motion, one of the armored men came around the corner. Aubry was braced above him, limbs braced against walls and ceiling like a spider.

"Jesus Christ," the general murmured.

Aubry dropped to the attack.

The armored man went down. The knife—

"This is where we made our mistake. Because the shock armor will repel a forty-four-grain slug, we felt that knives would be no real danger. We were wrong. The edge of that knife is as fine as the edge of a samurai sword. It is used in the art of durga. Where he learned it, we don't know. Combined with the focus and incredible strength and speed of this man, it went right through the armor."

"Dead," Koskotas said. An ugly sound. "One of *my* men."

Another image flashed on the screen. A man with eyes opened wide in terrible fear.

"Dead."

And another image—a leg bent at an unnatural angle,

as if the shock armor had broken at a joint. The next picture showed a raw wound in the neck joint of the shock armor. Blood oozed.

Gagnon's voice was soft, brutal. *"Three* men dead. They tried to hurt him, General. I suspect on *your* orders. He defended himself."

"This man is out of control," Koskotas said. "I don't want him as part of this operation."

Gagnon froze the image. "And just why not? What do you have against him?"

"YOU HEARD HIM IN THE BRIEFING!" Koskotas screamed. "He admires Swarna, that black bastard!"

"To which black bastard," Major Gagnon asked softly, "do you refer?"

Koskotas glared at her. "This is *my* operation," he said.

"Knight's training is almost complete. Once he is inserted into the pipeline, it will be beyond your control."

The little man stood abruptly. "Well, he isn't there yet." He glanced at his watch. "In fact, right about now, he should be making his final error."

"And what would that be?" she asked.

"Kim. They should be meeting just about now."

Gagnon looked at Koskotas, disbelieving. "After all you've seen, you still believe that Kim can take Aubry Knight?"

Koskotas smiled. "You just don't get it, do you?" he said, and left the room.

Gagnon brooded. What did he mean by that? "Guerrero?" she asked. The air clouded, and the little man appeared. "What do you think?" she asked. "You know Koskotas. You know Aubry. Aubry will kill Kim. What in the hell is this about?"

Guerrero's voice took on a tone of genuine regret. The simulacrum shook his head. "It doesn't matter who wins, or who loses," he said. "A brawl with an officer will give Koskotas the excuse he needs to cashier Knight out of the program."

"Will it work?"

Guerrero shook his head sadly. "I don't know," he said. "But look."

He played back the last seconds of the confrontation, after the three were dead, and the others flown.

On the holo stage Aubry stood, surveying the carnage. Then, one at a time, he took the shock rods that had rolled from limp and lifeless hands. He switched them off and placed them by their owners. He arranged the corpses' limbs neatly and carefully.

Then Aubry sat cross-legged, backs of hands against his knees, and waited. The sweat gleamed on his face. His eyes were closed. His lips moved without making sound.

Gagnon backed up the program, watching the lip movement again. "What did he say?" she asked Guerrero.

Guerrero smiled. "He said: 'I love you.' "

"Who was he talking to?"

"Himself. His younger self, I think."

Gagnon felt herself relax. "This isn't the man who came here, my friend. This is something different."

"Koskotas doesn't understand that," Guerrero said.

"I don't think he can." She turned the image off, allowing it to dissolve. "I think," she said, "that we've done our work." She looked at the hologram of the squat little man, and was overcome with a wave of affection. "You know—I wish that you were real."

"Why?"

"I'd like to buy you a drink."

24

Aubry sat in the garden dome, near an artificial waterfall, meditating. Meditation was something that had become a part of his life in the past few years. Often the journey took him into pain. Occasionally, into bliss. But however difficult the path became, he was committed to the journey.

The dome overhead reflected light, seemed to contain it,

and the soft sounds of water flowing made it a special place for him, a place so very unlike the city streets that had birthed him.

He heard Kim coming. He knew it was Kim. The footsteps were those of a man in complete control of his body. Almost flat-footed. The whisper of a step, sliding from ball of foot back to heel, always in perfect balance. No meaty athleticism here. No macho posturing. Kim's excellence was less a strength of muscle than a perfect alignment of bone and sinew. Aubry understood this, deeply.

Along a crushed-stone path leading past the waterfall appeared Kim. The slender Korean wore a white *gi* with a tattered black belt. He walked along the narrow path as if he had all the time in the world.

The man was thin. He moved so fluidly he seemed to have no bones. His eyes were as bright as coals. He might have been thirty or sixty. The nails of his hands were yellowish, and looked thick. He wore sandals, with thick cotton socks. Aubry knew he faced a master whose art was complete.

Kim stood before him. "You were expected at the gymnasium an hour ago." His voice was strained.

"It's peaceful here, isn't it?" Aubry said. Was this the man who hated him so much? Why? What had he done?

"Why didn't you come?" He paused, and Aubry could feel that the man was out of balance, and that this lack of equilibrium was far from Kim's normal state. "You are . . ." Kim searched for the proper words. "Disrespectful."

Aubry watched the water, and from somewhere deep inside him, he seemed to hear another man's words. Warrick? Perhaps. But had he had to stop crediting a dead man with all that was good in his mind.

He spoke carefully. "Everyone has worked carefully to bring us together. They say that you hate Nullboxing."

"It is whorish," Kim said, with a flash of anger. "And you have the same contempt for my art. We need not waste time on pleasantries. The only possible reply to your statements is action. Why do you sit? Has fear so paralyzed you?"

Aubry reached out and plucked a flower from its stem.

Its pink and blue petals lay neatly against his palm. "Do you see?"

Kim's posture didn't relax, but his eyes narrowed. "See what?"

"Either of us can do this," Aubry said. His hand closed on the bud, and when it opened, it was a smear of red and white. "Either of us can end life. I can't give it back. I . . ." He shook his head. "I can't mend the bones I break. Can't give sight back to the eyes I've taken. I can't make men breathe again. Can you?"

Kim looked at him suspiciously. Proudly, he said, "In hwa rang do, acupuncture and a form of chiropractory are requisites for advancement. Why?"

Aubry smiled sadly. "I envy you."

"You . . . envy me?" For the first time, Kim's energy seemed to shift. Rather than the focused blowtorch, it was more diffuse now, almost like a halo around the man. He kept his distance—Aubry would have to take steps to reach him—but sat on a bench across from him, watching and evaluating. "This is . . . not the kind of comment I expected from you. Tell me. What did people say to you, about me?"

"They said that you wanted to hurt me. That you were my enemy."

Kim nodded slowly. "I heard the same of you." He cupped a flower in his hands, smelled it without plucking it or damaging it. "Did you scent, before you destroyed?"

Aubry blinked, and again, there was that strange, sad smile. When he spoke, it was a whisper. "I never have," he said. He looked at the crumpled petals in his hands.

There was a pause, and into that pause came the sound of water flowing, and a distant insect sound, a soft chirping from the far side of the garden. "Come," Kim said finally. "This flower is sweet. Give yourself the gift."

Aubry hesitated, and then rose. He took a step forward. And then another. And sat. Now each man was within the other's kill zone. No physical response could stop an attack at such range. Only an intuitive warning, or a preemptive attack, could possibly suffice. Kim's eyes were dark and cool. Aubry bent, closed his eyes, and smelled the flower.

Then he sniffed the crushed, dead thing in his own hand. Its petals had released their fragrance fully, but the live flower's essence was greater still.

"Which do you prefer?" Kim asked unnecessarily.

Together, they listened to the garden.

Then Kim spoke. "If you had come to my class, in front of my students . . ." A rueful smile creased his mouth.

"The meekest woman becomes a tiger when protecting her cubs," Aubry said. A sudden warm smile split his face. "A friend of mine named Jenna told me that."

"When two tigers fight," Kim said, "one dies, and the other is crippled."

"Even if I won, I would lose." Aubry's big shoulders hunched forward. "Someone knew that."

"I do not know why you are here," Kim said. "Some say that you are being prepared for an assignment. Think, please." He laid his hand on Aubry's. Kim's flesh felt like parchment. "Think of the manner in which we were pushed toward each other. Someone wanted to see it. It was a test." Aubry looked up, and Kim peered directly into his eyes, as if measuring. "I think that someone read some old evaluations of you, and thought you an animal. Perhaps once you were. Now you are a man. I am not certain that even you completely understand this."

"You can *heal* as well as kill," Aubry whispered, close to awestruck. "You are complete."

Kim stared. "There is more than one way to heal, Aubry Knight. I can heal bodies. Perhaps you will heal something greater." He withdrew his hand, leaving behind a sensation of warmth.

Aubry stood, gazing at the garden around him, as if astonished and delighted to find it still there. "I think . . . I will walk in the garden awhile, Master Kim. I would like to smell the flowers."

Kim stood. And they bowed simultaneously, sincerely, two tigers who had offered, and received from each other, the gift of life.

3RD SONG

FIREDANCE

The fire spreads from the center out, or from the lower centers to the higher. Never from the higher to the lower. Thus, always, the emotions rule, the intellect acting only in their service. It is a conceit to believe that the head can rule the heart.

—Ibandi proverb

1

AUGUST 22. EPHESUS.

"Recommend that he be inserted into target." Leslie heard herself say the words, but they were remote, the distant, shallow echoes of a waterfall in a cave. She had no conscious awareness of having spoken them. There was only concentration, and escape.

Her toes dug into the golden path beneath her feet, and she spun back barely in time to avert disaster. A mountainous block of concrete thundered down, smashing through the path, spraying gilt dust and cement chips as it screamed its way into the abyss. Leslie peered over the edge, watched the block tumble endlessly into darkness, watched flames rise up to devour it.

She stood on a road of glowing golden bricks suspended in utter darkness. If she let any feelings creep past her shields, they manifested as screams of fear and doubt.

Her breathing steadied. The path began to heal itself, one brick at a time, until it rejoined with the far side. She moved cautiously forward.

Stop. *Sense.* She adjusted her mind, and *felt* what was waiting ahead. She couldn't see it yet. It *smelled* like a dragon. She was on the very edge of something, as if she had wandered into the wrong cave. There was a presence ahead, enormous, godlike in its power—and as yet, asleep. It dwarfed her, or anything she had yet encountered on the golden road. The presence metamorphosed from dragon to djinn. And then grew beyond even that fearsome potential. This was Death itself, and the only reason she had not been utterly crushed was that it was . . .

Asleep?

* * *

Leslie popped one level of reality out of the kinesthetic/ visual analog matrix she had so carefully constructed to penetrate STYX's computer system. Miles Bloodeagle had provided the key: Gorgon was cleared into select military data banks, and those contacts opened up myriad horizontal branch lines, cousins, related data links, a woven mesh of lines connecting communication, finance, research, and supply. As long as the lines were not completely sealed, there remained a chance that Leslie could wiggle through them.

Again and again she was challenged, her passwords revoked or annulled, and just as repeatedly she resolved impossibly complex security equations by transposing them to the kinesthetic or visual realm, dealing with them the way a basketball player executes a lay-up shot. Once they were solved by her motor cortex, her forebrain converted the equations into numbers, into bits and bytes of data.

The ripostes and challenges of the computers were a world of dragons, plunging stalactites, trolls, and killer robots to Leslie, and she raced, or squirmed, between them. There was no fighting back. There was only avoidance, evasion, and escape.

Asleep . . . ?

Leslie was no longer on the golden path, living the experience. She was watching herself experience it, a half-step removed from total immersion. And something was wrong. She might well risk tiptoeing past a sleeping dragon, or a djinn.

But did Death ever sleep? She had the oddest sensation that everything she sought was just the other side of this chamber, but . . .

Pride is a terminal disease. Jenna had said that a hundred times. Leslie crept back, snuck away, and—

The path retracted like a slidewalk, rolling away from Death, away from the cave, out of the dark, and—

Leslie flew upright on her couch, her eyes 'strained wide and wild. One thin hand clutched at her chest.

Her hands shook. She felt at her mouth, touched something tender, and glanced at her fingers. They bore a smear of blood. Only then did she focus on the white-tiled walls of Ephesus's virtual-communications complex, in the science building.

Jenna's hand gripped her shoulder, eyes narrowed fiercely. "Leslie? Are you all right?" Jenna held a blood-dappled handkerchief in her left hand, and daubed at Leslie's lip.

Leslie held up the bloodied fingers. "When?" she asked weakly.

"About a half an hour ago. You bit your lip, and were muttering something about inversions."

Leslie thought for a moment and then said, "Inversions. They were testing Father with one of the standard muscle-memory confusion programs, switching input under stress during a flying exercise. Gorgon technique. I pulled it out of a low-priority medical file."

"How did he do?"

She waved dismissively. "Fine." A sudden darkness fluttered across her face. Fear perhaps. Or shame. Her eyes locked with Jenna's as if seeking absolution. "I had to end the session. There was a major, big-time trap set up, and I almost fell into it. Catch me, and they catch Uncle Miles. Catch Uncle Miles, and they'll trace it all the way to Ephesus."

Jenna daubed at Leslie's torn mouth. "Shh. You did fine, darling."

The child was still reorienting herself, but began to smile shyly. "Daddy aced their training. They're going to use him." Leslie frowned. "But they don't expect him to survive."

Leslie steadied herself, breathing carefully, her chocolate brown eyes vast and unfocused. "He's disposable," she said coldly. "Swarna probably knows that he exists—after all, a PanAfrican kill team came after him, right? The army didn't want to send Daddy in, but the White House forced their hand. So STYX's attitude is: no real backup."

"What are you talking about?"

"All of the emphasis is on getting him in. The route out isn't half as secure. Extraction of a kill team, setting up decoys and diversions—that's half of a successful assassination. Check the computer—Kennedy, '63. Textbook case. By the time they unraveled the false trails in '97, all the primaries were safely dead. Daddy doesn't realize how delicate an extraction is, and STYX doesn't care at all. He'll die if we don't help him."

Jenna sat staring at the blood on her handkerchief. "I trust your instincts. What can you say about the insertion point?"

Leslie's brow furrowed and a holographic globe popped into view next to her head. It was garishly colored, not at all the usual staid world globe, with bright peppermint pinks and frosted greens. It twirled on its axis, and Leslie zoomed in on the northwest section of the African continent. "Somewhere here, in North Africa. I know he's supposed to rendezvous with a contact in a little town here, called Ma'habre. September fifth."

Jenna's hand stretched out, and she stroked the point on the globe. Ma'habre. She could believe that. Ma'habre was far enough from the border of New Nippon, from the PanAfrican Republic, to avoid the kind of direct and total surveillance found to the south. And yet, it would also be close enough to ancient trade routes. Land, sea, or air routes, a day's travel at most, would take Aubry across a stretch of border too vast to be patrolled effectively.

Ma'habre . . .

Jenna tousled her niece's hair. "Thanks, sweetheart. I'll take it from here."

"You . . . and Uncle Miles?"

"You think I need him?"

Leslie nodded soberly. "Aunt Jenna, you've hardly ever been beyond Ephesus. You don't know the PanAfricans. Uncle Miles has worked against them. Gorgon's most consistent mission was sabotage and terrorism against Pan-Africa."

"Which makes it more of a risk for him. They'll have files on him."

"That won't stop him. He owes Daddy. Twice. Please, Aunt Jenna." Leslie's slender fingers were on her wrist, small and firm and cool. "Pride is a terminal disease."

"Sometimes I hate you. All right. I'll talk to your uncle Miles. But this is our secret, right?"

Leslie's face was a child's. It was unlined, and firm-cheeked, glowing with health, and beautiful. And hadn't aged a day in four years. But if Jenna looked more deeply, beyond the bright brown cheeks and dark brown hair, to the eyes . . .

The eyes were furnace-hot, and frighteningly intelligent, and as old as God. And for the first time in Jenna's memory, just a little bit afraid.

Aubry and Promise, together, were Leslie's lifeline from hell. Together, they were the closest thing to a normal family's dynamics that Leslie could ever know. The memories of what she was, had been trained for, had done . . . of the lethal potentials and calculating, murderous intellect wired into that little mind, were corrosive.

A race car wants to race. A swimmer wants to swim. And a murder machine wants to murder.

What did it take to keep those impulses in check? To allow Leslie to function as anything even close to a normal child? Goddess . . .

Jenna sensed the unspoken challenge, the mortal promise in Leslie's eyes. It crackled there, dusty and electric as a summer storm.

Find my father, it said. *Go, and help him to come back. Or I will go myself. It will destroy my mother, but I will have to go.*

Jenna took Leslie's hand. There were two creatures within her niece—the death machine, and a child about to lose the only human being who could ever function as father.

"I can't make you any promises, Leslie," Jenna whispered.

"Find him. Save him. Or . . ."

The animal was there again, a thing she had seen in Leslie, a thing she had seen in Aubry, and she felt a chill.

"Find him. Bring him home."

And all Jenna could do was nod.

2

AUGUST 30. NORTHERN PANAFRICA.

"The primary has made his decision," Sinichi Tanaka said. "If he failed to appear at the opening of Swarnaville Spaceport, it would be seen as cowardice." His hands were light on the skimmer controls. At his command, it hovered two hundred feet above the carnival grounds. He set the panel to automatic and spun in his seat, facing the Four.

All wore silver-blue shock armor, reflective faceplates in place. All four were huge, calm, alert, and at ease.

Ni, San, Go, Roku. The Four. Once there had been six, Tanaka thought sadly. Ichi was sacrificed in the white medical room beneath the Citadel. Shi died in America, on a pointless mission of vengeance.

"Tanaka-san," San said politely. She was the female. Almost as strong as the others, and with greater endurance, she was the best marksman among them. "Have you decided upon our positions?"

"I will have regular security forces throughout the carnival," he said. "The primary will be covered at all times. We will have a disruption field functioning, of course. I want to hold you and your brothers in reserve in case of emergency."

Ni inclined his head. "Whatever you wish, Sensei."

Sinichi Tanaka allowed himself a tiny smile. "I am proud of you," he said. "I know that you will make me prouder still."

"Yes, Sensei," Go said. Go cleared his throat, and then spoke again. "This is our first opportunity to speak freely in many weeks," he said. "We know that you disapprove of the way we handled the American."

Tanaka sighed. "You disobeyed orders. Instead of executing your target, you challenged him."

"You have never criticized us," Roku said.

"I have access to classified reports," Tanaka said. "I disapproved of the mission, but I knew of it. I know of your origins. I know who the American is. I know what happens in the white room."

San's voice was almost as deep as her brothers', a catlike purr. "We have no mother. We have no father. You are the only one who cares about us, and even you, Sensei Tanaka, are not of our flesh."

"I love this land," he said. "It is in my blood." He looked out over the carnival site. Two square kilometers of bazaars, games, eateries, entertainments. From all over PanAfrica they would come, awaiting the launching of PanAfrica's first shuttle. This land was alive, and vital. Part of him. But the Four were right. He had no home but PanAfrica, and PanAfrica was not his home.

"You understand us, don't you?" San said, sympathetically. "It explains why you have treated us as human beings. Not merely as weapons."

"You are human," Tanaka said. "But you are also bound by your obligations. As are we all." He could see the little people down below him, laboring at their tasks. Thousands of them, building, and clearing and preparing. Most of them would never even see the man they labored to serve. One or two might meet him.

And none would ever know him, as Sinichi Tanaka knew him.

He shook his head, clearing out the dark thoughts. "We will take a walking tour of the area now," he announced, spinning back to the controls. "I am receptive to your security suggestions."

He released the autopilot and spun the skimmer down for a landing. But even with his concentration on the flying, in the mirror above his eyes he could see the Four behind him. Armored, loyal to him, and to the primary.

Incredible students, absorbing everything he could teach them of armed and unarmed combat.

And that last thought made him wonder, once again, about the American. Aubry Knight. Knight had slain Shi, childlike Shi, whose visit to the white room had dimmed the light behind his eyes. Knight had killed a child.

For the thousandth time, Sinichi Tanaka remembered training Shi and his siblings. Watching them grow. Goading them on with curses and candies. Holding their hands when, at maturity, they received their ritual tattoos.

Shi, gentle Shi, had so loved songs and flowers. For all his massive size and strength, Shi was the least of his clan. Shi was a baby in an adult's body.

With savage intensity, Tanaka wished to meet Aubry Knight, who had slain his gentlest student.

We know you can kill children, Tanaka thought blackly. *But how are you against a man?*

3

SEPTEMBER 4. INDIAN OCEAN.

Aubry checked the manifest against the computer records of the cargo. He was one of the crew of the *Saint John's*, out of Newfoundland, headed to port in North Africa. He had been aboard for the past week, and tomorrow would see the coast. There had been bad weather for the past few days, even worse than the terrible North Atlantic chop. The twin stabilizers had roared and groaned. Every step tested balance. The deck rolled wildly underfoot, and Aubry experienced a wild and foreign hunger.

For long hours he buried himself in work, suppressing the desire that raged within him. Finally, close to midnight, he climbed the narrow steps up to the main deck, felt the rain and wind lash his face, and grinned ferally.

What would the crew say if they saw him there near the

railing, hammered by the storm, but unyielding? What would they say if they saw him moving slowly through his exercises, disdaining the terrible power of the wind, the sheets of water battering his face?

He didn't care.

Eyes blinking against the pelting rain, Aubry began the Rubber Band. The deck rocked beneath him. Aubry extended his left leg to its farthest reach, grasped his big toe, and felt the simultaneous stretch in the bottom and top of his thigh. He pulled backward with his arm until the leg was almost parallel with his chest, tensed until the entire side of his body was rigid with strain. In the midst of effort, his face was completely placid, disassociated. That was what his father had taught him: *Stay calm, be the eye of the hurricane. Be strong.*

If you are, then the winds of chance can blow you, but not harm you. You can tumble, but won't break, flatten, but not be crushed.

So Aubry breathed, going into himself. Odd how it seemed somehow easier to do that, here in the midst of the terrible weather, than at Manitou Springs. There, he had felt observed. Even in the privacy of his own room, he had never felt the desire to perform his morning ritual. There were too many eyes in that place, and the Rubber Band was not for public consumption.

It was . . . sacred.

He had never seen waves like this, and had he acknowledged their overwhelming power, the fear would have been nearly paralyzing. He understood cities. They were, in the meat of it, all that he *did* understand. Cities, and human violence. Even the Ephesus forest fire hadn't seemed real, not a natural thing at all, because it had been instigated by human beings. It had been an attack.

And *attacks* he understood. World as war, life as combat, this he knew as certainly as his own heartbeat.

The Ephesus commune had been a strange place to him, until he gained the ability to see it as an armed camp. He understood the feminist separatists. The NewMan Nations were different—they felt frighteningly comfortable from the first. He felt so at home there that it terrified him—he didn't really want to look at that part of himself.

But this. This weather . . .

There was no one to conquer. No human was involved. There was no hope of "winning." Even a city rat like Aubry understood that no human could defeat a storm by force of will. How then to survive?

For too long, he had reacted almost passively to circumstance, allowed others to direct and guide him, to send him screaming against targets. But he was a *human* missile against *human* targets.

How to face the storm? He had to be more than he was, more than a human being, and completely willing to accept death. He had found that place within himself before, more easily in the past few years. But now he had to surrender to it absolutely.

So Aubry narrowed his eyes against the driving wind and the lightning, and ran through the Rubber Band's litany:

Contract the anal sphincter. Contract the abdominals. Spine extended, and usually straight. Exhale on twists and contractions. Inhale on expansions. The Rubber Band was not a series of combat movements. It developed the *potential* for movement—strength, balance, concentration, flexibility, endurance.

In the midst of the rain, sweat poured from his body as his arms and legs extended and wove. He slipped, and tucked into a roll, slamming into the steel deck, grunting. He gasped, mouth widening with pain and fear. Slapped out of his trance state by the elements, stripped of city, stripped of family, the child within Aubry Knight wanted to scream in anguish, but when he went inward, and saw the child . . . the child that he had been . . .

Leslie was there, beside him.

The fear tried to find another place to run. *You are weak and feminine,* it whispered to him evilly. And it attacked his feminine side, disappearing into the darkness in Aubry's heart.

Then, during an instant when the wind seemed to die just a fraction, he heard a voice. Promise's voice.

"Aubry," she said. *"We are family. If we can't be together, I can accept that. But you are the father of my child, and will always be in my heart. If my strength its needed, it is yours."*

He reached out to her, finding nothing because he searched in the wrong place.

He cried, until he felt a comforting touch within his chest, a comforting *ssshhh.* . . .

She was there. Promise was beside him, above him, within him. He could not see her, but could hear her, and feel her. And he could see Leslie.

And Leslie smiled.

The ship yawed and pitched. The crewmen huddled in their stations. And Aubry came back upright, and finished the exercises that he had begun.

4

The steward approached Aubry as he checked the manifest again. It was simple work, taking time but not too much thought, visually identifying crates in their storage racks, scanning their ID numbers into the clipboard linked to the *Saint John's* central computer.

The steward was African, as dark as Aubry, two inches shorter and probably fifty pounds lighter. He spoke thick-tongued Swahili.

"Hey, boy," he said. "Seen you dancing out on the deck. Thought I'd seen something like that before, but can't say where."

Aubry's mind took a little jolt. He heard the words, and they were strange to him, but also tamped down in some way. Simultaneously, he felt himself slide sideways, as if another part of his head were taking over, and he heard himself answer in the same tongue.

"Nothing special," he lied. "Just something that I picked up." He heard his voice, and marveled at the overlay of Brazilian on the Swahili.

"You speak our language well. My name is Abedi, and I am from the Republic." He lit a cigarette, and offered one to Aubry. Aubry declined, but watched the smoke drift up in the confined space, curling around the bulkhead.

Aubry's interest was piqued. "You must have been born just about the time that the Republic was created—so you don't remember much. But maybe your parents . . . ?"

Abedi laughed bitterly. "Yes. My parents. Whoever they are, and whatever became of them."

He inhaled again, and then exhaled a long, thin stream. "They were landowners before that communist bastard Swarna. His soldiers came, and took their land, and drove them off to the camps."

"His soldiers? I thought that he was just an advisor to the rulers of Kenya."

Abedi leaned his head back. His dark, thick nostrils flared. "Yes. That is the way it was described, wasn't it? Don't kid yourself. He was in charge from the beginning." He leaned closer. "Hundreds of thousands. Maybe millions died. The Westerners have never really understood. Or cared."

Aubry nodded. "Why do you go back?"

"Oh, it's not bad right now—and I have nowhere to go, and nothing to go to. I have a good job. And that bastard only *seems* to be immortal."

"What do you mean?"

"How old is he? How old does he *have* to be? Near a hundred? More? The pressure must be insane. The Japanese . . . ?" Abedi examined him craftily. "Well, you'll find out. What do you call that dance?"

"Capoeira," Aubry lied. "It is from Brazil. My father taught it to me, long ago."

"Well." Abedi flicked his cigarette toward the wall. It wheeled into the darkness, leaving a trail of sparks. "Keep practicing. Maybe you'll get good one day."

5

The *Saint John's* docked at Ma'habre at 11:42, local time.

Jumping ship was much easier than Aubry would have expected: the customs agents met him at the bottom of the gangplank, and gave his papers only a cursory examination. Afterward he simply shouldered his rucksack, walked into the crowd thronging the pier, and disappeared.

His first impression of Ma'habre utterly destroyed his mental picture of Africa. Near the docks, low buildings of steel and concrete shimmered in the awesome heat. Farther into the city international conglomerates were creating a corporate forest: office towers sprouted toward the sky like beanstalks of silvered ice. Black and brown and white men and women in native garb or Western business suits bustled about, obsessed by the same daily business prerogatives as their cousins in New York, or London, or Moscow.

The Scavenger part of his mind immediately began to study the building techniques, wondering whether he could do the job better, or as well, or cheaper.

Rucksack over his shoulder, he closed his eyes for a moment.

A series of hypnotically implanted images, hologram-sharp, flashed against the darkness. He opened his eyes, and began to follow the implanted map.

The tang of fresh fruit and roasting meat led him to a native marketplace reminiscent of the Maze's Free Market. His inoculation record was current, and his digestive system adjusted to cope with the local viruses, but there were dangerous local parasites—*so don't eat anything that you can't cook. Much of the fruit was fertilized with human waste.*

Treated waste, certainly—that was part of Swarna's land-reclamation program, a program successful enough to migrate north. But there were always problems—if no one was watching, how could they be sure that the compost/cesspools were properly treated?

So, bacterial and parasitic levels in the fruit stands were regulated in a series of spot checks. The results were not always appetizing.

A red and black flag hung suspended from a pole at one of the buildings. It immediately clicked with his mental image. *Contact point.*

It was dark and a little close inside the building, perhaps ten degrees cooler than the street. Men and women moved quietly, as if striving to conserve their strength and body fluids in the incredible heat.

They drank coffee from small cups, and talked in low voices, mouths mere inches away from each other, as if a breath away from passion.

Aubry sat back, trying to shrink. A dozen different languages burbled in the air. The combination of microprocessor and hypnotic implantations translated them into two dozen different conversations. His lips moved clumsily. His words sounded like English to him, but his lips twisted to construct alien combinations of consonants and vowels.

At length a stranger sat at the table opposite him. The man wore a light half-burnoose, belted at the waist, over American-style denims. He was dark-skinned and Semitic, and stood perhaps five and a half feet tall. His left index finger tapped the table, three times. "I am Hafid. You seek?"

"Food," Aubry said, remembering the identification sequence. "I have had influenza."

"You should boil your water."

"I heard the water was good."

"Don't believe everything you hear." The flicker of a smile crossed the man's face. "Come to my home," he said. "I think that the selection will be more to your liking."

And, it was unspoken, *there will be greater privacy.*

Aubry shouldered his rucksack and followed the little man out into the street, past the hawkers and the myriad craftsmen, past the sailors of a dozen nations, and deeper into the heart of an alien land.

6

The streets reminded Aubry of the early days of the Maze. Not only the Maze—but Death Valley Maximum Security Penitentiary.

After he had counted three dozen eye patches, or staring, cheap, obviously plastic eyes, he began to feel sick. The crowd was marked with scars, and limps, fingerless hands, and artificial limbs, and faces flensed of skin.

"Hafid," he said at last. "What am I seeing, and why am I seeing so much of it?"

"It is the free market. Swarna, he has been . . . *kind* to my people. He has provided health-care services across the continent. You will find that the level of sickness has dropped . . . precipitously. The infant-mortality statistics have become negligible. On the other hand . . ." And here he appeared to choose his words more carefully.

"For centuries, the people of Africa have been seen as raw material. Our continent has been raw material. 'White man's burden'—do you remember that? It was applied to the people of India, of Africa, of the Arab nations. We were to be taken care of. It gave the Europeans the moral justification to come in and take whatever they wanted. They took goods, or services, or freedom, or our life itself and gave us the holy gift of Western education and Christianity. We lost our own souls, in exchange for the white man's god."

He spat into the dust.

"Now, thanks to Swarna, we are raw material once again, but in a new and more degrading sense. When an American, Japanese, or Brazilian needs a kidney, a gonad

. . . if a woman needs a new uterus . . . the medical banks of the PanAfrican Republic are immediately accessed. A tissue match is found, and a price is quoted."

Aubry felt a chill. "And if the person with the desired organ isn't willing to sell?"

"There is always someone willing to sell," Hafid said. "Always. Examine the contracts signed, in order to buy food on credit from Swarna's grain storehouses, or to borrow money to buy land. The debt can be called due at any time, due to 'emergency.'

"It is a clause which has been invoked many, many times. One case at a time. The borrower has a choice—to lose everything he has worked a lifetime to earn, or to donate an organ." They had reached a two-storied white clay building at the end of a twisting, narrow street. Hafid unlocked the door and stepped aside for Aubry.

The room was furnished simply with wooden chairs, and rugs upon walls and floor. Hafid smiled crookedly and threw a rug back from the floor, revealing a trapdoor. He pulled it up, revealing a flight of stairs, leading downward into the earth.

The stairs were hewn in stone, and purpled by a wavering overhead light. A faint buzzing filled Aubry's head, but he had the feeling that the buzzing wasn't external sound—something was happening to his electronics.

"You may notice a little discomfort here," Hafid said. "An unfortunate necessity—our null-field suppresses electronics. It has the dampening effect of a thousand feet of rock. Only a combination deep scan and seismological study could detect this safe house. Your friends were very relieved."

"My friends?"

The stairs opened out into a larger chamber, also of stone. A simple refrigerator and stove sat in one corner. On a desk next to them were a small stack of books and a gaslight.

"My friends?"

Aubry's emotional alarm bells began to chime. Something was wrong. Hafid was hiding something. And in the background of the room, he caught a scent—there were other human beings here. A man . . .

The rug suspended from the far wall was swept back, and a huge sunburned man strode out, followed by a lithe woman with short brown hair.

Aubry was speechless. His carefully programmed Arabic malfunctioned, and he could barely find the English words. "Bloodeagle! Jenna!"

Halfway around the world, Aubry Knight had found Home again. The three of them embraced. Hard.

7

The map was of soiled yellow paper, spread across a rude table and lit by the gas lantern.

"How in the hell did you get here?" Aubry was still dazed, and confused. And very grateful.

"You can thank Leslie for that," Jenna said. She examined his new nose. "Aubry, that face! You look like someone flattened it out with a hammer! All that scar tissue . . ."

"It's the real you," Bloodeagle said blandly. "We don't have much time—listen to me. Some of the details of this operation are simply not available—STYX is using isolated data systems, with no reference to the outside, no linkages at all. And others have security which was simply too tight, even for Leslie. But we knew you were coming into Ma'habre, and we had a list of probable contacts from a four-year-old Gorgon operation. Hafid was on the list—we got lucky."

Jenna leaned forward. "Tomorrow, you disappear down the pipeline, in a truck caravan carrying workers out to a bauxite mine. We'll be with you. We break away. A sand skimmer will be waiting for us. We cross the border here—" Her finger touched the map lightly, very close to Aubry's hand. "And then we're on our own. Intelligence suggests that Swarna will make an appearance at Swarna-ville, on the thirty-fifth anniversary of the creation of the PanAfrican Republic."

"Anniversary of the defeat of the United Nations forces?"

"Exactly. It fits his psych profile. So we join a group of seekers, traveling across the wastes, and planning to enter the sacred city. We'll have trouble at this point—there are weapon scans. Bloodeagle and I will depend on the underground which supported Gorgon's operations in the past—"

"I was told that those channels were corrupt."

"They probably are—but we don't have a lot of choice."

Aubry considered. "My weaponry has been built into me," he said quietly. "The bones in my forearms and lower legs are hollow. They are shielded, and shadow-imaged. Ultrasound or X ray will show nothing."

"Jesus," Jenna said quietly. She laid her hand on Aubry's shoulder, and looked deeply into his eyes. "Aubry—are you sure?"

"I don't have any choice," he said. "Promise and Leslie are the only family I have. I have to take the chance. Any chance."

Bloodeagle rubbed his chin. He held a finger to his lips. Then he took a piece of paper and wrote down the following: *If they applied such invasive procedures, and you agreed to a hit operation, there may be more inside you than they told you.*

Aubry was about to protest. Hafid had said that the room was shielded. But what if he was wrong?

He took the pen from Miles's hand, and wrote in turn. *More? Like what?*

Explosives, Miles wrote. *If you are captured, and Swarna interviews you personally, they will detonate the charge.*

"Jesus."

Aubry looked at both of them. "Why did you come?" he asked.

There wasn't any answer from Bloodeagle. Jenna just

leaned forward and kissed Aubry's cheek. Bloodeagle looked a little drawn, a little thinner. He smelled of old perspiration and diesel fuel. "You just don't understand, do you? Even after all this time. You have family."

8

Night had fallen over the city, and except for far-off traffic sounds, and a distant call to prayer, Ma'habre was quiet. They sat on a terraced balcony on Hafid's second story, and listened to Bloodeagle.

"Four years ago, we became aware of an attempt to embarrass the neutral government of Zimbabwe. Swarna's people kidnapped several Energy executives, had them locked in a limo, and pinned on a bridge. They would be killed at the first sign of trouble."

"Did Swarna actually take responsibility for kidnapping a head of state?"

"Well, no—not officially, but it was his people. It wasn't hard to trace the trail back. We went in, and stopped it. I was in-country for maybe four days, and I can tell you— even in that short a period of time, the image that I got of Swarna was a hell of a lot different than the one we get in the media at home."

"Man of Mystery? Tough negotiator?"

"We know that he displaced families in his efforts to create the Republic, but there was more. Europeans were resented enough in Africa. But there was a simmering discontent about the Japanese."

"The Japanese?"

"Absolutely. You think that they were seen as the great liberators? The Educators? As far as the locals were concerned, they were Swarna's instrument of enslavement. After all—New Nippon is right in the heart of PanAfrica, and it's Swarna's private preserve. His bastion, and that's what has made it so damned hard to remove the man.

Every European or African who enters New Nippon is registered. Every Asian has to be tied in to specific business, and is watched even more carefully. Somewhere in the middle is Swarna's stronghold. Ten thousand acres of land, and in the middle is his private game preserve. The inner moat is his damned dinosaur preserve. Get through that, and you have the fortress itself. His private guard is on the premises at all times—and they have a hell of a rep. Their equivalent of the Airborne Rangers is maybe fifteen minutes away by skimmer or helicopter. Hard target."

"But this festival, at Swarnaville Spaceport . . ."

"It's a guess, but it's a damned good one."

They looked out over the balcony. A Jeep roared by. In it were four soldiers, very black, roaring a drunken song in Japanese. Aubry smiled thinly.

"Disorienting, isn't it?" Bloodeagle nursed his drink.

Aubry grunted. "The worst part is the way the switch in my head keeps flipping back and forth. Some combination of a microprocessor and deep hypnosis. The information is running back and forth so fast . . . on one level it feels like a stream of insects—that's the kinesthetics. On another, like a flow of light beads. But the weirdness is that I can actually talk it. We did a lot of work on that, on the actual phonetics."

"Phonetics?" Jenna grinned. "There's a word I wouldn't have expected from you."

Aubry's dark face creased amiably. "Well—would you have expected to see me on the ass side of the world, in the first place?"

Hafid, nursing an iced coffee, shook his head slowly. "You are all mad, but less mad than your countrymen. I have had many of you come through my house. And I have had . . . many houses. I have to move from time to time, to keep my head upon my shoulders. But I mostly get hard, cold men. Smuggling, spying. They do not laugh very much, and when they do, it is about women they have left behind. Men they killed, and the expressions upon their faces."

"I don't want to kill anymore," Aubry whispered.

Bloodeagle turned to look at him. "Yes, my brother?"

"I can see them. They tried to kill me, most of them. But I can't . . ." Aubry lowered his voice, bent forward until his face was in shadow. The rest bent over until they were in a conspiratorial huddle.

"Until I had Leslie, it never really hit me. I used to watch Leslie sleep, and he looked so innocent, beyond the cares of this world. And then I realized that Leslie is, pound for pound, the most lethal human being who has ever walked this planet. A killing machine. And I became enraged that someone would corrupt my child like that.

"But I grew past that. At Ephesus I realized that every child is born innocent, and then we twist them. We turn them. We condition them with cruelty or kindness. And so the killers who came after me were once children, as well. Maybe genetics determined what they were—in which case God rolled the dice, and they came up the losers. Or they were born into the wrong world, one in which being a predator made them the outcasts. I can understand that. Or they were blank slates, and we wrote on them. And what we wrote on those slates was a death sentence. Executed by me.

"There has to be another way," Aubry whispered. "We can't keep killing each other. I used to wonder why I had been allowed to live. Why someone . . . like me existed."

Bloodeagle reached across and clasped Aubry's hand. "We all have our place in the world," he said patiently. "Every star in the heavens, every animal in the Earth, has its place in the natural order. You have been among buildings, on paved roads, all of your life. You have never had a chance to feel the natural order. And you have covered those feelings up. Now they begin to break free."

Aubry looked at him. "You had your traditions. From the time you were a child."

"Yes. Myths, stories . . . they make us, or break us. Stories of heroes have been with us from the very earliest days of mankind. Even though my people's world was transformed by the Europeans, we still retained our languages, and our religions. The yellow men who came here had their languages and myths. But you, as a man of African heritage, had your language, your names, your religions, and your myths stripped away from you. You have no history except that of America—and yet that is denied you as well. You must find your own myths. You must grow into them."

Aubry looked up at the stars. His thoughts seemed to stew far back in the recesses of his mind. "And you, Jenna?"

"My myths aren't old," she said. "They are only as old as the communes. It is true that women's myths have been lost over time—but it is also true that if women breed, it changes their relationship with the world. Women who choose not to breed have options which nature gave them, and men took away. But women who have children . . ."

Her voice lowered. "Men didn't make us different. Nature did. It is nature who dictated that children grow inside women's bodies. If men and women make . . . love, it is the woman who will bear the children. Nothing I can say, none of my anger can change that fact. And a pregnant woman is not a hunter, or a soldier. That one fact divides the human race into two halves: women, who bear children, and men, who do not. Layer upon that the exigencies of child rearing, and of survival, and you have many of the roles which men and women play with each other. Of course, many of those have been perverted." She was silent for a time, her fingers woven tightly together. There was a storm brewing in Jenna's eyes, but at length she smiled.

"You, Aubry—you showed me that a man could be strong, and gentle. You gave me hope."

Aubry's eyes were stinging, and he reached out and took her hand. At length, after a time, Bloodeagle reached out and placed his there as well, and they were quiet together.

When Aubry spoke again, he found that his voice was unsteady.

"I have always known myself as a fighter. Kevin Warrick, a man long dead now, tried to show me his version of what a warrior was. But . . . I am not that. I don't know exactly what I am. I do know that I've become something I

don't have a label for. And I know that I am contented."
He smiled, almost bashfully. "It's all right."

There was silence on the balcony.

Bloodeagle was the first to break it. "Aubry, my
brother," he said. "All that I have is yours. My people are
your people." He drew a knife, long, thin, razor sharp, and
cut the palm of his hand. And he looked at Jenna.

She smiled crookedly. "This is so much macho bullshit," she sighed. But she shook her head, as much at her
own folly as anything else, and drew her own blade. And
she drew it across her palm. "Aubry—we don't have a
warrior ritual among my people—but I welcome you in
my heart. Men and I . . , oh, to hell with it. I just love you.
You are my brother, and would be even if you weren't my
sister's husband. Let's do it."

Aubry hesitated for a moment. "Either of you have a
Spider?"

Jenna smiled tenderly. "Fuck you."

He cut himself. And the three palms formed a triangle,
and their blood ran together, and mingled there, beneath
the stars, in a foreign land, where, very soon, death would
be in the air.

9

SEPTEMBER 7. CHINA SEA.

The slightest touch of her hands on the controls made the
skimmer shudder in response. As they flew toward Hong
Kong, Promise had the feeling that they were approaching
the doors to another world, a world of brutality and awful
potentials.

Anything at all might live behind those doors. She
hoped that one of the possibilities was an answer to the
riddle which was Aubry Knight.

The first challenge came at the 100-mile limit, when her

computer was automatically scanned for identification, her flight plan cross-checked. She felt a moment of nervousness as her on-boards responded to the query, but she knew that the flight plans had all been filed with the central control, and her mercantile licenses were flawless.

The mainland came into view another minute later. With it came the second challenge. This was the moment of greatest danger, when there was a possibility that one of Hong Kong's notorious air pirates would race in to intercept. If that happened, it was problematic whether Promise's small skimmer could outrun them before their disruptors took control of the guidance mechanism and the inevitable boarding occurred.

But—and she was not completely mystified by this—a silver escort skimmer materialized out of a cloud bank. It matched her speed, beamed the proper codes to downgrade the alert status, and accompanied her into Kowloon port.

Beside her, Leslie played with a coloring book, her perfect coordination leading the crayon between the lines effortlessly. She could have juggled grenades with her feet and done the same.

Promise switched on the guidance system, and the green markings appeared on the windscreen. She took the path marked out for her, following the silver escort vehicle.

That meant that her path was precleared, that there would be no problem with customs, or immigration, or any of the ordinary agencies that most visitors to Hong Kong had to deal with.

It meant, in short, that a man named Wu had cleared the way for her. They slid through a forest of spires.

Thirty years before, the world feared that when Red China took over the city of Hong Kong, chaos would reign. What hadn't been taken into account was China's desperate need for the 398.5-square-mile economic pore that Hong Kong symbolized. Hong Kong meant access to computer skills and electronic equipment. Hong Kong meant access to a world market that both feared and coveted China's emerging power.

Without foreign investors, Hong Kong was just another ghetto waiting to deteriorate, rather than the most expensive patch of real estate in the world.

The green-dot path led Promise toward a series of spires, and the second tallest of them was, she believed, the one that beckoned her.

She was within a mile now, and the automatic guidance system, tied in with the security network, had taken control of her on-boards, and she was able to relinquish the hand controls.

There *were* critical moments when human skill was really required—but this wasn't one of them. On leaving dock in Oregon, she had to keep control of the skimmer and pilot it until it cleared the coast, when she could hook it into the Pacific Network. Once she was on-line, her flight registered in advance, it rarely took more than five minutes' waiting while her flight documents were scanned and compared to those of the thousands of other vehicles making the trans-Pacific flight. Her vehicle batteries were automatically inspected, her on-board security lines were checked—in other words, the Pacific Network protected itself from her incompetence. After all, it just wouldn't do to have her skimmer flop out of the air and smash into a passing trawler.

Then she was on her way. The federally controlled Pacific Network disengaged a hundred miles off the coast, in accordance with a battalion of treaties. A dozen different guidance systems vied for her traveling dollar. In one sense, a more genuine open market existed in the Orient than in the United States. It was much like choosing a primary vidphone carrier, with differing rates and services. But Promise didn't need to worry about any of that. All she needed to worry about was what she was going to say to the man she had flown halfway around the world to see.

Smiling broadly, Leslie took her mother's hand. "It'll be all right."

"How can you know that? How can you be so certain?"

"Because I'm with you, that's why. And if I'm with you then there isn't really anything that can go wrong, is there?

I mean, if something was going to go wrong, you would have left me at home. After all, I'm just a kid."

"When you say that, it all sounds so reasonable." The communication beacon coaxed her skimmer toward the dock. Promise settled back and tried to relax. What would it be like to see this man again? Wu had once been their enemy, but had also cleared Aubry of rape and murder charges.

And now, with Aubry ensnared in a different sort of web, a deadlier web, one from which there might be no natural exit, Wu might be the only one who could create a doorway.

The car settled in, and a slender black African boy met them and eased the door up. He smiled, with perfect, brilliant teeth.

"Good evening." He bobbed his head enthusiastically. "I am Jamal. It is my pleasure to welcome you to the house of Wu."

Leslie stepped down with exaggerated formality, a calculated stiffness to conceal her natural, perfect fluidity of movement.

Promise noticed that Jamal moved well, also. A certain feline ease suggested a movement art. Dance? He was willowy enough.

She walked beside him to an escalator, humming a tune to herself. Jamal's movement automatically entrained to the rhythm. Yes, a dancer.

"That's nice," he said, and his smile once again was astonishing in its clarity. "What was it?"

"A song of my people."

"You are a dancer," he said. It wasn't a question. "Not ballet, and not formal modern. I would have thought something Middle Eastern, but your muscle groupings are wrong."

"Once again, it is from my people. I come from a community of women in Oregon. Suzette Freleng, who established the commune, was a dance enthusiast. She felt that physical movement could be used as a tool for spiritual development."

Jamal nodded sagely.

"She pulled elements of dance from a dozen different cultures. Not ballet."

"Why?"

"Mother Freleng felt ballet was a movement against nature. It tries to create an illusion of weightlessness in the women, a separation from gravity. She felt that it bred an unhealthy contempt for the physical body. She saw too much smoking, too much drug use—amphetamines, cocaine. And too much anorexia. So she took very strict modern dance, and melded it with Indonesian and Polynesian dance, and created something. I began my practice of it as a child."

"You move beautifully."

There was something unaffected about his enjoyment of her, and Promise gave him a little treat. She allowed her control over the plastiskin to fade. It began to sparkle, to wash with color, visual poetry, an arc of rainbow stolen from a bright and rainy day.

Leslie squeezed her hand, laughing.

10

The escalator wound through the slanted side of the building, an enormous wall of glass opening out onto the night-lit menagerie which was Hong Kong.

Promise held her breath. Never in her life had she seen such a dense, immediate tangle of lights, and sounds, and shapes. Out there, in the highest population density on the face of the Earth, fifty million people lived and loved and fought and strove and died. And in the midst of all of this, there rose one of the greatest economic centers of the world, surpassed only by Tokyo, Berlin, and Monkoto, capital of the PanAfrican Republic.

"How is it for you here, Jamal?" she asked.

"It is . . . very vital." He seemed to be choosing his words carefully. "Mr. Wu is very kind to me."

"You are a student?"

"Yes. I study mathematics at the university, one part of the exchange program which SwarnaCom has established."

Promise felt a moment of discomfort. So . . . near Wu, quite near him, was at least one human who owed allegiance to Phillipe Swarna. She would have to be very, very careful.

They stepped off the escalator, and walked through a gorgeously appointed hallway. Hides decorated the walls, and with an intake of breath she realized that several of them were illegal. Endangered species. Zebra, lion, ohmigod—black leopard! And there were delicate carvings of bone, what kind of bone she did not know, although if pressed she would have guessed elephant.

The aroma of oolong tea drifted to her through the hall as she was guided to a series of low, comfortable seat cushions. She had, of course, smelled the tea before, but this was the first time that the scent was so . . . vital?

A rather plain Caucasian woman drifted into the room. She seemed a bit vague at first, and Promise wondered what it was that gave that impression. Then she realized that she was almost sleepwalking. A faint smile lifted the corners of her mouth.

She carried a silver tray inlaid with gold. Upon it steamed a pot of tea. She nodded languidly to Promise, and set the tea tray down. She folded her legs beneath her carefully, with the precision of some dreaming insect.

Promise recognized that look, but couldn't quite place it.

After a moment's pause, the woman turned two teacups over, and set one each before Promise and Leslie.

Leslie held her cup out, nestled between her delicate pink palms, rosebud of a face upturned sweetly.

The woman roused from her reverie for the first time. There was a very slight change of expression, and Promise would have called it jealousy, except that it was overlaid with something so serene and confident that Promise envied her.

The curtains at the far end of the room parted, and Wu entered.

Wu (the only name by which she knew him) was perhaps five foot three inches tall, and weighed about a hundred and ten pounds. He would have seemed emaciated, were it not for a feverish life force raging within him. Although generally half-lidded, at the moment his eyes were as bright as newly minted silver.

He was related to the Ortegas by marriage, joining his inherited opium empire with the South American cocaine trade. Those empires had grown more legitimate over the past decade, but the illicit roots remained.

The Ortega empire was still largely drug-based, but they had diversified into many, many other realms.

Wu had done even more, steadily converting his illegal capital into as many other ventures as he could. Ten years ago, Tomaso Ortega had murdered his brother Luis, using Aubry like a guided missile. Then Tomaso's treachery was exposed, triggering civil war.

Tomaso ended up in an asylum. Wu had, after the death of Margarete, inherited the world.

On the three occasions that Promise had met Wu, she had been impressed by the man's serenity. Now, not for the first time, she was tempted to call his demeanor not serenity but . . .

Impenetrability.

No matter who plotted what, and no matter how it went, Wu ended up on top. He had an uncanny knack for positioning himself to profit by any turn of fortune. Chance? Manipulation? Luck? Genius? A level of duplicitous strategy so sophisticated that he had, thus far, eluded detection? She wasn't sure.

The one thing that Promise depended upon was Wu's genuine interest in Aubry Knight.

He bowed to them, and raised one elegant eyebrow at the sight of Leslie.

"Your child—" He paused, rolling the word *child*

around in his mouth, tasting it like a sip of wine. "—is superb."

Promise inclined her head. Wu floated down beside his woman, and served them tea with a hand that was absolutely steady. When he moved, he was both totally absorbed in the movement and, in some bemused manner, separate from it, as if his attention was elsewhere. Promise recognized its similarity to the demeanor of the professional dancer. Such a woman performed at such intensity that the audience believed her thoughts and feelings to be one hundred percent with them. But there was some private part of the dancer that was always separate, always . . .

Safe.

That was it. No matter what Wu did, or where he was, or who was about, Wu was . . . safe.

"Drink, please," he said. She sipped. Heat flowed through the china like a radiant fluid.

"Now," he said. "I know that you have come for my aid. I do not know what it is that I can do for you. There may be a possibility. I make no commitment."

Promise nodded.

"Can you think of any debt which I owe you? Any reason that I should place myself or my affairs at risk to aid you?"

Promise could not.

Wu watched her. "Proceed."

"I need information, and perhaps help," Promise said. "If the situation is as bad as I think, there may not be anything that can be done. But I have to know." She lowered her voice. "I have to know."

Wu examined her, and then turned his attention to Leslie. "You take after your mother," he said. "In appearance. I have heard rumors about the quality of your movement."

"Rumors?" Leslie asked, very precisely, in perfect Cantonese.

Wu inclined his head, and barked out a few rapid-fire

phrases. Leslie answered in kind. Promise sat very still. She had not known that her strange child spoke Cantonese.

Wu sat back against his chair, and his expression was bemused. "Yes," he said finally. "It would give me a great deal of pleasure to see Leslie's movement."

Leslie rose from her seat. Her baby-blue jumpsuit was made of some stretch material that clung to the declivities of her body almost affectionately. She didn't warm up—Leslie never needed such preparations. Nor did she *need* to exercise, in any formal sense of the word. Leslie's world was a world of facts, of flows of information, and one of the ways in which she sorted that information was kinesthetic. So Leslie was in constant movement.

For Leslie, *breathing* was exercise.

"Would it be presumptuous to assume," Leslie said, "that you practice the Wu family form of t'ai chi ch'uan?"

Wu inclined his head. "Not in the slightest."

"Please excuse any imperfections in my movement," Leslie said gravely.

She brought her heels together, and began.

With a single slow, steep inhalation of breath, Leslie raised her hands, as if she were a flower greeting the sun. With perfect balance she floated to the left, floated to the right, arms expanding or contracting, face perfectly placid, and Promise tried to hide her astonishment. She knew that Leslie had practiced durga, and a modified form of Null-boxing, and whatever killing arts that the NewMen and Gorgons had taught him. But she had no idea that Leslie practiced t'ai chi.

She didn't know whether the movements were correct, but it seemed that every motion flowed from Leslie's waist, her legs always a little bent, but firmly planted on the ground.

Her hands were as expressive as a mime's. Hypnotic, lulling Promise into a deep and pervasive sense of calm, as if there were a magical quality about the whole performance. Leslie possessed the power to still the passage of the sun, to quiet the air around them. There was no sound in the room. Hong Kong's eternal traffic burr simply . . . evaporated.

Promise kept her peripheral vision on Wu. The little man's casual attentiveness had given way to true interest, and then rapt attention, and then excitement.

Suddenly he sprang to his feet, crying, "Wait! Wait! This is wrong. You move magnificently—truly a credit to your teacher—but the middle phrase is wrong."

Wu demonstrated. It was strange, to see that skeletal frame corkscrewing and unwinding with such savage power. Even given the state of total relaxation that Wu entered, it was impossible not to see the focus and power of his movement. His hands extended like the rays of the sun, and he was grace incarnate, the product of a lifetime of study. . . .

But . . .

There had been a spontaneity about Leslie's performance that Wu could not even approach. Her child projected the impression that the movements were being . . . *discovered* . . . ?

"Here," Wu said. "In this phrase, you have moved incorrectly. It proceeds from Snake Creeps Down, to Golden Cock Stands on One Leg, to Repulse the Monkey. You have performed the same movements, but see how your angles shift?"

Leslie watched. Politely, he said, "Please, sir. If I might. Would you extend a series of straight punches? Slowly, for the sake of the demonstration."

Mystified, Wu did so. Leslie evaded the slow punches easily, moving straight back as Wu had demonstrated.

"So," Wu smiled. "You understand now."

"Yes," Leslie said. "Now—would you do the same with me?"

"You may come at speed, if you wish."

"If I may," Leslie said politely, "I will move at three-fifths speed."

Wu's face darkened in displeasure. Then he looked at Promise, and for a moment she imagined that he was thinking, *This is the child of Aubry Knight. Perhaps. Just perhaps* . . .

"I am ready," he announced.

And Leslie flew at him. The acceleration was so great that it looked as if the world had suddenly tilted sideways, and Leslie had dropped off a wall. With Wu backpedaling frantically, the first punch missed, the second grazed Wu's brocaded robe, and the third one would have crushed his throat.

Wu stopped, and smiled. There was something in the older man's face that Promise had never seen there before: delight.

"Yes," Wu said. "And that was three-fifths speed!?"

"Yes," Leslie said. "However, the problem was that you moved straight back. The secret is in the angulation. Take a twenty-degree, twisting the hips as I did on every slide-step. . . ."

They tried the movement as Leslie suggested, and this time, although she came at Wu with even greater speed, intensity that narrowed her beautiful face until she resembled some sort of hunting animal, speed which left Promise breathless, able to think only . . .

Aubry . . .

Even moving backward, Wu was able to glide a quarter-inch out of range. At every moment his body was perfectly positioned for the counterstroke.

"It's simple," Leslie said. "I can always run forward faster than you can run backward. Your only hope is to move off line. By cutting the angle properly, you can even compensate for an opponent's superior speed."

"I see." For a full minute Wu seemed lost in thought, as if replaying memories in his head. "And which of your instructors taught you this?"

"Ibumi," Leslie said, "was most responsible for tactical education."

"And he taught the t'ai chi? Superb. I must know his instructor. And his instructor's instructor. There must have been a link to my ancestor's most secret teaching. A son, or daughter . . ."

Leslie blushed. "I . . . I hope not to offend you, but no one taught me t'ai chi. I learned it from a book."

"Ah. A . . . book. Not even a holo . . ." Wu returned to his seat. His face looked deeply troubled, his brows coming together, his eyes deeply socketed, as if he were contemplating far-off vistas. "Are you telling me that you achieved this insight on your own?"

Leslie blushed. Promise was delighted—she rarely saw Leslie losing even the slightest control. "Well, yes. Did I do something wrong?"

"Amazing," Wu said, to Promise this time. "Without formal instruction, with no live movement at all as guidance, your child not only performs a superb t'ai chi form, but has also, in all likelihood, corrected an error which has gone undetected for two hundred years."

Leslie stood very still.

Wu nodded his head. "Very well. Now, Leslie. I am very pleased by your demonstration. I would like to give you a present in return. What would you like?"

Leslie looked at her mother, and Promise nodded.

"I would like information about my father," Leslie said.

11

SEPTEMBER 9

Promise and Leslie were guests in Wu's home that day, and the next. Promise had trouble allowing herself to enjoy the amenities. Leslie, with her absolute focus, swam and played and read with endless energy.

On the afternoon of the second day, Wu returned to Promise, his face neutral. "I have news for you," he said. He sat next to her on the bed, and took her hand as if she were a fond daughter. "Do you know what an Alpha team is?"

"First team?"

"Yes. In military parlance, the Alpha and Beta are the first and second teams. Very good. But the terms in and of themselves have little meaning. Now. What I have discovered about Aubry is disturbing. He is considered both Alpha and 'bird dog.' In other words, Aubry is being backed up. But the backups consider him to be a distraction. Something to draw fire. And he is considered vulnerable to sacrifice."

Promise felt her emotions boiling just beneath the surface. "But . . . after the pardon? After the service to President Harris? How could they?"

"The president doesn't plan such operations. The man in charge is named Koskotas. General Koskotas. A venomous racist, a Swarnaphobe. A man capable of hating Aubry Knight for his skin color alone. Aubry used his connection with Harris to force his way into the operation. Koskotas would hate that. Therefore . . . Aubry is expendable."

He clapped his hands, and a map appeared in the air before them. "It seems that Aubry will be brought to this point, where he will be substituted for an athlete performing at the dedication of Swarnaville Spaceport. There may be a chance to make contact."

"Why? What is happening there?"

Wu's eyes narrowed. "I do not know. To tell you the truth, I now have more information than it is safe to possess. I am unsure of the game."

"When is he due there?"

"In five days, on the fourteenth."

Promise looked at the map, and nodded. "Do you have any word on the second matter?"

"Kanagawa? Yes. As Swarna's minister of public works, he not only handles contract bids from organizations such as your Scavengers, he also pockets a huge amount of bribe money. Two years ago, your bid was rejected for insufficient side profit."

"Damn."

"I have had dealings with this man. I believe that if . . . say, the Scavengers and Wu Industrial were to propose a joint venture, Kanagawa would be receptive. Would you be interested in such a proposal?"

Promise had to laugh. "Can you even sneeze without making a profit, Mr. Wu?"

He coughed modestly. "It is quite unlikely."

She extended her hand. "We'll work out the details later."

"Beware, Mrs. Knight—my lawyers know no mercy."

"A happy coincidence," she said. "How nice to know that we two can remain civil, while our minions go to war."

"It has ever been thus, Mrs. Knight." Wu's green eyes sparkled. He clapped his hands sharply. "Tea?"

12

SEPTEMBER 14

The flavor of festival was in the air.

Aubry, Bloodeagle, and Jenna slipped through the crowd, feeling almost invisible.

Truckloads of Zulu mercenaries roared past. They swaggered through the streets laughing and joking in Japanese. Alarm buzzers triggered in the back of Aubry's head.

"What is it that bothers you?" Jenna asked.

"Zulus are part of the inner circle. Bodyguards. Agents. Spies. Armed forces. They are Swarna's eyes and ears." He spoke urgently. "This is your last chance," he said. "There's still time for you—both of you—to leave. Once I take the next step, that opportunity disappears."

They remained motionless.

Aubry nodded and strode away, feeling, presciently, that within the next few hours one of them would be dead.

* * *

The tracer in Aubry's ulna hummed when he took the correct directional turns. It pulsed when he was within thirty feet of his goal, and then he saw the tent with its red flag flying, with the tiny river symbol upon it. He slipped into the tent, closing the flap behind him.

Within the tent, three women talked in low voices. When Aubry appeared, their conversation stopped. They wore facial veils. One of them waved a hand to the other two, and they rose. He saw nothing but had the distinct impression that he had just been scanned.

The lead woman came to him, and said in a low, throaty voice, "Can I help you?"

"I seek food," Aubry said. "I have had influenza."

"You should boil your water."

"I heard that the water was good."

She nodded sympathetically. "Don't believe everything that you hear. Come in."

He stepped through a flap in the back of the tent, and into another tent, and stopped breathing.

The man who lay there, in a coffin-sized box, was him. Not the old him, but the twin for his new face.

"What in the hell is going on?"

"He is . . . was . . . Faakud Azziz," a small, bald Caucasian man behind him said quietly. "And he was the favorite for the PanAfrican Nullboxing tournament."

"Who the hell are you?"

"My name is Jacobs. Azziz's manager."

With those words, Aubry heard voices talking in his head. Memories, images flashed into existence, as if Jacobs had opened a floodgate. *Samuel Jacobs. Expatriate American Nullboxing trainer.*

Agent of STYX.

"Is he . . . ?"

"Unconscious, and will be for twenty-four hours," Jacobs said coolly.

Two silent coveralled black men entered the tent and sealed the box. The word EQUIPMENT was stenciled on the sides. They lifted it up and carried it out.

"Where are they taking him?"

"You don't need to know," Jacobs said.

"Just like that?" Aubry's throat was terribly dry. "Why wasn't I told?"

"There was no need for you to know, Aubry," he said. "If you'd been captured it would have placed other aspects of the operation at risk. You were evaluated physically— you trained as a Nullboxer eight years ago. I guess they're betting that you can do the job."

"The . . . job?"

The little man snorted. "Where have you *been*? The climactic event of the festival will be a Nullboxing match between Azziz and Thu, the North African champion."

He remembered the man who lay sleeping in the box. In body, in musculature, they were nearly twins. For a moment he was stupefied, did not hear the babble outside the tent as it flowed around him, and filled him.

His body felt different.

He held a hand up in front of his face, and it seemed a stranger's hand, not his at all.

"Why?" he said at last.

"If you can win the tournament tonight, you will meet President Swarna. You will shake his hand. And then you will pass him *this*."

Jacobs turned over his hand. It seemed to be empty. Aubry looked closer, where Jacobs pointed. He saw a thin wedge of plastic, clear plastic, perhaps half an inch square.

Aubry's implanted cybernetics whispered to him.

Adhesive, both sides. Nanoassassins encapsulated on the top side and layer of polyacrylic to protect you. It will adhere to his skin, penetrate. Death within seventy-two hours, from apparent heart attack.

Aubry took the tiny chip from Jacobs and studied it.

Death, nestled in the palm of his hand.

Death for Phillipe Swarna. And life for him.

"And all I have to do to shake hands with Swarna?"

"And whip Thu, the sixth-toughest man in the world. By his rules."

Aubry looked at the invisible thing in his hand, then back at Jacobs. "Piece of cake," he said.

13

Aubry walked smoothly through the crowd, followed by
Jacobs. It parted for him, as if waves before the prow of a
great ship. He looked neither to left nor to right, but
seemed guided by some internal sensor.

The festival was a celebration of the opening of Swarnaville Spaceport, with clowns, and food stands, and acro-
bats, and dancers, as well as exhibits of every kind. The
Nullboxing was just another dimension of spectacle. There
was a part within Aubry that could not understand how
anyone could consider it "just another" spectacle.

Two men, locked in the most extraordinary combat,
risking life and limb for the entertainment of the people
below. He was a warrior, and Thu was a warrior. . . .

(Although there was a part within him that whispered
that, although Thu, a former world champion, was considered in decline, no living man could take a Nullboxer in
zero gravity without actual experience. The force vectors
were unique to the situation. It was simply impossible.)

He presented his passes at the appropriate checkpoints
and was probed by security apparatus. The guards nodded, with grudging acknowledgment, and once, just once,
he saw one of their eyes open wide, as if receiving a reading
he hadn't expected.

He didn't care. It didn't matter. He was approaching a
moment he had awaited for half his life. Today he was a
Nullboxer, and no matter what happened later, nothing
could ever take this moment away from him.

14

Jacobs closed the door behind them and stripped Aubry's robe away. He hovered solicitously. He peered into Aubry's eyes, and examined his body, poking and prodding, and making Os with his tightly pursed little mouth.

"You're looking great," he said, in pidgin Swahili. Then he lapsed into English, almost as if talking to himself.

"You look terrific. Better than ever, you know?" Aubry noticed that Jacobs's left eye was artificial. "You're gonna do it. You can take Thu, and when you do, you will get the laurel directly from the hand of the Man himself. I heard it on the grapevine. He's coming. He'll be here, regardless of what they say. Wouldn't miss it."

Jacobs smiled grimly, as if nurturing a private joke. "Wouldn't miss it."

Aubry lay back on the table, feeling his body, the machine that was his instrument, as it rested in preparation. There was a cool towel over his eyes, and as he inhaled and exhaled slowly, he felt its weight against the lids of his eyes.

And then he fell deeply asleep.

15

Two hours later, they came for him. There were three Japanese men, with a portable medical scanner, and the suits and other apparatus he would need for the coming journey. They checked all of his vital signs, measured them against his records, and found him in excellent health.

Deep within Aubry's body, a series of beacons performed flawlessly, providing a false "shadow" to the instruments, adjusting Aubry's medical signs so that they matched Azziz's profile.

Jacobs scowled. "My boy is in perfect condition! We don't need all of this crap. . . ."

The smiling, professional Japanese nodded. Aubry was hooked to a series of neurological testers. One at a time, they fired his voluntary muscle groups, observed the reactions, continued to make him leap and twitch until he was covered with a fine sheen of perspiration.

Then, they again tested his cardiovascular recovery rate, his blood pressure, skin conductivity, and a dozen other indicators, and nodded approvingly.

"Mr. Azziz," they said in halting Swahili. "You are even better conditioned than your last check. Good luck to you."

Aubry/Azziz nodded.

He was led down a long narrow hallway, to an elevator. The hallway hummed, as if enormous pressure were upon it from above, and Aubry knew himself to be beneath the shuttle dock.

He stepped into the cubicle, and it began to rise, humming. Aubry and Jacobs were silent, until the little man looked at him, and spoke, his eyes nervous. The little man was talking for the invisible cameras.

"This one is for all the marbles, kid. You get past Thu, and it's the international circuit, for sure."

Aubry felt excitement pulsing in his temples. A tiny voice whispered to him, boiling his blood:

How many years have you spent wanting this? Craving this? How many times have you dreamed of entering the cradle of the heavens, of taxing your body and mind against the best that the world has to offer? How many times?

And were there times when you awakened in the middle of the night, and went to exercise, to stretch, or to tax your heart and lungs because on some level you knew that this day would come? Is there a part of you which understood these things?

Are you prescient? Can you see the clouds even now above you, awaiting the steel and ceramic touch of this shuttle—

He was guided along a vertical ladder, and strapped into his seat by a technician, who slapped him on the shoulder.

There was another compartment on the other side of the wall. A compartment wherein rested, reclined, awaited . . .

Thu. Tradition dictated that the two combatants have no sight of each other until the moment of truth. So the bays were sealed and compartmentalized, each man brought in separately.

He turned, looking back over his shoulder, wondering what Thu was feeling at the moment.

Time passed, as the thousand system checks on the Japanese shuttle were completed. A digitalized monitor in front of him gave the countdown.

Twice, the flow of numbers retreated, as some small glitch was detected that required the attention of the technicians, and then the numbers continued to march onward, toward the inevitable.

In front of him, Jacobs turned around, and gave him a shaky thumbs-up.

"I'm always nervous about now," he said.

"You and me both."

The motors roared.

16

In the crowd over a mile away from the launch site, Jenna and Bloodeagle watched as the red and white cylinder of the Japanese Tsunami-style shuttle roared, clouds of white-hot sparks and gas erupting from the boosters. The ground shook as the vehicle climbed, slowly at first as if mounting some agonizingly steep ladder, then growling throatily and leaping into the clouds. An impossibly bright tongue of gas and flame seared Jenna's eyes.

"There isn't a damned thing we can do to help him now."

"Isn't *that* the truth."

Jenna smiled bleakly. "What say I buy you a brew, and we enjoy the show?"

Miles laughed and offered her his arm. She hesitated a bare moment, and then slipped her arm through his, and together they went in search of a beer vendor.

17

Aubry felt the acceleration right down to his bones. It was a driving, pulsing pressure that flattened his ears against his head, and the flesh of his cheeks against his skull. In a recessed cavity in front of him, a flat-screen monitor displayed the angle of the ground camera: a sleek ship rising on a tongue of flame, catapulted into the sky.

For a moment, he felt a sliver of fear. So much power! So much—

And then the fear faded, and something very like wonder took over. After the long thrust that carried him up and up, he slid finally into a state where, instead of the constant sensation of pressure, there was . . .

No pressure at all.

And, in fact, no weight.

If not for the constraints of his belt, he might have floated entirely free.

Jacobs glanced at him. "Wild, huh?" he croaked. "I never get used to it. How are you feeling?"

The little man was talking in idiomatic English instead of Swahili. Aubry dimly understood it, but something kept him from answering. The little man's face went through a spectrum of changes. Confusion, understanding, a flash of fear, and then adjustment.

"Sorry," he said in pidgin. "I forget sometime. How are you?"

"Ready," Aubry said.

He looked back over his shoulder. In the compartment behind them was Thu.

18

Aubry's muscles ached for movement. It had been seventy minutes since the launch, and they were gliding into docking position. There was nothing to see but the confined space of the capsule. There came a gentle, oh, so gentle bump as the ship docked, and then there was, somewhere distant, a series of clicks and hissing sounds. Pressure equalizing, perhaps.

A door opened to his side. A door in the side of the shuttle? It wasn't the one he had entered through, and he hadn't really noticed it.

A metal tunnel loomed beyond it.

Aubry unlocked his belts, and pushed himself very gently, afraid of the lack of gravity. He drifted away, disoriented, senses struggling to adjust. Dammit! Who was watching? Who might expect Faakud Azziz to have undergone extensive zero-g practice?

He pulled himself hand over hand along the passageway, his toes grazing the ground.

Above him, the Earth loomed like a swollen blue teat. A pressure-suited woman on a scooter of some sort hovered just outside the tunnel, videoing for a distant audience.

An audience. Aubry's audience. Again, something uneasy stirred within him, and he took a moment to study the hazy colors of the globe above him.

Wonder stirred within him, and his eyes, inexplicably, misted up. Why should it move him in such a manner? It was the same planet he had seen a thousand times, in globes and newsfax and holos. . . .

And yet . . . and yet . . .

Something within Aubry's chest felt as if it were going to

tear open. Tears welled in his eyes, ballooning without rolling down his face or breaking free. He blinked hard, and a tiny droplet of water floated free of his face, drifting like liquid smoke.

19

Aubry entered a red-tiled chamber. The door closed behind him. Sets of looped thongs were affixed to the walls. He went hand-over-hand until he could place his wrists in one set of loops, and allowed Jacobs to place his feet in another. The loops pulled taut, and his manager began to work on him, massaging.

It seemed . . . so long since he had allowed someone to stroke and touch his body like this. So long. And barriers compressed, even though they wouldn't disintegrate.

When Jacobs finished with him, he was gleaming with sweat, completely relaxed, and ready. And limp.

Jacobs leaned close, and began to speak.

"You know what this is for?"

Aubry nodded.

"This is for everything. Everything you have worked for all of your life . . ."

The door opened with a *shush*, and a stocky Japanese woman in overalls floated in.

"I'm Sawa. Referee. I know that you are familiar with the rules of Nullboxing, but it is still up to me to remind you of them. There will be no biting or scratching. No striking into the joints once the joints are pinned. When I say, 'Break,' you will break.

"The fight is scheduled for three ten-minute rounds. More than enough time to die—so be alert, and protect yourself at all times. Good luck to you." She pulled herself out of the way, exposing the transparent tunnel beyond. It was as wide as Aubry was tall. Plastic ropes attached to its walls ran the length of the tunnel.

A great sense of calm descended upon Aubry as he swam along the lines. The inside of the clear tube was bubbled with some sort of yielding substance. When he bumped against it, it gave spongily.

The entire thing rotated slowly. The Earth was to his side now, a blue-white frosted crystal, vast beyond his imaginings, hypnotic, calming. Concentrating on the task at hand made his temples pound.

The bubble was twelve meters across, and there was a second tunnel leading into it, from the far side, painted red. Aubry's side was painted blue. There were two robot cornermen, one blue and one red. Nipples extruded from the walls of those corners, through which the trainers could send a variety of recharging fluids.

He could see Thu now, swimming in from the far side. And in his heart, he saw the crowds far below.

This was only a local event. The cargo bays of both shuttles must have been filled with goods to be delivered to one of the space stations or the power satellites. No sporting event, by itself, could justify the cost of a launch. Invariably, it was combined with some industrial payload.

His muscles felt loose and springy. He perspired slightly and was grateful that the air temperature was about seventy degrees. It kept him warm, but not too warm. The exertions to come would take care of that.

The door ahead of him at the end of the tunnel opened to his slightest touch, and he entered.

Thu entered at the same moment. They swam about the bubble, making the customary three circumnavigations, and then settled, Aubry in the blue corner, and Thu in the red.

And then the referee entered the ring.

Sawa was compact and muscular, as she would have to be to cope with the action to come. She bounced around the bubble carefully, and tested walls and handholds.

Thu was a stocky Mongol, almost six and a half feet tall, and broad. Very thick through the body, he still moved like a ballerina.

His arms and legs seemed as flexible and coordinated as

a squid's. They reached out almost on their own, finding the little anchoring loops set into the walls, testing the grips, and turning him around and around. He scrambled about the inner surface of the bubble like a monkey.

Aubry pushed himself off, spinning, coming very close to Thu, who ignored him. Thu bounced off the far side and returned to his point of origin. He nodded with satisfaction, and then came to a rest.

"*Ladies and gentlemen,*" the entire globe vibrated in Arabic. "*We present, at the blue station, the regional champion of the PanAfrican Republic, Faakud 'Suliman the Conqueror' Azziz!*

"*And in the red corner, former world champion, Olympic Gold Medalist in Boxing, Tae Kwon Do and Judo, presently reigning North American champion—Pham Thai Thu!*"

Aubry nodded, his eyes riveted on Thu. He had watched the man for three minutes now, looking for a flaw in his psychological or physical conditioning. So far, zip.

Thu looked back at him with the steady, neutral eyes of a machine.

The corded muscle in the man's arms flexed impressively. His red spandex leotard clung to every muscle of his perfectly conditioned torso.

Aubry pushed himself out toward the center of the bubble. Without a moment's hesitation, Thu did the same thing.

They floated out toward each other, each on a glide path that minimized tumbling. Neither was fool enough to present his back to a potentially lethal opponent. Their arms were splayed like a pair of cats'. Aubry felt his body cant slightly to the side, presenting Thu with a shoulder.

Shit! That was a gravity move, a move that worked when rapid changes of balance and posture were possible. Tactical advantage to Thu! He tried to scrunch himself into a ball, to increase the speed of his revolution, but Thu was on him in a flash, spun him, and now was coming in behind him. Legs as solid as pillars clamped around his waist, and began to squeeze.

Linked together, they both spun against the wall, and

Aubry gripped for one of the handholds, and found it. He torqued his body powerfully, and hammered Thu against the wall. The wall was too soft to do any damage, or even drive the wind from Thu's lungs, but as he rebounded, Aubry bent back and caught him in the ribs with an elbow.

They broke, drifting toward the sides, spinning. Hands found handles and increased the torque. From the corner of his eye, Aubry saw Sawa flash to the side with uncanny agility, avoiding the thrashing bodies.

Thu caught his wrist, and hammered a powerful leg up into his ribs.

Aubry twisted away, backpedaling, fighting panic. He strove to regain some sense of control, or at least *participation*. Thu was dictating the pace of the fight, and unless Aubry could steal it back, he was screwed. Smelling blood, Thu swarmed over him, seemingly everywhere at once.

Aubry's world was dark with confusion and pain. All of his skill was evaporating. His strength, gone. His endurance, caught in his chest like a bird struggling to escape the nest.

Gone.

Thu struck again, directly under the chin, and the world exploded into red. He tasted blood against his mouthpiece. Thoughts came in fragments, reflexes refusing to transfer from brain to limbs. Thu was a machine, coming at him from every conceivable angle, utterly without mercy.

Aubry knew terror. A childlike cry of anguish and—

(Daddy. I'm afraid, Daddy—)

(Shhhh. Daddy's here. And no one's going to hurt you.)

And there was another blow, and then Thu was behind him, torquing him around. Aubry knew that he was being maneuvered into position for a merciless hold, and he knew that he was supposed to tense, to spin.

But he did neither. Instead, there came a moment of calm.

Aubry felt as if he were gazing into a furnace. And deep within the furnace was a flame so hot that it consumed identity. In that moment, Aubry couldn't have remembered his own name.

Thu grunted, forcing Aubry's arm into a lock. The man was strong! The leverage he had was irresistible, and muscular fatigue should force the matter to a conclusion in seconds.

Then Aubry relaxed. Thu slid his arm in deeper, solidifying the hold—

But for the moment when Thu made that adjustment, the hold was no longer absolute. As he slipped to a more secure position, he created an instant of instability. Suddenly there was give in it. Aubry wiggled to a position where he could reach around, reach back and grasp Thu in a makeshift reverse headlock.

It shouldn't have been possible. There shouldn't have been enough give in that hold to reach around like that. For a man of Aubry's muscle mass to have that level of flexibility was almost *obscene.* It surprised Aubry—he had never done such a thing, and had had no idea that he possessed that much give in his shoulder joint. Aubry's thumb and fingers gripped at Thu's larynx and his opponent gagged reflexively. Aubry's arm slipped out of Thu's grip.

Thu turned into a buzzsaw, striking and striking, hammering with fists and elbows as Aubry strove to reverse the hold. They were tumbling now, in full engagement. Blood misted the bubble's air as elbows and knees smashed into lips and scalps, and fingers fought for purchase.

Nothing human could maintain that intensity. For Aubry and Thu, the pace was like sprinting uphill, carrying each other piggyback all the way. But for Aubry there was no pain, no exhaustion. The fatigue toxins flooding his body were simply overriden by a mind that screamed to go *on* and *on* and *on,* that raged at him, saying that a moment's weakness would cost the lives of everything he loved. Thu's blows split his lips, split his eyelid. Dislodged two of his teeth. Ripped the scalp above his left ear and fractured a rib. And every nerve in Aubry's body screamed that he was careening into the abyss.

I'm ready to die, you bastard. And I'm taking you with me.

Aubry saw the fear, naked and consuming, in Thu's

eyes. Thu, his face masked with blood, tried to turn away, strove to break away from this crimsoned, battered demon who seemed to have forgotten that this was a sporting event, who had turned it into something primal and absolute. And as he turned Aubry's arm whipped across his neck and locked in with a blood and nerve strangle that was unbreakable.

Unconsciousness followed swiftly and mercifully.

20

An armada of reporters surrounded Aubry as he stepped out of the shuttle. They trailed him from the gantry to the waiting skimmer, and they followed him as he sailed back in toward the great carnival.

How did it feel to beat an ex-champion? Would he go on to try to get a match with the current champ? Why had he suddenly changed his fighting style? Where had he learned those moves, and why hadn't he ever used them before? Curiosity burned in their eyes, and Aubry found his mouth speaking a language that he barely understood, saying things he didn't believe in, but that seemed to satisfy them. And that was all he cared about.

Jacobs stripped him out of his combat uniform and helped him on with his street clothes. Adrenaline still flamed in his blood. He had done it! He had finally ridden the big rocket, had done his thing up in the stars. . . .

It would have been the proudest moment of his life, save for the realization of what lay ahead. Save for the knowledge that it had all been a sham, and that his victory was in the service of murder.

Cold-blooded murder.

(But the man you will kill tried to kill you. . . .)

And where had he heard that before? Was it eight years before that he had escaped from Death Valley Maximum Security Prison, swearing to kill Luis Ortega? And how long after that had he realized the entire thing had been orchestrated, that he had been used as guided muscle?

And yet . . . he *had* killed this man's son. He *had* disrupted Swarna's vengeance. And it was reasonable, perhaps even inevitable that, although they lived on opposite sides of the planet, one of them would have to kill the other.

Mira was dead. Her death should be avenged. And his family had been threatened.

The aircade approached the fair's central plaza. His manager had finished all last-minute preparations. Aubry felt something pressed into his right palm. It was just a moment of pressure, but Aubry knew what it was, what it would be: a machine so thin as to be almost invisible. A few millimeters of clear plastic.

Aubry stepped down out of the vehicle, and a security man came up smiling. The man was half Japanese and half Zulu, a strange mixture that created a shorter, muscular man with epicanthic folds and a disconcerting habit of looking through you.

His hand was extended. "You were superb," he said. His hand remained suspended in air, awaiting Aubry's shake. His smile faltered.

Shit.

The Afjap's fingers began to curl, the gesture of greeting withering.

Aubry bowed stiffly and said, *"Hai."*

The Afjap grinned. "This way, please."

Aubry turned to look back over his shoulder. Jacobs was swallowed in the crowd as Aubry was hustled forward. A security shield surrounded him, protected him. Trapped him. The mood of the crowd was expectant and almost hushed. The other athletes were parading up, along with musicians, and poets. It had been a day to remember, the Nullboxing match merely another of its events.

Ahead of him was the platform. Narrowing his eyes, he distinguished a shimmering distortion field. And behind it was Phillipe Swarna.

Aubry looked at the faces around him. They weren't

watching the parade of notables, the parade of athletes, poets, and dancers who moved up to receive the PanAfrican ribbon. They were watching Swarna himself, and in their faces lived myriad emotions.

Who was this man? Was he a messiah? A madman? A Hitler? A Gandhi?

In every face there was a different answer, a different dizzying perspective.

Aubry passed through a gateway—

21

One of the huge silver skimmers parked at the edge of the festival coordinated the security arrangements for Phillipe Swarna. One of the protection systems was new, and unknown to the inner circles of STYX. It was a long-range genetic deep scan, probing every human being who approached the presidential platform. Each genetic code was compared to computer records filed in advance.

As Aubry approached the platform, a red Alert light flashed in the skimmer, and the computer screen suddenly read MISMATCH, and every head in the control room turned, suddenly alert.

The slender Zulu Afjap at the control said: "What in the *hell*?" her voice near panic.

And then the computer added a rider: *"Security override. Regulation 7503."*

There was a tangible sensation of tension in the room. One of the young women turned to her supervisor, a pureblooded Japanese man in his fifties. "What does *that* mean?"

His voice was very calm. "It means," he said, "that there are security procedures of which you need not be aware. Do your job." And he smiled. This man Azziz was nothing to worry about. In fact, quite the opposite.

22

The announcements were being broadcast simultaneously in Swahili, Japanese, English, and French.

This close to New Nippon the crowd was disconcertingly mixed, thick with Afjaps. Never in his life had Aubry seen so many human beings—and more to the point, so many human beings of his own color.

It was a new sensation, and as he moved forward, and saw that many of them were cheering for him, for the feat of arms that they had just witnessed, something happened within him.

He looked down at his own skin color, and then up again at the people surrounding him. It seemed as if he were moving in slow motion. Flags waved in the air, hands saluted with the same holovid artificiality. A forest of dusky arms surrounded him. Countless faces with block-toothed smiles, glittering with pride and cheering, cheering.

Then he saw the platform ahead, where stood the most famous black African who ever lived. A man of power and genius and protean evil.

And on the word of men paler than either of them, Aubry was prepared to murder Swarna. Had striven to murder him. Had dedicated his life, and quite likely his death, to the cause of murder.

Hadn't there been enough death? And what would replace this man? Even if he was evil, wouldn't his death merely destabilize the continent further?

And what then?

But then the line moved forward again, and he was in the final approach.

23

Twelve miles away, nestled in the woods beyond the town, lay two men. They utilized a more traditional form of camouflage, but it was completely adequate to the job. They were actually burrowed into the ground.

Red One turned to Red Two, and said, "I wonder how it feels to be a walking bomb?" He laughed.

"Well, considering the size of the capsules, I doubt Knight feels anything at all."

"Think we'll get to trigger it?"

"Don't know. The minidot is in position. If he executes his instructions, he could be home in three days. If he blows it . . . we blow him."

Red Two smiled. He was watching a satellite television hookup of the entire event. Some of the cameras were just cameras. Others peered deeper, security scans smuggled into the area by forces sympathetic to American interests. And these scans were sensitive to the specific optics of the implants. The images were directly uplinked to the satellites above, and then sent back down again to the STYX operatives. This gave them an excellent view of the security shields, and of Aubry Knight.

"Good fight, though," he said.

24

In Hong Kong, one of Wu's men interrupted him in the midst of a delicate trade negotiation, leaned close, and said softly, "The woman, Promise, says that you should see channel thirty-three-B."

Wu nodded, offered an apology to his Filipino guest,

and whispered a request into his desk console. A screen appeared. It was a news flash, a delayed broadcast from Swarnaville.

A Nullboxing match. Interesting, but why urgent? The action became brutal, and suddenly his eyes widened. What he witnessed was not sporting technique. It was intended for life-and-death only, and the only human being capable of executing it was a man named Aubry Knight.

He rose and excused himself. "I am willing to fulfill the contract on the basis of the most recent offer," he said.

The Filipino's eyes widened. "Why . . . you are being most gracious," he said. Something had just happened, he realized, making Wu divide his attention. Otherwise he would never had surrendered such a favorable position.

Something had just happened, clarifying Aubry Knight's situation. This minor diversion with the Filipino was of no further interest to Wu. It might have been interesting to pry an additional few tens of thousands of dollars out of the mineral lease. But Wu, and only Wu, already knew that due to lack of water access, the piece of land would be worthless in two years. Twelve million dollars was profit enough for a single day.

It was time for him to rejoin Promise.

25

The line winding behind the bandstand had almost reached the presidential platform. Aubry's heart thundered in his chest. What was right? What was wrong?

And then there was no further time for talk. Or thought. He mounted the steps, only three people ahead of him. One of the security men smiled thinly at him. An Afjap. Big man, maybe thirty-five years old. Maybe one-eighth black. A thin scar ran down the left side of his face. His eyes were as penetrating as stainless-steel skewers.

Sinichi Tanaka. The rest of Tanaka's dossier flashed

into Aubry's mind instantly. This man was Swarna's chief of security, of Japanese and Ibandi blood. A bridge to the Yakuza Divine Blossom *keiretsu*. This Afjap would sacrifice his own life if necessary, to save his primary. To Tanaka, Aubry was a monster, a coward, a masked assassin, striking from darkness.

Aubry was in sight of Swarna now. In another moment they would be face-to-face.

Once, Swarna must have been tall. Not so broad as Aubry, but a huge man nevertheless. His face was heavily lined, hard years etched upon them.

There was an avuncular feeling about him. His full lips laughed easily as he handed out scrolls with his left hand and dealt hard, flat handshakes with his right.

Aubry's heartbeat accelerated. This was the moment. The crowd, and the banners, and the cameras and everything else shrank to nothing.

And then he was next in line.

The two men faced each other, and Aubry felt himself falling into the depths of those eyes. They had seen so much, and done so much, and the weight of a monster mind was behind them.

How could he stand calm when such eyes bore into him? It was like entering twin tunnels, and how could a man enter into two tunnels in a single instant? Only by becoming two men. Aubry felt that happening, felt himself divide almost helplessly beneath the scrutiny of those terrible eyes.

Falling. Falling.

There was something he was supposed to say at this instant. Something that he was supposed to do.

In another world, another life, could this man have been his friend? Swarna had conquered an empire. Had united a continent. Had stood against all enemies, and all odds, and survived.

Survived for . . . God, how many years? How long had Swarna been alone?

Men had tried to destroy Aubry. They had tried to destroy this man, Phillipe Swarna. And now one had been

aimed at the other. But how did he know? How could anyone ever really know the truth?

All Aubry knew was that at this moment, he faced a
man he longed to question, longed to know, and there was
no time for that. No time for anything.

And Swarna, with a wisdom savage and old, seemed to
understand some of what Aubry had been through, and
what he thought.

"You fought well." His was an old man's voice, belying
the burning eyes. "And now there are larger things for
you, yes?"

"Yes," Aubry whispered hoarsely. The scroll was held
out to him in Swarna's left hand. Aubry watched, hypnotized, as Swarna's right hand rose ponderously. Aubry
watched his own hand rise as if it belonged to a stranger.

He clasped palms with Phillipe Swarna.

The cement on the front of the microdot adhered to
Swarna's palm. His sweat and body heat began to dissolve
the thin layer of organic plastic holding back the nanoassassins.

Was that a spark of recognition? Realization? Was there
something in Swarna's eyes that remained unchanging as
something deeper *shifted*, as some awareness sparked into
existence?

Swarna released Aubry's hand. Aubry stepped off the
platform and looked back over his shoulder at the man,
hoping that Swarna would turn his head and look at him.

What did he want? Benediction? Absolution? Forgive-
ness?

What have I done?

Part of him wanted to scream with rage, with pain, with
shame. Part of him was joyous. He had done it! He had
killed the bastard who had killed Mira. . . .

Hadn't he?

Oh, God . . .

Jacobs was waiting for him, tried to hustle him away
through the crowd. Aubry looked back.

Swarna was already handing a scroll to the next recipi-
ent, an artist. Tanaka was looking at Aubry, an embryonic

question gestating behind his eyes. His face remained neutral.

But those *eyes* . . .

Jacobs's small thick fingers tugged at his arm and spirited him away through the crowd. A few people slapped him on the back. Behind him, Swarna continued to pass out scrolls.

As they returned to the tents, no one noticed when two people, a man and a woman, fell into step behind them.

The first bits of the microdot had broken free. They were molecule-sized semisentient machines, nanotech free radicals, and their eventual task was the commandeering of Swarna's central nervous system. But first they began to scavenge. They had to acquire the raw material necessary to multiply into the billions. *Then* they would attack. Suddenly. Massively.

26

In the changing tent, Jenna shucked Aubry out of his clothes. "We've got to get the hell out of here. How long did you say that you've got?"

"They sa-said that the stuff will take effect within s-seventy-two hours, giving me t-time to get the hell out." Aubry quaked, his body on the thin edge of adrenal overload.

Bloodeagle nodded. "Then let's assume that the window is actually a tenth as long. And that the exit hole they have for you is corrupt."

"I'm s-supposed to take a Jeep waiting for me on the west side of the fairgrounds. Drive s-south to a little farming village, and make c-contact with a private air shuttle. . . ."

"Forget it."

"W-why?"

"Because they'll be in diplomatic communication with Swarna's successor."

"S-so?" Bloodeagle opened a small suitcase.

"All right—lay down."

"You've been t-trying to get me to do that for years."

"Don't flatter yourself." Bloodeagle set up a miniature disrupter. It hummed, broadcasting electronic chaff. Aubry lay down, and the NewMan went to work with a hand-held scanner.

Electronics. Bloodeagle saw the false shadow outline equipment, and the translators hooked into the language centers of Aubry's brain. There was nothing that he recognized as dangerous, except . . .

He tensed. "I've got a tracer here. I've got to disable it *fast.*"

Bloodeagle took out a laser scalpel and focused the beam onto Aubry's leg. Aubry's world dissolved into a red flash, bordered by white. There was a moment of searing pain, as the beam burned through Aubry's leg, through the muscles, and into the capsule.

"It *burns.* . . ."

"No time for anesthetic, dammit. Just hold on . . . got it."

The tracer fuzzed out. The whining noise died. Bloodeagle sat down heavily, tanned face pale. "Now . . . listen, Aubry. When the shit hits the fan, America's going to scream innocent. That's why STYX gave Harris his way. You're a civilian, and black—and Koskotas is a racist bastard. They probably had six different scenarios running, including entering a ringer in the Swarnaville Sport and Arts Jamboree. Your Nullboxing background made you perfect. Not just because you would be willing to go in and do it, but because they could claim that you had a motive to assassinate Swarna that had nothing to do with American policy. But there is classified shadow-imaging tech implanted in your femur.

"If you are caught, analysis of the imaging gear will prove that you were given high-level assistance. This would give Swarna's successor leverage—he won't make

favorable deals with America. It'll push PanAfrica further
toward Japan."

Jenna and Jacobs went to work, sealing the wound with
synthetic skin, numbing the tissues, bandaging. Aubry
hissed with pain, then steadied himself.

"Who . . . oh *shit*! Who would that successor be?"

"No idea. Ibumi was his only acknowledged child.
Swarna's office is a political/economic creation, and Pan-
Africa might go belly-up. Japan will back *someone*, probably Kanagawa. Kanagawa is minister of public works, and
a Yakuza boss to boot. America will back someone—
probably De Thours, the Dutchman. Minister of finance."

"Not a black African?" Aubry said quietly.

"Are you kidding?"

"What about Tanaka?"

Bloodeagle shrugged. "No political ambitions that I
know. His obligation is to Swarna—but he belongs to the
Yakuza. He will probably back Kanagawa." He tapped
Aubry's leg. "For America to successfully back the Dutchman, she has to claim innocence. Therefore, if there's any
risk of your being caught, you'll be terminated. I can block
the signal. I pulsed the bomb's processor, scrambled the
codes. I can do that—once. It's a built-in safety precau-
tion. Prevents an enemy from triggering destruct codes—
for about two days. That's how long it will take them to
run through all the codes, at the rate of a thousand per
second—that's the fastest the receiver will take them.

"But we've got to get the bomb out by then. Otherwise,
the explosives will trigger, and there isn't a damned thing
that I can do about it."

Aubry sat up, and winced. He tested his leg, cursed, then
said resignedly, "Better than being dead. I guess. Thanks,
Miles."

"There's only one thanks I want. Getting out of here
alive. Let's go."

The three of them shook hands with Jacobs. Aubry
looked at the little man. "Why did you do it? Wasn't Azziz
your fighter?"

Jacobs shook his head. "I'm hired help. Azziz's manager

had an . . . accident. I'm a backup. Nullboxing's a rough game over here—controlled by the government. Two of my guys died matched against state-bred boxers." His smile was small, weary. "I just wanted to get my own back."

"You have a way out?"

He tapped his chest. "Bad heart. Maybe a year left. No money to get a new one."

Aubry took his hands. "But can you get to America?"

"Maybe. There are ways. But why bother? Here, there. Now, later . . . what's the difference?"

Aubry squeezed his hands until Jacobs's eyes popped with pain. "Because if you get there, find the Scavengers. Talk to Promise Cotonou. Tell her what you did for me. They'll get you a new heart."

Jacobs looked into Aubry's surgically altered face, and after a long breath, he nodded. "The Scavengers. I've heard of them. Then you must be . . . ?"

Aubry nodded.

"Shit. You would have been great, kid."

Aubry gave him a brief, firm hug—and then turned and left with Bloodeagle and Jenna.

Jacobs watched the tent flap flutter behind them. He was alone now. Soon, no place on this continent would be safe for him. But Jacobs had a soft, speculative look on his face, and a feeling in his tired heart that he hadn't had for years.

Hope.

The microdot had dissolved. The nanoassassins had been busy, attacking bones, stealing material to build the generations to come. There was an artificial cyst the size of a pinhead lodged near Swarna's right ear, near what physiologists refer to as the tenth, pneumogastric, or vagus nerve. There, behind a biologically neutral membrane, they massed for the attack.

So far, Swarna felt nothing.

* * *

Their Jeep was twenty miles from the border of the Central African Republic. From there to Daglia was the work of a few hours, and Daglia was large enough, and international enough, to hide them.

"The tracer is blocked. Jeep is clean," Jenna said. Her long brown arms were sure on the wheel. "And canopied. Unless they knew where to look for us they couldn't pick us up with their best satellite. We're just another Jeep. On the other hand . . ."

Within Swarna's body were countless scouting nanobots, searching for microtumors, weak arterial walls, damaged nerve cells. They constantly repaired, rebuilt, and remained alert to the possibility of invasion.

The vagus nerves are uniquely important to the human body. They emerge from the cranium as a flat cord of woven filaments, carrying messages to the organs of voice and respiration, and the stomach and heart as well. They are, therefore, an ideal target.

The cyst fluttered, and the first few hundreds of nano-assassins crept out into Swarna's body. They were scouts, designed to appear innocuous, disguised as friendly nano-bots, exchanging proper protocols until the moment that they would become instruments of destruction.

But their vast numbers guaranteed some minute percentage of errors in duplication. And the inevitable finally happened.

Near the posterior pulmonary branch of the pneu-mogastric, one of the monitoring nanobots nosed against an invader. It sent a microsecond recognition signal checking for program corruption in its brother . . .

And received static in return.

Swarna's monitor nanobot sent out an alarm. There were dangerous rogue or alien nanobots and an unidentified, near-critical biomass near the vagus nerves.

The monitors were free-radical destroyers, were cancer-cell destroyers, but were tied in with central processing to the extent that they could send back information for that processor to evaluate.

And it did send in a report.

Mere seconds after it did the biomass broke open, and billions of killer cells spread into Swarna's system, in an action both precipitous and deadly.

Swarna's biomonitor sounded an earsplitting alert.

Reflexively, Tanaka said, "Code two-two," and the pilot immediately changed his heading. Then Tanaka was with Swarna, checking his vital signs with a hand-held monitor.

"Nothing . . ." he said, suspicious.

Phillipe Swarna sat back into the seat of the transport plane, and a puzzled expression spread over his face. He clapped a large palm over his stomach.

"It is odd," he said quietly. "I feel . . ."

Kanagawa, minister of public works, leaned forward. "Are you certain there is something wrong? A little indigestion . . . ?"

Tanaka glared murderously.

"I feel . . ." Swarna groped for words. Suddenly he sucked in air massively, and couldn't exhale it. His fingers clawed at his heart, and his face swelled, purpling. His eyes rolled back up in his head, and suddenly, as if with some masterful effort of will Swarna had managed to retake momentary control of his breathing, he *screamed.* . . .

The nanoassassins operated in three main groups. One attacked and took control of the vagus nerves, one sped for the spinal column, and one for the brain itself.

In all cases, they began broadcasting mutinous signals, and triggering every pain response in Swarna's body.

Die, they said.

Or that is what they would have done.

But the biomonitor that kept Phillipe Swarna alive was alert to the possibility of such an invasion. One of the invading cells was captured by an artificial phagocyte, and taken to a capsule the size of half an aspirin for analysis. The threat was perceived almost instantly, and reserve phagocytes were releasing into Swarna's system.

The battle was joined.

27

Wu paced back and forth, a worried expression creasing his face.

Promise tried to keep the fear from her voice. "Do you have an opinion about what you saw?"

Leslie was watching the screen without comment.

"Yes," Wu said. "It was Aubry, disguised to get him close to Swarna. He made physical contact. Something happened in that moment. There is no other reason for going through such an elaborate deception. But why . . . ?"

Leslie's eyes were vast. "Reference. NewMan Nations. Subheading, Assassination. There is a technology, not yet perfected, called microdots. Poisons and even tracer apparatus can be passed from one body to another, through direct contact. I suggest that some type of timed, coded assassination device changed hands. Swarna is walking but dead."

Promise thought about that. It was sensible, and, in fact, it made more sense than Aubry taking a shot, or planting a bomb, or even, for that matter, trying to attack Swarna directly. Thank the Goddess, *that* would have been a farce.

"I suppose if it had to happen," she said, "that is the best way."

"Yes," Leslie said. His eyes were far away. "But there is something wrong. I can't scope it. Ah. He has limited time to get out of the PanAfrican Republic. *Very* limited. Swarna is protected by the best security in the world. They will detect the problem, and move swiftly. Everything will mobilize against him."

Promise turned to look at Wu. "What can we do to help?"

"You can be there, in Swarnaville. Much construction is being conducted in that region. From there, you can move most quickly. From there, it just might be possible to do something positive. The arrangements with Kanagawa have been made. You and I can complete our negotiations later, in good faith."

Promise extended her hand. "You are a friend," she said. "One of the best that we have."

"Nonsense," Wu said politely. "Aubry Knight amuses me, and always has. The world would be less interesting without him. And you. And your child, Mrs. Knight. Please, do what you must, and then return to us safely."

His thin dry hand was warm in hers. Impulsively, she leaned down and kissed his left cheek. He smelled like cinnamon.

28

Immam Igrandi, border guard at the Swarna Bridge between PanAfrica and the CAR, squinted his eyes. A storm was blowing from the east, bringing with it countless flecks of sand and gravel and dust, a microscopic speck of which had lodged near his left pupil.

This was not good. The bridge was crowded. It seemed that everyone in the world had come south for the day and now, having seen the living legend himself, was returning to the Central African Republic, where they belonged.

Immam was twenty-two, and liked his job immensely (he had inherited it from his father). The money provided his family with a house and good food and comforts, and Immam with an Afjap mistress who gladly performed acts his own wife would castrate him for suggesting.

He was thinking about his mistress, a thin, big-titted slow-moving delicacy named Nikomo, when the fleck flew into his eye. *The gods are watching you today, Immam,* he clucked, rubbing the sore orb. *Maybe it's true. Maybe only white people and monkeys are supposed to fuck like* that. He wasn't to be relieved for another hour, and the six lanes of

traffic heading north wouldn't wait for any of the glass-
boothed border guards to head to the lavatory. Hell, he
had peed in a bucket more than once, and he could
damned well suffer through a bit of grit.

He waved a few cars through, after giving them a per-
functory scanning. His laxity was understandable: after
all, normal immigration pressure was in the opposite direction. Anyone who wanted to leave the paradise of
PanAfrica was welcome. Assuming, of course, that they
carried nothing of value to Phillipe Swarna.

But still, Immam had the task of recording every face
that passed, and he took that obligation seriously.
Through a haze of pain, he saw a face that he recognized,
and he suddenly forgot the throbbing eye. He stepped out
of his booth, shielding his face from the wind. He saluted
the occupants of the Jeep snappily. "Azziz, nex' champion
of world!" Immam said between chipped and golden teeth.

Aubry Knight smiled, and started to speak, and felt
something shift in the back of his head, and suddenly he
was speaking in Swahili. "Thank you, my friend. Blessings
to you and your family." Jenna and Bloodeagle regarded
him with amusement.

"My brother-in-law," she said. "The polyglot."

Immam waved them through, cheering, fingers inter-
laced, hands raised above his head in the Victory sign.

And no one, not even Immam, noticed that an automatic camera had recorded every face in the Jeep.

29

DAGLIA, CENTRAL AFRICAN REPUBLIC

Compared to Ma'habre, the town of Daglia seemed almost
somnambulant. It still revealed more Arab than European
influence, and few of the buildings along the twisting, narrow streets were more than three stories tall.

Daglia was crowded but not unclean, a town of perhaps seven hundred thousand souls. Aubry hoped that he could lose himself here for a few hours, and that his subsequent escape would be a possibility.

But for now . . .

They pulled up at a hotel, its bright neon sign speaking in a language Aubry knew, but had never learned. The implanted translator was disorienting as hell, and he wondered if it was possible to get used to it.

He imagined so. He was beginning to believe you could get used to anything.

30

Phillipe Swarna's skimmer crossed the twenty-two hundred miles between Swarnaville and Caernarvon in just under three hours. Long before the skimmer entered protected airspace, the autodocs had taken complete control of Phillipe Swarna's body. Twelve miles out from the castle, the first of the electronic challenges blipped off their computer, as the security systems decided whether or not to blow them from the sky.

At the ten-mile mark they passed above one of the protected townships, the encampments of workers who served the Menagerie—it took ten thousand men and women, working full time, to service the Menagerie and Phillipe Swarna's palace. That number didn't include Swarna's airborne battalions, quartered less than twenty miles from his inner sanctum.

The skimmer screamed through the air above the inner preserve, heading for an emergency landing at the northeast port. By the time it touched down, the entire life-support system in the skimmer was running on independent batteries. A swarm of technicians detached the steel-lined life-support cot, hooking it to the maglev medic tram and floating it into the main facility.

Despite a flood of countermeasures, the nanoassassin synthetic viruses were erupting all over Swarna's tortured body, disseminated in pods that spread widely in non-irritating sheaths before making a damaging presence known.

Tanaka watched them wheel his primary away, knowing that there was nothing he could do anymore. One of the doctors, a native of Kyoto named Saito, remained behind in the courtyard, and offered Tanaka a cigarette. Then Saito remembered who he was dealing with, and fumbled it away.

"Is there anything you can tell me that didn't come across the air?"

"One minute he was talking, the next . . ." Tanaka shrugged his big shoulders. "The next he was foaming and dying. I've never seen anything like it."

"He's really dead right now," Saito said. "The life-support systems keep his brain oxygenated. The trick is to rebuild faster than those damned little machines can tear him apart."

"What are his chances?" Tanaka asked. His face was unreadable.

"I wish I knew." Saito blew a feather of smoke out into the air. With the fall of evening, it was beginning to chill. The wind shifted, driving smoke and a slight saurian stench back in his face.

"I hate this place," Saito said matter-of-factly. Tanaka didn't react.

"I hate this country," Saito went on.

He watched Tanaka, who stood looking out across the concrete pad, to Caernarvon's white outer walls—thirteen feet thick and forty feet high. They were topped with electrified wire, a touch King Edward would have appreciated. Beyond its rebuilt walls was the moat, thirty feet wide at its narrowest point, and fifty at its widest. Beyond that—the Garden, and the Menagerie, and creatures which should have been dead fifty million years before.

"I don't care," Tanaka said. "I don't care that you say these things. He is my primary."

"Do you really care about that man? Or is it just a job?"

"I gave my word. I gave my honor," Tanaka said. "I will do everything in my power to protect him. Not for him. For me. Because honor is all that a man has. Just as you, Saito, will do all in your power to save him. Because a man without honor has nothing. Not even life itself." He looked Saito squarely in the eye, and Saito felt himself driven back, as if by a white-hot physical force. "Do you understand?"

"Ah . . ."

"I do not love him, although I have come to love this country. This land. It . . . touches me. But I know that I will do my best. And that all who are involved in this . . . tragedy will do their best. For me. And for themselves. And their families." He stepped even closer to Saito, until the doctor could see the pores on Tanaka's nose, and the network of tiny veins in his black eyes. "Do you understand?"

"Yes. Yes, Tanaka-san." Saito bowed and dropped the cigarette from his mouth, grinding it underfoot. He gave Tanaka a last, hurried bow, and then scurried into the medical center.

31

Promise folded a thin, blue-flowered coat and packed it carefully, every movement as precise as a machine's. She was aware that Leslie sat watching her, that Leslie had not moved for a quarter hour. Had barely blinked. She knew that if she inquired after Leslie's state of mind she would hear, "Fine. I'm just fine." That the control she, Promise, used to keep her fears and speculations under control was as nothing compared to what her child employed.

Within that calm, thin frame there raged a fire, very

close to out of control. Leslie's eyes were unnaturally bright, the pupils contracted. There was a light dew of perspiration on her forehead. Her hands, so small and delicate, lay upturned on her knees.

Promise whirled. Wu stood in the doorway. She didn't know how long he had been there.

"Yes?"

"Our flight plan has been logged and accepted. We have to tie into the PanAfrican Network *now*," he said. "The moment any word about Swarna's condition leaks out, there will be an automatic moratorium on traffic."

"I'm ready. Leslie?"

Without a word, her daughter stood, calmly. With total relaxation. Balanced perfectly. Her pupils contracted, tight.

Promise shut her suitcase and carried it over to Leslie. "Would you carry this for your mother?"

Leslie smiled, perfectly. Perfect teeth shining in her small, perfect face. She accepted the suitcase into one perfect hand, and fell into perfect step alongside her mother as they moved rapidly to the waiting skimmer.

Everything is just perfect, Promise thought, fighting hysteria.

Just fucking perfect.

32

At the moment, Sinichi Tanaka's entire world consisted of Phillipe Swarna's medical readouts. He didn't understand the majority of the symbols or words that flashed before his eyes, but he was determined to understand what he could. "What is the primary's condition?" he asked, when Saito finally approached him.

"Tanaka-san," Saito said nervously. "Right now, his body is under attack. Any poison we could have countered—indeed, would have overridden almost immediately. But billions of nanocytes are literally eating him alive. We have countered them with our own units, but it is a delicate matter."

Saito spoke a few rapid words, and the computer fed them a vastly enlarged representation of a nanoassassin. It looked like a chrome aspirin tablet. "This is one of the invaders. They reproduce themselves by scavenging calcium and iron. We are killing them as fast as possible, but . . ."

Tanaka's face was dark. This was grave. Never had he lost a primary, and it would be an intolerable blot on his reputation. He was not a man used to failure.

Nanodot technology. That ruled out all but a small handful of commercial rivals, and perhaps a nation or two. America. Germany. Even National Japan might not be able to afford such a thing. A dozen Japanese corporations. Two or three American corporations.

But when had it been introduced into Swarna's system? The primary was so carefully screened. There had to have been active penetration. . . .

"I assume," he said slowly, "that the primary was compromised within the last twenty-four hours. At the festival. I warned him of the risk." Tanaka sat in a canvas-backed chair, facing a flat video screen. Heavy lines creased his brow. "The Swarnaville Festival." He raised his voice a click. "Tanaka. Reply Swarnafest. Stay with the primary." There was a pause of perhaps seven seconds, and then the computer displayed the moment that Swarna's skimmer first came floating down from a gray southern sky.

It touched down, and the primary disembarked, to the cheers of thousands.

And the hatred of how many?

Tanaka would have to examine every second of the six hours Swarna spent at the festival, retrace every interaction. Everything touched, everyone greeted.

Merciful heaven.

So little time, and so much to do. But at the very moment when despair threatened to rise within him, one of his lieutenants, a muscular Zulu woman named Qui, approached him, a scrap of printfilm in her hand. "Sir?" she said.

He remained hunched over the screen. There had to be a way to sort the vast collection of data. . . .

"Sir?" Qui repeated, patiently.

"Eh? Yes. What is it?" His eyes were still riveted to the flow of images. Here was Swarna at a frozen-ice stand. And here, congratulating a particularly fat pig at the agriculture booth.

"Sir," Qui repeated patiently. "We have news. There was an accident off the road, thirty kilometers south of Swarnaville. The Nullboxer, Azziz, is dead."

Tanaka sat bolt upright. The Nullboxer. A succession of images flashed before his eyes. In the midst of the excitement, during the festival, there were too many separate bits of information for him to pay maximum attention, to thoroughly interpret any single event.

But now he ran the boxer's body language through his mind . . . then, even more revealingly, his martial technique. Not sport technique. Not a *do,* a "way of living," or a sport. It was *bugei,* a warrior art. A killing technique, barely repressed.

Yes. The boxer Azziz.

Tanaka's eyes glittered. "Seal the borders," he said.

33

Swarna's body was under constant scan. Bones were being torn apart and rebuilt. Armies of nanocytes warred within him for his life.

Saito examined a sample of the enemy nanocytes, and his eyes suddenly widened. He recognized this. His doctoral dissertation at UC Berkeley had been on nanosystems, and the present model was an offshoot of a Korean design. He thought that he recognized the design modifications. Hadn't there been a Canadian researcher . . . ?

"Lower his core temperature," Saito snapped. "I think I know what we are dealing with."

His coworkers hesitated only a moment, and then sent coolant flowing into the coils surrounding Swarna's ashen, wasted body.

The chief physician, a black African named Mgui, supervised the process, and then approached Saito. "I assume that you have a damned good reason for this?"

"Yes, sir," he replied. "This nanotech design originated at Montreal University. There was a small scandal when it was discovered that American Intelligence had funded the study."

"And?"

"The whole thing smelled, sir. The nanocytes were designed to break down when the patient's core temperature reached eighty-six degrees. In other words, utilizing the Moritz formula and estimating average ambient room temperature, when the patient has been dead for about two hours."

"An assassination nanocyte."

"Yes. And under normal circumstances, an untraceable one. Phillipe Swarna is one of perhaps three men in the world who would have any chance at all."

For the first time in hours, Mgui smiled. "Very good," he said. "Very, very good."

Together, they watched the life signs as they flashed from the medical scanners. Slowly now, very slowly, the rate of damage slowed. And then dropped to zero.

And Swarna's tame nanobots began to rebuild.

34

It was dark now. Tanaka finally breathed easier. His primary had stabilized, and would live. Damage assessment would come later. There had been extensive nanoactivity in the central cortex, but Tanaka had faith that repairs could be made. They had always been made in the past.

What was more important was determining the source of the nanoassassins. After Swarna's stabilization, Tanaka had flown to see firsthand the site of the accident, a godforsaken stretch of hard-packed desert road south of Swarnaville. There were no villages in sight. There were no major trade routes, and the nearest main highway was almost a hundred miles east.

It was, all in all, a miserable place to die, a back road leading to a tiny half-deserted farming village. All rocks and scrub and burnt sand, with nothing but dusty mountains to ease the starkness of the horizon. This is where Azziz had died, in a car that stood upside down in a ditch, black skid marks creasing the road like twisted railroad tracks. The car was burnt and blackened, a broken box that smelled like charred rubber and metal.

He had insisted that the local police officials leave the accident site as they had found it. Tanaka turned his collar up. Desert nights were cold, and miserable, with no redeeming feature save the exceptionally clear star field overhead. There was no moon. "What was he doing out here?" Tanaka asked, of no one in particular. He crawled into the inverted vehicle, repressing his revulsion, and examined the body, scrunched up between the collapsed ceiling and the dashboard. It was burnt, but not beyond recognition. Azziz's neck was broken.

Tanaka crawled back out and inspected the engine. The power cell had exploded. On impact? Perhaps. Or . . . it had exploded and then the vehicle had plunged from the road. Either could be the case. He guessed that it had happened upon impact. A loss of control, followed by impact. Murder? Perhaps, but Azziz hadn't been greatly disfigured, so there had been no attempt to conceal anything. . . .

Or had there?

"I want a complete scan on this man. Now."

His assistant brought a portable scan from the skimmer and brought it into play. Within seconds, he had part of his answer. "Tanaka-san. This man was dead before the crash."

Tanaka squatted by the side of the car. He trickled a handful of sand through his fingers. So many grains. The wind blows them from everywhere, he thought. How unlikely, how incredible that they somehow end up here, together in the same handful. No meaning there, but no meaning to anything.

His eyes were dead, his soul sang.

He stood, dusting his hands on his pants. "This is a decoy," he said. "The man in this vehicle is not the man who shook hands with Swarna. By now, undoubtedly, the genuine assassin is gone."

He stood, smoothing out the wrinkles on his pants. Where were the Four? They had been out of touch for hours. Maintaining radio silence. That might well mean they were stalking prey in enemy territory. They had their own ways, those Four. . . .

"We will find this man," he said finally. "I want to know everything. One last thing. He is extremely dangerous. Take no chances. I'm invoking the mutual security act of 2031, regarding pursuit into the CAR."

"Central African Republic?"

"Yes," Tanaka said. "That is where he is." He looked to the northern horizon. "I can smell him."

35

Aubry sat in their rented room, staring out the window at the street below him. As far as his eye could see, the streets were lined with shops and merchants, street carts and banners proclaiming FINE MEATS! BEST CLOTHES! IMMIGRATION SERVICES!

A shrill whooping sound filled the air, and a security skimmer dropped into view, cruising just meters above the heads of the nighttime shoppers, scanning, searching. In the distance, he could hear other skimmers, questing restlessly through the night, like a flotilla of air sharks.

Jenna knelt upon the couch next to him. A searchlight slid across her face, making her eyes shine. Bloodeagle leaned against the wall, watching them both.

"We should be safe," he said.

"But the man at the border recognized me. We don't have very long," Aubrey said, unemotionally. "How long will it take to arrange transportation?"

"I could be wrong," Bloodeagle said. "Perhaps you should have gone through the escape route STYX planned for you."

Aubry shook his head. "I don't think so, Miles. I think that you were right. They wanted me dead."

36

A mile outside the small farming village south of Swarnaville, two STYX operatives named Red One and Red Two were waiting. If Knight had shown up on schedule, with no complications . . . he might have been allowed to live. But the slightest hint of a problem, and the termination order would proceed. There had been, one might say, more than a hint of a problem. The real Azziz had already been killed, and planted. If Knight managed to make it here to the village, he would be killed as well, and his body strategically hidden.

But so far, no sign of the target.

"We're getting no reading," Red Two said. "Don't know where the hell he is. Somebody disabled the tracer. Could the entire unit be destroyed?"

"And him along with it?" Red One said. "I don't think so."

Red Two was irritable. He hated the country, and hated the job. Any interest in the operation was long dead. Now he just wanted to get out, and get the hell home. "Should we trigger?"

"Just in case? Yes." Red One opened a slender case, and began to tap in a series of commands. He uploaded the in-structions to a geosynchronous STYX satellite, which bounced the message of death back down. "Well," he sighed. "That was that."

"Poor bastard."

"Yeah. Hell of a fight, wasn't it?"

"Hell of a fight."

Bloodeagle's case beeped.

"Shit," he said nervously. "The self-destruct is trying to activate."

Aubry looked at his leg with horror. "Can it?"

"This jammer is supposed to be working. The satellite is changing frequencies to get around the jam. The two units are trying to talk to each other."

"And if they do?"

"The room goes."

"What are my options?"

"We can hope that it will stop trying, or . . . shit."

Bloodeagle watched in horror.

"A chunk of undigested code got through. It's a crypto-gram, in unbroken form. The leg unit is attempting to break the code. At its present rate of decoding, I would estimate it might take . . . two hours."

"Two hours," Jenna whispered.

Aubry's voice went hard and very flat. "Get the hell out of here. You've done everything that you can."

"No," Bloodeagle said. "There is one more thing I can do."

Jenna sat at a bar across the street from the hotel. She was not dressed as herself. She wore too much makeup, and a dress that was uncomfortably tight. It was long and black, but the mere revelation of her figure, combined with her lack of male escort, made her every gesture and movement an open invitation.

A tiny transceiver lay concealed in her ear, and a match-ing microphone nestled almost invisibly against her throat.

While she sipped a bitter local brew slowly, trying to fit into the nighttime bar crowd, she kept her eyes on the room. Her heart was pounding. It was all up to Bloodeagle now. Otherwise, Aubry Knight would be dead in just over twenty-three minutes.

Leslie's head whipped around. Promise had settled into the suite of the New Nippon Hilton, and she was trying to get her thoughts together.

Wu said, "Is something wrong?"

Leslie's nostrils flares. "I . . ." Her brows furrowed, and she seemed terribly troubled. "There's something wrong. I can't . . ." Leslie closed her eyes.

"Father . . ." she whispered.

37

Aubry lay unconscious, his great dark head lolled onto his left shoulder. Bloodeagle stood above him, his breathing meticulously controlled to prevent a panic response. He was fully trained in medical procedures, and just as well trained in bomb disposal. But the combination of the two areas was enough to give him nightmares.

The bomb and its triggering processor were sheathed by a titanium-ceramic tube within the living core of Aubry's left femur. Access could be gained through the thigh muscle. The muscle grain had been split once, and reentry should be relatively simple.

Still, under conditions like this . . .

Aubry's leg was completely covered by a plastic bubble, through which Bloodeagle performed his terrible, delicate miracles. He peeled back the epidermis. He went in between the adductor magnus and semitendinosus, angling toward the side. The blood vessels were carefully peeled back and arranged by the thin delicate arms of the Gorgon field-autosurgeon unit. But the autosurgeon didn't know how to remove a bomb. Its textbooks and tapes could guide Bloodeagle, but not replace his judgment.

And so he fought panic. So far he was winning, but the fight wasn't over yet.

There. He gripped the end of the capsule and began teasing it out. He stopped, and whispered into his throat mike. "All clear?"

Jenna's voice came back to him. *"All . . . shit. A Jeep just landed on your roof. No, the roof next door. This doesn't look good."*

"How many? Just a little more time."

"Maybe three. Could be a random patrol."

"Can you buy me some time? I need five minutes."

Jenna smiled grimly. *"Or die trying."*

"Jenna . . ." Bloodeagle said softly. "That's not your job. Remember your promise to Aubry. Stay peripheral. Somebody has to get word to the Scavengers if . . . anything goes wrong. Promise me. Like you swore to Aubry."

"Damn you."

"Promise me, dammit!"

There was a long pause, filled with nothing but electronic crackle. Then: *"All right. I promise."*

38

The building next to their hotel was crowded with a hundred small sounds of living and survival. Jenna slipped silently through the shadows, surprised at her own nervousness.

She understood perhaps five percent of the words she heard, the occasional snatch of French or English. She had never experienced the shock of being in a completely foreign land, had had no preconception of how that distorted your sense of identity.

She had the odd sensation that she didn't completely exist. Paradoxically, at the same time she felt more substantial, more essentially *real* than the things and people around her.

In shadow, she waited, counting minutes. Her thumb tested the sweetly curved six inches of her durga blade.

How accurate were the enemy scanners? They couldn't be maximal, or they would have landed on the correct building.

A man came down the stairs. Japanese. A team leader.

As his weight transferred from one stair to the next her hand snaked out, grabbed his wrist, and yanked him. She sliced his throat in midair. He thundered through the railing, smashed into the floor, and was still.

Good.

Then she heard shouts, and shots from the hotel next door, and realized that she had been terribly wrong.

This was just the first ship. They hadn't landed on the wrong roof—they had surrounded the building, cutting off escape, and the sounds of shots next door—

She considered running to their assistance. Goddess—it was death. The radio button in her ear began to speak.

"Jenna! For God's sake get out."

To hell with her promise—

Voices. Steps on the stair. She dove for the dead Japanese, snatched up his sidearm, and pivoted before the first man came into range.

Split target, dammit. Two on the stairs, one in the door. Perception had slowed to almost stop-motion. She dropped into the Weaver stance, right arm rigid as a rifle stock, left hand reinforcing the right fingers around the pistol butt. Left elbow down. Flick off safety. Double action. Good.

First man. Flash of light. He had gotten off a shot. Jenna squeezed her trigger, twice. Two in the chest. Second man coming in the door. She addressed him, two shots—one chest, one head, dead center. His head flew back, and he crashed against the wall, but Jenna had already swung back to the stairs. First man had fallen. Third was almost down, in range. There was a second shot. Who? She wasn't sure. Legs visible. She squeezed off three more shots, at the legs and hips, before the third man could descend to firing level. Third one caught him. He tumbled, sprawling over the first men.

She swung back to number two—

Ripping, terrible pain in her side. Japanese bastard wasn't dead. Blood gushed from his gashed throat, but he had managed to draw a boot knife and clip her side as her attention was focused on the other three. She spun away from the pain even as it bit into her, and addressed him. Firing twice, both into the head at close range.

Jenna staggered back against the wall, sobbing for breath, knowing that when the pain came, it was going to be bad. She needed time to stanch the wound. But Aubry and Bloodeagle needed help.

No. They were depending on her to do her part. To keep her word. She hated herself, hated the necessity, but Jenna ran, ran through the back of the building as a jarring explosion tore the side out of their hotel.

Aubry. Bloodeagle . . .

She was in an alley. Screams filled the street, and the sound of whooping skimmers filled the air. Jenna swallowed her pride, and her fear, and disappeared into the night.

39

Bloodeagle was trapped. Aubry was still unconscious, his leg partially sutured up. A little blood still leaked onto the table, and he was finishing when he heard the scream in the hallway.

Doubtless there were undocumented laborers, and drug dealers, in this building. The result was that armed men, even having no interest in anything but Aubry, would cause a stir.

Shots.

Carefully enfolded in an oilskin was the detonator he

had removed from Aubry's leg. It did not hum. It did not tick. But he knew that the mechanism within the blood-smeared steel tube continued its relentless progress toward zero.

Bloodeagle concealed it under the bed and dragged Aubry into the bathroom, leveraging his enormous body into the bathtub. The unconscious man lay there, breathing shallowly.

Bloodeagle reached out and stroked Aubry's face.

"Aubry," he said gently. The barest smile crossed his face. So beautiful. And utterly incapable of seeing the possibilities. Aubry stirred gently, groaned, and lapsed back into unconsciousness.

Bloodeagle bent over and, very gently, kissed him. He tasted Aubry's sleeping breath, rubbed his stubbled cheek against Aubry's.

"In another life, my brother," he said.

Then the front door exploded.

40

The concussion jolted Aubry into consciousness. He struggled to his knees, then heard the first blast of gunfire, and crouched again, humiliated by his own weakness.

He peeked up over the edge of the tub, and saw Miles Bloodeagle die.

Singing his death song, Miles charged them. There were three black men, security forces of the Central African Republic, and they had no idea what it was they faced. Miles Bloodeagle was no ordinary man. He was a NewMan, one of the beings spawned in the Gender Wars, a creation of superior strength and speed and intent.

Their guns roared at him, and any ordinary man would have died then. He took a grazing shot in the shoulder, and another one in the hip. His mind simply shut down the pain, and he was onto them, and for what happened next, Aubry's heart sang.

Bloodeagle was not as fast as Aubry, not as strong, although perhaps his musculature was thicker.

But he shared Aubry's total, mindless commitment to the moment, and its impact was awesome. The amplitude and speed and sheer *clarity* of his movement were virtually balletic.

One of the men dropped where he stood, spine shattered. Bloodeagle fought from a crouch, moving up and down, side to side, throwing, and landing low kicks, constantly maneuvering, and the men were in each other's lines of sight.

He had his hands on the second, and slammed him into the wall, and Aubry could hear the bones shatter.

And then the third. But Bloodeagle was weakening now, and the man got his hands on Bloodeagle. It didn't matter—the Cherokee *twisted* him like a doll, and threw him aside.

He turned, and the next man through the door fired, catching Bloodeagle again, along the side of the head. But the NewMan pivoted as he fired. In an eye-baffling movement he whipped a chair up and around, hurling it the way an Olympian hurls the hammer, and the security man's head rocked back so fast that his neck snapped and then—

And then the death machine that had been secreted in Aubry's leg triggered. There was a moment in which the entire world was devoured by white light. There was the sensation of heat, and then of cold. And then there was nothing at all.

41

The street boiled with police. Jenna immediately switched out of combat mode, softened her face and body language, and shut away her pain. She wore a stolen coat over her hastily bandaged wound, and prayed that the blood wouldn't seep through.

She cut a sidewise glance at the next man who examined her inquiringly. He was thickset, with a puffy face and an effeminate mouth.

He jerked his head and said something in a language that she didn't understand. She nodded and followed him.

Behind her, a squadron of skimmers lifted away from the hotel roof. She didn't need to be told what they carried.

Aubry . . .

Miles . . .

My God. What did I do? What have I done?

She walked up a winding staircase with the man, and into a dingy room. He closed the door, and as he did, saying something else in that singsong voice, she slipped up behind him and her arm twined around his throat.

Her rage was homicidal. She ached to complete the torque and break his neck. But his only sin was in finding her attractive. He had not been rude. Perhaps he would even have been gentle. As gentle as a man could be.

She changed the grip. He passed out, and slipped to the ground.

Jenna sat on the edge of the bed. She held her face in her hands, and contemplated her next move.

42

Outside, in the street, Daglia's chief of police, an African named James Danessh, considered the evening's catch. Two men. One dead, one unconscious. Seven of his own men were dead, one probably crippled for life.

What in the hell was going on here? Alerts from the goddamned PanAfricans had brought heat down on his neck. Informants had pinpointed the foreigners rapidly. And then he had put his people into motion.

Seven men dead. "Search," he told his assistant brusquely. "There is another man."

There was more to this than met the eye. Much more. And he would extract payment for his dead men. He had something that the PanAfricans wanted, and they would pay dearly for it. There were rumors. Swarna had fallen ill. Suddenly. Perhaps this man Azziz had tried to kill Swarna? A shame the attempt hadn't succeeded. But still, if he could find the third conspirator, alive, there was advantage to be gained. . . .

43

"I have tried to be an honorable man," Harris said.

Jeffry Barathy thought that the president would seem a larger, broader man. He realized that the weight of office, and perhaps something more than that, had shrunken him over the years.

"I have tried, but personal and national interests rarely coincide."

"I can understand that." The image was crystal clear, but Jeffry understood that the computer links were as secure as technology could make them. A plainclothes member of the Gorgon antiterrorist task force, which—it was an open secret—sometimes acted as a security arm of the executive branch, had hand-delivered the descrambler to Jeffry personally, and insisted that he prepare for a message from the president. Jeffry had been skimmed to a safe house outside Las Vegas, a room in the basement of a building labeled only GENERAL PRODUCTS, INC. He had descended in an elevator and wheeled himself through a short maze of passages. He had seen no other human beings, save the two enormous men behind him. And they had waited outside the room. He wondered, a little alarmed at what would happen to someone who tried to enter, to get past those two utterly foreboding men. He decided that it would probably be better not to know.

"How can I help you, Mr. President?"

He was quite certain that he had not been brought here on a whim.

"I am nearing the end of my second term. A breach of security such as we are about to discuss could severely imperil my party's ability to hold on to the White House for another four years." He smiled bleakly, raising his shoulders a little as if in apology for being a politician.

"But," he said, "there are things which go beyond politics."

"Like Aubry Knight?"

The president smiled. "Yes. Like Aubry Knight. I would like to ask you point-blank: What have you been able to discover about his whereabouts and activities? I believe that Koskotas is lying to me. I can bring pressure to bear, but time is of the essence here."

"Virtually nothing. He hooked into the Denver sky line, and then disappeared."

Harris drummed his fingers for a moment before speaking. "Please listen closely. I will only say this once. Aubry Knight was prepared for an operation against Phillipe Swarna. He was inserted in Ma'habre, and traveled south to Swarnaville and there made contact. The attempt failed, although Knight performed . . . admirably." Harris removed his glasses, and wiped them with a gesture that was pure stalling tactic. "He is a . . . remarkable man, isn't he?"

"That's what everyone seems to think."

"Tell me . . . how much personal contact with him have you had?"

"Not a lot. Just the operation four years ago."

"I see. You have a reputation, and you have the personal incentive. I wish to make certain . . . information available to you. At three-forty-five A.M., your time, your computer banks must be prepared to receive a transmission—approximately twelve megabytes of files pertaining to something called Operation STYX. It is the most I can do. Afterward, all references to this conversation must be destroyed. It must never be spoken of. Do you understand?"

Jeffry swallowed. "Of course."

"Very well." Harris allowed himself the tiniest ghost of a smile. "You know, one makes do with what material one can get. You are . . . more interesting material than most."

And the image dissolved.

44

There was no *air* in the room. On the other hand, perhaps it was the hanging upside down that did it. Aubry's diaphragm was exhausted. He was gasping for breath in a manner that utterly terrified him, or would have, except that he was somewhere beyond terror. His leg bled, and a trickle of blood ran down it and into his mouth.

"Who are you?" James Danessh said. He was speaking in pidgin English, and Aubry found it difficult to understand some of it.

Other aspects of the conversation he understood very well indeed.

He hung upside down in a room that felt as cold as a meat locker. He was dizzy, and tired, and in so much pain that he could barely think. His circulation was gone.

"Cut him down," Danessh said.

Aubry tried to brace himself, tried to relax, and it meant very little. He crashed into the ground shoulders first, and barely managed to get his head out of the way.

"Cut him loose," Danessh suggested.

They did. There was no circulation. No blood to his limbs. Despite the pain, Aubry wanted nothing more than to curl up and go to sleep. Two men, almost as large as Aubry, hauled him upright, and one of them drove a fist into his gut.

"I think that you will talk to us," the first one said. The

second agreed, heartily, and slammed a fist into Aubry's gut to demonstrate the practicality of the suggestion.

Aubry tried to move. He tried to steady his breathing. He knew a dozen ways that he could have killed both of these men. They were clowns, with soft bodies to match their blows, which ordinarily wouldn't have bothered him more than gnat lashes.

But he was so tired. And hurt. And cold. And all he wanted to do was sleep.

So tired.

His world flashed red as another fist smashed into him, and he sagged.

The second man looked up from his work. "Excuse me," he said, and slammed his fist into Aubry's face.

"Nullboxer? Shit. I could have killed him at his best. Now, he is a nothing. Step back. Stand him up."

Aubry fought with himself, momentarily shaken out of his dream. Wasn't there any strength at all? There wasn't, and he felt as weak as a baby. But . . .

But he feigned complete torpor, allowed himself to seem weaker still, and weak to the point where they not only had to stand him up, but hold him up, as if he were dead. And as he did he concentrated all of his strength in one leg. His right leg. Still not enough strength. Then just in his right foot. There was a slight tingle of light if he concentrated that precisely. And then he managed to feel as if the strength in his body were a thick, viscous syrup, and he concentrated the entirety of it in his right toe. The rest of his body was a thing of numbness and death . . . but there was a spot of light in that darkness. The big man stepped forward, and with the greatest effort of his life Aubry sent that single point of light arcing into the juncture between his tormentor's legs. The moment of contact was electric in intensity.

Oh . . .

It felt so good to have that moment, as if it was something long denied him. To see the flash of surprise on the fat, flabby face. To see the eyes start out from their sockets, to see the hands fumble to the crushed and ruptured genitals, and watch him bend over . . .

To see the thin stream of vomit. Then there was a sound like a bell, ringing against the side of his head, and all was darkness.

Danessh glared at the man with the ruptured testicles, and shook his head. "You are a fool," he said. The man could not answer. He was far too busy cupping himself, and perhaps bemoaning the loss of his sex life.

"Perhaps we are all fools." He nudged Aubry Knight's senseless form with his toe. "There is much here that I do not understand." He watched his breath form frozen puffs in the cooler, and shuddered, drawing his thick woolen coat tighter across his thin shoulders. "And I'm not certain how much time we have to understand it."

Aubry awoke in the cell. It was, perhaps, a little warmer. He curled onto his side, and there was not enough heat for him to feel that he could move. He was dying, and it didn't seem to matter much. He had done all that he could to protect his family. To regain his honor.

And more than that no man could do.

Golah, senior guard at Daglia Prison, was used to many things, but there was an unaccustomed sense of excitement in the air.

There had been many official visitors, and the vidphones were still humming. Everyone wanted to see, or speak of, the man in the security cell.

There was a sense of excitement. This had, in some way, been a coup over the hated PanAfricans, and the sense was that there would be a way to turn it to their advantage.

It wasn't the same as holding a member of a royal family, or even an ambassador, or something of that kind.

But what happens when you hold a man who attempted to assassinate a head of state?

Attempted? As yet, there had been no further word on Swarna's condition. . . .

Golah lit a cigarette and looked out at the desert. There could be a garden there, if they had the technology to make it bloom. The Jews and the Ibandi had done it. And there could be benefits . . .

He lit another cigarette, inhaling deeply, never realizing that it was his last.

Two miles away, three men and a woman met, shaking stones from a leather cup.

"Whose task will it be, siblings?" Ni said.

"Should we even go? He allowed himself to be taken," Roku reminded them.

"Any man can be taken," San said. "He was in a foreign land. He had no training in such things. He was betrayed. Surrounded by enemies. Still, he performed superbly." She lifted her head, almost sniffing the air. "I think it likely that he endures torture superbly."

The bones rolled out, and tumbled to a rest in the sand. Go took his turn, rattled them, and sprawled them out.

The bones came to a rest. Go smiled. "It is mine."

The four of them shook hands in a curious four-way clasp.

"The honor is yours, my brother."

"It is mine."

"Have a good death."

Clouds had stolen the moon, and the wind off the desert was a low, moaning thing.

Golah thought about another cigarette. He craved it. He knew that he was killing himself, slowly, but in his considered opinion, the taste of another cigarette would be worth its infinitesimal reduction of his life span. One should live for today, he mused. The future took care of itself.

He shook a cigarette out of its pack, then looked down and saw the dot on his chest. He said "Oh . . ." a moment before the bullet slammed into his breastbone, a single .22 slug that tore through bone and cartilage and delivered a ghastly load of hydrostatic shock to his system. He was dead before he hit the ground. The guards in the other towers died next, one after another. In more advanced environs, they would have had more armor, more protection. But they were poor, and had endured a lifetime of indignities owing to that simple fact of birth. In the final analysis, death was just one more.

A shadow moved away from the periphery and toward the front gate.

The guards in the outer towers were dead. Now it was time. Moving toward the front gate was a curious figure, blocky and yet somehow lithe. He was an essential contradiction, simultaneously almost comical and immensely dignified.

He leveled his arm at the gate.

45

3:07 A.M.

The men inside didn't have time to think, no time to lower their weapons, no time to do anything but die.

The front doors exploded inward, and before the flame had ceased spewing, or the roar of the metal and wood and plastic peeling away under the assault of the rocket had died to echoes, the armored figure walked through.

The first three men died almost instantly, taking eight to twelve rounds each from some kind of fast-loading machine pistol that spewed twelve hundred rounds a minute, delicately tapped to give a microburst per man.

The alarm went up.

On the second floor, a mass of guards were heading down to the ground level. Monitors showed some kind of armored enemy, and a primitive computer hookup gave them the information that it was a Mitsubishi armor suit, pointed out possible weaknesses, and warned them that it had been reinforced.

The guards were ready to repel tanks and armored vehicles. They had enough weaponry. What they needed was the time to get it into use.

On the ground floor, men were dying. They had poured over three hundred rounds into the advancing monstrosity, and some of the rounds were explosive, and some of them armor-piercing, and nothing seemed to slow it.

It rounded a corner, and then paused, as if checking some kind of internal sensor, attempting to determine its direction and intent.

It turned the corner.

"What is it?" Danessh screamed.

"We are being invaded, Captain. I don't know how many."

"What do they want?"

"They want to kill us all!"

The first of the rocket men had arrived on the site, and they locked on to their target quickly.

Inside the suit, Go read his infrared readouts and knew almost instantly that lock-on had been achieved. He spun, and took out the first rocket man before he had time to depress the trigger, blowing him back into the wall in bleeding bits, two hundred rounds slamming through the protective barrier, ripping his body into shreds.

The second rocket man managed to get his off.

The rocket slammed into the back of the armored suit, blowing it off its feet, slamming it back into the wall with a roar like a dying titan.

Go gasped. He had never felt an impact like that, despite the cushioning in the suit. He switched to manual, unable to be certain that the suit's servos would be worth a damn after such an impact, firing as he did. A stream of rounds tore into the second rocket man, by which time some of the suit systems were back up, and he found a third man, who was behind a wall, trembling as he tried to bring his unit into play.

He was dead an instant later.

There was nothing but mopping up to do now, as the man in the suit fought to his knees and made his way into the maximum-security block.

Three more guards died, and the general alarm had been out for four minutes. It would take another ten before any reinforcements could arrive. He knew the direction from which they would have to come. There would be confusion, and uncertainty: the prison's power had already been dampened, a communications buffer thrown over the entire installation.

Go was limping. Bone and muscle had been torn. The medical units inside the suit struggled to repair the damage, but there simply wasn't enough power to keep the suit moving and the medical units working simultaneously.

He reached maximum security.

He grasped the bars of the door. There was no time to search for keys. Distantly, he heard screams and moans. *Ignore them.* He heard a hiss of pain emerge from his own mouth.

Ignore it.

He ripped the door from its hinges, aware that his hydraulics were rupturing with the strain.

Inside the cell, the limp figure of a man lay on a cold floor. He looked near death. The armored figure moved in carefully, with great tenderness, and scooped Aubry Knight into his arms.

That these *animals* had done this to a brave man.

He spun, and blew another guard back out of the door.

Then, carrying the wounded, unconscious man gently in his arms, he stalked toward the front door, killing everything in his way.

Go's biological monitors were edging into the red. He had to stop and allow himself to repair. He knew that he should. The man with him was an enemy, and yet . . .

Bleeding badly, Go carried Aubry Knight out into the desert.

46

The first two reinforcements arrived at the prison five minutes later.

The wind blew sand and dust through the corridors, and set up a low, sighing moaning sound that echoed and filled the entire building with a kind of slow moan.

"What happened here?" the first man asked. He attached scans to the external monitors, sent in auxiliary power, and got the monitors running. They scanned the halls. They heard sobbing, and screaming.

"A force moved in. Maybe a dozen men, a light assault tank—"

They were getting the image now. They saw a single armored figure wading through a sea of blood, flame washing from that damned gun. They saw their men die. And then they saw no more, the cameras themselves canceled out by some sort of disruption field.

The dead sprawled twisted and broken, everywhere.

"What did he want?"

"Guess."

"The assassin?"

"Yes. And that battle suit was NipTech. That means PanAfrica."

"Can we prove that?"

The first man laughed bitterly. "Of course not. But we know. We know. Damn those bastards."

"What do they want him for, that they would do this?"

"I don't know," he said, putting away his weapon. "But the poor bastard was better off here, with us."

47

Aubry came slowly to consciousness. He lay in the sand, and it blew over him, a thin curtain of dust dancing across the horizon like a line of ethereal imps. It moaned, low.

He struggled to an upright position. Where? His limbs didn't want to work. They had been severely traumatized, and there seemed no end to the small aches and pains that there remained for him to discover.

It was early morning. He could tell by the slight sweaty moistness in the sand beneath his cheek, and the cool of the air. Soon it would be blazing hot.

He might have lain there, unmoving, except that from the corner of his eye he saw the aircar. It lay in the sand at an angle, as if it had crashed.

What? He had the vaguest of memories. The sounds of struggle. The sound of screams, and explosions. He had been in darkness, but even in the cell, his cheek frozen to the floor, a single tear gelid on his torn cheek, there had been sound. And screams. And then the blissful release of darkness.

He turned onto his side, struggling as if heaving off boulders. And saw the kneeling, armored figure. The armored man had knelt there, waiting for Aubry to awaken for . . . how long?

They stared at each other, and for a long time Aubry thought that the man wouldn't, or couldn't, speak.

Then he heard the words. They were foreign, accented, and labored. As if it took an unbelievable effort to speak them at all.

"*Greetings, my brother,*" Go said.

"Who . . . ?"

"*Do not speak. I . . . do not have much time.*" A sound very like a laugh came from the armor.

"I was to rescue you. And then I was to kill you."

"Kill . . . me?" Aubry was dazed.

"Yes. But neither of us is prepared for that. I am afraid that I am dying. You are badly hurt. But the Ibandi will help you."

"Ibandi?"

"Wait. You will learn. I should have given you to the others, but . . . you deserve a chance to heal."

Go began to fiddle with the faceplate.

"You are . . . a man. When you have healed, seek out the others. Finish what has begun. Promise me."

"Promise you what?"

There was another time of silence, and the man finished fumbling with the face mask.

It hung on a hinge, obscuring the face. Aubry looked at the rest of him. The shoulders must have been unusually broad: the armor was built for a giant.

And then he saw the blood, seeping out of a gaping hole in the side of the armor, and heard the wheezing. It was true: the man was dying.

"Promise me . . . there is struggle. You must find the others."

"What do I have to do with this?"

The man laughed. "You will see," he said. The mask fell free, and Aubry found himself looking into his own face.

Once again, as in Tyson's All-Faiths, the face was not exactly Aubry—it had eaten different foods, grown beneath a different sky, perhaps. There were keloid scars across it, and a front tooth was missing. But it was Aubry's face, the unaltered Aubry, before the plastic surgery.

"What is this?"

"We have all asked that question," Go mused. *"And only one of us can answer it. Oh, it hurts . . ."* He pulled himself back from some far place, and faced Aubry. "Take this." He fumbled, managed to pull a slender cylinder of metal and plastic from his belt. It was slicked with blood. *"A tracer. When you are ready, trigger it. You will find the others. Listen. I called to the Ibandi, and they will come to you. Trust them. They are your people."*

"My . . ." Aubry looked at the man, and didn't understand.

"Look at your skin. You speak the white man's language, and you think his thoughts, except that your body doesn't belong to his family. Do you not feel that there is something more?"

Aubry faced him and said, "I was born in the city of Los Angeles. It was all I knew. My father died when I was eight. I know the streets. That's all."

God, it hurt even to talk, but it felt like the words were being dragged out of him one at a time, with fishhooks.

"Aubry Knight," Go said. *"With no past, and no future. With no one to love you, or help you find yourself. Wallowing in corruption, and plagued by violence and anger. How did you survive?"*

Aubry felt a terrible weight hanging over his head, almost but not quite something that he hadn't seen there before. "I don't know . . ."

"You will learn."

And Aubry felt a sudden jolt of unreasoning fear. "What do you want from me?"

"You," the man said. And then he sagged.

Aubry dragged himself over to the armored man and touched him. There was no movement. The sand blew across the desert, a low call that powdered the kinky hair. But there were no more words.

"Who am I?" Aubry whispered in a drugged voice. But there was no answer, and could be none, ever again, from those lips.

The sand danced across the desert like a curtain in the wind, and the sun touched the edge of the horizon. The light changed with fearsome speed, and became a shadow play of oranges and deep purples.

Aubry tried to drag himself to the crashed vehicle. It was easy to find it, he thought. Just follow the trail of blood. So much blood.

And it was junk, wrecked. And the radio. Oh, yes, he could use the radio. And call what down upon himself?

He was terribly far from home, and surrounded by enemies. There were, he reminded himself, things worse than death.

So suppose he just settled back, him and the other Aubry, and they looked at each other, one whose eyes were sightless, and another whose sight grew duller by the moment.

There came a shadowy figure. It came from out of the wind, and he thought, for a moment, that he knew it. Was it himself, again? He essayed a laugh, but it came from somewhere too deep in his chest, and blood bubbled with it.

There were more than one figure, more than one man. They walked with staffs, and they walked with a curious dignity, as if these sands, this patch of ground, were theirs, and no one else's, and their bodies knew it in a manner that went beyond and beneath all logic or calculation.

There were six of them, and Aubry watched them approach, and as they did, the leader bent down to him.

For a long time the examination continued. Or it seemed like a long time. The truth was that there was no way that Aubry could be certain how long it actually was, because by that time he had slipped off the ends of the earth, into a cold, infinite darkness.

4TH SONG

DEATHDANCE

Those who fear death cannot win. Those who love both life *and* death cannot be defeated.

—Ibandi proverb

1

Jenna pulled her coat up around her face, so that the wind—a hot wind, blowing off the desert—didn't sear her face. There was a moment of desperation, in which she felt lost and fragile. Then she put it away. There was no time for that. There was no place for feelings like that. She had to control herself, to find the strength to go on, although she wasn't certain which way to turn.

Separation from both Aubry and Bloodeagle left her in limbo. Were they alive? Her heart sank at the thought of Aubry's death.

Her side ached. With every step, she felt her makeshift bandages pull.

Daglia's streets were crowded with vendors, people shuttling this way and that, on their way to a thousand marketplaces. It was a very *alive* city, and she felt a stab of guilt. How much of that life was due to trade with Pan-Africa, due to the man that they had killed? She had to assume that by now Swarna was dead, and that the alarms ringing around Daglia were the result of that death. She had heard no official announcement, but . . .

A Jeep loaded with soldiers rumbled down the street. Oh, Goddess—did they have a description . . . ?

A very dark-skinned man in a full-length leather cloak smiled at her. Keloid scars crisscrossed his face. Jenna instantly assumed a facade and took a hipshot position, a display of her "wares."

Even bundled up as she was, there was nothing visible to give any man a cause for complaint. Her legs, concealed by her garments, nonetheless met at hips that tantalizingly swelled the enfolding material. Her waist was muscularly narrow. Her eyes glittered with mischief, with challenge. She knew how to focus her *ki* through her eyes, and warrior *ki*, a blend of sexuality and physical mastery, could be focused by a mistress of durga to emphasize the former.

A twentieth-century master of yogic sciences, Swami Satyanananda Sawaswati, defined it precisely: *"When Kundalini has just awakened and you are not able to handle it,"* he said, *"it is called Kali. When you can handle it and are able to use it for beneficial purposes and you become powerful on account of it, it is called Durga."*

The would-be customer was actually rocked back on his heels as if struck in the face with the force of her sensuality. He recovered swiftly and began chattering at her, holding up a handful of fingers, bargaining. Jenna used sign language to argue back at him, laughing. The soldiers passed, barely giving them a second glance.

As soon as the Jeep disappeared around the corner, Jenna laughed, waved the scarred man off, and hurried away. He called after her, probably raising his offer, his voice musical with disappointment.

She turned down a side street, trying to think. She had no money, and no friends. She didn't speak the tongue, and had no way of communicating beyond the simplest sign language. She was hunted. *Goddess.*

Another squad of soldiers passed along a perpendicular street, and she shrank against the wall, breath rasping in her throat. A gray tide of hopelessness rose within her.

There was a sharp wrench on her elbow, and she turned. The scarred man held her, painfully tight, and his eyes were bright with lust. He motioned toward a nearby alley with sharp, urgent flicks of his head.

She tried to tug her arm away, and he only tightened his grip and said something ugly. One hand brushed his coat back, exposing the hilt of a knife.

Something inside her both tautened and relaxed in the same moment.

This was his game? All right then, he had called it. She allowed herself to be dragged back into the alley, feigning fear. He dumped her against the wall, behind a stack of trash, and reached for his belt, grinning now with a mouthful of huge bright teeth. He was talking quickly, excitedly.

He was still talking excitedly when she kicked him dead in the balls.

There was a shocked expression in his face, and something behind the shock—anger. And suddenly she knew that she had made a mistake. Her foot struck something solid—a groin protector? Her mind blanked for a moment. A soldier. Plainclothes? Some kind of security? Oh—

His eyes glittered, and he whipped the knife out of its sheath. Before he could clear it, she had already dropped to her hands and knees, and mule-kicked up into the side of his left knee.

It is true that it takes an average of twenty-seven pounds of pressure per square inch to rip off the patella. It is also true that an adult human being with decent reflexes can bend with a blow so as to minimize that damage. He was clumsy, but not stupid. And she remembered the strength of his grip.

So when he rolled with it, she followed in, staying down like a crab. She struck at the knees once, twice, again and again—never letting him catch his breath, keeping him on the recoil until he almost forgot that he had a knife in his hand, so that he was reeling in a nightmare of defense, until he stumbled and fell. He slashed at her. Both of them were on their knees now. Jenna blocked with her forearm—a jarring sensation—and grasped his wrist, twisting massively and torquing so that his body arced as he tried to flip. But when you are already on your knees, there is no room to somersault out of such a wristlock. He went forehead-first into the pavement, smashing his nose and most of his upper teeth. Still, Jenna didn't release the arm. She wrenched the knife from his hand, flipped it smoothly to get the correct grip, and struck him in the temple with its pommel. Hard.

He collapsed.

She rolled him over. His face was a mess—blood bubbled from between smashed teeth. His breathing was ragged, but he would live. She searched his pockets and found his wallet.

A communications card. Goddess. An off-duty soldier. Was there a tracer on it? Maybe. She tossed it away. There was also money. Not much—just a few low-denomination bills. But right now, it looked like a bloody fortune. She pinched his sleeping cheek. "I could almost kiss you," she laughed. "I've never been happier to see a rapist in my entire *life.*"

She looked both ways up and down the alley, and left.

She took the train into the center of town, to get the hell away from there, and her temporary exuberance began to wane. There was still no path out of the Central African Republic—maybe not even out of Daglia. If she tried to get a room, she might betray herself. If she searched for someone who spoke English, that alone might betray her—although she might have no other option.

Jenna found a tavern and bought a bowl of hot cider, letting her robes cover her as much as possible. She didn't think she would withstand any additional attentions. She hadn't the spirit to join in the music and gaiety. Her side felt sticky and sore, and she fought with flittering dizziness. Her skin felt hot.

Just what I need—an infection.

She concentrated on the conversations around her, desperately seeking to strain any fragment of information out of the cacophony.

Listening harder didn't make the language barrier less inpenetrable. She began to wish she had killed the man in the alley. Why hadn't she? *Damn, damn damn.* She was an alien, in a land where she was surrounded by enemies, and she had left behind her an enemy who could describe her. Why had she *done* that?

Aubry would have killed Scar-Face without a second thought, and tucked the pain away where it would never show on the outside. She was one of perhaps three people who knew what the deaths, the murders, the destruction of human life and body had cost Aubry Knight. Others saw an external shell, a husk of a man animated by an enormous vitality, a man of gigantic melancholy and rare mirth. But as he sloughed off his sociopathic shell, the violent memories emerged to haunt him.

Aubry Knight was paying the price of being inhuman. As she was now paying the price of being human.

For all of her theoretical martial knowledge, except for a single foray into Death Valley Jenna had lived a sheltered existence. *Welcome to the real world.* And this was the world, the world of blood and death that Aubry Knight had lived in for forty years, somehow managing to hold on to his humanity.

She was not, could not be Aubry Knight.

But neither could Aubry be Jenna.

She paid for her drink and left the bar. Night was coming to Daglia, and police patrols filled the streets. Her first task was to find a place to bed down.

2

In any society, there are those who live on the edge, those who will not or cannot conform, who slip through the cracks between welfare and social services, who cannot afford housing and yet do not resort to crime. And it is fashionable for the forces of law and order to turn their gazes away from the temporary shantytowns erected beneath bridges, on dark corners, and in the back alleys of every major city in the world.

Jenna sought them out, and they were not hard to find. The wind coming in off the desert was cold, and it was time for settling in. She followed an elderly woman who walked with a bowed body and trembling step, toward an uncertain destination. The streets narrowed and darkened. The sounds grew thin and wavery, sounds of music played on someone's radio, a news report, perhaps a soap opera.

The buildings looked as if they had been thrown together with pasteboard, and patched and repatched until they resembled, more than anything, the homes of termites.

In this land, the faces were dusky, but they echoed similar faces all over the world. They were fatigued beyond any ordinary meaning of the word, and had lived at the edge of hunger for too many years, but there was also fierce pride there. Jenna hunkered down with her back against the wall, her hands folded over her chest, and looked at the old woman as she enfolded herself in a sheath of pasteboard, preparing to bed down.

The woman stared at Jenna, a quizzical quality to her expression. She smiled, broken yellow teeth shining in her black face. From her paltry stock of pasteboards, she offered a broad sheet. She spoke a few sharp words, loudly. Nearby stacks of rubble quavered, and dark heads poked out, speaking in questioning tones. The old woman chattered back at them. The other men and women rustled in their meager stores, and likewise offered.

There was not much, but they shared what they had. They drew a bit closer together, and there was laughter in a language that Jenna didn't understand. These men and women offered each other bits of cheese and bread, the heartbreakingly small substance of their lives, sharing without reservation. She wondered if they knew each other's names. It probably didn't matter. Even if they had never seen each other before, they knew each other. Their stories were the same. And they didn't need to inquire as to the particulars of Jenna's story. She was of no language, no land, an orphan like the rest of them. How she had reached this alley was of no importance.

She was just another homeless face, who, for this night, had found a home.

Jenna ate, and forced her voice to laugh with them. Despite her fatigue, her pain, and the increasing dizziness, she felt herself relax for the first time in twenty hours. And with that relaxation came a series of massive yawns. The well of fatigue was so deep that it seemed bottomless. The old woman showed Jenna how to construct a bed of pasteboard and rags. In the company of strangers, Jenna fell into a deep, deep sleep, from which she did not awaken until morning.

3

Jenna awakened before any of them. The sun had not yet risen, but the first feathers of its warmth were stirring the air. A distant dog was barking, as if shaking off the filaments of night, preparing to greet the new day. Jenna's companions were still asleep. Their faces were incongruously clean for the circumstances, and relaxed, as if in poverty they had found great peace.

She felt an almost absurd kinship with them.

Her side throbbed as she reached into her pocket and removed the thin sheaf of bills that she had taken from Scar-Face. After a moment's consideration, she peeled off one of the larger bills and slipped it into the old woman's withered hand. What was her savior's name? How had she come to such a state? And how had she managed to keep her humanity? What beliefs had sustained her?

Soberly, Jenna wondered if she could have done half so well under similar circumstances. Then again, she reflected, she might soon have an excellent opportunity to find out.

Jenna walked the street for an hour before she found an open bakery, where she purchased a hard roll and a mug of coffee.

Her money wouldn't last long. And when it was gone, what then? Would she be reduced to mugging? Or worse? A floatcar, early-morning patrol, whisked past. She shivered. By sign language she pointed out the coffee brew that she desired. She walked down the street, nursing the cup with tiny sips until the liquid grew tepid and she was almost down to the dregs. The street was coming to life, filling with tradesmen and citizenry. She dared not linger anywhere, for fear that someone would recognize her.

How long could she keep moving? She had to find a place to rest, a place to lay her head, to make plans. Despite the night's sleep, she was dead tired, her skin was fever-hot, her side ached like hell, and she still had no plan of action.

A tiny brown man hurried down the street ahead of her, wrapped in saffron robes. He looked as if he were a half-breed, part Indian and part African. He thumbprinted the front door of a curio shop, and it sighed open. She walked past, almost walked on, when she noticed the sign in the window. It was written in a language that she didn't understand, but contained a small, grainy picture. Flat. Color. Clipped from a local newsfax.

Pictures of two African boys. Thirteen years old, perhaps. Underfed. Intense.

They faced each other across the warlocked expanse of a chessboard. Each had a trophy by his side. The trophy of the boy to the left was almost twice the size of the other.

Behind them, smiling like a proud father, was the little mixed-blood proprietor.

Jenna's mind whirled. She opened the door and followed him in.

It was warm inside the shop, which was crammed to the rafters with boxes and trays, toys and artificial flowers and blown-glass widgets, gewgaws and knickknacks and tiny figurines, books and scrolls and oversized pencils and plastic fruits, framed paintings and dusty motors and jars filled with strange dust.

The proprietor, a thin-faced man in his sixties, prattled at her in a singsong voice. She supposed that he was telling her to leave, to return in ten or fifteen minutes, when he was ready to open. What he couldn't know is that she *couldn't*. She was running out of options, and had to take her desperate gamble *now*.

She said a single word to him, and made a motion with her hands.

To her delight, his eyes widened.

He narrowed his eyes, as if evaluating her anew. He went to a counter on the far side of the room, one that was in shadow. He turned on an overhead light.

The room was filled with toys. With children's books. With puzzles and gewgaws. She prayed that she was correct.

He reached down under the counter and brought out a checker plaid board, and carved ivory Staunton pieces.

The chess set was beautiful. Even in the low light, she could tell that the pieces were hand-carved from ivory, and that he was justifiably proud of them. She looked at his eyes, and knew that she had made her choice well. This man could easily be the sponsor of the local chess club. Or at the least, a devotee. He owned a knickknack shop, with an emphasis on games of logic and skill.

Swiftly, Jenna set up the pieces, her every movement as controlled and careful, as smooth and practiced as she could make it.

Then, from her pocket, she removed her largest remaining bill—equivalent to about five dollars American—and placed it next to the chessboard.

For a long moment he said nothing; then he opened his wallet and placed a matching bill beside it.

Jenna moved her queen's pawn forward.

He responded by matching her, refusing to relinquish the center of the board.

She responded, moving out a knight to protect the pawn. Three moves later he was engrossed, a thin, intense smile creasing his face. A customer came in, and the little man excused himself, sold the woman a selection of ancient phonograph albums, and returned to the chessboard.

A truck loaded with soldiers floated past the front window. Jenna tensed, praying that she wouldn't be noticed.

The little man had her a pawn and a knight down. Despite his scarred face and broken teeth, his thick skin, intelligence fairly *seethed* behind those eyes.

Outside the window, a floatcar *shoosh*ed down. Still, the little man's eyes were upon her.

He carefully moved one of his own men, and studied her face.

There was a ringing at the front door. He glanced up. Two soldiers stood at the threshold.

Jenna felt trapped. He watched her. She slowed her breathing. As deliberately as she had ever done anything in her life, Jenna studied the board.

She focused her attention down to a pencil point. There might have been no sound at all, nothing in the world but the two of them in that shop. The board swelled until it filled every nook and cranny of her mind, until she saw the interactions of the ivory pieces as if they were alive, and dynamic. He wanted to see something. He wanted to learn . . . something. . . .

Jenna moved her queen forward, and a slight smile tugged at the edge of his mouth. He took the queen with his bishop, and then watched her. She moved a pawn forward, revealing check with her own bishop. He sighed, and tipped his king over.

Something inside Jenna almost snapped. The two soldiers entered the shop.

The little man looked at her. Jenna was as still as death in that shop. Both soldiers were armed. At this distance there was nothing she could do. She and Aubry *together* could have done nothing. The little man spoke out to them, once again in a language that she couldn't understand. He pointed at her, then he pointed outside, and the soldiers nodded. They left the shop.

The little man came back to her, his eyes filled with humor.

Jenna touched her own throat. "My name is Jenna," she said.

He pointed to himself. "Name . . . Pattabhi," he said. "You . . . good play. Play more?"

"Please," she said.

Neither of them said another word. Without moving his eyes from hers, his hands scrambled with practiced precision, setting up the chessboard once again.

4

What followed was a time of hallucination and confusion, a time when the chasm between reality and fantasy threatened to swallow Aubry whole. Life devolved into a dream, something that roiled at the edge of his consciousness and never spilled over into awakening.

He remembered transport in a canvas-covered flatbed truck. Beyond the roar of the engines he heard other sounds, wind and animal sounds as they traveled a rough road that extended to an infinite horizon.

Within the truck there were touches and words, and occasional sharp pains that pierced the constant dull ache. Medication sweeping through his veins like lava. Voices sweet with song urged him back from the precipice. He was, for the moment, content to follow their advice.

The desert howled outside the truck, battered at its canvas walls. Sometimes he slept, and sometimes he awakened to its dusty call, the scrape of its fingers against rough fabric.

A dark woman bent over him, her face young-old, her hair tightly rowed. She had seen much of the world—perhaps too much—but was still beautiful. In a way, she reminded him of Mira.

There was a sense of peace about her that let him slip more deeply into his coma, down and down to a single spot of light. Just a single . . .

In it, there was warmth.

And then darkness.

When he awakened again, there was no movement, and little light. He lay in a room with a low ceiling that looked as if it might have been constructed from corrugated tin. It vibrated thinly in response to a distant, rhythmic thrumming.

Aubry lay listening and thinking, too weak to move. He couldn't feel his arms or legs, or his lower body. He slept for a while.

When he awakened the next time, an elderly man sat by the side of the bed, a man who gazed upon him as a father might examine a fond child. He held a broad spoonful of some steaming broth under Aubry's nose.

It smelled delicious. Aubry's mouth found the edge of the spoon, and he suckled greedily.

"Slowly," the man said. It was in no language that Aubry had ever heard, and yet the electronic thing within him translated it almost instantly. "Slowly. We have time. No one can find you here."

"Who are you?"

His benefactor smiled. "You can call me Old Man."

"Where am I, Old Man?"

"You are in the Iron Mountain, in the south of what was once called Rwanda, which existed between Tanzania and Zaire." Old Man's mood darkened. "All gone, now. All PanAfrica now. You are safe. You are with the Ibandi. Your people, my son. Your people."

5

SEPTEMBER 18. SWARNAVILLE, PANAFRICAN REPUBLIC.

It took the better part of a day for Promise to receive her call. The air shimmered, and there was a brief surge of light, and Phillipe Swarna stood before her.

"Good afternoon," he said gravely. "And welcome to the PanAfrican Republic. I trust that your journey has been comfortable."

A chair materialized in the middle of the room with him, and he sat in it. She observed him closely, trying to open her senses to the drama unfolding before her. He was tall—in his prime he might have been almost as tall as

Aubry—but his face was thinner, his shoulders narrower, although there was every evidence that he might once have been quite muscular. His face was wrinkled and shiny. She could believe that he might have been well over a hundred years old, and marveled that any technology could have kept him so very well preserved. The shiny skin . . . she supposed that this was the result of several generations of differing, increasingly sophisticated regeneration treatments. She wondered: How many of the problems that they sought to correct had been caused by the previous course of treatments?

"It is regrettably impossible for me to see you personally, but my very good friend Dr. Kanagawa will see to your needs."

There was the very slightest suggestion of a pause, and Promise suddenly had the feeling that Swarna had never heard of her, knew nothing of her visit. That this was a mere construction, a computer-generated image, programmed for the occasion, but based on some core template of Swarna's movements and word patterns.

It was eerily effective, but she was certain of its artificiality: there was no way that a head of state like Phillipe Swarna could afford the time to see her personally, or even make tapes for every minor dignitary who wanted his time.

And . . . she had heard the state-of-emergency bulletin. And knew that Aubry had disappeared into PanAfrica to kill this man. Could there be a connection? Could Swarna be dead?

While her mind had drifted, Swarna disappeared, and Kanagawa took his place.

Kanagawa could have been anywhere between forty and sixty-five, his black hair graying around the sides. His body was comfortably padded, but healthy and somewhat sun-bronzed.

Kanagawa rose from the couch where he had waited politely. He extended a hand, and a smile curled the edges of his mouth, although his eyes remained cool.

"As President Swarna said, welcome to the PanAfrican Republic. I am Dr. Kanagawa, PanAfrican Department of

Public Works. Although your initial bid did not meet with our needs, Mr. Wu has vouched for you. He has yet to fail us. The possibility of a joint venture between the Scavengers and Wu Industrial is intriguing. Your portfolio is impressive. Your bids for construction and demolition are quite competitive."

"Our use of local labor makes it possible," Promise said quietly. "We are interested in expanding our interests into the international market. Given that that is the case, we are willing to take a loss on our first project with you, to demonstrate the quality of our work."

"And your track record is your guarantee of quality." Kanagawa watched her shrewdly. "I suppose there is no way you could know that your bid undercut the nearest competitor by seven hundred thousand dollars."

"No." *Yes. Bless Wu's flinty little heart.* "The bridge construction is identical to a job we completed last year in São Paulo. I think that we can modify local materials. Two months for the training program. We will be turning a good portion of the cash back into the local economy, so there is an additional benefit to you."

Kanagawa's gaze locked with hers. "The situation seems . . . if I might hazard to say so . . . almost too good to be true."

His eyes flickered to where Leslie, wearing a charming pink dress, sat in one corner of the room, reading by natural light.

"Your daughter?" Kanagawa inquired politely.

"Yes. Leslie? Say hello to Dr. Kanagawa."

Leslie smiled politely. *"Kanagawa-san, ohayo gozaimas."*

Kanagawa's left eyebrow rose in surprise. *"Nihon-go ga dekimasu ka?"*

"Hai, sukoshi dekimasu. Hon no sukoshi."

Kanagawa laughed out loud. "I hope to meet you." He regarded Promise. "Your child is delightful."

Promise nodded almost shyly. "I am very proud of her."

"Well . . ." Kanagawa's eyes shifted, as if weighing a thought. "There is a state of emergency at the CAR border town of Daglia, more than a hundred miles north of Swarnaville. I think we can provide sufficient security forces. It should be safe to recruit labor here."

"For that," Promise said, "I would be extremely grateful."

He paused, and seemed to be checking a set of off-camera notes.

Promise's only safe assumption was that PanAfrican computers would turn up the assassination attempt in Los Angeles. But that was not necessarily disastrous: if that operation was directed by Swarna's covert-operations people, Kanagawa was unlikely to have been informed. The entire operation would be classified. And it was equally unlikely that the originator of such a "black bag" operation would concern himself with a minor engineering bid in a northern province. Swarna's holographic simulacrum was boilerplate. Dr. Kanagawa, an important enough man in Public Works, would have no reason to suspect that Swarna had ordered the assassination of an American named Aubry Knight.

Bureaucratic inefficiency was her greatest protection.

"I think that we can do business, Ms. Cotonou. What is your next step?"

"Checking materials, and recruiting labor. I will want access to the following areas." She scanned Kanagawa a list. A holofax appeared before him, so quickly she might have handed it to him.

Kanagawa examined it without hesitation. "None of these areas are secure. I will run them past the computers, but once again, I think that we can do business."

6

SEPTEMBER 25. IRON MOUNTAIN.

A succession of men and women nursed Aubry, cared for him, tended to him. He began to recognize them the way a child knows the adults in his neighborhood. He felt safe, and warm, and drifted mindlessly from dream to wakefulness to sleep, and back again.

The woman who had been with him in the truck was named Tanesha. Despite the wrinkles starring her eyes, her skin was very fine, and he grew to anticipate her touch when she checked his temperature, or helped to change him.

From time to time, there would be quiet visitors, men and women who appeared in the doorway filled with smiling curiosity, almost as if they shared a private joke.

They were clearly worker-folk, dressed in dust-stained overalls. And he saw them as being a kind of Scavenger, and felt himself at home among them.

On the fourth day, Aubry awoke feeling famished. A delighted Tanesha ordered food for him: a kind of coarse rice, meal pancakes, and an enormous salad. Fresh fruit for dessert. He bolted it down almost without thinking, and only after finishing did he realize that he had eaten no meat since awakening in Iron Mountain.

He rent the air with a long, satisfied belch. Tanesha laughed wholeheartedly. "Good," she said. "I believe that you will live."

"Where is Old Man?" he asked, and then paused. "And why . . ."

"Why does he call himself that?"

Aubry nodded.

"He has a name," Tanesha said. "But it is a custom of

our people—if there is an enemy who has dishonored us, our warriors forsake their names until honor has been regained." Aubry's expression changed to one of puzzlement. "Do not concern yourself with this thing. Old Man is in the conveyor room. I will take you there."

For generations, the Ibandi had worked Iron Mountain, the most productive source of ore in Central Africa. A hundred years before, they had used the methods of their ancestors. Then, inevitably, the modern world had caught up with them, and the technology had changed.

But one thing remained the same—these mountains belonged to the Ibandi, and had through all tribal memory. In the last forty years they had pulled back into the mountains, had tunneled deeply within, creating a network of shelters and protected domiciles that could withstand a nuclear attack.

And the mining continued. Beyond the mountains, there was farmland, land that had been carefully irrigated and fertilized over generations. With the growth of Ibandi financial power, experts from around the world had contributed to their knowledge of agriculture and land reclamation, until their thirteen thousand square miles of land, a kingdom within the PanAfrican Republic, was self-supporting, as well as an exporter of textiles, ore, and food.

The living spaces within the Iron Mountain coexisted with the mining operation itself. Conveyor belts rumbled twenty-four hours a day, as steady as the beat of a mother's heart.

The halls were seven feet high, with arched ceilings and darkly tiled floors. Living quarters were often on one side of a hallway, while on the other was a cavernous, glass-walled hole. To peer into it was to look into the heart of the Iron Mountain itself, to look down into the labyrinth of tunnels, seeing men and women who seemed the size of ants laboring, running machines and ore cars, supervising the conveyor strip carting iron ore from the depths of the

Earth. The dry stench of burnt and powdered rock hung in the air like a curtain.

Tanesha led him down a complex system of elevators and slidewalks, and into the heart of the mines, where, finally, he saw Old Man.

The Ibandi patriarch wore overalls and a hard hat, and was in conference with a younger, larger man whose hard, dark face was spiderwebbed with smile lines.

Tanesha said, "I have other business. He will speak with you when he can." He turned to thank her, but she was already gone.

After about four minutes, Old Man slapped the younger man on the shoulder, pointing at something on a clipboard. They both laughed uproariously, and then Old Man turned to Aubry.

He waved his hand in greeting, and motioned him over. "Aubry," he said. "Peter Challa."

They shook hands. Challa was three inches shorter than Aubry, but still a large, powerful man with an infectious grin. "I've heard of you," he said. "You don't look so abominable." Then he laughed and shook his head, going back to his work.

"So," Old Man said. "What do you think of all of this?"

"All of this belongs to the Ibandi?"

"Yes. We have mined these mountains for a thousand years—and will until the Earth has no more bounty."

"Swarna didn't try to nationalize it?"

"He tried." Old Man grinned. "The price we made him pay is too high. So now, we pay each other tribute. He gets the ore he wants, at a fair price. And he gives us . . . other things."

"And who are the Ibandi? I've heard that name." He searched his memory. Suddenly, his tired eyes opened wide. "Now I remember—the Ibandi were Swarna's people. He was a priest, wasn't he?"

"We are *your* people as well," Old Man said. "When Swarna took power . . ." He paused, perhaps searching for the right phrasing. "He was careful to remove those who might challenge him. There was utter chaos—remember, in creating PanAfrica he consolidated six different countries into a single entity. Hundreds of thousands sought to flee the continent. You were one of the refugees, when you were only a baby."

"How . . ." Aubry took a moment to digest that. "My . . . father brought me to America?"

"No. Your father died before you were born."

"Then who . . ."

"The man who brought you to America was Thomas Jai, a great Ibandi warrior. He was sworn to protect you."

Aubry could hardly hear his own voice as he asked the next question. "Why? Why me?"

Old Man smiled. "You were helpless, and needed aid. You need make nothing more out of it."

Aubry was quiet, and he looked out over the factory from inside the control room, the conveyor belts carrying the ore from the mountain down to the loading docks.

The windows were slanted out at a thirty-degree angle, and the glass, he sensed, was tinted so that those below couldn't see up into the control room. Most of the men and women working the conveyor belts were as dark as Aubry. Some were not. There were a few Japanese, and a few scattered Indians.

"This is all so confusing."

"Of course. Nothing is as it seems. Everything is as it is."

Aubry looked at him, and realized that Old Man was laughing at him. Gently, but definitely.

"I don't know what is next," Aubry said.

"Next, you finish healing. And then, if you wish, you can return to America."

7

The mining equipment droned steadily through the night, never completely dying away. Nor did it ever completely grasp consciousness. Aubry lay in bed thinking about the people he had seen, and the things that had been said, and realized that for the first time in . . . weeks? . . . he felt whole.

He levered himself up to sitting position, and decided to attempt the Rubber Band, the series of exercises that he had learned in childhood.

A series of exercises taught him by . . .

His father? No. Not his father. By *Thomas Jai,* a warrior who had given his life for Aubry. Who had given this one piece of his heritage to a small, frail boy, that that heritage might not die completely.

Aubry stood, feet close together. Breathing deeply, he felt a swell of warmth in his feet, let the warmth roll up his legs, connect with his hips, let himself begin to sway.

He bent backward, feeling his back muscles contract as his chest expanded. His muscles, unstressed for days, moved stiffly beneath his skin. He arched powerfully, expanding as he inhaled, swaying. Then he thumped down into an inverted V and placed his palms flat on the ground; as he had been able to do, with absolutely no warm-up, for all of his memory.

All his weight went onto his hands. His tendons creaked as they began to bear the load. The first of a long, unbroken series of breaths hissed from his mouth.

For the next ten minutes he was lost in the movements, as he transported himself to another time, and place.

He was once again in the city of his youth, a warren of alleys and sewers and abandoned shops. It was a place alive with memories. Sometimes the movements mimicked the shapes of the city, and sometimes the air in his lungs escaped like steam, mimicking animal sounds.

At the fifteen-minute mark, his breath began to grow ragged, and he felt the first trembles of exhaustion. And at seventeen, his entire body was shaking.

Sweat was pouring from him in a torrent, and he could no longer control himself. Then, during a complex movement where his weight was balanced on his arms, his entire trunk rotated to the side and parallel to the floor. Aubry could take no more, and collapsed, lying on the cold tile in a pool of sweat. Trembling.

But not unsatisfied. He was on the way to recovery.

From the doorway came five sardonic claps. There stood Challa, an enormous smile splitting his lips.

"Is good," he said, in stilted English. "You have no teacher, for long time, yes?"

Aubry bit back his retort. This man suddenly reminded him of something . . . of himself.

Challa didn't have Aubry's size, but he conveyed the impression of concealed speed and effortless, efficient movement.

Aubry wiped sweat from his forehead, spattered it from his fingertips onto the ground. "You know this?"

"Every child know fire dance," Challa said, still in English. "You do high form. I know low form. You want see?"

Aubry nodded, almost foolishly grateful.

Challa said, "You want see, you come to the dance tonight. You see!"

And he laughed, and left Aubry lying in the stink of his own sweat, thinking on things that he hadn't considered for many years.

8

Aubry showered, shaved, and dressed himself, and for the first time left the complex of tunnels and catwalks that composed Iron Mountain. The tramway took him to a balcony next to an elevator system, from which he could look out over a valley.

From where he was he could see train tracks stretching off into the distance, warehouses and geodesic domes, and a four-story concrete block ventilated with steam and smoke pipes.

Below him and to his left, a huge conveyor belt rumbled. It seemed to Aubry that a million tons a minute flowed out of that mine. Then it would be down the chute and onto boxcars at the foot of the mountains, where it would be loaded again and sent to the refineries.

He took the elevator down and trotted to the four-story concrete block, testing his body gently, and cautiously pleased at the results.

The building was Iron Mountain's small private refinery; most of its ore was carried a hundred miles to the south in boxcars, to more extensive refineries. But here in the valley at the foot of the Iron Mountain, coal was carted in, ore was heated and pressured to extract the iron within, and molded and tested by Ibandi workmen whose fathers had mined this ground, and refined its fruits, for a thousand years.

A corrugated-steel door opened before he reached it, and closed automatically behind him.

The air within was hot and dry. Most of the refinery seemed to be automated, but there were human beings everywhere, checking pipes and conveyor belts, wiring and scanning systems with sober, dutiful care. A thin stream of liquid fire gushed from an enormous vat as he watched. Even at a hundred meters, the heat crisped the hair on his arms.

He climbed a winding metal staircase to a small surveillance platform, where Tanesha stood checking a clipboard against a readout meter. She didn't notice him until he squeezed her shoulder with one large hand. She gave him a short, pretty smile that made him burn. "How did you build all of this?"

"These mountains," she raised her voice to pitch it above the roar of the machinery, "have always belonged to our people. Many have tried to take them. None succeeded. In the end, the Europeans, and later the Japanese, helped us build factories, and brought in the mining equipment, and we built what you see here. It has grown. We mine the mountains, and we plant trees and brush to cover the scars. We brought water to our desert." She looked at him sharply. "And we are a free people."

She turned, very lightly and tightly, with a physical grace that he recognized. "I know someone who would appreciate you," he chuckled. *Jenna.*

Grief for loss of Bloodeagle, and fear for Jenna, hit him like a wave of fever. *God.* Was she even alive? And where was she? And was there even any way to find out?

She looked back at him, over her shoulder, and the light made her face seem a liquid opal instead of a human form. The liquid steel gushed sparks. "Really?"

"Yes," he said quietly. She waited for him to continue, but he remained silent.

She paused, and let her clipboard slide into a slot on the ceaseless machine. "Are you going to be at the dance this evening?"

"What kind of dance?"

"It is a celebration. All the mine workers will be there. And many of our people from the entire Ibandi nation. It is almost time for our boys to become men. Almost time for the Firedance."

—you want to see, you come to the dance tonight . . .

"You mean the morning exercise routine?"

"That also carries the name. The emphasis is different. Say it as if one word."

"You mean Firedance, instead of fire dance."

"Good," she said, almost shyly. "It is very good."

9

At dinnertime, Tanesha came to him in his quarters and took him back outside. She wore a dress composed of earth browns and sky blues, dense, heavy fabric that looked handmade and much more traditional than anything he had seen her in.

Pungent food smells, the aroma of onions and garlic, potatoes and spiced beef drifted from kitchen units set up farther down the valley. There, the communal meal was being prepared by the young men and women of the tribe, in a ritual as old as the Ibandi themselves.

But now, before a circle of flaming torches, hundreds of young Ibandi men and women stood in a huge circle of packed earth. They stood swaying, gazing up at the sky, bodies moving in response to music that Aubry could not hear.

Then, at some unspoken signal, they took in a deep, sighing breath, and began to perform the Firedance, what Aubry had always called the Rubber Band.

The first thing he noticed was that they seemed boneless. Their motion was effortlessly fluid, and absolutely synchronized with their breathing. Somewhat shamefacedly, Aubry realized that he had allowed his own morning rituals to become unsynchronized, shamelessly sloppy when compared with the precise rhythms of this group.

They rolled and somersaulted backward and forward, making strange music with the thrum of their breathing, the impact of their young bodies against the hard-packed earth.

There was a fluidity to it that he had never achieved in his own practice. He wanted to weep.

The ritual lasted an hour. By the end of that time, they had twisted and contorted their bodies into a variety of shapes and clusters, and a very faint memory, far back in Aubry's mind, said that what they were doing correctly was what he had done incorrectly for decades. . . .

Old Man came up from behind Aubry, so quietly that Aubry was almost unaware of it until they were shoulder to shoulder.

"This is the first level," Old Man said. "And you see that they have the fluidity that you lack."

"Yes—but it is still beautiful."

Old Man nodded. "But there is more than beauty. There must be function. We have little need of the higher levels, the warrior levels, now. Thomas Jai was one of the last who understood the warrior-hunter ways of our people. We are miners, now." Something in Old Man's smile put the lie to those words.

He gripped Aubry's shoulder. "But you . . . we would have you show us the extent of your knowledge. Some of us remember the old ways. . . ." He smiled. "For tradition. Tradition is important."

10

SEPTEMBER 28

Trucks and trams, and men and women traveling on foot and in private cars, small skimmers and light airplanes, appeared continuously throughout the following day. Dinner was an unending stream of meats and fowl and fruits and vegetables and fish, serving at least five thousand who had gathered for the Firedance celebration.

Aubry hadn't eaten much of it. He was being observed,

and *knew* that he was being observed. The whispers of *"American,"* and *"Abomination,"* put him on edge.

The trays were cleared away. The diners formed a gigantic circle on the ceremonial earth mound where the Rubber Band had been practiced earlier.

The youngest Ibandi men of the tribe stripped down to loincloths, and carried six-foot spears—the traditional weapon of the Ibandi. Old Man and another dozen elders gathered in the center. Old Man used his spear as a walking stick, leaned on it, and began to speak.

"In the beginning," Old Man said, "there were the wild grasses, and the animals, and the sky. And then came the white people. The white people tried to take our mountains. They tried to move into the deserts, and sent their soldiers. They rode the trains into our territory. And they died, all of them. And we still have the spears whose heads we made from their railroad spikes!" He slammed the butt of his spear upon the ground, and the night was filled with hooting.

"But the days in which we roamed free were at an end. The world reached out for us, and we could never go back to the old, free ways. This we knew, this we understood from the very beginning. The white people knew it as well."

"We had our own ways and our own gods. And one day, one of us rose up. This man was a priest of our people. He knew our ways, knew the Five Songs, the traditions of our wisdom. The power of our priest is the power to heal the hearts of the men who kill to protect the tribe. He reached out to the warriors of Uganda, of Zaire, of Tanzania and Kenya. And the soldiers listened to him, and followed him, and rose up to throw off their leaders."

Old Man looked directly at Aubry.

"His name was Phillipe Swarna. He left his people, left the Ibandi, carrying with him our knowledge of the heart and body, and went out into the world. And when he was in the world, he shared his wisdom with many who were not worthy. And we watched. And were not pleased.

"And when he rose up in the world, we sought to remind

him that he had betrayed his roots, sought to expose him
to his own incongruency. And when he refused to listen,
and we strove to warn the people, he sent soldiers against
us, and drove us into the strongholds of the Iron Mountain. And further than this he could not go. He tried, and
we fought back. And we killed his soldiers here in the
mountains.

"Then he signed the paper with us, and this truce he has
never broken. When he made parley with the men from
Japan, he offered education to our children that would
allow them to grow in the world of the present, and we saw
that many of our ways had been the ways of the past. And
there has been peace."

Old Man walked a somber circle on the axis of his spear.
"But now one calls, who has the right to call. There are the
old songs, and the old ways, and we must answer, because
to fail to answer is to lose ourselves, lose our hearts. And
so we bring to our bosom, bring to the Iron Mountain, a
lost child."

Old Man bade Aubry rise. He did, and walked to the
center of the mound and paused, deafened by his own
heartbeat. And he scanned their intelligently inquisitive
faces.

"Who are you?" Old Man asked.

Aubry opened his mouth and started to answer, and
then remembered another man, or perhaps the phantasm
of a man, who had asked a similar question, long ago. And
there was no rational answer. He felt himself floating, rid-
ing on inner rhythms, and said, in a small voice, "A child,
glad to be home."

He expected laughter, or derision, but instead, there was
a nodding of heads. Those wise, dark faces creased in
smiles.

"Show us," Old Man said. "Show us what you remember."

And Aubry began. He already knew that there were errors in his practice of the Firedance. He also knew that it
would be dishonest to try to correct them now, to change
what he had done so many tens of thousands of times.

So he performed his morning exercises, and became so locked into the flow of the breathing, the power of the movements, that he was hardly aware that the night sounds around him had faded completely away.

When he stopped an hour later, his body steamed with sweat. Every muscle was stretched and strengthened and wrung to its maximum, there was *still* no sound.

Old Man strode forward and took his hand.

"This you did," Old Man asked, his voice trembling, "with no teacher for thirty years?"

Aubry swallowed hard, realizing that something enormous hung in the balance, that his next words had some devastating impact on the remainder of his life.

"Yes. Father . . . Thomas Jai, the man who I called my father . . . taught me these things, and then he died."

"How did he die?"

"There was a fight. He tried to help. I remember . . ."

He closed his eyes. . . .

11

It was a cold night, and the man Aubry called Father was walking with the child he called his son. As they passed by one of the alleys in the area called South Central Los Angeles, both heard a scuffling sound.

The sounds and the sights, even the smells came back to Aubry clearly, closely, and he was murmuring aloud without even realizing that that was what he was doing.

"I saw him. There were three of them, attacking a woman. All of them had weapons. My father . . . tried to stop them. He was large. Strong. But the one that held the woman down was larger. My . . . father pushed him. It was a small thing, it didn't look like much, but the man flew. He flew. My father reached out with the tip of his . . . walking stick."

Old Man's eyes widened. "Ah. He used a stick, then?"

"Yes."

"But he did not hit the man?"

"No. I remember. He reached out slowly, and not until the stick was in contact with the second man's body did he push. I heard a snap. The man flew away, and smashed into the wall. The man looked . . . very surprised."

"Yes, I imagine that he was."

"The third man stabbed my father, and then ran away. I tried to help him. . . ."

Aubry shook his head, and then bowed it.

"And you have been alone since that time?"

"Yes."

"Which of the Songs do you know?"

"Songs?" Aubry asked, mystified.

The old man closed his eyes. "Songs. We sing them to help the memory. Europeans would have written them down as books, five books of sacred knowledge, knowledge of all things external and internal. So. You do not know the correct form of the movements, and you do not know the Songs. And yet you have achieved all that you have." He clucked, smiling. "It is a tribute both to you, and to the movement system taught you by Thomas Jai."

He took Aubry's hands. "I would like to welcome you home. I would be honored to complete your education."

Aubry's head swam. "Complete . . . ?"

"Yes," Old Man said. "Every movement of the Firedance has an internal component. Each has a sound. Together the sounds make up the Songs. The songs that you should have learned."

He called out two of the youngest boys, and they flowed through the movements, each limb moving in perfect sequence, every joint rotating in perfect order. It was a miracle of motion. and their breathing shaped itself into words, into music. Into a kinetic rhapsody. It took him into another world, into a place inside himself, where colors and geometric forms danced and swayed.

"What is this?" Aubry whispered.

"We are the Ibandi. Every people on this planet has their gift to give. The Ibandi have a special gift. We have known of the arts which are called yoga, and called karate or aiki, for thousands of years. The human body has not changed. Instrumentation has changed. We developed ways of teaching our children the laws of mind and body, in a balanced matrix. Mind, body, spirit, together. None more important than the others. Thomas Jai gave you your body. He did not live to give you the keys to mind and heart."

Aubry was entranced, bound by strands of melody, by patterns of perfectly synchronized movement. His own body twitched, responding to the deeply etched memories of that motion. Each separate sound seemed to reverberate in a different part of him. There was a high note that made his head ring like a temple bell. He was intoxicated by light. "Today," Old Man said, "beginning tonight, you will be given the keys of your manhood ceremony.

"Aubry Knight," he said. "You may leave this place, and return to your world."

"No," Aubry said quietly.

"What? What did you say?"

Aubry's eyes felt as if they were swelling. "I said no. I want it all."

"You wish to claim your manhood."

"Yes."

"You wish to become a warrior of your tribe."

"Yes."

"You will let no fear, no pain, no past bitterness stand between you and your destiny."

"No."

"You are willing to belong first to yourself, and then to your people, and only after that to the things of the outer world?"

He swallowed, hard. "Yes."

"Then you will join us. We will light the fire within you. You will bring that flame to the Firedance. And there you will make your choice."

12

Aubry awoke from a fantasy of open veldt and clear night sky. The awakening was sudden, but not abrupt, as smooth a transition from dream to wakefulness as any he had known.

Tanesha knelt by the side of the bed. She wore a cloak of elegantly woven cotton, and smelled like honey. Her face was very clear, and direct, and at peace.

Aubry sat up, staring at her. "What is this?"

"The ritual begins," she said.

"What am I . . ."

Her face tilted up, and he almost fell into her eyes. There was depth enough for five of him. "You must leave behind everything that you have known. The Songs are five. Songs of Earth, Wind, Fire, Death, and Birth. Body, Mind, Emotion, Spirit . . . and Void. Void is the emptiness, the unknowable. It is woman. You must be born anew, into the Void, or you will never survive the Fire."

The blood roared in his ears. What of Promise?

You must belong first to yourself . . .

And if he belonged first to himself, then what happened between him and Tanesha had nothing to do with his vows to Promise.

Did Promise belong first to herself? Yes. Always. More than he ever had. And she did what she did because it served her, and the world she sought to build. And if their places were reversed, how would he feel . . . ?

Terrible. Jealous. Betrayed.

But *would* he have been betrayed? If she needed to heal herself; if, away from him, she needed to learn or experience something . . . would it be a betrayal if she returned to him? So what if he hurt. Did he own her body even if not there to love her?

If she belonged first to herself, the answer was no. Even if it hurt him . . .

No. That was the lie.

Even if *he hurt himself* with the knowledge of what she had done. She had promised to love and cherish him, to grow with him. She had never promised to be his property. He would hurt, if he knew. But the hurt was his concern, not hers.

She cannot hurt me, unless I make it so.

And I cannot hurt her.

God. Is this the truth?

Tanesha knelt by the side of the bed, awaiting his decision.

His hand shaking, Aubry threw the cover back, and drew her into the bed next to him.

13

"I am you," she said. "I am the Feminine side of yourself. It is through interaction with the Feminine that the Masculine is defined. It is through interaction with the Masculine that the Feminine is defined. To one who has never seen light, the concept of darkness has no meaning."

She took his hand and placed it on her left breast. Through the robe, he could feel her heart beating, a steady, healthy dance of life.

"Have you ever felt a woman's heartbeat?" she asked quietly. "Or have you always been too eager to reach the fire?" Her voice had a hint of tease in it.

"You were not born of woman, Aubry Knight. You never knew the call of your mother's heartbeat, floating there within her body, warm and safe. You never knew this." Puzzled, he started to speak, but Tanesha shushed him with her lips. She parted the robe, and Aubry smoothed her skin with his hand, seeking to feel the steady pumping flow within her, seeking the source of her aliveness. Her flesh was smooth, and very warm.

Gingerly, Aubry laid his head against her chest, his ear above her heart, and listened to the *ka-shoosh ka-shoosh* as it rumbled through its hundred thousand daily contractions.

"Find my breathing," she said, "and match it with your own. Synchronize. Listen to my heart. I have no limit, Aubry Knight. Take from me the comfort you have sought for a lifetime. Take from me, and build the woman inside you. Everything that lives is born of woman," she whispered. "And tonight is your time to be born."

14

How long he lay there, he didn't know. But it seemed to Aubry that in listening to her heartbeat, and breathing as she breathed, a great calm settled over him. Perhaps solely because of the focus of his concentration, it seemed his body was filled with light.

Her hands urged him gently to move up, to touch his lips to hers, to part them slightly so that their breath could join, so that her exhalations became his inhalations and vice versa, so that it seemed they were feeding each other. The sensation of lightness, of ascent to some far peak, grew even stronger.

It's the carbon dioxide, his mind said, and he noticed that the part of his mind that questioned and judged and evaluated was a distant, chattering thing, sounding more and more like a chipmunk.

Her eyes held him. Her heartbeat held him. He was enthralled by her breathing, each measured breath taking him simultaneously deeper and higher, until he felt intoxicated, *above, outside of, beyond* his mind.

Her eyes rolled up slightly, as if she were slipping into a deeper trance, and her breathing and heartbeat slowed, and he slipped deeper, suddenly losing awareness of his body as a thing separate from hers, not even noticing when her hands searched his body, stroked between his legs and caressed him, drew him down and into her. She clasped him in warmth and wetness, in a soft, sweet vise that rocked him, cradled him, and her body arched, pulling him more deeply inside as her hands gently urged him to keep the rhythm of the breath, as her heart took him deeper into the Void.

It was a sensation beyond his knowledge, a dance on the edge of destruction, a loss of self that was simultaneously a grasping of something . . .

Something . . .

Beyond his conception.

He didn't know when it happened, but he slowly began to take control of the pace of the breathing. Her heartbeat began to follow his. His hands urged her body to greater, more sinuously sensuous effort. . . .

The shared breath became, at his urging, the ultimate kiss, a melding of wetness and fire that spurred them on blindly. Their eyes locked, breath locked, heartbeats locked, their hips drove as their stomach muscles rippled in harmony, her eyes flew wide—

There was a strangled scream, a twisting of her body as she strove to break contact, when she felt her fingers twist in his, as his body drove her into the sheets—

And there was a great *roaring*, a physical sound like the rolling of a great wheel or the changing of a tide, and he felt the bottom of his world fall from beneath him, and *he* struggled to escape her, suddenly realized that somehow in the moment of surrender she had gained control, and he screamed without sound—

And his body cried out—

And hers—

And at the last moment they achieved some kind of savage parity, gripping as a wall of fire swept them both, taking them through all harshness, all strength, into a softness that was the essence of life itself.

And into darkness.

* * *

Aubry lay on his side, not thinking, not dreaming. His body hummed like a slumbering dynamo.

He stared into the darkness. He stared at his hand, seeing it for the first time. Listened to his breathing, finally realizing what a marvelous thing it was to breathe, to drink air, to be alive.

He turned to Tanesha, and ran his fingers wonderingly along her face.

"Thank you," he said at last. And as soon as the words were out of his mouth, he realized how absurd they were.

A single tear glistened at the corner of her right eye. As he watched, it spilled over and trailed down her dark cheek. "I have to go now," she said.

Stay with me. . . .

"Tomorrow, you will have to face the same choice made by every young Ibandi. Most venture no closer to the flame. I think that you will want more. I think that you will want the Firedance."

"What is that?" he asked.

She wrapped her robe around her and slipped from the bed. She stood at the doorway, and looked back at him as if she were leaving a piece of herself there, with him.

"You will find out tomorrow," she said, and left him.

15

SEPTEMBER 29

When he awakened, Old Man stood over him.

"Yes?" His head was still muzzy. He patted the sheets, as if disbelieving that an experience so intense could ever end.

"It is time," Old Man said.

The mine was at a standstill, the conveyor belts motionless. The gigantic factory was almost preternaturally cool and quiet. He scanned the valley, and saw no people, no sign of life.

They walked Aubry down to a skimmer landing pad, where a four-man vehicle awaited. He squeezed in, Old Man right behind him. Its engines thrummed beneath his feet as it spun into the air, taking him up and over the refinery, above the railroad tracks, over the Iron Mountain itself.

Through the window he looked down upon savagely stark valleys, crested with rock and speckled with scrub brush. Off between two peaks, he caught a glimpse of irrigated farmland, green and laid out in checkerboards, stretching off to the horizon.

The skimmer's humming suddenly became more urgent, and they dropped toward a landing pad on the outskirts of a network of weathered brown brick walls and huts. An immense amphitheater of some kind lay at the north corner of the complex. The amphitheater was at least a hundred meters in diameter, and both ancient and modern in construction: its lower levels were of weathered brick. Its upper levels and the domed roof were of ribbed steel. Even from the air, Aubry could see that there was some sort of a shutter system that could close the dome to the elements. Right now it was open. He thought he saw a flicker of motion from within, but couldn't be certain.

Hundreds, thousands of people were clustered around the weathered walls. He couldn't begin to count the throng. As the skimmer landed, his stomach began to sour.

Old Man led him to a corrugated-steel hut at the edge of the complex. "Disrobe," Old Man said. Aubry complied. Old Man took the clothes and folded them over his arm. "You enter a boy. When you exit, it will be time to become a man."

He held the door open.

There was no light within, but from the sliver of daylight through the opened door, Aubry could see at least two dozen young men packed into the tiny shed. Wordlessly, they made room for him.

The door closed.

Aubry crouched down, and finally managed to seat himself comfortably.

The heat was killing. Every breath was a struggle. He listened to the breathing of the young men around him, and realized that he wasn't alone in his suffering. More humbling was the fact that these others had endured longer.

The boy next to him sobbed for breath, and Aubry fought to think of a way to help him. He touched him, shoulder to shoulder, and matched breathing with him. His own breaths were shallow, searing with the heat, but he forced himself to deepen them, deepen until he felt as if he were traveling someplace deep within himself.

Until it felt as if he sat cross-legged on the bottom of a fiery lake. Where he was, there was cool, clear water. Above, there was fire.

Beside him, the boy's breathing had calmed. Around him in the darkness, one after another of the boys linked into the calm, centered breathing, and escaped the fire.

Aubry sat at the bottom of the lake, breathing smoothly. He felt cool, and at peace. As an experiment, he touched his own cheek with his fingertips.

His fingers burned.

16

When they opened the door, stars filled the sky.

Aubry crawled out and collapsed on the sand. He gasped and stared into the night sky while warm water was sprayed over him.

When he rolled to his knees, his eyes focused on two rows of half-naked men. Each held aloft a flaming torch.

Every young man of the Ibandi was there, in tribal garb, and the sound of the drums beat behind them. Seen like this, in the torch- and starlight, in their endless rows, their scarred black cheeks made him feel naked and feminine.

Old Man came to him, and said, "You are a warrior. The scars of your battle were upon your body when first you came to us—we need not put your courage to the test. There is another ceremony which you must complete."

"I am ready," Aubry said.

Old Man nodded, and as Aubry stood there, two dark old men came to him. They carried a spear before them, its tip fresh from the fire. It glowed a dull coal red. They extended its searing tip.

Lightning struck his marrow. He smelled his own flesh burn, saw the steam and smoke curling away.

Aubry bit his lip, and tightened his fists into knots. His knees sagged, and the room spun. Air caught raggedly in his throat, and he was certain that he was going to vomit.

Light infused and surrounded him, accompanied by pain so intense that it was a kind of ecstasy.

The glowing spear dipped again. He clenched his stomach muscles, as the world wheeled again and the sky and ground played leapfrog with one another. Then he found his center again, and the world began to steady. . . .

And then the spear again . . .

Then repeated three times on the opposite cheek. He still stood tall, but in some odd manner he had passed beyond consciousness. He wasn't present in the same world and in the same body as the indignities. He sat at the bottom of the burning lake.

Old Man raised his thin arms. "You are men now. You can stop, or go forward. You can be trained for a worker, or a priest. But being a warrior is not about training. It is a thing of the heart, a decision made not over time, but in the depths of understanding. If you choose the path of the Firedance, there is no turning back. Which of our children take this path?"

Of the thirty youths, twelve stepped forward. Aubry hesitated.

Old Man seemed tired. "The Firedance is as ancient as our people. It is Death, it is courage, it is blood. In it, we pit the men of our village against the most awesome natural foe they might face. In times past it was the lion, or the elephant. I have no choice—the test must be terrible. Only one who has endured it can claim to be an Ibandi warrior."

Only a warrior of the Ibandi could do what Aubry had to do. He could not let anything stop him now. *Mira. Bloodeagle. And my God, Jenna.*

Someone had to pay. Aubry stepped forward.

17

The base of the wall was of ancient brick, and stone that had been weathered when the pyramids were new.

How exactly do they train their warriors? Koskotas had asked.

We do not know. There are rumors . . .

And before them was a bed of coals, forty feet long and twelve wide. The air above it shimmered with heat, rolled and wavered like a window into Hell.

To one side, a clutch of women mashed herbs and mushrooms in stainless-steel bowls, dipped gourds in the vile-looking fluid, and handed it out. Aubry was handed a gourd, and drank deeply of the fluid within. It tasted like shit. But he almost immediately sensed the tiny, warning buzz of the Cyloxibin mushroom.

Some of the old, and some of the new. Just another wondrous example of God's cosmic sense of the absurd.

Some of the substances in that potent brew were as old as the Ibandi themselves. Others were quite new, vegetables that wouldn't exist at all but for two human beings named Aubry Knight and Promise Cotonou.

Promise . . .

He drank it, and something within him, some great well of grief, bubbled up and came right to the surface of his consciousness, trying to erupt.

Promise . . . what have we lost? How much have we paid? . . .

But another voice whispered to him, whispered quietly, strongly. *If you don't own yourself, you have nothing to give to anyone else. Not Promise. Not Leslie.*

Nothing at all.

Aubry drank.

His head began to swim. And he danced.

Right at the edge of the coals, he danced. With the heat searing his loincloth, he danced.

His cheeks, newly seared with the marks of manhood, still burned. The worlds whirled. He had barely enough strength to stand, but he danced.

He looked about himself. These were his people. Yet the people of America were his people, too. Black, white. Brown.

But these. Their bodies bent and twisted, so knotted and corded, so muscular, so beautiful. Their faces were his face. Their hearts his heart. And the music that swirled about them, and around them, spoke to some part of him so deep and primal that he barely noticed when the change occurred, when the sour mash he had imbibed began to swell within him, lifting him up to some point above the clouds.

He was light.

He was divinity.

The first of the thirteen initiates began the Rubber Band, dancing with it, the missing rhythm there at last. The last piece of the puzzle, Aubry's arrhythmical performance of a morning exercise was transformed into terpsichore.

They twisted and hopped . . . and some far part of Aubry's mind noticed, almost accidentally, that he was . . . they *all* were . . . upon the coals.

His palms did not burn. His feet did not burn. He moved steadily and smoothly through the motions, and he smelled the singed fibers of his loincloth, but his flesh did not burn. The drums beat and sounded for him, for them, for them all. Aubry was in a place beyond pain, beyond fear, and the fire did not touch him.

A roaring surrounded them, a primitive thunderous

wail, something that called from within the amphitheater. A call of challenge older than time. *I am here,* it called. *I am Death. Come to me.*

And then it was over.

They stood to the side, and Aubry's eyes were on the fire, on the terrible pit where the fire burned and wavered in the air, and he heard his own breathing, deep in his chest, and it spoke to him of another man, and another time, and he was separate from himself, watched himself floating up and up away and apart from himself, and hovered there. And watched the thirteen of them.

The old women of Iron Mountain, toothless crones, came to them, and laughed at them, and mocked them, spitting on them.

They did not move.

Then came the old men, men whose hands were crippled, who walked with time-twisted backs, who blinked through rheumy eyes. They carried paddles and switches and whips of braided rope. And they thrashed the young would-be warriors, laboring especially over Aubry, lashing him mercilessly.

None moved.

Then, most cruelly of all, the young women of the village came, and displayed themselves. Thighs and breasts and loins presented boldly, gleaming, undulating, gyrating, with wild cries, and japes.

He noticed that Tanesha was not among them.

And none of the initiates moved—then one boy broke from the ranks, and followed the girl. Right there on the ground, for the sky and all to see, he coupled with her. She laughed over his shoulder as he ground himself into her, hips pumping frantically.

She laughed, and she cried, because she had won, and he had lost, and he would never be a warrior. *This* was why Tanesha was not there. This was an escape hatch, a ritual of failure, not a lesson.

Aubry ached for the boy, knowing the staggering cost of that moment's weakness.

The sound of thunder called to the twelve who remained. The earth shook again, and he knew that the time had come.

The gate opened.

The path to the gate was covered with kindling, leading to branches, and from there to a matted floor of logs and shaved wood. He knew that there was a single door, a single door on the far side of the arena, and in times past, between them and the door would be a lion. Or a chained, rogue elephant. Or whatever the elders could acquire to test the mettle of their young warriors. Sometimes chained. Usually not. Maddened by fire. Creatures that must be killed before the fire consumed them all.

His senses were sharper than they had ever been. The entire world narrowed to a pinpoint. Aubry heard the beast's roar, and knew what he would find within.

18

The beast gleamed, flanks heaving in the firelight. Its tiny dead eyes glared from sixteen feet above them. In his heart, Aubry felt that this was the most beautiful creature that he had ever seen. Dead for sixty million years. Revived through the NipTech nanobots, genetically engineered by machines functioning on the molecular level.

The *Tyrannosaurus rex*'s stubby nostrils quivered as it sniffed the air. Did some subcellular memory within it quest about, wondering where the swamps and fat-flanked brontosaurs had gone? Was there brain enough behind the sloping brow, within the pebbled flesh to ask what pygmies these were who approached it, twelve weak, tiny, spear-carrying humans . . . ?

Did it feel anything at all? Toward them, or toward the fire that burned behind them? Toward the first of twelve brave lads in that line? This boy had no name, had nothing but hope, and a belief that within him lived a spark of greatness. Even in the face of the greatest predator that ever walked the Earth, his stride was calm.

Nerves and veins seething with the potent brew, Aubry was both terrified and exalted.

But there was a line of fire that each of them had to cross, a line separating the spirit from the flesh.

By striding past the women who used their bodies, the old women who used their laughter, the old men who mocked and beat them . . .

From love. For what but love could motivate the grandmothers and grandfathers of Iron Mountain to dissuade the children from their terrible destiny? What but love?

Ringing the top of the amphitheater, a hundred men, armed with spears, chanted their excitement. Any young warrior who stepped into this arena would find no retreat, no escape. Here, it was conquer or die.

Aubry's heart opened to these people, to this magnificent beast, to the world within the Iron Mountain, and most of all, to himself. His emotional skin peeled away to reveal a man he had never known before.

A man who wanted to live and love and laugh.

But first had to kill.

The rex's jaws flashed down. The teeth snapped shut just a foot away from the first boy. The youth reared back, and the beast squalled as the chain brought it up short. Its great tail thrashed as it spun, seeking a moment of freedom, an inch of slack, any slight opportunity to destroy these fleas.

Behind them, the coals touched the wood chips. The chips smoldered and burst into flames. The logs beyond them began to burn. The initiates weren't endangered yet—but the threat was real, and nearer every second.

The magnificent beast sniffed the air, and its dead eyes came to life as it sniffed the smoke. Fire it understood.

The King could lie down and die. Or it could kill them all. And die. There were no other options for such a beast. There was fear. There was heat. There was flesh.

The attack began.

And Aubry, in that state outside of his mind, remembered teeth and claws, and the fire creeping up behind them. The rex's lashing tail almost caught him twice, strobing in the haze. Aubry sprang, higher than he ever had before, over the tail to land lightly on spring-steel quadriceps. He felt no pain, no fatigue.

The spears dug, and the rex was bloodied in a dozen places, but unslowed. Two of the young warriors were down, unmoving . . . no, one of them groaned and cried.

Atop the arena, the spearmen stared down pitilessly.

A spear rolled from the hand of the dead man. Aubry snatched it up, and looked at the left side of the terrible, wonderful beast. As he stared at it, it seemed to expand, filled his field of vision until the only thing that existed in his world was its dark, cold eye. Its head shifted, Aubry's hand and eyes in synch, until he felt a part of it.

He knew this tyrant king. His *ancestors* had known it, chittering things that were the size of squirrels when beasts the size of houses ruled the earth. Back that far, before anything with the awareness of life had lived, he and this thing had known each other. Sixty million years before man it had lived, but within Aubry was the germ of cells older than man. Something that understood. That had always fled from creatures such as the King. That hid in shadow, and upon occasion ate the eggs of such beasts.

The spirit of a million generations of living things witnessed this moment. That place within him was tired of waiting, impatient now to come face-to-face with fears older than thought. It guided Aubry's arm, so that the cast began in his legs, which pulled their strength from the earth. The cast twisted at the hips, and whipped the shoulder forward. He loosed the spear.

It flew true, and buried itself in the beast's eye.

The rex reared up, howling anguish and rage and perhaps, at last, fear.

This thing from the deepest depths of their nightmares feared men! And all of the young warriors heard it in the rex's cry. Fear. And Aubry's heart sang: *There lives within you a force equal to the most terrible creature ever to walk the Earth!*

The rex threw itself at them, the spear waggling from its bloodied, ruptured eye socket like a flagpole. The tail smashed at another young warrior and he howled, nerve breaking, trying to flee up the wall of the amphitheater. The spearmen on the wall pushed and poked him back down, hooting. He fell sprawling into the flames and screamed, racing up blindly, his hair burning—directly into the range of the blood-maddened, half-blinded rex.

Its head, as large as the cab of a truck, lunged down and snapped, the teeth clacking shut. Half the boy's body protruded from its jaws. The legs twitched spastically, intestines sliding down the front of his loincloth like Christmas treats exploding from a ruptured piñata.

But one of the other boys lunged in while the head was low, and thrust with his spear. And then another.

Blood flowed from a terrible gash above the single, unblinking eye. The beast scraped at its eye with those ridiculous forepaws, trying to clear its sight. But the gash was deep, and although it blinked and wiped, it could no longer see.

There were nine young warriors remaining, nine against this thing resurrected from their darkest fantasies. Behind them, the flames crackled, nearer now. The rex stopped, shook its head until the dangling human legs fell free. It stood tall, head cocked slightly to the side, smelling the air, feeling its wounds, and perhaps in some saurian manner singing its own death song.

It lunged at them and the chain broke, snapped with a sound like a dying dream. The hairless apes evaded but did not flee, harrying it, screaming and and tormenting, but scoring again and again with their spears. The rex stood with its back to the fire, tail thrashing, face and jaws crimsoned. Its pitifully small paws wiped at its cuts, and failed to do anything but widen them. The stench of burning flesh filled the air. Blood flowed from wounds in chest and flank. Its chest labored.

There was a moment of quiet, a moment when something in that arena shifted, *quieted* in respect for what was about to occur.

Another spear was launched, catching the rex in its exposed throat. It pawed at the spear, splintering the shaft. It charged again, so fast that one young warrior hadn't time to get out of the way and was trampled.

But the spears flashed now and, every time they did, left another thread of crimson. The rex was laboring now. Had its tiny mind been capable of irony, it might have asked why it had been born again, after cold eons, to die so. Still, when it walked, the Earth thundered; and if its walk was hobbled by shorn tendons, it was still the walk of a king.

An old, and tired, and wounded king, but a monarch nonetheless.

The rex's mouth opened to the artificial sky above it, and it screamed. In that scream was all of the rage and pain of a lost race, a vanished time. Then another spear struck it in the throat. A third spear, cast by Aubry's arm, thrown with all of the strength of his body, and powered, this time, by love.

And the rex regarded him. Aubry swore that it looked directly at him, blood flowing from its mouth, looking *into* him. Something passed between them, some moment, some *aliveness*.

It took a step toward him, and Aubry didn't move. The fire was close behind him. He could, in some distant manner, feel its heat. And the beast, dying now, blood bubbling from its gouged flanks, seemed almost intelligent. Almost inquisitive, as if wondering who had done such a thing to it. To Aubry's mind it was no longer a monster but merely an animal that, like all living things, must at last confront its own death.

And they knew each other.

One of the young warriors dashed in, and slashed the right leg once, twice again, until the giant bunched tendons were laid bare by a flap of skin the size of a flag. The rex twisted on the axis of the ruined leg as it buckled. It fell into the fire.

It struggled to climb out, but was prodded back at spearpoint, unable to walk.

It lay on its side now, thrashing for a few moments, then

quiet, then thrashing once again. The great chest heaved, striving to pump blood to legs that would no longer work. Tiny clawed hands scrabbled for purchase it couldn't find.

Aubry ran forward and buried his spear in the rex's eye. He drove it in, ground it in, pushed with maniac strength until it broke the wall of bone and pierced the brain.

He remembered fire.

He remembered floating in the air, as its head jerked reflexively.

He remembered striking the ground, his arm slapping hard, his body relaxed, taking, breaking the fall.

He remembered standing, looking at the King upon its pyre, flanks still shuddering.

He remembered the survivors, heaving, bloodied, exhausted, filing out the door as the flames rose up to consume the amphitheater's floor.

He remembered his last thought:

The King is dead.

Long live . . .

19

SEPTEMBER 30. SWARNAVILLE.

The crowd was immense, and the police control of it merely adequate. Faces of every hue—but mostly dark—stretched through the streets. The men and women in the line were carded, one at a time, by the police, and by the recruiters for Scavengers Ltd.

Promise watched the crowd, her heart thundering. Had the announcement been made early enough? Often enough? There was no telling, but there was not enough fear in the world to stop Promise from coming.

She didn't know where Aubry, Jenna, or Bloodeagle were—or if any of them were even alive. But she had to try.

She had to gamble that if any of them were alive, they would hear, and come. But so far, she had seen nothing in the throng to tell her her gamble was a good one. She saw no one resembling the three of them, and a terrible heaviness engulfed her. On some core intuitive level, she *knew* that someone close to her heart had died.

She wanted to cry, she wanted to do anything except continue to supervise the endless rounds of interviews.

Have you had experience in construction? Would you be available for classes, in special camps where for the first two months the only wages would be food and shelter? She watched the expressions of the people as they filed past. These were the lost and lonely, more so than in even the Maze. And they looked at her now as if she were some plutocrat from afar, the head of some ethereal Areopagus, swanning down from the heavens, offering to lift them from their misery with a wave of her pen. They didn't know. They just didn't know.

She caught a flash of white in the monitor, and her eye focused upon it. A handkerchief, a fold of white cloth, edged in red. A man wiped his face with it. A thin, brown-skinned man. He wiped his face again. And lowered it. And five seconds later, almost like a metronome. She zoomed in on him. Her heart froze. She knew that cloth—it was of soft leather, and she had seen Jenna clean her durga blades with it a hundred times.

The man was nervous, but resolute. Again and again, in that repetitive nervous gesture, he wiped his shining brow. And she was quite sure that the sweat upon it was caused by more than heat.

Promise had four team leaders, each in charge of five men and women. The interviews were going fairly rapidly. She crooked her finger at a man named Amel and said, "Third row. Small man. Gray shirt. I want you to walk him through personally, Amel. Find out if there is anything special. Anything we should know of."

Amel nodded. He was a trusted contact, the brother of one of her Denver crew chiefs.

She continued to pretend that she was concerned with

the flow, and consulted with a few of the other chiefs, so that it wouldn't seem that she had given undue attention to Amel. She had to assume that she was under constant surveillance—any other assumption was suicidal.

The line crept on, and finally the little man made it to the front. He didn't look at her, but the cloth was gone now.

Strange. His clothes were not new . . . but they had been cleaned. Almost as if they had come from a secondhand store.

Amel came back to Promise's side with a clipboard, and gestured widely to the crowd, and then made a small gesture to the clipboard. There, at its side, was the cleaning cloth. It was dappled with blood. At the lower left corner was a single initial, scrawled with a shaky hand.

J.

Without changing expression, Promise said, "Find a way to bring him in. With at least twenty others."

Promise went to the bathroom and vomited. She washed her face, and stared at herself in the mirror. Some of the tense lines around her mouth had eased. New ones had appeared.

This could be the deadliest of traps. This could be salvation for the people she loved most in this world.

The thin man was the thirteenth to be admitted to see her, and as soon as the door shut, she ran him through the standard questions. He answered crisply. In badly broken English, he said that he owned a small shop in Daglia, across the border in the Central African Republic. Business was poor at present. He had, in his youth, worked as an engineering assistant.

Promise took his information with little encouraging hems and haws, then examined the completed form and nodded with satisfaction. She pressed back into her chair. "You say that business is bad in Daglia?"

"I own . . . small shop in Daglia," he said apologetically. "Business . . . not good. Neighborhood gone bad. Not many customer. Have much time for . . . hobby. Chess. You play?"

"Sometimes, yes."

His eyes grew intense. "Variation on Queen's Indian defense. Known as durga. You know?"

Promise's heart soared. "If you would give me the address of the shop, I would like to visit sometime."

"I would suggest that you do so soon."

"Very soon?"

He bit his lip. "Merchandise . . . spoiling." He gave his address, stood, bowed deeply, and turned to leave.

Promise stopped him. "Why do you . . . seek employment here?" she asked, mystified.

"I gamble when I play chess," he said, his eyes amused. "Lately, have lost much. Need to repay."

"You should play on the rooftop, in the moonlight," she said. "It is very beautiful."

"Tonight, might be beautiful moon," he said.

"Tonight would be fine."

20

The skimmer was protected with a Gorgon-quality distortion shield, and betrayed no trace but a heat shimmer as it crossed above Swarnaville, heading north to Daglia. Dead to radar, dead to the visible spectrum, still it would show up as an infrared blur if such instruments were trained upon it.

A little distraction was needed.

At the south end of the recruitment camp, a truck blew up, and there was the sound of machine-gun fire.

PanAfrican security forces appeared as if by magic, and Promise's own people hovered about. "It is not safe here," they said. "The rebels are active. You know that there was a state of . . . emergency not a hundred miles from here?"

"No," Promise said. She was dressed in her finest robe. It hugged her figure in the moonlight, and in the slight wind blowing in from the desert, she was quite a sight.

They never saw the skimmer lift silently from its pad and head north across the desert.

21

Amel piloted the ship across the city. He bore the scars of torture upon his back, and had little love for the madman Swarna. He was glad to do something to help. Still, he was afraid, and remained so even when he maneuvered the ship in between the buildings. The moon was clouded over, and the sky was very dark.

The girl beside him made him nervous. The girl . . . Leslie? . . . said little, just stared into the city with those huge eyes. Amel sensed that those young eyes had seen things no child should ever have to witness.

In a gust of steam, the ship descended to a rooftop. There was no sound as the door opened. The girl vaulted over the side of the ship, and landed on the roof as lightly as a cat's dream.

At first, there seemed to be nothing there. Then, bundled in one of the corners, Amel made out two human shapes. A man. A woman. The man helped her to her feet. She seemed weak, but determined. Leslie flew to them, and helped the woman into the skimmer. She looked like death, but was muttering something. "Pawn to king's bishop five."

The man helping her looked at Amel desperately. "Help us," he whispered.

Amel left the controls and carried the woman to one of the seats. She swallowed hard. Her eyes seemed incapable of focusing. "Pawn," she whispered hoarsely, "to king's bishop five."

The thin man smiled sadly, as if his heart was breaking. "Bishop to queen's knight four. Checkmate."

Jenna was silent, and still. For a moment, Amel thought

that she was dead. Then, very softly, she spoke. "Yes," Jenna agreed. "You win."

And then she fainted.

The little man looked at her, and then at Leslie. "You . . . Leslie?"

Leslie nodded, stroking his aunt's forehead. Then the child smiled shyly and looked up at the little man. "I don't know your name," he said.

"It doesn't matter. Your aunt—she good. Almost dead. Hold me to . . . fifty-seven moves."

Leslie took the chessplayer's hand. "You are a friend," Leslie said. "You brought Jenna back to us. We won't forget."

"You go. Care for her. Tell her . . . she owe me one more game."

The little man tousled Leslie's hair, and backed out of the skimmer's doorway. Leslie pressed his face against the window as the skimmer floated free of the roof, heading east to circle back south.

The last thing that Leslie saw was the chessplayer's small, slender figure on the roof, watching as they floated into the clouds.

A pawn, who had, for a critical moment of time, become a knight.

22

Aubry Knight lay on a pallet in his room, staring at the wall, unmoving. From outside the room there came the sound of celebration. It was not a surprise to him. It was a day for celebration. Last night, he had been born.

Where and who was he? He wasn't certain. He remembered . . .

Another life. Long ago. A life without rhythm or purpose. A life filled with vague regrets, with anger, with hatreds.

And now, he was at peace.

"And what will you do now?" Old Man said.

"I will go home," he said, clearly. "I will see what is to be seen, and do what is to be done."

"And your business of death?"

"That was another man's business, not mine." He lay, considering. "I feel sorry for that man. He wanted so much, for so long, and now that it is here to be had, he is not the one who gets to enjoy it."

"It is God's."

"Yes." He stopped, and thought. Listened to his breathing, hissing through a throat that had breathed fire. "It is God's."

"There is only one thing that you should know," the old man said, slowly. "And that is that your woman was in Swarnaville. It is said she has gone south, to New Tokyo."

He opened his eyes. "Promise," he said.

"Yes. And your child is with her. They are in danger."

"They came to try to help me," he said.

"Yes. To help you."

"And when cornered, Leslie will revert to the most basic mode he knows. He will try to finish the assignment I began."

Old Man nodded. "Death is not so easily cheated. One way or the other, you have an appointment."

Aubry Knight looked at his scorched hands, and looked out through eyes that, for the first time in his life, were cleansed of anger. "There are things to be done."

"Women can Be. Men must Do. All that is meaningful is in the Doing, and the Being."

"Can you help me?" Aubry asked.

"It is our fight. We can help. I think that you are the one. I think that this is why you came home to us."

"Home," Aubry said. "Home is what I have never had, except in the hearts of the people who loved me."

"This is your home," Old Man said.

"Yes," Aubry said. "This is my home."

5TH SONG

BIRTHDANCE

Everything in Life is born
of woman.

—Ibandi proverb

1

"**Y**ou are the American. Tell us why we should trust you."
The rebel's voice was flat, empty as his left eye socket. He
was old now; his skin was as dark and sun-cracked as the
earth beneath them.

Five of them crouched around the fire, eyes shifting suspiciously from Aubry to Old Man. Five of them: three
leathery men and two thin, dusty women. Elder represent-
atives of Five Songs. Farmers and traders from Pan-
Africa's northernmost province, still called Matundu, in
what had once been Zaire. They were all, in one way or
another, crippled. Blind. Stumps for legs. A missing hand.

Phillipe Swarna had cost them much, and they now
wanted nothing other than his death. They had traveled to
Iron Mountain at Old Man's urging, to hear what the
American had to say.

"Swarna is your enemy," Aubry began slowly. "He betrayed your people, he betrayed your trust. He is your
demon, and he is mine." He paused, seeking to organize
his thoughts into some sort of coherent order.

"Five years ago I killed his only son, in fair combat.
Now he wants to kill me, and my family."

"And you came here to take your vengeance?" one of
the men said. His cheeks were burnt black, sun and genetics, age, fatigue and tribal branding iron combining to produce a shade beyond blue-black. It was the blackness of
despair and death.

Aubry nodded, waiting for what had to come next.

"But you didn't kill the bastard. Came face-to-face with
him, and you failed."

He bristled. "I administered the poison. If anything
failed, it was the American technology."

Scar-Cheeks laughed. "You are a coward and a fool. Do you know what any of *us* would have paid for a chance to die with Phillipe Swarna? You failed because you wanted to live."

" 'Those who fear death cannot win,' " Aubry quoted. " 'Those who love both life and death cannot be defeated.' "

They murmured approval. "You know the Songs?"

"I am learning them. And the Dances."

One-Eye turned to Old Man. "It is true?"

Old Man nodded, the corners of his dry, cracked lips lifting in the ghost of a smile. "Truth. He was lost. He has come home. He is one with us."

They studied him, as if comparing him to some mental pictures of their own. Then Stump-Leg said, "And one of the Six was found near you, when you were rescued."

"Yes."

"And he rescued you from the prison. Where you were being tortured to death."

"Yes."

"Why?"

"I . . ." He paused. "I'm not sure. I believe that he was cloned from my flesh."

There was an ugly murmur at this conjecture. "He did not look like you."

"My face has been surgically altered. However they raised him, some feeling of kinship for me remained. He wanted to kill me man to man, but was unable to complete the rescue. He was wounded. This is all I can say."

The one-armed woman stood. She seemed so thin that Aubry was afraid the wind might sweep her up screaming into the sky. But there was an intensity within her, a fire raging behind her wide, accusing eyes. "We cannot believe this. Swarna sends death to you across an ocean. And fails. You strike at him, with America's deadliest weapons. And fail. One of the Six attacks you in Los Angeles, and then another tries to save you here. And now you want us to expose Five Songs to you, to get you into Caernarvon Castle. How do we know you are who you say you are? How do we know that this entire story has not been concocted to draw us into the open, and thence to destroy us?"

"You are already exposed," Aubry observed quietly.

"We are old," One-Eye said. "And already damaged in the fight against Swarna. And we are but a single note in the Five Songs. If we die, or are captured, we will expose little. Our contact will flee, or commit suicide if we do not send the clear signal." A knife appeared in One-Eye's gnarled, rusty hands. "We believe that we have been betrayed. We will die, and we will take you with us." The knife hovered near Aubry's throat. Aubry met his eye evenly, unmoving.

Old Man spoke quickly. "No! He is one of us. He is a child of the Ibandi, raised in America."

Scar-Cheek held up a hand, and One-Eye retracted the knife half an inch. "We heard that there was such a child," Scar-Cheek said, "but how do we know that this is the one? He could be another clone, grown, implanted with a shadow soul. I mean no insult, but he would fool even you, Old Man. How would we know? How would *he* know?"

Aubry, about to argue, suddenly felt a sour question poisoning his confidence. "What do you mean?"

"Swarna and the Americans could have created you. Programmed you in America. Sent you in to uncover us. Perhaps their animosity is a sham."

"But . . . they didn't want me to come. I forced their hand."

"So you say. Or think. But it need not be true."

Aubry stopped, considering that. Then he shook his head. "Once, I might have doubted myself. I might have wondered. But I am no longer a man who doubts. The fire burns clean. I will kill Phillipe Swarna. No matter what the cost. I can do it—all I need is another chance."

"Old Man," the second woman asked. She bore no visible scars, but when she moved or spoke, it was with evident discomfort. "Why do you vouch for this—American?"

"Because of the Firedance," he said. "It is known only to my people. Only to the *warriors* of my people. Swarna was a *priest,* not a warrior. He did not know the Firedance. This man did. Thomas Jai, who took the fetus to America, and claimed to be this one's father, was a warrior. *Thomas* knew the Firedance. Aubry performed for us. It was flawed. It was partial. It was magnificent."

"Could Thomas not have been captured, and the Firedance extracted under torture?"

"Information can be extracted, yes. But not the *joy.* Firedance holds the joy of our people, our love of movement. It must be taught, one to another, hands on, over a process of years. Love, given father to son, uncle to nephew. Protector to protected. You can steal the external shell, but not the nectar it holds. Aubry Jai was given the nectar. He is our child, come home."

"Jai?" asked Aubry, confused.

"It is High Ibandi. It means protector. Guardian. Warrior. Knight."

Old Man came and stood by Aubry, grey head rising only to the level of his shoulder. There was silence, save for the wind passing over the Iron Mountain. Passing as it had passed for ten million years, and would for a billion more.

The three men and two women gazed at Old Man, and at Aubry, and at last they nodded. "You risk your own people. You place their lives on the line. Five Songs will stand with you."

2

OCTOBER 5. THE MENAGERIE.

The world was a nightmare of black and white streaks, frozen, edged in shattered color, like paintings glimpsed in a thunderstorm.

I hunched into my seat. Unfeeling, almost unseeing. I felt my heart dying.

Father. I cannot stop myself.

The rain blew against the skimmer windows. I saw the lightning. In that rain-dappled window, I saw my face.

I had not seen it before. It was so small, so drawn. So empty.

How had I survived, enfolding such an angry void? Surely, only by denying its existence.

Father.

Rain whipped against the window in rippling sheets. My reflection looked wet. Cold. Alive.

The transport skimmer struck an air pocket, shuddered. The seat beneath me trembled in rhythm with the engine. My feet did not touch the floor.

I turned. Mother peered at me. She looked sick. Her cheeks were drawn tight against her cheekbones. Her slender fingers gripped my shoulder. I did not feel them.

"Leslie . . ." she said, something present in her voice I had never heard before. Her heart, like mine, was dying.

Everything I touch dies.

She bore me within her body. Protected me with her life. Gave me her family. When I die, she will blame herself. Forever.

And still, I had to do this.

"Leslie. Darling." She gripped my hand. Strength in slim fingers. Soft oval of face, caught in flash of lightning. Glint of moisture on cheek given fire. A falling star. I wanted . . .

I wanted . . .

Father.

"Isn't there anything I can say?"

The room shifted minutely, left to right.

She stared straight ahead. I recorded line of jaw. Luminous eyes. High, lovely hairline. Firm mouth that had kissed mine so often.

Then, burned memories away. Suicide to take such softness into combat.

"If I stopped you—"

You could not.

"—and your father died, you would never forgive me." Her voice labored. She swallowed thickly. The cords in her neck stood out like bundles of vine. Hands went to her face. Fingers flitted like butterflies, as if questioning the reality of the flesh they stroked. "If you . . . if anything happens to you . . . I will die, Leslie." She looked at me. I saw how she would have been, in labor with me. Animal. Pure commitment. No turning back. This woman would not use drugs, or surgery. She would plunge into the sensation.

One life to live. One. Feel it all. Even the pain.

"So . . ." She wiped the back of a hand against wet cheeks, managed the travesty of a smile. "I have to let you go, don't I? I have to pray that you'll come back to me." Her smile faltered. "Somehow. And bring your father, if you can."

The rain was harder.

Soon, now.

I heard my own voice. I didn't know who spoke the words.

"Trust me, Mother," I said. "If Father is alive, I will find him. If I find him, and we are together, nothing in the world can stop us."

That voice came from somewhere far away. I wanted to reach out to her, to comfort her, to say something more to her. For her sake I wore the dresses. For her, the makeup. For her, I strove to be human.

But human beings are such frail, vulnerable things. They love what cannot last. They cling to what they cannot keep. They think that passion, and caring, and love, can build a fortress against that night which claims us all.

Pitiful.

I wanted so much to be human.

But I am not, and never was. I am Gorgon. I am Medusa-16. There was no time for softness, not then. Not ever again.

I made a little adjustment, focusing on the line of light that starts near my anus, and travels up my spine. It pulsed with my heartbeat.

I was within myself. There was a sound of small, balanced feet. Amel, returning from the pilot's compartment. "Two minutes, now," he said quietly. I did not respond. "I suppose—it would be fruitless to try to talk you out of this?''

I could not hear Amel. He was a decent man, a good pilot. He did not, could not, understand a creature like me.

All I could think of was my father, and Aunt Jenna. Bloody. Aunt Mira. A tattered target. A harmless, sallow woman with nimble fingers and an open heart. A woman who never thought of herself. And who was killed to get Father's attention. My aunt.

Pain.

If there was no Hell, I swore to make one. I would tear open the earth with my fingers, and cast Phillipe Swarna into it. And climb in after him.

Father.

Oh, Father, I thought. *What have I brought to your life? It was the Medusas. And Gorgons. You came to save me. And killed a man called Ibumi. Swarna's only son. And PanAfrica reached out for you and destroyed your home. I cannot forgive myself. If evil exists, I am that thing.*

I took Mother's hand from my shoulder.

Mother. I am sorry. You tried so hard.

You can't love the evil out of an evil thing.

I had to remain calm, in a world of vectors and velocities. Too many people to find and kill. Too much to do.

Sensed my inner clock. It was time.

I moved to the door. We were two miles above the Menagerie. The radar was scouting us, even then. A parachute would be picked up, at once.

Strapped to my back was a three-foot fiberglass turtle shell. It was all I needed. The door opened, and a wall of wind hammered me.

Amel touched my shoulder, then drew his finger back, as if he had brushed a piece of dry ice. I looked up at him. Behind him was my mother.

Her face.

I had to forget . . .

Must imprint it upon my heart . . .

And in the last moment, it bloomed with light, revealed

to me a sunrise in the midst of a storm. No longer controlled by me, my eyes burst with tears and I screamed "Mother . . . !"

And I stepped through the door.

3

Promise stared at the door, lids fluttering but not blinking, long after Amel sealed it. She sat, and raised her hands until she could see them. They shook, picked at each other, acted as if they belonged to someone else. Someone she didn't know.

She thrust them into her mouth, and pressed herself back into her seat, staring out into the storm.

What have I done?
The only thing that could possibly save my family.
Aubry. Leslie. Forgive me.
Goddess, save them both.
Or let me die, as well.

4

The wind gut-punched me. Then nothing. I was of the wind, whipped by it, skating on little eddies that whipped my hair and spun me. But I saw only the skimmer, which was drawing apart and away from me. I flew, sinking slowly. The skimmer pulled farther away from me and disappeared into the clouds.

The Menagerie's largest lake was far below me, a shimmering white patch in the rain, still radiating yesterday's heat. I tucked my body tightly and headed for it, wheeling through space.

I had already performed the calculations: thirty-two feet

per second, per second. The wind pressure: rain seemed almost to buoy me up, as my emotions could not. Terminal velocity.

I was ready. Flip to land butt-first, on fiberglass turtle shell. The patch of day-heat swam up at me, slowly at first, and then more swiftly, swiftly, and then with phenomenal speed, and I felt my way through the wind. I canted, coming at the angle, using wind pressure to change my declination. Perpendicularity would prove fatal.

I saw the sky.

White/red/black. Concussion.

World spun as fall translated into forward motion, stone-skipping across surface, back, side, then front, my body curled into a ball, forearms over face. Lost control of spin, control of everything as concentration splintered, revolving white/black/white, then pain in a flash so hot and brief it was barely registered and—

5

Awakened, coughing water. Kicked free of shell, not thinking, just moving. Water, reeds, rain in my face. Cheek against mud, mouth half in water. Puking swamp muck. Shaking. Body like bag of broken glass.

Checked inner clock. Sun still an hour below horizon.

Check: location. The Menagerie. Dead center. Around me, legs rising like dark columns from the swamp, the herd of *Apatosauri.*

Bioengineered small—averaging only forty feet in length, only twenty tons. Saurian. *Brachiosauridae.* Middle and Upper Jurassic. Sometimes erroneously referred to as brontosaurus. Herbivorous.

One raised its head, lazy-gazing at me. Struck from sleep by the din? Were there sound monitors? Were computer relays then opening, waking to the predawn even as these

flea-brained creatures? Did my splash source more sound
than a sleep-staggered apatosaurus sagging in the swamp?

Gasping, I made my way to shore, and dragged myself
out. Sore—ache lived in every limb and joint.

Pain is life.

I lay flat. Waited, and watched. Nothing moved . . .
or . . . ? I heard something sniffing in the bushes.

Something was called by my impact in the water. Not a
security 'bot.

Allosaurus. *Theropoda.* Iguana-head. Powerful claws,
sharp, thick-nailed fore and hind legs. Carnivore. Not
more than twelve feet long, seven feet high. Wind shifted,
carrying putrid meat stench. Small, even for Swarna's
Jurassic bonsai brigade. A baby. Should have still been at
the clutch-hunting phase, under mother's watchful eye.
But it was hunting on its own, its head swiveling slow to
scent the air, rubbing the long grass against its nose, trying
to read spoor.

I pretended to be a tree, a rock, an unliving extension of
the night. Where was I? The lake map blossomed in my
mind. A quarter mile to the nearest sauropod-secure concrete bubble-blind.

Felt no urge to match skill and strength against something like this. Irrational thing to ask of an injured, woozy
body.

Conversely, was also uncertain of locomotive capacity.
Hip felt as if smashed with a sledge. Throbbing grew more
intense by the moment. Think positively: *Pain is life.* Still,
it was hardly a desirable sensation for one pursued by a
famished carnosaur.

I rolled back into the swamp slowly, carefully, and
watched. It couldn't catch my scent—

And then I exploded from the water. Something almost
had me, something that moved through the water so quietly and stealthily that I felt nothing, sensed nothing, until
the moment before its jaws closed upon my leg. Teeth
grazed me as I twisted away onto the land.

The allosaurus was after me instantly, its underlegs
thundering along, lifting it with every stride, propelling it

forward. My hip began to burn, and made a slight click with every step. Couldn't keep up the pounding.

Swift inventory told me that I had my flexibility, and that my skeletal alignment would tolerate one more shock.

No choice but to fight, while defense was still possible.

The beast was almost on me. I sprang forward, dug in my left heel, balanced on my left leg, and snapped back, allowing the shock of deceleration to flow through muscles that were perfectly relaxed. My right leg cocked, everything in slow motion as the allosaurus came for the kill, not even trying to brake itself.

And I hit it with a Korean-style *yop chugi* side kick, focusing through my heel. I possess 99.98+ energy efficiency. My focus was the best, even among the other Medusas. And every bit of focus, every bit of energy, with perfect alignment and everything else I could muster went into that blow, timed perfectly, and aimed for the plate in the center of its chest. My heel struck cleanly, delivering in excess of thirteen hundred psi precisely on target, and I heard the ribs crunch, felt impact. Heard my own scream as my hip protested, but held.

The allosaurus registered surprise. If you tied a log to the side of a truck and ran it into a rhino at precisely the correct point, you might get a similar effect.

The lizard spun off into twelve o'clock, and I into six. Energy transference wasn't quite perfect.

My hip roared. Now that it had done its job, it was appropriate for it to complain. The carnosaur roared as well—far more audibly.

It would attract others of its kind. The sun would be up soon. Unless one of the Menagerie wardens took pity on it, it would be torn apart by its brothers and sisters.

I felt as if my hip and knee were on fire. I dragged myself the rest of the way to the shelter, leaving the dinosaur thrashing in the dirt.

The shelter was a low concrete bubble with a keypad and a voice box. The computer codes were easy to break. I dampened the security system.

I was in.

6

The canvas-covered truck had traveled for three days across the hardpack, and beneath a lazing day's merciless sun. It was old, and rickety, a gas-driven relic capable of no more than forty miles an hour, bumping and jostling every foot of the way along a road that was maintained too rarely.

There was method to the apparent madness of Five Songs: the air, and the rails, and the seas were swept constantly, but the caravan routes across the great grasslands in PanAfrica's north country were the continent's lifelines, and had been for a thousand years. There were too many small merchants, too many trade routes to monitor. For those who spoke Swahili, the path was open wide.

Aubry's eyes were cold, his hands firm upon the wheel. On the dash before him was the small tracer device handed him by Go. Its digital display read *17 K.* Not far now.

In the truck bed behind him were a dozen men, registered as general workers. The entire truck was one of thousands carrying human machinery from one village, one township, one province to another, seeking a place where the work might be more plentiful, the salaries a fraction higher. The men knew no explicit details of his mission, but were allied with Five Songs. They had sworn to fight and die at its call. They were of a dozen tribes and, through them, connected to other committed men and women. Sometimes, when the truck's engine quieted a bit, he could hear them singing.

Death songs? They came to him, in the language of his people, floating on the wind. The three-quarter moon cast protean shadows upon the land, sharp darkness and cold light that transformed the landscape into a thing of dream. He felt cool, and at peace, and within himself.

Beside him, Tanesha was quiet. She had been silent for over a hundred miles, lost in her own thoughts, no energy to waste on talk. Her hair was tightly braided in ceremonial rows. She carried a gourd filled with smalls rocks and seeds, and shook it occasionally, as she hummed and chanted to herself.

She seemed so calm.

Mountains that had been distant slumbering beasts loomed up now, revealed as insensate tumbles of black rock, cairn upon cairn heaped on each other like broken building blocks. The earth beneath the truck grew rougher. The truck's ancient suspension groaned in the attempt to level the ride.

Tanesha raised her hand. Flat, short-nailed fingers together. Aubry braked the truck. He turned and looked through the slit in the back of the truck, beneath the canvas. It smelled of old, burnt oil. The night wind carried the dust of a long, weary day.

The digital display read *1 K.*

She turned to him. "This is the place," she said. "Once, long ago, this too was our territory. This was our land, before we were driven to the Iron Mountain as elsewhere. Before we chose to make our stand. This is where they will come. You must go. And you alone. We will wait."

"Thank you, Tanesha. For everything."

"You are certain about this thing?"

Aubry smelled the night. The night was clean, and taut. Dawn was coming. Even if he couldn't smell it. It was coming. "Yes," he said. "I am."

She nodded. Aubry climbed out of the car, and headed up into the rocks, and began to climb hard, his body working like a perfect machine.

There is more than emotion. There is more than body. There is the thing called spirit.

There was a cave up ahead, one of a network of old mines, and he knew what would wait for him within, in a circle of blood.

He paused in the mouth of the mine, waiting for his eyes to adjust to the darkness.

He smelled them before he saw them, smelled their heat, sensed their . . . energy. There, squatting like so many machines, so many primal animals waiting for him, for something, to come out of the darkness and join them, were what remained of the Six.

They watched him. Two were male, one female. All were naked. The males balanced their heads on thick, sinewy necks. The female's body was more slender, her body fat low, her breasts carried high upon solid muscle. The impression of fluid power was unmistakable. Their skin was heavily tattooed. Both males had shaved heads. The female wore densely knit cornrows. Male scalps were graven with keloid scars. Their brows were plucked clean.

"Welcome, brother," the female said. "I am San. These are my brothers Roku and Ni. It is time for us to speak."

7

"You are . . . made from me?" Aubry said.

"Make the circle, brother." Ni handed him a knife. Aubry cut his hand and let the blood flow into the pot. The pain was a deep, silvery thing, and he felt something within him draw back from it, but he was unmoved.

They handed him the pot. He walked around the circle, adding his blood to the thin line of black that encircled them. Then he stepped within.

"Within, we are more than brothers and sister," San said. "Within, there are only the Three. Once, the Six. Now, we are Three."

"We are Four," Aubry said.

"Within this circle, there is only truth."

Aubry waited.

Ni looked at Aubry. "What is your truth?"

"I came here to kill Phillipe Swarna."

Silence.

He continued. "I know that you were created from my

flesh. That you were sent to America to kill me. Why you rescued me, I do not know. But we are all brothers. I believe that you and I share more than blood. And flesh. And bone. I believe that you and I share a dream."

"And what is that dream, my brother?" San asked.

"I dream at night. All men do. But in waking, my dreams slip away, leaving only the taste of the dream to suggest its journey through my mind. I know the dream I have lived. I have awakened. I will kill Phillipe Swarna. I will take his life for what he has done to me, and done to my people. And I want your help."

There was a long pause. "You are our brother," Ni said at last, "but you still don't understand."

"Understand what?"

"We were not made from you," Roku said. "You, and I, and all of us, were made from Phillipe Swarna. We are the Abomination."

8

San continued. "We are what Phillipe Swarna created to keep himself alive. At first he did it to continue his work. Then, he did it because he was mortally afraid of death."

"Death," Aubry said.

" 'Everything of Life is born of woman,' " San quoted. "In creating us, he created something not of life. We were his extra hearts, and brains, and livers. When a piece malfunctioned, he took from us. There were three generations of clones—you were first generation. You are the only survivor of the original Six, forty years ago. Fifteen years later he grew six more. And when he had used those up, he created us, the last. The nanotech is more efficient than transplantation. We are the last generation. Only one of us, Ichi, was sacrificed in the white room. The other five became his most private enforcement arm. His personal bodyguard."

"Then why did his own son go to America?"

"During the PanAfrican war, Swarna's only wife and daughter were killed." Roku's voice was a bass rumble. "Ibumi's mother and sister. The vengeance on President Harris was Ibumi's dream, his driving ambition. More his plan than Swarna's."

Aubry considered this. "So this is how he survived six assassination attempts? By taking pieces from bodies grown for him?"

"Yes," said Go. "By the creed of the Ibandi, it was unholy. An abomination. When it became known, he was excommunicated."

"Yes," San agreed. "And the Ibandi tried to rescue some of the clones. And failed. Only one was liberated."

"Me."

"A warrior named Thomas Jai betrayed Swarna, and carried you to America. Took you far beyond the reach of Swarna's security forces. A futile gesture, saving a single child. But it had to be done."

Aubry's mind opened, as if someone had pulled back the night and the stars, and exposed the sun. He felt the light flowing through him, and his body began to shake. "So . . . I accidentally killed Swarna's only son."

"And he sent us to kill you."

"Didn't he know? Didn't he know who and what I was?"

"No. There was a single order: 'Find the one who killed my son. Kill him.' We came to America. We traced the information. We found you. And when we did, we knew. And we didn't tell Swarna."

"Why?"

"Because we had an allegiance beyond Swarna. Beyond even Tanaka Sensei."

"To each other."

"To each other," San said. "To Swarna, we were spare parts. And his security. But we were the Six. Three years ago, he needed a heart transplant. He took it from Ichi, our brother. We were then the Five."

San leaned forward. "We have only each other . . . we

are family, We are not of Life. He created us thus. We never knew anything of that world. We came to America, to kill you, and discovered for ourselves who you really were. And saw in you what we never knew for ourselves."

Aubry's voice was soft. He felt as if he could barely breathe. "And what was that?"

"A family. A woman. A child. A great child." Suddenly, the cave seemed hotter. "You are what we could have been, had we been human."

"You *are* human," Aubry said.

Ni shook his head sadly. "No. To be human, you must be alive. To be alive you must be born of woman. You found a woman to share her fire with you. Your woman *made* you human, brother. You are our hope."

"Your hope?"

"Despite the transplants, despite the nanobots, Swarna grows ever older, and more fearful. Divine Blossom, the Yakuza combine, is a vulture. Soon, they will take what they have coveted for so long. There is nothing to stop them—"

"Why do you need me? Why haven't you done something about this, if you hate him so?"

"Divine Blossom waits, knowing that PanAfrica cannot survive Swarna's death. If we kill him, we have to deal with Divine Blossom. But you are our brother. You have Gorgon. You have the ear of the president of the United States. You have the Scavengers. If you will add your knowledge, your connections, to our strength, what Swarna did might yet become a thing of good. Without you, we are a rabble, unable to hold what Swarna created. So much death and misery . . . all for nothing. Will you do this thing? Will you join with us?"

Aubry considered.

If this was why he had been born, not of woman, a creature of Death . . .

If this was why he had been reborn, through Promise, through Mira, through Jenna . . . and through Leslie . . .

It made sense. The world was smaller and stranger than

ever he had imagined. But now, for the first time, he could see a pattern behind the chaos.

My life, he thought.

I can have my life. Complete.

Or, no less desirable, a good death.

He leaned forward. "We have a commitment from Five Songs," he said. "A thousand men and women of the underground. Ready to die, if I can promise Phillipe Swarna's death as well."

San's eyes shone. "I have a plan," she said.

9

It was raining by the time the security skimmer passed the Citadel's gates, running the codes through its computer. It landed, and scanners showed that Ni, San, and Roku were aboard. They disembarked, still wearing shock armor and faceplates, and seemed as tall and strong as the mountains from which they had just returned.

The courtyard below the Citadel was of concrete, with high, stark walls, and the raindrops hit and spattered, steaming against the asphalt.

Tanaka met them at the lock, with his own group of Divine Blossom guards. "And?"

San's face shield depolarized. "No sign of Go, or the rebels. It was a false sighting."

Tanaka cursed. "And you let him go into that prison alone. Alone!"

"He was the strongest," San said coolly. "If he had succeeded in extracting the assassin, he would have gained much honor. You, more than anyone, should understand this."

In their armor and helmets Ni, San, and Roku were a half head taller than Tanaka. He glared at them, then nodded curtly and turned away.

He returned to the electronic-scan station and watched

as they filed in. One at a time, the computer scanned their retinas and palm prints. One at a time, they entered the Citadel.

Tanaka watched, suspicion narrowing his eyes.

Inside Ni's armor, Aubry Knight sweltered as they walked the halls of the Citadel. There was no cover here, no place to hide.

They marched, down the graven stone hallways beneath the Citadel, until they came to the bank of elevators.

Then San and Roku turned to him, and raised their hands, touching palms to his palm.

"One dies, we all die. One lives, we all live," she whispered, and armed her rifle. She turned abruptly, and ran down the hall.

The elevator opened. Aubry and Roku entered.

The door closed.

10

Roku reached the control room first, and Aubry, disguised as Ni, a moment later. There was a door with a wide glass window in it, and within they saw the control room, a series of flickering panels, and holographic displays of the Menagerie.

Their eyes met. They synchronized breathing, their bodies and minds becoming one. They smashed through the door.

"One chance," Roku barked. "Away from the panels." One of the technicians moved toward the alarm, and Roku fired instantly. The hapless technician flew back against the control board, bullets stitching his body.

He slid down slowly, leaving a slick of blood and tissue.

The other Japanese and two Ugandans stood, raising their hands.

Roku linked his shock armor's tactical computer into

the main boards. Circuits appeared, crawling in the air before him; one of them blinked red.

"No—!" one of the Japanese said. Aubry pulsed him in the leg. Cloth and skin burned. The Japanese crumpled, cursing.

Roku dominated the circuit.

He scanned the holographic model of the Menagerie. He weakened the inner electronic barrier's signal, then killed it. He pumped up the outer barrier's signal, trebled it, and then trebled it again.

He disabled all electronic alarms and safeguards on the drawbridges across Caernarvon's moat.

Aubry fired his pulse rifle into the control panels themselves. Bits of steel and plastic fountained flaming into the air.

Roku looked at the men and women cowering on the floor, and his voice was deadly. "Stay here," he said. "If we see you outside, you die."

Roku turned, then turned back, an instant too slowly. One of the technicians had a pistol, aimed at Roku's open visor.

They fired at the same instant.

Roku's finger remained on the trigger, hosing the room with death, even after the visor slid down, concealing the ruined cavity that had once been another of Aubry Knight's faces.

Aubry stood silently, breathing hard. The room was full of death. Blood trickled from beneath Roku's visor. He fought the urge to lift it. Instead, he turned, and ran from the room.

In the halls outside, the alarm was blaring.

11

When the drawbridges began to lower across the concrete moat, the tower guards were at first unconcerned. Somewhat distractedly, they checked to see what dignitary might be arriving.

But the rain and driving wind puzzled them. Who would come now? Why not virt in? What could they want?

And then, through the rain, they saw the first of the sauropods. It was a scelidosaurus, only twelve feet long, the oldest known ornithischian and the first of the plated dinosaurs. A sort of protostegosaurian oddity from the lower Jurassic. Lightning reflected dully from its crocodile plating as it waddled across the drawbridge, lowing with pain.

The guards froze for a moment. The beast was considered harmless, its tiny skull holding barely enough brain to coordinate its heart and lungs. It was almost comical, wobbling on those powerful hind legs and short, stubby forelegs. Clownlike, rolling its eyes as if about to request an aspirin.

Someone laughed. The laugh died in mid-chuckle, as someone realized the implication: the inner electronic moat was down . . . ?

And in the dark beyond the moat, there was a throaty, rumbling cry, a scream of insane pain and rage, echoed in a hundred saurian throats.

And then, through the rain, they came. Herbivores and carnivores, tiny nanosaurs and full-sized giants, they thundered toward the Citadel. Blind with agony they charged, driven onto the spikes by those behind, climbing up and over and falling into the moat, where they lowed and scrabbled with broken spines, tearing flesh from each other's backs and flanks.

Thundering on the most powerful legs any animal had ever possessed, whipped into a frenzy, the creatures fought and snapped, boiling out of the darkness. The guards, disbelieving at first, loosed all of the alarms.

Some brave Zulu dashed onto the drawbridge, trying to raise it with the manual winch. He was a moment too slow, and was ensnared by the jaws of an eighteen-foot megalosaurus. He barely had time to register pain and disbelief before the carnivore's jaws flashed down. He howled as the teeth clamped around him. Blood spurted, blackly. There was a frenzy of smaller predator activity, and the Zulu was ripped to pieces.

The external alarms sounded.

And then—from the strip of mined ground, the wedge stretching from northwest to west—there was a shrill whistle and an arc of fire. Something flared out of the darkness, rose high, and plunged down onto Caernarvon's north wall, exploding. Chunks of stone and mortar tumbled, flaming, and there was a shriek of pain and fear.

The rebels were attacking.

12

Tanaka's nerves burned. Something was terribly wrong. Somehow, Five Songs had nullified crucial—but not critical—elements of the defensive system. With the cover of the rain, and the confusion caused by the sauropods, and the sudden failure of the communications and security systems, it would take perhaps seven minutes to get everything under control. Seven minutes—but he wasn't certain that he had that much time.

The Four had failed. Go had died in the Central African Republic, and somehow in the process, the assassin had escaped.

Hadn't he?

He didn't like any of this. And in fact, he knew where he belonged.

He had to get to the throne room, protect Swarna. Whatever else happened, the primary must survive.

He grabbed a pulse rifle from the rack in his office, and then stopped, staring at the object in the glass case. His great-grandfather's sword. He suddenly had the sensation that it was calling to him.

That this was the last night of his life.

He smashed the case with his elbow, and reverently removed the blade and scabbard.

His African blood had isolated him from the Japanese society he craved, but no one could deny him his great-grandfather's sword. Another explosion shook Caernarvon. He strapped the scabbard to his waist. So be it. If he was to play out the last act of the comic tragedy that was his life, he would do it as a man, as a samurai.

And by all that was holy, he would die before one hair on that monkey dictator's head was harmed.

13

I was in a ventilation duct on the second story. Through the floor and walls of the duct I could feel the reverberations. I could smell smoke. Hear distant screams.

Five Songs.

Needed data. What resources existed? Surveillance fiber optics ran in parallel with the duct. Low-security lines, running to outer guard tower. I compromised them, and began to scan. Tactical input—maximum three hundred troops. No air support. Moving through narrow cordon between sauropod pens. Minefield ahead activated. Attack useless. Would be pinned down and destroyed. Why attempted?

Unless . . .

Two hundred and seven separate camera feeds from inside Caernarvon. Eighty-seven infrared scans. Over a thousand pressure plates. I referenced them all in seven seconds, and stopped.

Two images, walking side by side. Armored. Almost identical bone structure. One was a paragon of physical power.

The other moved perfectly.

Father.

Five Songs "rebellion" was a feint. Father had infiltrated Citadel guard. On his way to kill Swarna? Video was pure visual feed. Contained no reference code for location. Did not know where Father was.

Body seethed with pain, rage, fear. Excitement. Had never felt anything like it. I was at sea. Arms and legs shook as adrenals dumped. I crouched in the duct. Must have resembled an animal, eyes wide, with the hair standing up on my head. Filthy, bloody, wounded.

I hurt, but I shut down the pain. Must help Father.

Video input projected chaos. Rebels surged across minefields, sweeping it with their own bodies. Guards terrified by sheer ferocity. A few external guards overwhelmed.

Excellent—sauropods being driven into inner garden by pain collars, the Menagerie turning against its masters. The guards were frightened, but regrouping. If only the saurians were intelligent, they could . . .

If only . . .

Swarna's entertainment center. His pleasure—entering mating carnosaurs. I saw better application of technology.

I crawled along the duct and headed to the entertainment complex. All computer centers were underground. Sealed during initial alarm. There was no direct access. Nothing human could reach them.

I am not human.

I am Death.

14

I couldn't breathe. The conduit was too narrow for a human body. It was barely large enough for a cat.

But if my head could fit through, then the rest of me could. Pain was nothing. I felt my hips slip out of their alignment, and there was a *stretching* sensation, overwhelming pain as I torqued my spine.

Mustn't sever the spinal column, but the conduit was threaded like a corkscrew. I slithered along, taking out filters as I went, ripping them from their moorings, and pushing them ahead of me. A bone in my hand broke from the pressure.

I ignored it. There was nothing for me but to continue.

I was at the window of the entertainment control center. It was grated. An air purifier was set into the wall, controlling the air flow. It made the computer room impervious to attack by gas, by germs, by almost anything.

It was set into the back of the wall by welded struts, and glued into the base by a new polyacrylic cement, with a breaking strength of seventeen hundred pounds.

The human body is an odd thing. If every muscle in the human body pushed or pulled in unison, it would be capable of exerting fantastic force. Most people care about hurting themselves, and never reach their full potential physically or mentally.

I was wounded, and had very little purchase. I set my toes, finding some kind of grip on the tunnel. I set my hands to the unit, and I pushed.

Father.

I could not move this thing. I had reached the limits of my strength.

Father.

I had to stop, stop before I died.

But I am a thing of evil, and the only way that I can cleanse that evil is by dying. Dying at that moment, in the service of something that I

(Love)

I could hear the metal whine as the purifier began to move.

15

The Nigerian at the first security monitor saw the first alarm go red.

Until that moment, the entertainment complex had been secure. The rebellion couldn't possibly reach them, down where they were, beneath walls of concrete and steel. There was no way that anything could be done to compromise them, and there was security here as there would be in few places in the world.

But he saw the tiny red light come on, and interpreted it quickly.

Air system compromised.

There was a faint rumble of an explosion up above, and they looked at each other. What had gone wrong?

Then they heard another sound, a sound that was much, much closer, and it was something that came from the wall itself.

The wall plaster was splitting, cracking and peeling away a foot back from the reinforced ventilator grille.

Their eyes widened. Beneath the plaster, one-eighth-inch steel sheeting, welded at the seams, was coming undone, peeling back, screaming. A trickle of thin red fluid ran from within.

They watched, hands hovering over the alarm switch, horrified, not quite able to move, as the wall gave birth.

There was a gasping sound, rising above the dying hum of the ventilator, and a child's bloodied head came through the hole. The technicians were frozen. The child *couldn't* have been alive. It was torn, and dusty, and one ear was almost torn away. Blood drooled down its neck. But its *eyes.* Its eyes were so alive. They *burned.*

There were three men in the room, and the child fixed each of them, in turn, with those terrible eyes.

They still had yet to move, frozen, horrified, watching the dreadful process.

The child fell out, and slid down the wall, leaving a slick of blood. Thudded to the floor.

It shuddered like a puppet with tangled strings. No man in the room had managed to move yet.

The child-puppet stood, wavering, as if its strings were being mended, strand by painful strand, under the urging of a will that was stronger than death.

With dreadful slowness its head rose. It blinked blood from its eyes. Its clothing was torn to shreds. The body beneath the clothes was so thin, it seemed starved.

Then it opened its mouth, screamed, and flew at them.

16

I rolled the last body out of the way and crawled into the seat in front of the security monitor.

I shut pain somewhere far, far away, but set my body to healing in the best way that I could. What I needed to do was to crawl somewhere quiet and dark, and allow my body to begin its process. But there was no time for that. No time at all.

There were multiple intake devices available, and I had to find the right one, and find it quickly. With bloodied fingers, I ripped out the paneling, and found the fiber-optic cables leading to the main processor. Split them, and reached back to the base of my skull, found the input dock, and spliced the cables in.

I died.

I was the room, the cooling system, the environmental

unit. My eyes filled with light. My brain is a puny co-processor. It can perform a pitiful few billion functions a second, but that would have to be enough. I raced through the wiring wide as railway tunnels, my consciousness a ghost in the machine.

I ranged beyond. I was the outer walls. I could disrupt communications. I tied into main security systems, found them already compromised.

Father.

He changed settings on Menagerie pain-fences. Froze drawbridge controls. A good beginning. I could do more.

Cracked codes on emergency security shield, broadcast recall code to backup troops. Energy weapons were being used. I could dampen and disrupt. Swarna's troops would fall back on explosive weaponry, which would place them on greater parity with the rebels. Father's pulse rifle would now be dysfunctional. But he had . . . other skills. It would throw things further into balance. But it was not enough. Not nearly enough. There must be more.

The Menagerie.

Last radio reports stated Five Songs rebels were streaming through the minefield. Heavy casualties. I disarmed it.

More.

Swarna's private codes were the work of a moment. I would enter the mind of the ankylosaurus.

17

Ni watched Stump-Leg die. In one moment the rebel was beside him, cursing gutturally and firing his ancient rifle at unseen guards. He was probably unaware that the man he fought beside was a Swarna clone. Ni was just another rebel, firing at guards and soldiers with lethal skill. In the next moment, Stump-Leg's head was aflame, slagging, and then the skull exploded in a shower of brain and bone and smoldering hair.

The men and women of Five Songs had converged in the night. Maps supplied by the clones revealed safety corridors through the Menagerie and the garden, protected by electronic pain transmitters. The safety corridor was mined—and every day the security computer selectively armed and disarmed different segments of the minefield. They could only hope that their map was up to date.

They were wagering their lives that it was.

So far, it was a poor bet. They had made it as close as the garden, but were pinned down in a cross fire, faces in the mud and muck, drowning in the torrential rain in a night that threatened to last forever. When they tried to move, the mines blew them to pieces.

Screams of pain and frustration churned the air, some of them originated in the throats of the carnosaurs behind them. The sound, the shock, the smell of torn flesh combined into an overwhelming sensory collage, paralyzing the warriors of Five Songs where they crouched.

And then—

The energy bolts, pulse-rifle plasma blasts ripping them in unending salvos, just *stopped*. The sky no longer rippled with fire, was no longer seared with an angry aurora borealis. A guard screamed in frustration and fear and confusion, cursing his suddenly useless weapon.

Ni smiled grimly, gripped his machine rifle, and charged across the minefield. Behind him, the rebels gasped at his lone, headlong plunge, expecting to see him blown into bits in the next moment.

But—there was no explosion.

Bullets exploded around him as the guards switched to the non-energy-based weapon. Ni charged directly into the fire, a lone figure screaming defiance, and for a long moment the rebels watched him. Watched as he fired, cutting down two guards atop the wall. Watched as the bullets finally found him, and tore his body to pieces, throwing him this way and that, until he lay, in the rain, unmoving.

And then, something broke among the rebels, and they charged. Charged across the dead minefield, charged the inaccurate rifles and machine guns. Charged the ancient walls of Caernarvon Castle.

They died the way Zulus died at Roerke's Drift, by the hundreds. But over their shattered bodies came more, and yet more, and the guards were overwhelmed, screaming.

The earth shook. And in the light of the flaming wreckage, a giant shadow fell upon the rebels from behind.

Again the carnage paused, and all turned to look.

One of the great placid plant eaters stood watching them. A speaker box chained at its throat suddenly crackled with sound.

"Hello," the box said. *"I am an ankylosaurus, an herbivore of the Cretaceous—"* Then it stopped, and seemed to shudder. Then there was . . . a change. Something happened in its eyes, and it no longer gazed at them dully. Suddenly, its eyes were focused, intelligent. And the speaker said, *"Follow me. We have taken control of the Menagerie. Follow me . . ."*

And the ankylosaurus charged, directly into Caernarvon's suppressing fire.

They watched as the machine-gun fire ripped into it, and then a rocket, blowing a great piece of living armor from its hide. It screamed in an agony that was too human, the scream coming from its throat and the box at the same time, and it collapsed, dead, tail twitching. But its enormous bulk gave them cover closer to the wall.

Then there was a scream from behind them, as a thirty-foot iguanodon charged. Bipedal, carnivorous, a relic of the lower Cretaceous, it shrieked, folds of loose flesh beneath its jaw puffing and deflating with each scream. On thick, gnarled legs it plunged through the deactivated minefield. The earth thundered as it approached, and the men on the wall screamed, pivoting their weapons as the creature, suffering unimaginable torment, charged through the electronic barrier and went to the attack.

On momentum alone, it made it all the way to the wall, and slammed into it headfirst. The men on the wall screamed, as much in sheer terror at the size of the beast as anything else.

And as they fired—

Another iguanodon came out of the smoke, through the barrier, and attacked at the northeast corner. . . .

And then another, and the rebels of Five Songs watched, amazed, and then raised their arms to the sky, screaming and shrieking their pleasure.

Truly, the gods were with them.

18

I was in a world of split attention. I rotated my consciousness between the creatures a hundred times a second, controlling their actions, feeling their agony as the bullets poured into me.

I transferred out of their bodies when the pain grew too great. I had to suppress my physiological reaction when the bullets hit, or I would slide massively into shock.

My physiological pain reactions hammered at the gate of my mind, almost more than I could bear.

Through saurian eyes, I could see the flashes of light. Now the rebels swarmed up, climbing over the gates on ladders of dead dinosaur flesh. Although they died, they killed as well. Guards were confused, terrified.

I allowed my attention to be distracted

It hurts—!

The pain. I took a direct hit. Explosive weapon . . . bazooka-type. Chest. My attention shrunk.

Must get out.

Must get out.

Must . . .

Couldn't transfer.

It *hurt*, more than dream or nightmare. I never dreamed of pain like this. Mind wouldn't work. Felt heart shudder slow stop.

Blood pressure dropped.

I was . . .

I . . .

19

Tanesha watched as a rebel died planting a satchel charge against Caernarvon's main gate. The guard who shot him died a moment later as the charge detonated, sending steel and stone and flame into the night sky. This was the moment!

Her ears still ringing, Tanesha grabbed her rifle and charged forward, buoyed by the joyous screams of the other warriors of Five Songs, all about her.

This was a moment to remember, for whatever brief minute of life remained to her. The guards were actually falling back, cut to ribbons by the guns of the rebels.

But there was no illusion. Within minutes, reinforcements would arrive, catching Five Songs in pincers. Then it would be over. Then, all of the death would be for nothing. . . .

Unless Aubry Knight, Aubry *Jai*, could succeed. But that was the future, for now there was the killing, and the dying, and there was enough of each to fill her world.

20

Caernarvon's great halls shook with the thunderous pulse of explosions as Five Songs battled with Swarna's guards.

Aubry was deep inside himself, only his senses beyond his skin. He was completely at peace.

His pulse rifle had failed, and the laser sight on his pistol wasn't working. Something had happened to the power all over the Citadel. As long as the guards were concentrating on the external threat, it helped him.

San was in the darkness, near him.

They were aware of each other, each mirroring and supporting the other's motions. They seemed able to read each other's minds.

Aubry felt utterly alive. Even in the depths of shadow, his senses seemed sharper, clearer, than they had ever been. His eyes were sharper than they had ever been before. Even in the shadows, he was aware.

There was a movement to their right, and he swiveled to face it, squeezed off a silenced burst.

Another burst of fire, and this time from concealment. The throne room was sealed off, weaponry projecting from slits in the walls.

Aubry depressed his trigger until it clicked, empty, clicked again and again.

San smiled at him, enormously. "Good luck, my brother," she said, and flew at the door.

She rolled a smoke grenade before her. It exploded in a dark cloud, and she rushed behind it. The wall cracked with fire, and San, sprinting faster than Aubry had ever seen a woman run, was caught a dozen times. Her shock armor dampened the impact of the shells, and her momentum carried her forward, screaming all the way. She slammed a disk-shaped explosive charge against the door, then hurled herself to the side and—

In the confined space, the detonation was almost unendurably loud, and Aubry's ears split. His head felt as if it had been smashed with a hammer.

Smoking wreckage was everywhere.

San lay sprawled in the wreckage, her arms and legs twisted and broken by the impact, shock armor torn and smoldering. Through her open visor her eyes stared up, sightless.

Then she blinked.

Aubry had her in his arms in a moment. She was too weak even to cough, but a bubble of blood slid from her mouth. *"Go,"* she said, almost too softly for him to hear the word. *"Finish it."* Then she lost consciousness.

The air was filled with smoke, and flame, and the moans of the dying.

There was no need for speed. He climbed over the rubble, and there, at the back of the room, at last, sat Phillipe Swarna.

21

Aubry walked forward slowly, with measured step. He felt as if his hair were on fire, and with every breath, the heat stoked up to a higher level.

Phillipe Swarna was old, old, but there was no doubt that when the man had been young, and in his prime, when he had walked with full utility, when his eyes and heart had been his own, before he had required marrow transplants to keep himself alive, he had been Aubry Knight.

"Who are you?" Swarna quavered, his voice an old man's voice.

"I am you," Aubry replied.

Swarna shook visibly. "Tanaka!" he ranted. "Tanaka!"

And near Aubry, to the left, something rustled. Covered with dust, and bleeding from where an ear had been torn away, Tanaka stood. He raised a dusty pulse rifle. It was useless, now.

Aubry leveled his machine rifle. His finger tightened on the trigger.

No response. It was empty.

His hand shaking, Tanaka straightened his scabbard and drew steel.

"This man is my primary," Tanaka said. "You may not pass."

"You are wounded," Aubry observed bluntly. "All I have to do is wait, and you will bleed to death."

"But you can't wait," Tanaka said. "Your feint outside will fail. Everything will be for nothing. Reinforcements will arrive in minutes. To kill him you must pass me."

Aubry turned, walked two paces, and plucked a rifle from the hands of one of the dead guards. He fired a short burst into the ceiling. Marble chips and plaster rained on them both.

"San told me that you were her teacher. That you are a man of honor. I would not kill you, unless you force me. You are armed only with a sword. Stand aside."

"Will you?" Tanaka asked. "You are a warrior of your people, as I am a warrior of mine. It would be dishonorable to shoot me."

"I am beyond honor," Aubry said. "I cannot put my honor above the lives of my people. I have forsaken my family, my past life, my country. I will kill you, Tanaka."

Upon his throne, Swarna cringed.

Tanaka's great chest heaved. "I will make a deal with you, warrior," he said. "If you will face me in fair combat."

A deal. Aubry could almost laugh. "What do you have to offer me?"

"PanAfrica," Tanaka said quietly.

Aubry lowered his rifle. "What in the hell are you talking about?"

"I can give you the computer codes."

"No!" Swarna's voice broke on that scream.

"Shut up!" Tanaka said. "It is the only way."

"He will kill you anyway!" Swarna screamed again.

"No," Tanaka said. "I do not believe it."

His eyes met Aubry's and it seemed as if, once again, Aubry was meeting himself. Across a gulf of cultures, and a gulf of years and miles. Yes. He and Tanaka were the same man, born in different worlds.

"Yes," Swarna said desperately. "I agree. All right. The code is my name, plus the letters QDX."

"Why so simple?" Aubry asked quietly, his eyes on Tanaka.

Swarna wiped a string of saliva from the corner of his mouth. "You have one chance to enter it, and then the system shuts down for twenty-four hours."

Aubry shifted his gaze back to Tanaka. "Is that the truth?"

Tanaka's gaze met his levelly. "No, it is not." His voice was as cold as the steel he held. "Do you agree to my terms?"

"And what are they? Exactly."

"To face me man to man, without projectile or energy weapons. No tricks. No loopholes. You are a warrior, not a lawyer. You know what I ask."

Aubry almost smiled.

"All right. I agree."

"The code," Tanaka said, "is a drop of my blood, and Swarna's blood, on the sensor built into the seat of his throne."

"Fool! Fool!" Swarna howled.

"Then why can't you activate it? Why can't you take over everything yourself?"

"The system is coded to Swarna's genetic scan. Only he can operate it. It was devised as such, from the beginning. His code, and that of his head of security. I am bound by honor. And impossibility. There is no spoken code. If I were dead, and my body beyond recovery, technicians would have to be flown in from Osaka, the entire system rekeyed. It would take a week."

"You crawling, puking imbecile. You traitorous *shit*! I'll kill you, kill you. You'll scream for *months*—"

Aubry's eyes cast around the room. To the right of the throne was a wall of traditional weapons cast in modern materials. A plastic bow. A composition aluminum staff. And next to it, crossed one over another, was the pair of stainless-steel *assagai,* a present from the Zulu.

"I choose these," Aubry said.

Tanaka nodded.

Aubry took it down from the wall. He balanced it in his hand and felt the spear come alive. It was for throwing. It was for stabbing. It held an edge as fine as anything made by man, an ancient fighting implement, refined to the standards of the twenty-first century.

He turned, and faced Tanaka.

22

There might have been the slightest inclination from Tanaka, the hint of a bow. Then he held his sword in his right hand, his scabbard in the left, tips down in a variation of the classic *happo biraki*—"open on all eight sides"—position. He advanced carefully, sliding his right foot forward, regaining his balance with his subsequent step.

Tanaka screamed and cast his scabbard aside. In that scream there lived the echo of ancestors dead a thousand years, men who had lived and died with steel in their hands, by their hands, who had perfected their art over the same bloody years that Aubry's ancestors had perfected theirs, and only Aubry's insane reflexes saved him from a thrust that was so fast that his conscious mind didn't register it at all.

He slid backward. Balanced, thrust. Tanaka blocked flawlessly. The tip of his sword danced back in, his body behind it—perfectly.

Aubry had barely enough time to shift to the side. The blade passed a half inch to his left. Tanaka recovered perfectly, slid forty-five degrees to the left, and lunged, recovered with impossible speed, and brought the blade down a completely different line, screaming.

Aubry knew that he would be dead in a few seconds. Tanaka had learned something. Cadence? Distance perception? Something. Perhaps he had merely sensed Aubry's lack of experience with the weapon.

And he would make his kill in the next engagement.

Aubry threw the short spear, and Tanaka flicked it from the air with the tip of his blade. Aubry ran to the wall, Tanaka just steps behind him, and snatched down the staff.

It popped away from the wall, spun into the air, and he caught it only a foot and a half from one end. It was six feet long, and ornamentally heavy. Heavy enough that an ordinary man would have labored with it.

But Aubry Knight was not an ordinary man.

And when he held it, he felt its balance, its truth, and it almost dizzied him. This, and not the spear, was the natural weapon of the Ibandi. Of Firedance.

Tanaka lunged. Aubry riposted and the tip lanced in. Tanaka parried, and Aubry stepped back like a swirl of smoke coiling. The staff spun in his hands, almost as if it were alive.

He saw Old Man.

Lion killers, that is what his people were. That they had been, long before Iron Mountain. The line of the weapon, the balance, the feel was so natural it was almost like an extension of his mind and will.

Tanaka drew back, eyes sharpened, and evaluated. He smiled, almost to himself, and Aubry circled him, using tip, using haft, spinning the staff, using its length to keep Tanaka at a distance, keep that deadly *katana* at a distance.

Tanaka lunged—Aubry countered, trapping the blade beneath the staff. In that instant, he realized he had made another mistake: he had allowed himself to think of the *staff* as the weapon. Staff, spear, knife, gun—none of these are weapons. They are merely tools. Man is the weapon.

Tanaka had not made that mistake. His sword down, Aubry's attention upon it, Tanaka's right foot hooked up and around, and struck Aubry Knight with perfect form and precision in the left temple.

Once again, Aubry's reflexes were all that saved him— he was rolling back even before he knew what was coming. His hands left the staff for a moment, and Tanaka was after him, not hesitating the instant that it would have taken him to reclaim his sword, following instantly and unhesitatingly after the kick.

Tanaka became a maelstrom of elbows and knees, clawing fingers and hammering feet. Blinding light and fire crackled in Aubry's mind and he realized that this man, Tanaka, trained from birth in the arts of Japanese *budo*, was the deadliest human being he had ever faced.

Aubry tripped over a guard's corpse—and it was all that saved him, because his head went down under a devastating hand-axe strike, a blow that would have nearly decapitated him.

He hit on his shoulder and rolled, backing away, and then pushed off to the side, springing to his feet.

Stars still scrambled his vision, but he stood, blinking, catching his breath. Tanaka was two paces away, holding his ribs, eyes narrowed, wincing soundlessly.

And Aubry realized—somewhere in that last exchange, he had landed something. His body, without the aid of his conscious mind, had done what it had to do.

Tanaka stepped back a pace, exhaled, fingers of the left hand fanned, crooked, and the right fist balled by his side. Eyes absolutely level. Breathing growing steady now.

The thing on the throne screamed out orders, screamed out pleas. All of which Tanaka ignored.

Aubry feinted with a kick to the groin, letting Tanaka fade back. He slid his right foot along the ground, catching chunks of plaster and gravel from the crushed wall, and scooped them into the air with the inside edge of his foot, kicking them into Tanaka's face. Tanaka blocked, and even though Aubry was behind it an instant later, Tanaka's counter caught him in the ribs. He felt them go, and caught the next blow in the neck, hunching his great trapezius muscles to cushion the shock.

Then he was in grappling range. He felt Tanaka's body slither away. In a movement that had been extracted from aikido, Tanaka threw him, and maintained the grip on his right wrist at the same time, in a hold that threatened to freeze Aubry's entire body.

Aubry went against the pain, against his wrist, and hammered a kick into Tanaka's side. His own wrist and elbow snapped from the torque.

It was the first clean blow he had landed, and it broke something.

Tanaka sucked air, his eyes watering, staggering back. Aubry, right arm dangling, touched down on the ball of the left foot, pivoted, and spun before Tanaka could lift his head to see. The heel of Aubry's foot impacted on the side of Tanaka's face, smashing him around, whipping him back against the wall. Bone cracked audibly as his head bounced back, and Aubry's second kick caught him in the midsection.

It was like kicking a tree, but Tanaka reeled into the wall again.

Now. Now.

In the single moment of advantage that his broken arm had won against this terrific man, Aubry Knight used knees and left elbow, side and palm of the left hand, and smashed Tanaka against the wall again. Trapped his hand against the wall with his heel, breaking fingers. Striking again and again, forcing himself past pain and fatigue, squeezing every last bit of speed and power out of his body. He never gave Tanaka room or time or a moment's respite, not once, until Tanaka screamed, his head lancing forward, and caught Aubry on the bridge of the nose.

Aubry staggered back, legs rubbery. His eyes refused to focus. Tanaka staggered up, jaw shattered, ribs cracked, right eye swollen shut, fingers on the right hand broken.

And came in for more.

Aubry watched him. Timed him. Caught Tanaka in the knee with a perfect side kick. Bone cracked audibly. Tanaka flew back against the wall again. He slid down, eyes rolling up with the pain.

The only sound in the throne room was harsh and labored breathing. He glared up at Aubry, sucked air, and levered himself up with shaking arms, sweat and blood drooling down his ashen face, leaning back against the wall for support. He took a step, and fell. His breath hissed in his throat as if he were some terrible reptile. His eyes focused on Aubry, burning.

Unblinking, he crawled forward.

"My God," Aubry said fervently. "I've never seen anything like you."

Tanaka crawled another foot and then collapsed. His nose cracked against the marble floor. As if each inch of motion were costing him an ocean of effort, Tanaka turned his head sideways, barely able to move now. He swallowed, and gazed at Aubry, as if the will driving the body had finally given out. "Kill me," he said.

"No," Aubry replied quietly. "Too many warriors have died today. There aren't enough left in the world."

Tanaka's eyes closed. "Kill . . . me."

Aubry felt the pain and fatigue descending upon his body like a cloak as the adrenaline burn diminished. He wanted to crawl somewhere and curl into a ball, and die. But there was still something left to do. "Only one thing," he said to Tanaka, "will release you from your oath."

He turned, and approached the throne.

23

The thing that had been Phillipe Swarna screamed as Aubry came at him. And the scream went beyond words, beyond fear, to some place where logic and rationality ceased to work. Where, perhaps, it had never existed at all.

Aubry took Swarna's face in his hands and gazed into his eyes. For the fraction of an instant logic returned, and a kind of animal recognition dawned in Swarna's ruined brain.

"You . . . are me," Swarna said.

And Aubry looked at the bones beneath the skin, and the eyes, and the flesh hanging on the body, and something within him said *yes*.

But he whispered, "*No.* I've never been you."

He twisted, once. Hard.

Tanaka had managed to prop himself up onto his elbows. He regarded the dead thing sliding from the throne, and lowered his head, letting out a kind of strangled sob.

His precious *katana* was only three feet away from him,

and with infinite pain, he dragged himself over to it. He wedged its hilt against a piece of debris, and fought to place its tip against his throat.

"No," Aubry said, fighting the fatigue that swarmed over him like a plague of shadows. "Help me rebuild PanAfrica."

"I failed," Tanaka said.

"I am Phillipe Swarna!" Aubry screamed. "I was cloned from the *meat* lying on that throne. By every legal right, I am Phillipe Swarna. What is a man? What did you swear fealty to? I am all that is left. Serve me. Serve *Divine Blossom.*" Tanaka wouldn't meet his eyes. "San said that you love this land. That you grieve for what has happened to it. If that is true, do the hard thing, Tanaka Sensei. Live. Fight for what you love. The real battle is just beginning. Live, Tanaka Sensei."

Their eyes locked, Tanaka searching for truth. And then, at last, the man upon the floor nodded.

24

The computer sensor was built into the arm of the throne. Tanaka showed Aubry how to open it. How to smear a drop of Tanaka's blood, and a drop of his own—of Phillipe Swarna's—blood. And the system responded.

The air before them blossomed. He selected the security monitors. The walls of Caernarvon were breached. Brick and stone masonry six hundred years old lay in heaps, smoking, shrouding the bodies of brave men and women who had fought to the death in the name of duty, or liberty. Only a dozen or so guards remained alive. Less than a hundred Five Songs rebels remained.

"According to this," Tanaka said, "someone gave the recall order for our reinforcements. They will realize it is a ruse, and arrive within minutes. The guards and rebels both will die."

Tanaka whispered hoarsely. "The guards fight for what they think right, Mr. President," he said. "Save them. Give the signal to withdraw. Talk to both rebels and the commandos, who must be on their way."

"I can do that?" Aubry asked.

"You," Tanaka said. "And no one else."

And so it was.

25

OCTOBER 8. CAERNARVON CASTLE.

Naked, suspended in clear nutrient solution, Medusa-16, also known as Leslie Knight, was healing slowly. Leads were attached to his eyes, his heart, his genitals, his nose and throat, to the inputs at the back of his skull.

He was scanned three thousand times a second. Within his body, nanobots scurried about, repairing nerve and tissue damage.

Aubry Knight slipped his left arm around his wife, Promise. His right was encased in a plastic cast. They watched their child breathing, each inhalation and exhalation carefully monitored.

"I still can't believe what she did," Promise said, eyes tearing.

"He," Aubry corrected.

Promise leaned her head against his shoulder. "Ordinarily I'd argue, Mr. President, but I'm a little too tired. I hope you'll understand."

He kissed her hairline, and they walked a few paces to the left, to another tank. In it was a woman who would stand over six feet tall, a woman whose voluptuous body carried the promise of savage strength and speed. She, too, was unconscious. But alive.

Alive, Aubry thought. *My God. I have a sister.*

"I want to meet her," Promise said.

"You will."

She smiled shyly. "You know, they're going to do everything to keep us apart."

"Not that they have to do that much," he said ruefully. "I'm needed here. You're needed in the States. I have work to do here."

"What do you think?" she asked. "Can a bicontinental marriage work?"

"It's going to have to," Aubry said.

Her hands traced the bruised contours of his face. "It will take a while to get used to this mask. . . ."

"What do you think?" he asked, almost shyly.

"Brutal, but vulnerable. Not like anyone *I* know."

"Right." He held her shoulders. "I crossed the world for us. I watched myself die three times. I will destroy anything that hurts my family, or that stands between us. Anything."

Promise gazed into the eyes of the man she loved, and nodded, feeling as if someone had rolled a stone from her heart. Her child was alive. Her man was alive.

There were a few little problems. For instance, Aubry was, technically speaking, America's greatest single enemy. Little things like that.

She had to return to America with her healing sister and child. Ephesus, the Scavengers, and perhaps even the New-Men needed her. So much to do.

And there would be trouble from the State Department if Aubry decided to give up his citizenship. America would try to keep husband and wife apart, or possibly play them off against each other.

They could *try*, dammit.

The door at the far end of the room clicked open. Aubry's liaison with the Divine Blossom *keiretsu*, Security Chief Sinichi Tanaka, limped in. His right hand and half of his face were bandaged. Goddess—what had *happened* in this place?

"Aubry-san," Tanaka said, bowing slightly.

"Tanaka Sensei?"

"De Thours is here with the Johannesburg men, concerning the palace."

Promise arched an eyebrow.

"The original deconstruction company," Aubry explained, "bidding on the repairs—" He stopped, suddenly realizing that he was talking to the head of the Scavengers.

"And what," Promise said, "if I guaranteed you that Scavengers Ltd. would underbid them?"

"There would be problems with visas and work permits. . . ."

Her smile was pure mischief. "All of which could be worked out," she said. "I have friends in the government."

"Do you now." He drew her closer. "I hope you understand," he said, his voice tautening, "that negotiations could be . . . lengthy."

She buried her head against his chest. "God," she said. "They'd better be."

26

Sinichi Tanaka stood, watching them for a moment. Then, the slightest of smiles creasing his wounded face, he backed quietly out of the room, leaving the two of them together. The men from Johannesburg would just have to wait.

The primary had business to attend to.

27

My body was asleep. My mind fluttered toward wakefulness. I heard *their* voices.

Father. Mother.

I was healing, coming back from the edge of the pit I

have inhabited all of my life. I realized that there was love enough in all the world to bring me out.

Aubry Knight. Promise Cotonou. The two of you were born to love each other, that is clear. What I do not understand is how you tolerate my intrusion into your lives, how you make room for a small, unworthy creature who needed you . . . needs you . . . so desperately. Miracle of miracles, you love me still.

We are family.

I drifted back into dream. In that dream, I saw us together again, in a world large enough to ignore us, to let us live our lives and hold each other while there is still time. Death is too close, always. Only love holds back the night.

All of the powers of hell or heaven may strive to keep us apart, but they will fail. I swear it.

Mother. Father.

You cannot understand what you have done for me.

But you will.

AFTERWORD

I would like to thank Jeff Learned, Harley Reagan, *Pendekar* Paul De Thours, Steve Sanders-Mohammed, Ray Doss, Bobbi Laurens, Danny Inosanto, and Richard Dobson. Special thanks to the *Awakening the Warrior Within* folks: Dawn Callan, Robert Humphrey, Bob Bailey, and especially Gary Sullivan, who gave me the best and cruelest gift any man has ever given me. Bless you.

Dr. John LaTourette (a true wildman) has contributed more to a *scientific* understanding of the psychology of combat than any single individual I know of. His highly recommended texts and tapes can be ordered by writing to: Sports Training Institute, 6252 Dark Hollow Road, Medford, Oregon 97501. Or call 503-535-3188.

These are friends all, and contributors to my understanding of the martial arts I love so dearly.

Michael Kerr and Dr. Richard Landers, for technical assistance. Larry Niven for encouragement.

Beth Meacham, for patience above and beyond the call of duty.

Eleanor Wood, thou charming and ruthless one. A warrior in agent's clothing.

To my daughter, Lauren Nicole Barnes, who taught me to love without reservation. And my wife, Toni, who waited patiently for me to discover that that was exactly what I needed to learn.

To my father. Dad, there has never been enough time. I think that we finally understand, and have said what we needed to say. If there is more, it has to boil down to: I love you. So I'll just say that here, now, for the record.

To my most beloved sister, Joyce, and her children, Steven and Sharleen. May life be sweet to you, always.

To Patric, Nanette, Tomme, and Tom. Family. Period.

To Casey, Sandy, Angel, Adams, Donna, Victoria, Dan, Pat, and the rest of the Lifewriting/Firedance bunch:

thanks for believing. Firedance is an actual technology that is being reclaimed from the mists of time. It promises to unleash the full spectrum of mental and physical capacities. It is currently in its infancy, and massive amounts of technical and practical research remain to be done. Those interested in what I call "Self-Directed Human Evolution" can write to: Ronin Arts Productions, 13215 SE Mill Plain Boulevard, #C8-243, Vancouver, Washington 98684. Or E-mail at lifewright@aol.com

A special thanks to Brenda, for a night with the Bolshoi, and to her malevolent spawn David, for Hide-and-Seek at Vasquez Rocks.

For Chuck and Mati at Yoga Works in Santa Monica, and K. Pattabhi Jois, whose beloved Ashtanga Yoga, thinly veiled, is the basis of the "Rubber Band" technique.

To Sri Chinmoy, whose astounding creativity (800 books, 6,000 songs, 7,000 poems, and 130,000 paintings!) and fully documented, unparalleled physical prowess (lifting 7,063¾ pounds??!) are evidence enough that miracles still exist.

And to all of the others who have added to my life, my understanding of the craft of writing, who have given me love and support and room to grow over the years. . . .

Bless you. Be gentle with each other. Life is short, and death lasts forever. Therefore, never carry anything in your heart which is heavier than a song.

Steven Barnes
Canyon Country, April 10, 1993